GHOST VOICES

Episodes from 373 Days in the Vietnam War

BARRY MORRIS

First published by THE KATES HILL PRESS
126 Watsons Green Road, Kates Hill, Dudley, DY2 7LG

ISBN: 1-904552-01-3

British Library CIP Data:
A catalogue record for this book is available from the British Library

Cover Design By: Julia Martin-Lane

Printed in the European Union by ANTONY ROWE, Chippenham, England

For my lovely Dad
George Francis Morris
1919 – 2002

ACKNOWLEDGMENTS

There are numerous acknowledgements, probably too many to fit on one page. Here's my selection – I hope those whom I've missed out won't be too offended. My wonderful parents whom I feel proud to call my Mum and Dad have helped more than they could imagine. Support from friends has been invaluable. My tireless proof readers: Dave Evans, Barbara Smith and Jenny Williams, who helped me with my sometimes-questionable grammar. Greg and Carol Stokes for their encouragement and help with getting my book published. Former Marines: Trevor Clarke, Graham Farr, Jonathan Jeffers and Greg Miller. Those in other countries or no longer with us: Chauncey Leigh, Mơị Phằn Bý, Billie Ebotée and Stephen Lane. Those left behind: Miranda Bell, Edith Graham, Julia Martin-Lane, Karen McFall and Irene Speed. Roland Powell for his support and advice on military matters. Jean Clarke and Barry Flynn for their abiding compliments. Former Marines from other Platoons. Nhợŷ Qụỉ Trơứng from the Vietnamese Embassy and copious Librarians – bless their cotton socks.

AUTHOR'S NOTE:

Some of the names and places within this text have been changed in order to protect the innocent and spare the guilty.

BM

GHOST VOICES

2: Bravo 6 Platoon Royal Marine Cadre

One Squad:
Lieutenant Nigel Derrick [The Lieutenant]
Corporal Stephen Lane [Bronco]
Corporal Derek Speed [Speedy]
Lance Corporal Colin Bell [Dinger]
Marine Jonathan Jeffers [JJ]
Marine Gregory Miller [Dusty]
Marine Clifford Vincent [Vinny]
Medical Attendant Stuart Moore [Moose or Doc']

Two Squad:
Sergeant Michael Edwards [Buster]
Corporal Graham Farr [Tommy]
Lance Corporal *Barry Morris* [Bazzer]
Lance Corporal Vernon Jessop [Jez]
Marine Trevor Clarke [TC]
Marine Gerald Collins [Jumper]
Marine Alan Cunliffe [Cowboy]
Marine Robert Lyle [Sugar]

Three Squad:
Colour Sergeant Ian Biffly [Biffo]
Corporal Nathan Alan [Nasher]
Lance Corporal Iain McFall [Macker]
Marine Peter Giggs [Giggsy]
Marine Shaun Gypsy [Tinker]
Marine Kieran Rippley [Blue]
Marine Jonathan Montford [Mongo]
Medical Attendant Dennis Hughes [Yozzer or Doc']

Four Squad:
Sergeant Brian Hoggs [Chopper]
Corporal Harold Biggs [Ronnie]
Lance Corporal David Bear [Huggy]
Lance Corporal Ricardo Barilla [Ricky]
Marine Anthony Fox [Wolfie]
Marine Gareth Bernard [Bruiser]
Marine Keith Taylor [Buck]
Marine Carl Woods [Woody]

In Sàigòn I always went to sleep stoned so I almost always lost my dreams, probably just as well, sock in deep and dim under that information and get whatever rest you could...

...A dead buddy is some tough shit, but bringing your own ass out alive can sure help you get over it.

Michael Herr

OUR COMMANDERS KEEP TELLIN' US WE GOT VICTOR CHARLIE ON THE RUN THAT SURE MAKES ME FEEL GOOD. IT WOULD MAKE ME FEEL A HELLUVA LOT BETTER IF SOMEBODY WOULD GO TELL CHARLIE!

MOONSHINE MANNY '68

MY HEAD'S SPACED OUT, MY BODY'S DONE IN, VICTOR CHARLIE'S EVERYWHERE 'CEPT IN THE CRACK O' MY ASS, LEASTWISE I DOE THINK HE'S THERE.

BADDIE 2-SHOES '69

[Sàigòn Graffiti]

Cry Việt Nam – let your tears wash the bitterness and pain,
Weep my beautiful land, for the dying & the dead,
Cry for joy once lost, soon re-found...

Mỹ Chự Lìun

THE JOURNAL

War knows no power,
Safe shall be my going.
Secretly armed against all death's endeavour,
Safe through all safety's lost,
Safe where men fall,
And if these poor limbs die, safest of all.

R Brooke

The California Bar, China Beach, Đà Nẳng, South Vietnam, April 1973.

The air conditioning was out of order yet again. The sweat-stained patches augmented on my cotton shirt in the humid atmosphere. Flies buzzed round my half finished plate of nasi goreng and tepid glass of San Miguel. Nothing seemed to work in that dilapidated cockroach infested building. Still, at least I was temporarily away from the war.

The bar was all but empty, save for two drunken former US Marines, two soldiers with nothing else to live for but their memories of a war they just couldn't stop fighting. Bob Dylan's *Lay Lady Lay* played on the crackling '50s Tannoy. Waves breaking on the bleached sands and the clamour of seagulls challenging for discarded fish heads stirred childhood memories of warm summer days on New Brighton Beach.

I sat updating my journal. Our period of Rest and Recuperation would give me time to catch up. Most of the lads were out on their jaunties: looking for cheap bar deals and top-notch arm candy. I wanted some time alone to reflect.

The barman, Mợi Phẳn Bý, was wiping the empty tables for the umpteenth time. I'd become acquainted with him during my time off. We both enjoyed testing out our language skills on each other. We also had conversations about the war. Mợi declared that he was neutral; for somebody purporting to be middle-of-the-road he sure had a lot of sympathy for the aims of the Viet Cong. He approached me full of curiosity.

"What you write?" he asked looking over my shoulder.

"My journal," I replied to his obvious confusion.

"Jour-nal, what jour-nal?"

"Diary…" I said deliberately, "record, chronicle of things that are happening."

"Legend!" he said with a smile.

"No not quite, though it is a story, a running story."

"You write book maybe, many-time future?"

"Yeah maybe, then again who knows, I mightn't even make it out of here."

"Your book when you write not be the same. You can only write now for future reads also. You write future, different picture; not see things the same."

"You mean I'll put a different interpretation on things?"

"Can't be the same," Mơị said becoming frustrated. "Not can see or feel like now. Only listen to voices in your head, they tell of what you've seen and feel, how you say, you experience. Only through voices... *ghost voices*."

"It's okay Mơị; I'll try and write as I feel now."

"Your book if you write, many-time future, what you call? What title?"

"That's easy Mơị," I said with a smile: "Ghost Voices."

1: SMOKIN' DOPE

There's something happening here,
What it is ain't exactly clear.
There's a man with a gun over there,
Tellin' me I've got to beware.
I think it's time we stopped, children,
What's that sound?
Everybody look what's goin' down…

David Crosby

06:00: Brize Norton Royal Air Force Base, 8 August 1972.

We sat in the Departure Lounge awaiting embarkation in a disconsolate huddle, moaning at the constant din from aircraft taxiing towards the runway. Waiting is an invariable feature of a soldier's life, a feature few master. Waiting leads to boredom, fatigue, numb arses and on that occasion thumping headaches. Hitting the town on our last night in Blighty didn't help. The whole Section went out of its way to dispose of every last coin of British currency before being introduced to the Vietnamese Đồng. Not that we had much to spend our cash on in the dump that surrounded the airbase, except booze, copious amounts of it.

The Section, four Pathfinder Platoons of the Royal Marine Cadre, was secluded from the usual human cargo waiting to fly out to sunnier climes. The operation code-named 'Check out Charlie' (quite novel considering that we were doing our utmost not to give the game away) was shrouded in secrecy. This made no difference to some of the daily broadsheets which had already announced our intentions: '...BRITISH ROYAL MARINES TO INTERVENE IN THE VIETNAM WAR', some of the headlines read, raising untold anxiety amongst our loved ones.

I was a Royal Marine Lance Corporal in 2: Bravo 6 Platoon whom, along with Alpha, Charlie & Delta Platoons, had been seconded to the International Peacekeeping Supervisory Force [IPSF] a peacekeeping component created by the United Nations [UN] to oversee an imminent interim ceasefire in the protracted war in Vietnam. We were to act as 'spearhead force', a frontline section placed to administer and monitor the anticipated ceasefire preceding the arrival of a more permanent United Nations Force.

Our Section numbered 128 men. It was beyond us how we were to facilitate our tasks in a country measuring 66,000 sq. miles and containing an active fighting force (which included 250,000 US Service Personnel) of 3.6 Million people. Nevertheless, our immediate concern was boarding the RAF VC10 covertly parked on the edge of number two runway; the sooner we took off, the sooner we'd get home. We were expected to board our special flight, a one-way ticket to Tấlận Chựí Military Air Strip Sàigòn, at 05:30. Doubtless, there were last minute snags none regrettably that would abort our departure, we were bound for Vietnam ['Nam or Charlieville] and that was that.

The enforced inactivity made everybody fractious. The overbearing silence was occasionally broken by a mutter or half-hearted joke. Marine Jeffers was persistently emitting noxious gasses from his distended colon.

"Put a fuckin' bung in it!" Sergeant Edwards said.

"I can't help it," JJ replied, "it's the legacy of a vindaloo special and fifteen pints of Courage Export—"

"You need fuckin' courage to smell it. Now you will be advised to start exercising your anal muscles, otherwise you're gonna find a Tabasco soaked cork lodged between the cheeks of your arse!"

The Sections finally boarded the plane at 0730 hours. As we settled we scanned the central aisle looking for the voluptuous Air Hostesses we'd been promised; all we could see were male stewards.

"Hey mate where's all the fanny?" Marine Lyle enquired as a steward swept past.

"You're lookin' at it sweetie!"

"Are-aye," Sugar groaned in his thick scouse accent, "all the 'ostesses are swinging dicks!"

The roar of laughter and wolf-whistles was followed by the usual banter associated with pre-take off. We were in fine form, shouting, jesting; taking the piss out of everything with a pulse that wasn't a Bootneck [Royal Marine Commando]. Then, as the VC10 prepared to speed down the runway there was an eerie pause in the babble. Up to that time the war in Vietnam was just another conflict; a far off struggle telegraphed to a largely undiscerning and uncaring populace on the early evening news. Now, we were about to soar into the eye of that confrontation, into the cruel actuality of war. Our intensive training and pre-contact briefings were complete. We'd apparently learned all there was to learn about Vietnam: its geographical position and history; the idiosyncrasies of its people; the ethnic, cultural and political divides and the fundamentals surrounding a hostility that had been raging for 9000 days. Nonetheless, as I gazed through the windows at the flashing runway markers, I was overcome by a feeling that we were about to enter an arena that we had little knowledge about – a place where we'd doubtless be unwelcome. I had left home on numerous occasions, but I'd never felt such an immediate yearning to return.

*

16:00: Tấlận Chựí Military Air Strip, Sàigòn, Wednesday 9 August.

Our flight to South East Asia was much the same as any other on-board military transport. Whilst in transit you're always on duty. No in-flight entertainment, save Sugar's usual jokes. Our plane touched down at Tấlận Chựí at 1200 hours local time. It taxied to the far corner of the runway where a small disembarkation team was waiting with steps and a large forklift truck seconded to remove our equipment. We disembarked as the ground crew unloaded our bergens [rucksacks] from the cargo hold; the secrecy continued.

We sat on the verge of the runway as the VC10 moved away, waiting for our airlift. We didn't have to wait long. Three Royal Canadian Air Force Chinook helicopters flew in, the aircrew signalling for us to board. Our flight lasted less than fifteen minutes. It was just as well; the noise from the double rotor thud was unbearable. Our ears continued ringing as we disembarked at the first of many United Nations Base Camps.

Our frenzied arrival was succeeded by a call to the briefing room. We'd hardly had time to find our accommodation, let alone unpack. We'd been in South Vietnam for less than an hour; my head was already spinning faster than a Chinook's rotors.

10:00: UN Base Camp 1, Bìen Hoâ, Sàigòn, Saturday 12 August.

We were all clock-watching. Two days of monotonous lectures were due to finish at 1030 hours. We had all been given a 24-hour pass; time to check out the delights of Sàigòn. The designated Translators: Corporal Lane, Lance Corporal McFall, Lance Corporal Barilla and I had escaped some of the lectures. We'd been given leave to check out our language skills in a local college. We had completed an intensive twelve-week linguistics programme (Vietnamese and associated languages) in the UK. In the latter six weeks of the course, during classroom hours, the lecturers forbade us to communicate with them or each other in anything but Vietnamese. The lessons were well and truly over – time to test things out.

Vietnamese is a monosyllabic and tonal language. It has no inflections, a large number of compounds and widely differing dialects. The tones were the most difficult element to master. The correct use of tones is vital: context and meaning can radically change if the wrong tone is employed in a given sentence or situation. We all struggled with initial introductions. The college lecturers had varying accents; they put us at ease with their humour. The four of us enjoyed our short time away.

Lieutenant Derrick could see we were anxious to get going. He dismissed the Platoon who exited quicker than a point .30 calibre round. We changed in record time, crowding into taxis waiting at the gates of the former United States Logistics Base.

11:00: Tư Đô Street, Sàigòn, Sunday 13 August.

We sat on the makeshift barstools outside *The GI Blues* bar sipping coffee in the forenoon air, watching the frenzied activity that was Sàigòn. We'd done our utmost to check out the Metropolis. Sàigòn [Big S] was a truly amazing city, a paradox, decadent yet unadulterated. I had been to some noisy places in my three years in the forces: Bombay, Naples and Rio de Janeiro during Mardi gras, but the racket was nothing compared to the hullabaloo that was Sàigòn. The din was constant: car horns beeping, vendors shouting for trade, traffic controllers blowing whistles, music blaring from speakers, low flying aircraft taking off and landing from the numerous airstrips surrounding the capital. The clamour was occasionally accompanied by gun and mortar fire; constant reminders that the country was at war.

Bronco, Jumper, Sugar, Tommy and I had spent the previous afternoon and evening attempting to walk the patch. We hardly scratched the surface. What we did discover was amazing. Parts of the city had been Americanised: Milk Bars that sold everything except milk; Ten Lane Bowling Alleys with lanes so worn and balls so unbalanced that the only way to get a strike was if you were pissed out of your brain, and Amusement Arcades with early 1960s games machines and one-armed-bandits. The arcades would be teeming with Vietnamese pinball wizards intoxicated by the flashing Gottlieb machines, their ears ringing long after retiring from their marathon games. The quayside contained Movie Halls fashioned out of giant dilapidated stores. The selection of films was mind-numbing: Ming Dynasty adventures overlaid with English and 1950s American cowboy films containing cowhands and sheriffs speaking Vietnamese. The shows would be frequently interrupted by propaganda pieces extolling the wonders of the regime. Richard Nixon walking beside President Thiều in the grounds of the White House: '...our friends in the USA'. What a joke! The US were never their friends and by August '72 they were planning to haul arse big time. We suffered the cheap three-screen auditorium for just over an hour, there were too many other things to checkout.

Tư Đô Street was the main drag of the city. It acted as an artery to the assortment of thoroughfares and side streets. The neighbourhood was heaving with bars, nightclubs, shabiens and dope dens. Vợ Van Trần Street had a collection of tightly knit alleyways lined with saloons that appeared to be frozen in the 1960s. Music was piped outside each bar in an attempt to attract customers; the result was predictable. Nonetheless, the compositions were magical: The Beach Boys, The Bee Gees, The Byrds, Donovan, The Doors, Jimmy Ruffin, Cat Stevens, Union Gap, The Yardbirds & The Youngbloods. It was like walking into a time warp.

Tommy and I wanted to look at some of the Gothic architecture. We sauntered down Đong Khởi Street towards the Cathedral of Notre Dame, a huge structure with its distinctive twin spires. Its presence was colossal amongst the drab stumpy buildings.

We noticed some large placards along Thừơ Chới Street. The posters contained twenty-five, 4-by-5 inch pictures of known revolutionaries topped with large captions—

WANTED DEAD OR ALIVE—ENEMIES OF SOUTH VIETNAM

The scene resembled something out of a 1960s Western, more Silver City than Sàigòn. One had been covered over with a picture of President Thiều, the large print replaced with—

WANTED, DEAD ONLY, BOURGEOISIE ENEMY OF THE NATIONAL LIBERATION FRONT!

We laughed at the irony. The sidewalks were full of street traders, many were disabled: deaf artists vying to create five-minute portraits with their Conté crayons and blind bespoke tailors that measured by touch. The traffic on Tư Đô Street was frenzied: battered Citroëns, immaculate Mercedes Benz and customised VW Beetles. Ox carts perilously competed for space as Lambretta scooters wove in and out of the fast moving vehicles. Traffic cops stood like robots in the central isles. They would stop the traffic every so often to allow a dignitary's car through. There seemed to be a lot of government cars in Sàigòn but not a lot of government order.

The city was crawling with Special Police [White Mice] with their distinct blue-white uniforms. Some of the peddlers skulked in shady back streets whilst others openly flouted the law, likely after giving backhanders. Creepy men stood outside brightly adorned saloons portraying peep shows and elaborate burlesque presentations. The bright neon lights looked incongruous aside some of the dull 19th Century buildings.

The Metropolis had a fragrance of its own: blue-grey incense mingling with choking smoke from charcoal buses; the aroma of spiced foods wafting down alleyways strewn with rotting garbage. The austere gave way to the opulent. The lower end of Tư Đô Street abounded with beggars. Within the blink of an eye you'd be greeted with uptown taverns containing découpage patterned furnishings. Fashionable middle-aged Vietnamese women dressed in western styles sipped cocktails served by petite bargirls; Sàigòn's à la mode.

We could see street kids laying out their bedrolls on the sidewalks at sundown, people walking by disinterested. Later that evening we saw the White Mice clear a whole alleyway; they waded in with four-foot rattan canes. Many of the children had to make an escape without their possessions, what little they had. We could do nought but look away.

Some street children survived by selling their bodies down Lê Đuân Street. Middle-aged European and American men would hide in the dark shadows whispering code words. A number of children, not unsurprisingly, went missing. Their beaten and buggered bodies would be found days or weeks later, the constabulary closing the cases as quickly as they were opened. Paedophiles existed then, as they always have.

In the evening we checked out Lế Chừí Street. Street girls called out in soft voices from doorways. We could make out their sloe-eyes, extenuated by pencil-lined make-up, in the dimness. Some of us visited *Mademoiselle Dieu Kiềm's* and *The Passage To Pleasure*, with their dope filled atmospheres and voluptuous courtesans.

Later that evening we bumped into Dusty and Jez outside *The Pussy Palace*; they'd spent the day drinking cheap absinthe. Dusty looked decidedly unwell as we piled him into the heaving nightclub. He spent the first half hour throwing up before mouth washing with San Miguel. The Lovin' Spoonful's *Summer In The City* was playing on the jukebox as young bargirls tempted us with their split áo dài gowns [wraparound dresses] and sensuous smiles. Mama sans patrolled ready to broker a deal.

We boozed until the early hours. I finally succumbed to the delights of a young bargirl. I don't much recall the night, apart from a lumpy bed, a packet of condoms that had a mind of their own and a rattling ceiling fan that made more noise than a squadron of Chinooks.

Sunday morning Sàigòn didn't seem any different than any other time; the day of rest meant nothing, despite the city being predominantly Christian. I met up with Bronco and Tommy at an agreed venue. We spent the morning looking round Sàigòn's lotus shaped Chùa Môt Cột [One-pillar Pagodas]. The ancient buildings were sporadically strewn with bullet holes; the city planners had clearly abandoned the stunning edifices.

We picked up the pace for our rendezvous with some of the others, enjoying the warmth from the early morning sun. Most of the lads were sat outside at *The GI Blues* bar when we arrived; they all looked worse for wear. Sugar tried drinking a hair of the dog cocktail which included turquoise crème de menthe; the strangest remedy I'd ever encountered.

We downed the last of our coffee amid stories of our exploits before hailing taxis back to barracks. Sunday was only to be a half-day of rest. More lectures were planned for 13:30. I gazed from the taxicab at the frenetic activity wondering if I'd get another chance to test out the delights of Sàigòn.

17:30: UN Base Camp 1, Bìen Hoâ.

The last hour of our afternoon lectures seemed to drag. We were treated yet again to a potted history of the conflict—

In 1959 the Viet Cong-sangannalese [Viet Cong, VC or (Victor) Charlie] challenged the repressive South Vietnamese Government. Brutal reprisals led to the formation of the National Liberation Front [NLF]. By mid '64 the NLFs guerrilla tactics had the Government Forces on the run. United States troops intervened late '64. The inclusion of US Forces had little affect. The guerrilla war – supported by North Vietnamese Forces crossing the Laotian and Cambodian border – continued. By 1968 US personnel totalled 500,000. US casualties matched the increase in personnel. The continuing arrival of body bags and news of massacres perpetrated by US Forces added to anti-war demonstrations in the United States.

In May 1972 President Nixon created a framework for a so-called, 'Peace and Withdrawal with Honour'. Talks on a cessation of hostilities culminated in an agreement on an Interim Ceasefire as a '...pledge to bring about a peaceful end to the discord'.

The tutorial was accompanied with non-stop, largely inconsequential, information on war zones and hot spots. Features on encounters of purported historical significance: the 1968 Tết Offensive (a concentrated attack on the South by North Vietnamese Forces supported by Viet Cong elements); the siege of Tẩy Nịnh City and bloody battle for Đắk Tơ. Embellished stories of endless frontier skirmishes with the Khmer Rouge [KR]. We spent over an hour being lectured on the ways of the Viet Cong: their cunning and treachery, and how they'd butchered hundreds of innocent civilians. We wondered why the lectures didn't include stories of atrocities carried out by US Forces and the South Vietnamese Army [SVA]. What any of the information had to do with the interim ceasefire was beyond us.

Our frantic briefings included advice on avoiding the exotic diseases familiar to the region, including venereal disease. A corpulent US Medic, Sergeant Larry Izzard [The Lounge Room Lizard] gave us one of the most entertaining lectures we'd ever received:

"...If you pretty boys can't keep ya delicate dicks tucked in ya tent then be sure to take one o' these to the cathouse," he said holding up a condom. "This here's a double rubber, specially made for your liddle ol' tools. Now don't you go thinkin' that any of you boys are free from temptation. Oh it'll all be fine 'til Suzy J Rotten-croutch comes on over rubbin' her quim 'gainst ya leg. Next thing ya know porky's pencil's got a new line o' lead; a throbbin' robin lookin' for a warm nest! Ya'll don't wanna dose in this liddle ol' cow town, no sir! Y'all get more mileage outa this than a Goodyear Tripleply."

We spent the evening hanging around barracks waiting for news. The final terms of the interim ceasefire were still being thrashed out. Rumour on Radio Sàigòn was rife – numerous futile news reports interrupting the music. Radio Sàigòn had three medium wave channels broadcasting in Vietnamese, French and English. Former US Army personnel playing contemporary music amid inconsequential babble, and Vietnamese DJs doing their utmost to emulate Emperor Rosco presented the English network.

I shut myself away for the evening at around 20:00. I'd promised myself that I would write a journal whilst in Vietnam. I stared at the first empty page of my A4 notebook. 'What do I write?' I thought. Hardly anything of note had happened. If our briefings were to be believed hardly anything would happen. Reports of heavy machine-gun fire broke the silence; the distant echoes reminded me of my tour in Northern Ireland. I hadn't written whilst in that conflict, a factor I later regretted. The gunfire abated as I started to write. By the time I'd leave the 'Nam I would complete a total of three books.

23:00: UN Base Camp 1, Monday 14 August.

I sat in-between Cowboy and Dusty in the back of the Military Police [MP] vehicle nervously waiting for Colour Sergeant Biffly. Bronco, JJ, Jumper and Sugar sat facing us. The handcuffs were digging into my wrists. I hoped I didn't look like Sugar; he had an ugly gash above his right eyebrow. I don't know who started the fight; it was probably Cowboy. We were sat drinking Tiger beer in *The Pussy Palace* when the yanks started. "Well I'll be dipped in shit if it ain' a bunch o' Limeys," one of the GIs yelled as we sat singing along to Martha Reeves & The Vandellas' *Dancin' In The Street*. What started as banter somehow deteriorated into a fistfight. The South Vietnamese MPs came wading in with their nightsticks three or four minutes after we'd kicked off. It was just as well: barstools, tables and any manner of loose debris were flying around the room. We were still hurling insults as we were bundled into the back of the Paddy Wagon.

Biffo was not a man to stand on ceremony. After we'd received a brief check from the medics he promptly threw the lot of us into the Guardhouse. I lay on the straw-filled mattress in my cell listening to the continuous noise of US cargo planes departing from the adjacent Bìen Hoâ Airbase, wondering why we were not at least asked to give an explanation. 'That's done it...' I thought, 'no more shore leave for me.'

22:00: Tuesday 15 August.

Our morning appearance on Commander's Report was brief. We were guilty and that was that. We each received a four hundred-Đồng fine and five days stoppage of leave. On dismissal I got a good look at my injuries. My phizog was hideous; I resembled a one-legged blind Thai Boxer. My knuckles weren't much better; it was as if I had spent an afternoon punching hessian fenders. The yanks had outnumbered us 3:1; we still gave as good as we got.

As it transpired our stoppage of leave was an empty sanction. Everyone was confined to barracks amid increasing tensions; the NLF was on the rampage. The furore had started after a terrorist attack on the Đon Bế Market. A young Viet Cong woman rode her explosive-packed bicycle into the crowded marketplace. Informers had tipped off the White Mice who were waiting in a Dillinger-stlye ambush. Unfortunately for them the insurrectionary managed to pull the pin before her riddled body gave-way. Thirteen people were killed, a combination of purported terrorist activity and gross incompetence.

The cancelling of leave meant that the base bar did a roaring trade. The Lounge Room Lizard joined us mid-evening. He had a talent for telling yarns. He talked of crazy days and wild nights from the De-Militarised Zone [DMZ] to Sàigòn. Manic excursions through moonscapes in Quang Trì; swallowing bagfuls of amphetamines during forty-eight hour firefights; crawling like moles through darkened VC tunnels; smoking cocktails of cannabis and opium through dumpy homemade hookahs in backstreet bars; three-day malaria induced zonks on sweat soaked sheets. He was as crazy as a shithouse rat. By end of evening, he and Marine Lyle were engaged in a double act – it was a hoot.

Captain Page, accompanied by the officers from the Platoons, interrupted our hootenanny at 2230 hours. The whole room came to standstill as Colour Sergeant Biffly banged an ashtray on a table.

"Listen up boys," the Captain said in the deathly silence. "An interim ceasefire has been brokered. It will come into force at 0800 hours local time Wednesday 16th of August 1972. The agreement is inclusive of a steady withdrawal of United States Forces from key areas, around twenty-five per cent in total. We can be sure that there'll be trouble; hence we've been put on twelve-hours notice. I don't want to spoil your fun, but I suggest you empty your glasses and turn in. Assignments will be handed out at first light."

I'd never known the mood to change so quickly; the bar staff slammed the shutters before anyone could get another drink. A few of us slinked off to a secret room at the back of the Drill Hall. Jumper, as usual, had a stash. We sat on sandbags with The Lounge Room Lizard. He had a sugar cube-size block of cannabis resin that he shared out. I elected to sip tea as he summed up his view of Vietnam in a dope-crazed tirade of verbal diarrhoea—

"Oh motherfucker, yo' all gonna love the 'Nam! Y'all either get fucked or hooked. Ain't no way out 'til ya get in. Shoot up to Quang Trì, kick-shit alley; war day everyday. The body bag emporium, select your bag, lie down and zip it up, save Charlie the job. Take a trip to Cambodia, go steamin' or dreamin'. Hoppin' the Hồ Chì Minh Trail; dodgin' mines an' zippin' through clouds of razor spiked 'squitoes, either way you're dead meat. Team up with the devils disciple's: winos, bunk brains and murder junkies – mad bastards with dead eyes and chronic halitosis. Ain't no choice – in the 'Nam you're either killin' or drillin'. Suck in Big S; get on to *Mademoiselle Dieu Kiềm's* down Lế Chừí Street. Girls, boys or girls an' boys if you're that way inclined. Don't make no mind in the 'Nam, fuck or get fucked, simple philosophy. If it's dick exercise ya need call in at *The Pussy Palace*. Cool beer, weird potions and blowjob jockeys. Sàigòn witches and tongue twistin' lick bitches. They can roll your dick into stretch popcycle that a cat could scratch; hard-on heaven! Get on down to Nợi Đưan Street; dope den alley. Say goodbye to fantasy-'Nam and hello to reality. Mosey down Vợ Van Trần Street: massage mommas and tattoo parlours. Call in at Rembrandt's; he'd tattoo the inside of your eyelids if you'd let him. Sell ya unused helmet graffiti, all that unique arty stuff, not the dogcrap most o' the Joe's slink 'round with on their lids [helmets]. Yes sir, Charlieville's one long fuck-boat; like suckin' on a hash pipe stuck to your lip. Constant delirium, gotta take it in afore you blow it out. It's surreal and unreal, a long drawn out beautiful nightmare. Like smokin' dope, d'ya hear me…just like smokin' dope!"

The Lounge room Lizard was the first of scores of crazy bastards we'd bump into in Vietnam; crazy but interesting.

07:00: UN Base Camp 1, Wednesday 16 August.

We sat in the lecture room awaiting our final address before deployment. There was a mixed air: quiet reflection, tension and excitement, the men generally wanting to get moving.

Captain Page entered along with the Lieutenants. One of the guys let go an arsehole-ripping fart just as the room quietened.

"What was that?" Colour Sergeant Biffly snarled.

"Judgin' by the stink in 'ere it wasn't the fuckin' doorbell!" Marine Lyle answered amid a roar of laughter.

The customary introductions were followed by our assignments – 2: Delta 6 Platoon would remain in Sàigòn; 2: Alpha 6 were to police the districts on the periphery of Chû Laị; 2: Charlie 6 Platoon was to oversee the removal of logistical services from Quang Ngaî Province, and 2: Bravo 6 the withdrawal of United States troops from Quang Trì.

The men sat muttering at the end of the briefing, particularly the lads from 2: Bravo 6 Platoon. We'd all heard horror stories from every province and district of Vietnam, but none were as prolific as Quang Trì.

Post breakfast we split into our respective Detachments for the specifics. Information was sparse. We'd likely be given the task of checking the final withdrawal of US Forces from two redundant firebases. It would be a mammoth task. The yanks were expecting trouble. The NLF was not going to make the US withdrawal easy; they had scores to settle. Moreover, the SVA would take every chance to round up suspected Viet Cong separatists. Refugees would be an added problem. Apparently, most felt relatively safe in the presence of the Americans, in spite of past atrocities. The Security Forces had scant regard for them, particularly immigrants from North Vietnam, Laos and Cambodia.

We'd have to protect the vulnerable at the same time as counting vehicles, checking itineraries and looking out for terrorist activity – whatever that was supposed to be.

22:00: Base Camp 1.

We spent the evening packing. Some of the men sat frantically writing letters home. We all wanted to get some shuteye. Unfortunately, at the very time we needed some peace the movement of aircraft to and from the nearby airbase had tripled. We could also hear artillery and rifle reports to the southeast. The South Vietnamese Army were apparently trying to flush out separatist rebels firmly rooted in the Plain of Reeds [Hell's Triangle]. The whole territory flanked the Sàigòn River. The National Liberation Front had long secured the area the Security Forces looking on in envy; they'd have given anything to flush out the paramilitary groups. The cessation may have given them an excuse to surreptitiously enter the area in the guise of offering negotiations, not that Charlie would be interested.

I sat writing my thoughts in my journal. Corporal Farr interrupted my scribing: "I see the interim ceasefire's been well and truly established!"

I smiled as I continued industriously writing. It was as if I was possessed. I don't know why I wrote so much. Maybe it was thinking of Quang Trì along with thoughts of home. Truth is I had an underlying feeling that somehow my days were numbered.

SONGS FROM THE 'NAM

Sàigòn Bars

THE BEACH BOYS *God Only Knows; Good Vibrations*

THE BEE GEES *Massachusetts; Saved By The Bell; Words*

THE BYRDS *Goin' Back; Mr Tambourine Man; Turn! Turn! Turn! (To Everything There Is A Season)*

DONOVAN *Catch The Wind; Universal Soldier*

THE DOORS *Hello, I Love You; The End*

THE FLOWER POT MEN *Let's Go To San Francisco*

THE LOVE AFFAIR *Everlasting Love*

THE LOVIN' SPOONFUL *Summer In The City*

MARTHA REEVES & THE VANDELLAS *Dancin' In The Street*

THE ROLLING STONES *Paint It Black; Ruby Tuesday*

JIMMY RUFFIN *What Becomes Of The Broken Hearted*

THE SMALL FACES *Itchycoo Park*

CAT STEVENS *I'm Gonna Get Me A Gun; Matthew And Son*

TOMMY [The Rock Opera] *Various Artists*

UNION GAP *Young Girl*

THE YARDBIRDS *For Your Love*

THE YOUNGBLOODS *Let's Get Together*

2: MURDER HOLE

Sleep well you lusty fusiliers,
Close your brave eyes on sense & sight,
And banish from your dreamless ears,
The bugle's dying notes that say,
Another night; another day.

S Sassoon

05:00: UN Base Camp 1, Bìen Hoâ, Sàigòn, 17 August 1972.

I was a child again on holiday on the Norfolk Broads. The cabin cruiser slowly cutting its way through the reed-flanked waters: my father at the wheel; my mother and sister sitting on the starboard side, their bare legs dangling beside the fenders. It seemed so real: the cool water lapping the side of the boat; the rumble of the motor; the bright sun shimmering on the channel; the warm breeze sweeping across my face. Picturesque, serene, uncontaminated. It was good to revisit my childhood; it was a good dream…

"Up, up, up!" Biffo hollered as he thundered down the dormitory.

I could never get used to frenetic mornings; I guess I'm just not a morning person. Having to down breakfast and haul your gear to an airstrip in record time whilst possessing a pervading feeling of anxiety was just too much to bear. The others were clearly feeling the same; there was no banter, just silent contemplation.

Alpha, Bravo and Charlie Platoons boarded the Royal Canadian Air Force C130. Delta Platoon had already left for Hell's Triangle. Our Platoon would be deployed first, with Alpha and Charlie disembarking at Chû Laị. The Canadian [Canucks] cabin crew were as friendly as ever. The Canucks had been seconded to provide air transport to UN Forces. We would learn to depend on them during our tour.

The flight was as noisy and monotonous as ever. The C130 had no comforts. The seats, set against the bulkheads port and starboard, were fashioned out of cargo netting. The vacuous space and curling ribs reminded me of a picture I'd seen of Jonah living in a whale. The crew handed out some lukewarm coffee. The foul tasting liquid looked muddy in the red-light glow. The vibration was playing havoc with my senses; I suddenly discovered new injuries from our barroom brawl. I couldn't remember being punched in the kidneys. I tried blocking out the numbness by playing songs in my head. Somewhere between a rendition of The Beach Boys' *God Only Knows* and *Good Vibrations*, I dropped off to sleep.

08:00: Quang Trì Military Air Strip.

The C130 touched down at Quang Trì Air Strip. Bravo Platoon unbuckled and made ready to disembark. We stood, port and starboard, in an ordered line waiting for the rear door to open. The unmistakable snap of the bolts withdrawing and the hum of the massive ramp lowering signalled our move aft. As the ramp continued to the full, a shaft of daylight streamed in making us wince; the noise from the wake of the turbine-propellers filled the cabin. Our earplugs offered little defence, particularly as we began exiting the plane. Alpha and Charlie Platoons offered their goodbyes as we disembarked. We touched hands with our compadrés as we sauntered past laden with our rifles [M16s] and bergens.

The Detachment gathered to one side of the tarmac as the C130 made a 180° swing on the turnabout at the end of the runway. We quickly squatted in a huddle as it revved-up to depart. The draught and reverberation from the enormous metal beast buffeted us as it came thundering past – destination Chû Laị. I distinctly remember looking at the C130 as it climbed skyward. As a Specialist Pathfinder Section we had eaten, slept, trained, fought, laughed and lamented together for five months. I had become acquainted with the lads from the other Platoons – even close to some. Separation felt strange. Jointly, we seemed so much stronger, even within the enormity of the Vietnam War. Alpha, Charlie and Delta had gone. I would learn sometime later that I wasn't the only marine that felt strangely alone.

09:00: UN Base Camp 7, Biên Duc, Quang Trì Province, Monday 21 August.

Day five of complete and utter inactivity, we were all frustrated. Our days consisted of endless hours on the base cleaning already immaculate equipment and reading up on the history of the province. I couldn't work out which was the most pointless.

Quang Trì, the most northern province of South Vietnam, had more than its fair share of misery and tragedy during the prolonged conflict. It appeared that politicians from the north and south considered the province to be a tabernacle. The heavily contested provincial town and surrounding areas were battle-scarred. The entire region was branded a 'murder hole' post Tết Offensive. Innocent civilians from all persuasions had been invariably caught up in the slaughter; there was no monopoly on pain in Quang Trì.

The province was flanked by the Laotian border to the west and headed by the De-Militarised Zone, hence, infiltration by North Vietnamese Regulars was simple. The infiltrators could easily mingle with the populace. The regulars would work in factions or link-up with long established Viet Cong

Cadres. Terrorist attacks on military posts and government buildings would be followed by brutal reprisals, some of which were recorded in a diary of horror. Post Tết Offensive, the Security Forces captured a dozen Viet Cong insurgents. All were sentenced to death. Major Phự Trấn Xàứ, wanting to make an example, arranged for three of the revolutionaries to be crucified outside the city gates. Their deaths were predictably slow and agonising. The strategy did have an affect; unfortunately it wasn't what the Major anticipated. The National Liberation Front went on a killing spree wiping out every government sympathiser they could lay their hands on. Major Trấn Xàứ mysteriously disappeared days later. Nobody could work out if it was the Viet Cong or his own side.

The outlying villages were open to constant threats and intimidation. Viet Cong militia would sometimes recruit young men from the villages; refusal was not an option. Days later the SVA would punish the inhabitants for collaborating with enemies of the state.

In 1970 the Vietnam War burst the borders of Cambodia and Laos. The border regions were swamped with migrants; people fleeing from incessant carpet-bombing or marauding rebels. Many Khmer and Laotian tribal people [Mân, Meớ and Nưng] embarked upon perilous frontier crossings only to be force-marched back by the SVA. Stories abounded of the Security Forces deliberately marching dislodged people into minefields – a final solution.

The surrounding districts contained a network of Viet Cong tunnels. Given different circumstances the warrens would've been considered a marvel of civil engineering. The elaborate systems were patiently fashioned by hand. They had no supporting beams or reinforced bulkheads, yet they withstood concerted attacks by opposing forces. An enemy who had the ability to disappear would challenge any military operation. The South Vietnamese and Americans tried any number of ways to flush out insurgents. The yanks provided the Security Forces with *sniffers*, gas-blowing machines that could pump CS-Gas into the tunnels. Soldiers would wait at designated points to accost rebels as they exited the labyrinths. One bright spark decided to force pure cyanide into a network of burrows west of Quang Trì Town. The results were foreseeable. Unfortunately, the composite also housed a come-at-able medical centre and school: 298 bodies were recovered from the complex including a large number of young children. The government controlled South Vietnamese Press Agency released a statement '...regretting the loss of non-combatants'. The statement went on to say that the fatalities occurred as a direct consequence of terrorist activities by the National Liberation Front. It would be a statement that I would hear many more times in my life; seems it's always the other guy.

*

10:00: Khê Sahn Firebase, Route 9, Tuesday 22 August.

We were on the road at last; a Chinook transported the Platoon to the outskirts of Khê Sahn early morning. We were to oversee the final evacuation of the infamous United States Marines outpost. The Garrison had been pounded by the North Vietnamese Army [NVA] for a number of years. The firebase was a kill junkie's paradise and coward's worst nightmare. Crumbling sandbag revetments surrounded the former fortress; it resembled a ghost town. Local people had already taken advantage of the withdrawal. Some of the small dwellings lining the road contained fittings that had either been sold or cannibalised in dawn excursions. One house looked like something from a Vietnamese version of *The Adams Family*. It had more additions and facelifts than an ageing Hollywood actress.

We'd been given a fleet of jeeps to watch over the withdrawal. We sat at the gates watching line after line of Troop Carrying Trucks and Armoured Personnel Carriers [APCs] leaving the firebase. Some people stood clapping whilst others had a look of trepidation.

We managed to take a closer look at the populace on the slow eastwardly drive towards Highway One. The war weary people seemed to shuffle around in a state of semi-catatonia. It's said that in war people look old before their time; in Quang Trì people looked dead before their time.

We reached the intersection of Highway One in no time. The worn carriageway was the main artery of the eastern coast. The main road hugged the coastline cutting through Quang Trì, Huê, Phu Baì and Đà Nằng, before bypassing Chû Laị, Quang Ngaî and Quì Nhôn. The road continued via Nha Trang before swinging southwesterly towards Sàigòn.

Once the Trucks and APCs were southbound we made a high-speed run back towards Khê Sahn to pick up another line – all in all, a pretty futile exercise.

16:10: Approximately 2 miles west of Highway One intersection.

We were on our last run of our triple point-to-point, expectant that we'd be returning to base. We were slowing before a staggered junction when we saw a unit of South Vietnamese soldiers by the roadside. Something wasn't right; they nervously stared at us as we passed. Lieutenant Derrick was in the lead vehicle. I didn't see him signal a halt; I was too focussed on the suspicious looking troops.

As we stopped I could see the reason why. There appeared to be a row of people squatting alongside a monsoon ditch adjacent to the highway. The Lieutenant, accompanied by Sergeant Edwards, walked up to what was likely the leader of the unit. After a brief interlude he summoned the translators. Lance Corporal McFall and I moved forward as Colour Sergeant Biffly continued escorting the convoy with around half the Platoon, the remainder pulled over and waited for directives.

UN peacekeepers had strict instructions to adhere to protocols. We could not intervene in situations unless we had clear evidence that non-combatants were being threatened. In that situation Command had already assigned tasks. To abandon an undertaking was a serious transgression, but Lieutenant Derrick was no fool. He was unlike many of the other officers. He was an experienced campaigner who had risen through the ranks gaining his commission in 1970. He and Sergeant Edwards were in their mid-thirties, it seemed old to us at the time.

Macker and I had a better view of what was going on as we approached. The soldiers had separated a party of men and women into groups. The women, who numbered about six, were sat on the verge around ten yards from around eleven men who had their hands tightly bound behind their backs. The men were squatting in what must have been an uncomfortable position; two of the men had small sacks over their heads. The more we saw, the more concerned we became.

Buster slowly pulled away as the Lieutenant directed Macker to ask the Vietnamese officer to give him a situation report.

Macker nervously complied. It was the first time any of the interpreters had been put to the test. I stood alongside him with the translation manual ready to offer assistance or correct any mistakes – we had to get things right.

"Khôngván dề dia diêm," (*There is no problem here.*) The SVA officer guardedly answered. "Tru sơ thực hiện. Liên hoừn không sợ," (*We do work for headquarters. These people have no need to be afraid.*)

Macker conveyed the information. As he did I noticed Sergeant Edwards rallying the squads in the background. The lads formed a line on each side of the road. I'm not sure if the South Vietnamese troops could work out exactly what was going on; they stood around looking at one another. I recall hearing one asking a Lance Corporal why United Nations soldiers were intervening; the atmosphere was fast becoming tense.

"Tell my counterpart that I'm very pleased that *these people* shouldn't be afraid, but I would still like to know exactly what's going on!" Lieutenant Derrick responded. He was in an uncompromising mood. The Vietnamese officer could clearly sense this. He tried smiling; the Lieutenant remained impassive.

"Chúng tôi, Việt Công Chiến sî, chiến cứơ sì. Không chống lý đơ xe chầ," (*We are looking for Viet Cong guerrillas, terrorists. You cannot oppose us here...not your business*!) the Vietnamese officer retorted. He was becoming flustered. In contrast, Lieutenant Derrick remained composed, deliberately pausing before responding.

I looked into the ditch as Macker conveyed the response. The people were of varied ages. They all looked terrified; they likely thought that we were American soldiers. The women were huddled together in a tight group. Many had been weeping. They all looked dishevelled. The soldiers had confiscated their possessions, what few they had. They were stacked in a bundle by the roadside.

"Ask him if they've found any weapons," the Lieutenant said.

The SVA officer responded by slowly shaking his head. He was wearing a sarcastic smirk as Lieutenant Derrick continued to survey the scene. His troops were also making derogatory comments, a factor he had no intention of correcting.

"Lance Corporal Morris," the Lieutenant said, "get down there and find out where these people were heading."

"What are you do?" the Vietnamese officer snapped as I jumped onto the side of the ditch.

"Ah ha!" Lieutenant Derrick said. "So…we can speak English—"

"Not for you, this," the officer interrupted becoming increasingly agitated. "Can not come here!"

The Lieutenant waited, yet again, before responding: "Now I don't know how much English you can speak, but you will be advised that my powers give me every right to be here. And ask questions, understand?"

"Not can be here, you go—!"

"Lance Corporal McFall!" the Lieutenant said maintaining eye contact with the officer. "Convert and convey my last sentence to my counterpart. Lance Corporal Morris, carry out my instructions."

I stooped down alongside two of the men. They must've been in their thirties. One was sweating profusely; his face was a picture of fear. I tried to calm them by smiling. Unfortunately, some of the American soldiers began shouting obscenities from the open trucks as they continued lumbering past.

I struggled with my words as I began to ask questions. The remainder of the collection were nervously looking at us as we eventually struck up a conversation. The two men who had sacks on the heads were to my left; one appeared to be sobbing. We had no idea why they were being kept incommunicado.

Meanwhile, the SVA officer, who had likely contacted headquarters, began frantically talking on his radiophone.

After some ten minutes I climbed out of the ditch to convey the information. The Vietnamese officer followed me as I approached Lieutenant Derrick. "Excuse us!" the Lieutenant said in a tone that he'd have understood whether he could speak English or not.

Sergeant Edwards joined us as I began to communicate the details: "They're from Mưì Sặn Thờưc, Sir, a hamlet about eight miles west. They say they were heading for Thầy Pưc, a small settlement south of Quang Trì. They had to leave their village for some reason, they wouldn't stipulate what."

"Are the men NVA?" the Lieutenant asked.

I considered for a second: "I don't think so Sir, the two guys I spoke to have southern accents. People from the north draw out their tones, a bit like Brummies; their tones had sharp closures."

"VC?"

"They admitted to being 'Cong-sangannalese—"

"That doesn't make them terrorists," Buster cut in.

"I know Sergeant," the Lieutenant responded. He yet again quietly surveyed the scene. I suddenly realised that the convoy of trucks had gone as he focussed on me: "I don't want to put you on the spot young man, but you and the other interpreters have had a bit more leave to study these people and their ways. So, what's your gut feeling?"

The Lieutenant and Buster stared at me as I thought out my response. I felt as if the whole world was resting on my shoulders. I wanted them to go free they looked innocent enough. But what if they were separatist rebels moving in the guise of harmless people. I could've opted out; said I didn't know. But I had a responsibility: "I think they're just very frightened people trying to get from one place to another Sir."

"Sergeant?"

"Lance Corporals Morris and McFall could try talking to one or two of the others. Maybe some of the women."

"Good idea, but I don't think we've got the time; this could turn ugly. We just about outnumber these little pricks presently, but they could have reinforcements here in minutes."

"We could ask headquarters for advice Sir."

"Yeah, we could ask," he responded with a cutting tone. "If this pathetic little lot are Viet Cong guerrillas then I'll eat my hat. Sergeant, round up the men. Inform them we're to take these people to, what's the name of the place Lance Corporal Morris?"

"Thầy Pưc, Sir."

"Yeah…there. We'll have to budge up in the jeeps but we'll manage."

Lieutenant Derrick instructed Macker to invite the Vietnamese officer for a consultation. Unfortunately, he was not interested. "You must go now!" he barked dismissively waving his hand.

"Oh yes, we're going…" Lieutenant Derrick answered with a scornful grin, "and we're taking these people with us!"

The SVA officer launched into a tirade of abuse, Vietnamese mixed with broken English. Macker and I jumped onto the side of the ditch to inform the people of our intentions. Some of the troop accompanied us; they started cutting the plastic ties on the wrists of the men. Lance Corporal Jessop and Marine Cunliffe removed the sacks placed on the heads of the two men; they winced in the bright sunlight. Some of the women began screaming, clearly unsure of the situation.

"Nghe. Khắp thế giời chiến sĩ. Đứng lo an toàn cà bây giơ," (*Attention, United Nations troops, don't worry, all safe now*!) Macker and I instinctively called out. The man that I had the discussion with also gave encouragement telling everyone to keep calm.

Meanwhile we could hear a commotion above. Some of the Vietnamese soldiers were eyeballing the lads lining the road. Many were attempting to evoke a face-to-face confrontation.

"Don't rise to it," the Sergeant advised, "just ignore the little twats."

Most of the men complied, stoically staring the opposition out with deadpan expressions.

Marine Lyle had other ideas. Sugar was the Platoon comedian an essential component in the dynamic make up of a unit. He was also incredibly cavalier; he was forever being reprimanded. Sugar shouted at a Vietnamese Sergeant as he attempted to engage Buster: "Well fuck me backwards if it ain't Wok-head Fred…who sent you, rent-a-cunt!"

A dwarf-like SVA Corporal joined in, meting out obscenities whilst cupping his hand around his genitals.

"Fuck me another pan-faced cunt!" Sugar derided. "…that's it skillet-head balls, you wanna go out an' buy yerself a pair—"

"Muffle that beak shitbird!" Sergeant Edwards barked.

Once free the men and women gathered together in an embrace. We helped them up the low banks beside the road. We needed to separate them in order to give them all a place in the jeeps. Once again the women became distressed – they clearly wanted to remain close to their men. One young girl appeared to have a learning disability; in addition she may have been blind. She held tightly onto the hand of a woman who may've been a relation; the poor girl looked terrified. 'How brave of these troops to pick on such a harmless and disempowered group' I thought.

Lieutenant Derrick worked out a compromise as the SVA soldiers continued looking on. The party would be placed in four jeeps with drivers. We would pack into the remaining vehicles, which would drive front and rear.

I placed some of the people's belongings into the second jeep as four of the group crowded in. I looked at the woman with the disabled teenager; both were trembling. I tried smiling at the escort but she remained impassive. She likely still didn't understand what was going on. Each vehicle had a wire whip-mast with the United Nations Flag [Blue Duster] attached; this failed to alleviate their anxiety.

The SVA officer pointed his finger at Lieutenant Derrick as we prepared to move out: "I report you! You will have kicking...**I report you!**"

"Be my guest!" he responded as we gathered speed.

We progressed down Route 9 at a swift pace. We needed to put as much distance as possible between the SVA Unit and ourselves. We drove through Quang Trì Town at a frantic pace. The convoy passed hordes of South Vietnamese soldiers in the streets and on the roadside. I kept on imagining they'd marshal us in and demand we hand over the group.

We were pulled over some ten minutes later by a routine roadblock. Macker accompanied Lieutenant Derrick as a collection of MPs asked questions.

"Those bastards had better not start," Jumper said. "We're not handing this lot over, not now we've come this far."

"Cool it," Corporal Speed whispered as the MPs scanned the vehicles.

They thankfully waved us on. We noticed a rust-spotted sign for Thầy Pưc on Highway One. The lead jeeps slowed as the principal of the compilation began gesticulating; the convoy pulled over.

Sergeant Edwards beckoned me. Lieutenant Derrick was standing next to the vehicle containing one of the men I had a conversation with.

"Find out what he wants," the Lieutenant said.

I asked the man, who by that time looked less stressed.

"Chúng tôi đến trang Lộng. Xin chơ phép liên hợựn bày giơ," (*We have arrived, this is our town. Please, may we go now*?) He asked.

I conveyed the request to Lieutenant Derrick who gave the man a gentle smile: "Tell him that he and his people are free to go anytime they wish."

The group disembarked from our vehicles. They hastily collected their belongings and made for the modestly sized settlement; they likely wanted to enter under their own steam. Being brought in by troops, regardless of our neutrality, may've compromised their safety.

The party trundled away. As they did, a woman turned and made her way towards Lieutenant Derrick. She grabbed his hand, brought it up to her mouth and kissed it gently. The Lieutenant looked embarrassed as she rejoined the others.

We were all feeling pleased with ourselves as we left. Later, Lieutenant Derrick disappeared for a day. Sometime after that we heard that Command had given him a roasting for '...intervening in an internal affair'. It would be the first of a number of admonishments that the Platoon would receive during our Tour of Duty.

*

19:00: UN Base Camp: 7, Biên Dưc, Tuesday 5 September.

We'd just completed a fifteen-day assignment of monitoring the continuing withdrawal of American equipment and personnel. It felt as if we had been camped on Highway One for an eternity. The ad nauseam of watching lines of troop-packed lorries making their way towards Huê-Phu Baì Airport had dulled our senses. We'd been lured into a false sense of importance by our act of mercy on Route 9. Seeing yourself, as a White Knight charging around the countryside was more than just self-satisfying – it was positively euphoric.

The monotony of our duties was occasionally broken by the remarkable panoramas. Quang Trì Province was an enigma. Sunrise would reveal a kaleidoscope of colour, a cornucopia of splendour: occasional rice paddies flanked by palm trees and dense rubber plantations; barren grounds unexpectedly replaced with fertile soils fed by Artesian wells. The serrated massifs assembling the Â Shàu Valley looked as if they'd been shaped by an army of giant sculptors, the stepped terraces below acting as if a stairway. The mountains gave way to gentle slopes abounding with vegetation. During the day the skies seemed to be forever filled with billowing snow white clouds, only to mysteriously clear at sunset.

The only thing that ruined the aesthetic pleasantness was the persistent remnant of war. The area was scattered with acre-sized remains of chemical warfare and napalm bombing. Swathes of earth cleared by defoliants and extended patches of scorched terrain that had struggled to recover.

We had to deal with the added stress of looking out for tripwire claymores and antipersonnel mines. Both devices instilled a chilling dread. The decapitating claymores would send a 360° spray of ball bearings at varying angles. The German WWII design Teller-mine was even more feared. The device was a vertical release mine. Once triggered the core would shoot upwards to groin level and explode showering the victim with thousands of tiny metal slivers. A man could be cut in half by the high-speed shards. It was rumoured that there were more mines in Quang Trì Province than in the whole of South Vietnam. You had to just learn to walk through areas with the hope that you wouldn't activate a tripwire or weight switch.

The infamous murder hole was living up to its reputation. The highways and surrounding districts were littered with dead bodies. Execution-style killings; bodies with holed and bloodstained pillowcases placed on their heads. Occasionally we'd find a body of an elderly person who'd either walked to their death after becoming separated from a line of refugees or had simply been left on the roadside or in the bush, the relations unable to carry the corpse. Some of the corpses had been lying in the sun for days, maybe even weeks. Cadaver eating animals grew fat on the feasts.

At 17:00 we witnessed the last line of United States troops heading for their long awaited departure – the GIs were all wearing grins.

We returned to barracks to the shocking news that eleven Israeli Athletes had been murdered in the midst of the 1972 Olympic Games. A group of *Black September* Arab guerrillas had broken into the Olympic village in Munich. Nine of the athletes lost their lives after a bungled rescue attempt by West German Special Forces at Furstenfield Military Airport. Until then we had no particular interest in the Olympics. It was strangely comforting to realise atrocities were being perpetrated in other parts of the world.

These horrors were quickly tempered by local news. A reporter from Radio Sàigòn gave an on-the-spot broadcast of a massacre in Hứ Đựìn, a renowned Viet Cong separatist village in western Quang Trì. The killings included women and children, many of whom had been herded into an underground rice store. The victims had been blasted to death by grenades [pineapples].

'Pass the pineapple' was a favourite game of indigenous troops in the region. Their victims would be locked into an underground store; the tormentors would then sporadically toss grenades into the space. The result would be predictable, the terrified people trying to cower away from the deadly explosives. Soldiers would take bets on how many pineapples it would take before the rice store quietened. They'd draw out the game for maximum enjoyment. The space would be checked once silent. Injured survivors would be executed. Surviving females, and often young-boys, would be raped before their termination – 'fuck the riddled body', another perverse game in their collection.

The reporter said that a government spokesman had suggested that renegade North Vietnamese troops were responsible for the barbarous act. It was highly questionable why North Vietnamese Regulars would want to murder supporters of Hồ Chí Minh.

I remember reading a column from Seymour Hersh of the *Washington Post* who wrote: '*There is no Geneva Convention in this place, in Quang Trì only barbarity rules.*' We'd only been in the murder hole for three weeks; already it was living up to its standing.

13:00: Chừ Mý Shựi, Â Shàu, Wednesday 20 September.

Day thirteen of a reconnaissance of the Â Shàu Valley; Command had given us the unpopular task of patrolling known Viet Cong hamlets. The villages were to be reminded of the terms of the interim ceasefire. The Â Shàu Valley was the core of the murder hole. The general population were predominantly Viet Cong-sangannalese. The whole region had been involved in numerous territorial battles throughout the protracted conflict, including the struggle to capture Hill 875 (depicted in the film *Hamburger Hill*). The settlements that made up the western reaches had suffered more than almost any others in South Vietnam.

Massacres are a feature of armed confrontation. Non-combatants have been slaughtered by invading armies and marauders since time immemorial. Vietnam had suffered more than its share of mass murder. The historical context of the war had left the VC with an understandable loathing of foreign troops; the SVA were bad enough, but at least they were Vietnamese. Victor Charlie had a particular loathing for 'round-eyes'.

We detested entering 'Cong strongholds, we always felt unwelcome. In 30 years of conflict the Japanese, preceded and succeeded by the Colonial French, and the repressive South Vietnamese regime supported by the USA had failed to break the spirit and determination of the people. The Viet Cong have their own inimitable culture based on a number of paradigms. They believe that the uniqueness of individuality is complemented by a common singularity, that of 'community', the primary concept integral to their very existence. They view themselves as a dynamic collective – consequently, if you pushed one of them around you pushed all of them around and you did that at your peril.

Victor Charlie just about tolerated our presence. On passing they would either gently nod or simply disregard us. Given the choice the Viet Cong would have ejected all uninvited aliens. Ironically, it was in their nature to welcome strangers, they were renowned for their hospitality. But successive invaders and 9000 days of bitter hostility had tempered their ways. The Americans tried to win over the masses with a sustained *Hearts-and-Minds* programme; it was a joke. At the same time that they were trying to convince the people of a change in attitudes by the administration they were supporting the SVA in razing Viet Cong villages to the ground. The whole thing was a complete failure.

The small hamlet of Chừ Mý Shụi was no different from any of the other of the settlements we'd visited. A rampart surrounded the immured community. It would've been totally ineffective against a sustained attack. I guess it simply made the inhabitants feel safer. It was apparent that the sparsely populated community had suffered numerous attacks. There were clear remnants of earlier fires: scorched areas where habitations once stood; small craters surrounding areas formerly used for livestock. Information on the commune suggested that it was well inhabited; the particulars were clearly out of date.

I was chosen as the primary translator with Bronco acting as backup. The Chû tuổi [village elder or honcho] listened as I translated. The people quietly stood round as the one-way conversation continued. The honcho interrupted

Lieutenant Derrick, as he was about to wind-down. He wanted to know what he was supposed to do about constant threats. We assumed he meant from the SVA. How surprised we were to hear that he meant threats from all sides. The Lieutenant instructed me to ask the Chû tuổi to elaborate.

The elder delivered a catalogue of abuse. Viet Cong guerrillas had been persistently entering their hamlet in search of new recruits. Once all the young men had been taken they began to demand older men and strong young women. The SVA would follow; they would refuse to believe that the inhabitants joined the NLF under duress. They'd burn the village and beat up a chosen number of people. The Americans offered the commune protection in the late '60s, providing that they relocated twenty miles east. The yanks sent in medical teams to offer the children inoculations against childhood diseases. Local Viet Cong militia heard of the proposal. They came in during the night and rounded up the people. They warned that they would cut off the arms of any children receiving injections. A demonstration was carried out on a young boy – he bled to death. Catholic missionaries offering salvation came into the village in the early '70s. Some of the people signed up, receiving crucifixes as a sign of their newfound faith. North Vietnamese Regulars entered in the early hours looking for Christians. Some of the inhabitants had their crucifixes round their necks. The soldiers ripped off the medallions and proceeded to score a hammer and sickle alongside a five-sided star into their chests with daggers. A fortnight later an American Infantry Unit entered accusing the inhabitants of being communist sympathisers. The presiding Chû tuổi was arrested and taken to a South Vietnamese Army Base for questioning; he never returned. The Security Forces said that he had fractured his skull after slipping in the shower. The villagers appealed for his body to be returned; the SVA granted their request. The Chû tuổi's corpse was full of bruises; the elder said he must've slipped about a dozen times. He concluded by asking what *we* could do for him and his people.

I was exhausted by the time the elder had finished. The translation had taken over twenty minutes. I was pleased that I'd done so well; I had to paraphrase a wide variation of often-complex words. My satisfaction was underpinned by a feeling of ambivalence; I wished the contents of the report were different.

Lieutenant Derrick was rarely lost for words. On that occasion he struggled. He looked at the honcho, apparently unable to give a response. After what seemed like an eternity he gave an answer: "Tell the elder that we'll write a detailed report to our superiors."

The honcho gave a lingering look after I'd translated: "Đồng chí bẩi đoc báo. Cám ơn," (*You write report...thank you.*)

The Lieutenant looked uncomfortable. What else could he say, or do.

We moved out of Chừ Mý Shụi after handing out detailed information on the terms of the provisional accord. I'm sure everybody was thinking the same as me: 'What's the point of handing people information on an accord that quite simply doesn't exist?'

My mind was working overtime as we walked towards our next objective. I had doubted our presence and effectiveness long before we arrived in Vietnam. Chừ Mý Shụi would be the first of a line of frustrating and negative experiences. I couldn't get the image of the honcho out of my mind, or his words. I wondered how long it would be before they would receive another visit, a visit a lot less friendly than ours.

13:00: Roughly 6 miles from the Laotian border, Wednesday 18 October.

October began with our first period of monitoring the movement of refugees throughout Quang Trì. I have seen numerous depictions for refugees: social misfits or economic migrants; victims of ethnic cleansing; dislodged or exiled people; nomads or banished émigrés. It's not hip in the politically correct 21st Century to talk of refugees in the negative. The term *Asylum Seeker* was ostensibly created in an endeavour to minimize unconstructive views of individuals or groups – people desperately in need rather than simply wanting an easier life. Terms like, foreign spongers; beggars and thieves and benefit scroungers, confined to BNP rallies or the whispers of the disgruntled. I have a supposition about the use of idioms: '*You can change the language, but this does little to change notions.*' Nobody wants to be a refugee, and refugees are wanted by nobody.

Refugees are an inevitable consequence of armed conflict, particularly Civil War. Nobody suffers more than the displaced; they are the epitome of disempowered people. They have no base; no status and virtually no control over, at least their short-term, future.

The chaotic passage of refugees throughout South Vietnam compounded the problem. Most nomads have a clear objective: a neighbouring country offering a temporary enclave; established ethnic groups or communities, or quarters containing UN or other security personnel. The movements around Quang Trì were disorganized and frenzied – people moving through every variation of the compass point. Việt Kieụs and Kiệuries escaping persecution from Viet Cong activists; displaced 'Cong-sangannalese fleeing from the South Vietnamese Security Forces; Laotian Clans people crisscrossing the border to escape oppression and fighting in their own country, and ethnic Chinese attempting hazardous journeys to a neverland.

When we were called upon to monitor a refugee movement that's precisely what we did – monitor. We had to adhere to a strict criterion. We could not intervene in a situation unless refugees were suffering overt abuse. The South Vietnamese Military Police had primary responsibility for guiding refugees to camps or distribution points. The administration had given the task to the constabulary to placate the aid agencies. Regular South Vietnamese Army Units had been accused of the maltreatment of refugees. In Trệng Nhôy an entire company was found guilty of the highway robbery of travelling groups. The Commanders were jailed, only to be released on appeal whereon they took charge of fresh units.

We spent our first week chasing phantom sightings or accosting people who were simply going about their everyday business. One afternoon we scared the life out a cluster of people returning from market. They became panicky as we approached to ask if they needed assistance; they likely thought we were about to rob them or pull them in for questioning.

We made our first real contact during the second week. Lines of North Vietnamese moving southeast passing bedraggled Meớ and Nưng moving northwest in the hope of re-crossing the Laotian border. Having to stand at the roadside whilst lines of refugees were marshalled to designated points sorely tested our resolve, particularly since it was obvious that the Military Police wanted nothing to do with the task.

We could do little but offer the people water and occasional medical assistance. One hot and sticky afternoon we spotted a woman lagging behind her party. She was struggling with a heavy load wrapped in a large sheet. She'd likely packed as many of her belongings as she could; the load was clearly slowing her down. The Military Police stopped her and told her to dump some of her possessions; she refused. On refusal a Military Police Sergeant pulled the roll from her back and tossed the belongings onto the road. He and a colleague then began throwing some of the items into a monsoon ditch. The woman became distressed. She fell to her knees wailing as the police sifted through her belongings. Members of her party continued walking; they were either too scared or too exhausted to protest. After dumping around two-thirds of the load the MPs handed her the wrap and ordered her to rejoin the line. She remained in a collapsed state on the tarmac. One of the MPs gave her a little persuasion with his rattan cane.

We all looked in Lieutenant Derrick's direction as the woman succumbed to the beating.

"Can't we intervene Sir?" Marine Vincent enquired.

"No! Stay at your posts."

"I'd like just two minutes with that little twat," Marine Collins muttered. "I'd turn that cane into a permanent arsehole-rod!"

I looked at the tormented woman's face as she struggled past. I felt sick to the stomach. Her haggard look made it hard to gauge how old she was. She gazed at me with her sunken eyes. I looked away feeling uncomfortable, ashamed. 'What are we doing here?' I thought. I can't think of many things more heartbreaking than being considered a refugee in your own land.

The following day we picked up a small crowd of people on the edges of Route 9. The terrified collection said they'd been constantly harassed by a band of VC insurgents. We bumped into a Viet Cong Cadre in the middle of providing an escort. The frontman sported a small red ribbon tied around the barrel of his Kalashnikov [AK47] an indicator that the faction were 'Minh Nationalists' (followers of Hồ Chí Minh). The Nationalists, who endeavoured to create a Unified Social Democratic Republic, were the most feared of the guerrilla movements. Separatists would do their utmost to recruit Viet Cong rebels from other factions; there were 'Cong revolutionaries who wanted nothing to do with a pact with the Communist North. Many simply wanted to be rid of the oppressive South Vietnamese Government; the National Liberation Front was not as indivisible as it imagined. The splinter group was openly carrying Rocket Propelled Grenade [RPG] launchers and an assortment of assault rifles. They eyeballed us as we walked passed. The refugees huddled close together between our Detachment.

Lieutenant Derrick instructed Marine Giggs to contact the Red Cross on the Radio Transmitter [RT]. We were supposed to contact the Military Police to request an escort to a safe haven. He considered that the group had suffered enough. We were all relieved when Giggsy announced that an aid section was to pick them up early evening.

Our satisfaction was cancelled out early on the following morning. Command directed us to muster at a grid reference on Route 8. We arrived to discover groups of refugees camped along the roadside. The vicinity was dotted with bomb craters. Refugees would sometimes utilise the craters constructing crude dugout shelters with discarded timber and army tarpaulins.

The Military Police, accompanied by Alsatian dogs, arrived with a convoy of lorries. They proceeded to wade into the conglomeration with the baying dogs whilst blowing whistles. The people fled in all directions only to be marshalled further down the highway by more soldiers; yet again we found ourselves redundant. It was beyond us why we'd been asked to witness the spectacle; the MPs knew exactly what level of force to use. What made matters worse was the refusal by the police to employ the lorries to help transport the refugees. Lieutenant Derrick pleaded with the Military Police Commander to use the vehicles to take the people to a distribution point. The principal refused saying it that was not policy. The trucks stood empty, their engines idling as the refugees set off on yet another trek to a nameless destination.

*

17:00: Roughly 1 mile west of Vả Thươì, Route 9, Friday 20 October.

We were all looking forward to end of day. The following Saturday was to be our first day off for nearly three weeks. Most of the Platoon heard the disturbance ahead, unquestionable reports of gunfire. We slowed in the jeeps adhering to the signal from Sergeant Hoggs in the lead vehicle. I was driving the third vehicle, Cowboy, Ricky and Vinny sat beside and behind me.

We could see Chopper requesting Lieutenant Derrick to come forward as he signalled a halt. I could only just see ahead. Apparently there was a body on the road. We crept up to the position to discover a horrendous scene. What looked like one corpse turned out to be around a dozen. The bodies were lying on the road and verge in various positions; they'd clearly been shot to death. A scattering of spent 7.62 rounds littered the opposite side of the road.

"Form a semi-circle round the scene!" Chopper shouted as we jumped from the jeeps. "Check out if there are any survivors. And don't forget to don plastic gloves!"

Some of the Detachment were posted as sentries front and rear and each side of the road as we set to work. It was a heartrending sight. The group of men and women were in close proximity to one another. They were of varying ages, though most were young. They had undoubtedly been ambushed, the perpetrators making an escape through the elephant grass in the surrounding fields. It was difficult at that stage to determine the motive.

One or two of the victims were laying face down on the verge adjacent to the monsoon ditch. Checking if there were any survivors was a largely fruitless exercise; the bodies were riddled with bullets. I approached the body of a man not much older than myself. He was lying on his back part on the verge. His head was back at an angle. The man's mouth was wide open. The air escaping from his lungs was slowly flowing up his windpipe, buffeting against the back of his throat. It would be the first – though regrettably not the last – time I would hear the death rattle. I nervously felt for a pulse on his neck, though I'm unsure why.

Some of the others slowly made their way through the undergrowth to see if anybody had made an escape. Macker accompanied them advising that we were UN troops. An ox driven cart carrying two adults and three children passed as we carried out our unenviable tasks. The caregivers covered the children's eyes as they gazed down at us.

The bloodstained highway was strewn with the victims' belongings. The perpetrators may've started rifling through the spoil only to rapidly withdraw when they heard us drawing near.

We were in the process of tagging the bodies when we heard, what appeared to be, the sound of a baby crying. "Can you hear that?" Lance Corporal Bear

asked. “Am I imagining something or is that a baby crying?”
“We can hear it,” Sergeant Hoggs replied. “Check the undergrowth and under the bodies, especially the women.”
The Detail began frantically searching as the crying continued. My mind was working overtime. I imagined that a distraught mother had flung her child into the bushes as a last attempt to protect it as the bullets riddled her body.
We were just about to widen our search when the wailing stopped.
“Relax,” Marine Clarke yelled from a deposit of low shrubs, “it’s a cat!”
“What?” the Lieutenant said.
“It’s a moggy, caterwaulin’. It’s scampered back into the undergrowth.”
“A song for the dead,” I suggested.
“Fuckin’ ’ell, you’re weird!” Marine Cunliffe said as we aborted the search.
“I ’eard a baby,” Marine Wood said, “…I’m sure I ’eard a baby cryin’.”
“It’s just wishful thinkin’ son,” Chopper followed. “There’s no baby here. Continue tagging the bodies.”
We sat waiting for the MPs once our tasks were complete. On arrival the law enforcement officers set to cordoning off the area whilst vociferously informing us that we could leave. I couldn’t help thinking that they were deliberately trying to get rid of us. What happened after that was anybody’s guess.
We left the scene as frustrated as ever. On our departure Ricky mentioned that he’d noticed three flash-scars slashed into the right cheek of one of the victims, a tribal marking of the Laotian Mân. They were likely making a final dash for the border. They’d probably been under the false impression that it would be safer to travel north through the western reaches of South Vietnam rather than dodging North Vietnamese infiltrators on the Hồ Chí Minh Trail. Their gamble almost paid off: they were less than 4 miles from possible sanctuary. The hackneyed adage ‘*A miss is as good as a mile,*’ never seemed so poignant.

14:30: Quang Trì Military Air Strip, Wednesday 1 November.

The Platoon stood on the tarmac waiting for our airlift. We’d just returned to Base Camp 7 after completing our tenth day of patrolling the outskirts of Quang Trì Town. Command instructed us to pack our gear in preparation for an immediate clandestine transfer. Impromptu relocations were something we’d need to get used to. Speculation as always was rife, claim and counter claim dominating otherwise prosaic conversation. Whatever the conjecture our destination would probably be some nice little spot where the masses were still trying to tear each other’s heads off.

The country was in its 78th day of the interim ceasefire. It had long become apparent that the word *ceasefire* had a multiple meaning in the Vietnamese language. The war continued on all fronts – none more so than in Quang Trì. Daily updates would kick off with a list of ceasefire violations. The peace would be broken by mad half-hours where reports of gunfire would fill the air. Charlie had been as busy in the provincial town as on the outskirts. On the night of the 25th the Platoon was treated to a complimentary fireworks display after Viet Cong militia scored a direct hit on a pyrotechnics factory. The mega exhibition could be seen as far south as Thơư Đế.

The following day we were informed that an adjacent Leper Hospital had been set alight by loose rockets and flying embers. The authorities abandoned the patients after a forced evacuation. Nobody wanted the unfortunates. We could see them scavenging in rubbish dumps and lining the streets of the town begging with their creased-leather faces and withered hands.

We spent the 27th & 28th dodging sniper fire in the south of the suburb. Our status dictated that we could not return fire unless under threat. It was beyond us how being targeted by marksmen hiding in bushes and buildings could not be construed a hazard.

All the same, leaving Quang Trì would bring no heartache, even though we were unsure of our new assignments. In our 77 days in the murder hole there had been a total of 489-recorded fatalities. A lot more had probably gone undocumented.

10:00: Huê-Phu Baì Airport, Sunday 5 November.

We sat in a makeshift lecture room awaiting yet more 'guess the location' briefings. Each duty appeared to have a gadfly-existence. The hullabaloo surrounding our expedient departure from Quang Trì turned into another damp squib. Our secret location was nothing more exciting than the open grounds surrounding Huê-Phu Baì Airport. Undercover agents had informed intelligence that local Viet Cong militia were massing in readiness for a concentrated attack on departing US personnel. None of us could understand why we had been sent to observe something that could've been dealt with by the SVA and remaining US Forces. I had my own theory: that the neutrality of the IPSF was being compromised by persistent United States vetoes on reports on the conduct of the South Vietnamese Security Forces. What better way to divert attention than advertising the behaviour of a purported terrorist organisation. As it transpired the whole thing turned out to be an elaborate hoax – either that or the IPSF were in cahoots with intelligence.

It wasn't all bad. On Saturday 3rd a dozen 12-hour passes were up for grabs. We held the accustomed lottery. Bronco, Dinger, Dusty, Tommy and I were amongst the lucky ones – time for us to check out the delights of Huê.

The former Imperial Capital still carried the battle-scars from the 1968 Tết Offensive. The Perfume River split the old and the new sectors of the city though it was hard to distinguish between the two. As in Sàigòn, the streets were adorned with enormous pictures of President Thiều and Vice President Trần Ván Hựơng. The lamp-posts along Lế Loí Street were festooned with multiple hanging baskets and the central reservations of Bấ Triệu Boulevard contained rows of azaleas and blooming forsythia. Though beautiful, the floral displays looked absurd amongst the squalor that ringed the old sector of the municipality.

Tommy and I separated from some of the others to examine some of the historical buildings. We quickly discovered that 12 hours was woefully inadequate. Huê was a truly astounding conurbation. Stunning Chùa Môt Cột's & Cậo Dai Temples lined the banks of the river. The western influence was evident: French built schools containing children singing Frére Jacques stood beside ancient halls of academia dating back to the 16th Century. The Christian influence was also evident. Mawkish people lined the streets trying to sell heavily bound bibles. The Buddhists tolerated them only because their teachings demanded that individuals should find enlightenment through their own paths. The Christian missionaries still did their utmost to proselytise those with alternative beliefs. I found myself locked in an altercation with a young American woman who did her best to sell me the New Testament. On informing her I was an Atheist she launched into a tirade of abuse. I accused her of caring not one jot about the abuses carried out by her own so-called God-fearing countrymen. She responded by quoting passages from the good book. Tommy dragged me away amid me shouting accusations of hiding behind text. I've always despised the moral justification some religious zealots profess: the concept of 'God on their side'.

We sauntered down Chớy Phặn Từ Street after I'd calmed down. The street was famous for its Tranh sơn mài (Lacquered pictures). A bronzed Eurasian adorned with jewellery invited us into his shop and back store factory to see the sơn màis being created. We wished he hadn't bothered. The tiny dimly lit sweatbox was full of children sat cross-legged on a stone floor – child labour before our very eyes.

I looked at Tommy whose face was mirroring mine: "I've just had an argument with one cunt! I don't want another, let's split."

We took a leisurely stroll to the Sông Chờ [Floating Market]. The bustling marketplace was incredible. Small boats tied up alongside bamboo pontoons with stalls teeming with river food, vegetables and al fresco eating-places. The open and covered stands were full of any number of assorted goods; live crabs in cages beside produce fresh from the fields. One stall had a cage crammed with jade monkeys. We thought they were on sale as pets until the stallholder grabbed a terrified monkey from the cage before proceeding to skin it alive. The man twisted its neck once the poor creature had been stripped. Apparently, the meat would taste better if the animal's heart raced before its demise. I thought that the practice was despicable; then again there were, and still are, some pretty appalling abuses of animals in my own country.

After some food we met up with Bronco and Dusty to try out some of the nightlife. Our passes ran out at 2000 hours, so we took it easy. Dusty showed us a small Tranh sơn mài he'd purchased for his mum. I didn't ask if he'd bought it from a small shop down Chớy Phặn Từ Street.

We returned to our small mess room at Huê-Phu Baì with time to spare. It had been an enjoyable half-day. Tommy and I would like to have viewed the Tombs of the Nguyễn Kings along with the Thiền Mứ Monasteries. At least we had the chance of leaving the mundane of listening to the persistent drone of aircraft taking off and landing.

11:00: Huê-Phu Baì Airport.

It was of no surprise that we were to be reassigned yet again; there was plainly nothing to do at Huê-Phu Baì. Imagine our delight at being informed that we were to be put on standby at an old US Naval Annex in Hoị Ẩn.

We packed at a leisurely pace for our short flight south. Marine Wood disappeared for half an hour. Before our departure we could see why. The base had a signpost created by passing servicemen: New York, Los Angeles, Phoenix, Hong Kong and Sydney, amongst the many arrowed signs. Woody added his own creation: 'Tooting Broadway'. He had fashioned it out of cardboard. It wouldn't have survived a squally shower, but it still tickled us. The sign would have been really cool – if the arrow was only pointing in the right direction!

20:00: Hoị Ẩn Naval Annex, Tuesday 7 November.

Being on standby was not as rewarding as we'd imagined. It wouldn't have been so bad if we were allowed some shore leave – no such luxuries were forthcoming. The Platoon occupied a long-standing barracks on the northern shore of the old Chinese Seaport. The annex was nought but a giant store for the United States Naval presence off Đà Nẵng. The silted harbour was lined with L-shaped jetties accommodating rusting tugboats, heavily barnacled caissons and half-sunken barges. The site had long been redundant; the administration hadn't even bothered posting sentries on the gates.

The location was lined with dilapidated Nissen huts. Our mess room had faded pictures of Che Guevara, Jimi Hendrix, Martin Luther King, Huey Newton and Raquel Welch posted on the drab walls. We enjoyed sharing our lodgings with nature: mammoth rats and well-fed mice scurried under the floorboards, whilst feral cats and mangy stray dogs competed for territory amid the mildew infested buildings.

Our perpetual boredom led to night excursions around the station. We found a broken down Automat at the far end of the base. The 1950s Nissen hut looked as if it had been boarded up since President Kennedy's assassination. We manufactured an opening with a friendly jemmy. The grimy and cobwebbed hut contained an assortment of vending machines secured by an enormous chain connected to a stout padlock. Sugar and I set to work picking the locks – I knew the skills we'd acquired in Approved School would come in handy one day. Half the machines still had goodies in the racks. Some of the goods were out of date, but it mattered not. We waddled down the quayside loaded with boxes of soft drinks, our pockets bulging with Twinkies and 50/50 bars. A chocolate feast washed down with copious bottles of 7-UP succeeded supper.

Colour Sergeant Biffly entered the mess room at 22:30. Biffo had the look of an avuncular man. He was anything but – Biffo was a fierce man who was intolerant of shenanigans. He demanded one hundred per cent from every member of the section, but he was still popular. "Listen up cunt-weasels!" he barked. "The caretaker's in a flap. He said a bunch of fuck-sticks broke into the Automat and emptied the machines. Any info'?"

We all gave him an innocent look – as pure as the driven snow.

"If I find out it's anyone from this fuckin' Platoon I'll 'ave their arseholes on meat 'ooks!"

I settled for the night by adding news reports to my journal. It would be a practice I would get used to during our tour. World news was as interesting as ever: in the UK the government announces an immediate compulsory prices and wages freeze following the failure of the CBI and TUC to agree on a voluntary deal to curb inflation. In Argentina Juan Peron returns after 17 years in exile – Government Forces increase security; hundreds of Human Rights activists are arrested in anticipation of civil unrest. Martial Law is imposed in South Korea amid increased political tension; the US backed regime states that they are '…trying to forestall militants infiltrating key institutions'. And in Washington, President Richard Nixon wins the US Presidency by a huge majority. The same day the US resumed the bombing of North Vietnam in an attempt to force the North Vietnamese back to the negotiating table. The broadcaster omitted to mention that the negotiators had left the peace talks because the bombing had never actually stopped.

10:30: Hoị Ần Seaport Naval Annex, Wednesday 8 November.

After an early morning of drills and equipment checks we finally sat down for an update on our position. Captain Page had travelled from Quang Ngaî to give us his obligatory lecture and praise. He said that we should be proud of our intervention. We'd apparently had an effect in Quang Trì – he could have fooled me.

The briefing concluded with the news that we were to be moved from Condition-1 [Yellow Alert or Stand Down] to Condition-3 with immediate effect. Things were bubbling, that was nothing new. What was new was the news that we may be called upon to participate in action. The Captain said that should it come to fruition it would revolve around protecting ethnic groups.

None of us were particularly spooked by the prospect. On the contrary, we would've welcomed protecting refugees against the ravages of the bullies that roamed the territories. It was to our annoyance that some seven hours later Colour Sergeant Biffly told us to disregard the information, and that we were being put back on Condition-1. Soon afterwards we reverted to Condition-3. Being categorised and re-categorised without the slightest inclination of what was going on was maddening.

Lieutenant Derrick finally pulled us together at 21:30: "As of now we are on twelve hours notice. Keep your gear packed ready for a rapid transfer. I can't give you any more information save that we'll be moving south…that's all."

The discontented mutterings were palpable. Being left further in the dark was the last thing we needed. We'd been on 12-Standby many times before. One instance lasted almost 23 days. Sugar said that being an élite Platoon meant that we were fed hybrid shit. We felt more like mushrooms than ever. It was as if we were riding a ghost train. I wrote a closing line in my journal—

'…The murder hole is behind us, where to next nobody knows. Windows frosted with breaths of tension; ears muffled by thunderous screams; incandescent flashes rebounding in claustrophobic labyrinths: the ghost train rumbles on.'

I smiled at my poetic analogy, though I'm unsure why – Charlieville was anything but a ride on the funfair.

3: TENTED CITIES – STEEL GRAVEYARDS

Imagine no possessions,
I wonder if you can,
No need for greed or hunger,
A brotherhood of man,
Imagine all the people,
Sharing all the world…
John Lennon

09:00: UN Base Camp 3, Nịhn Hoâ, Nha Trang Province, 9 November 1972.

The Platoon's transfer to Nha Trang was rapid. We were still holding onto a notion that we'd have a chance to check out Hoị Ẩn when the 'Supervisory Force Command finally placed us on Red Alert. The territory by all accounts had become the new hot spot.

The locality was subtly different from Quang Trì. It nestled in the fertile lowlands of the southeast. The coastal sector was once considered the Côte d'Azur of South East Asia. It was easy to see why. Seemingly endless golden beaches caressed by turquoise waters flanked the provincial town. The whole area was clean and bright. The roads were lined with palm trees and climbing bougainvillaea. Catholic Churches, Hindu Temples, Buddhist Shrines and Pagodas shared the same neighbourhoods. The layout of the white stucco buildings, their distinctive red-clay tiled roofs, added to the ecstatically agreeable presentation. The municipality appeared sleepy, people going about their everyday business without a care in the world. The provincial town, at least, seemed to have been untouched, as if the war was in another country. However, there was a sinister undercurrent. Viet Cong insurgents, hidden in the surrounding woods and long established havens within the borough, were slowly tightening the noose.

Nha Trang Province had long been a thorn in the side of those who attempted to administer control. The territory was the domain of the National Liberation Front. The Chơn Biên, Thộc Điếm, Shau Tiâ and Tchựin Districts were particularly problematic. Intelligence suggested that local Viet Cong rebels had been reforming into larger units. The traditional warfare associated with the revolutionary movement – infiltration, acts of sabotage, planned ambushes and attacks on small posts – had changed to one of open combat. The Security Forces had been incurring heavy casualties, particularly since the interim ceasefire. Victor Charlie, it appeared, was not interested in brokering deals.

Nevertheless, the Platoon still found itself in limbo; the urgency of our assignment wasn't mirrored by our duties. When not confined to base we were endlessly observing the Security Forces monitoring movements of the populace and refugees. It was a futile exercise. Charlie mostly travelled by night, or in various guises. Furthermore, they had certain elements of the Security Forces in their pockets. Corruption was rife. Post-terrorist activity, the police would blame the SVA – the SVA the police. Excuses, fabrication and deceit seemed to be the norm amongst the less than professional forces: an infinite circle of snakes eating their own tails.

15:00: Outskirts of Camp India, Nịhn Hoâ, Tuesday 14 November.

The Platoon was on day four of a specific United Nations mission. IPSF Command had ordered 2: Bravo 6, to monitor an expected influx of new refugees from An Hoâ, Côn Thiểm, Đắc Ân and Là Thứê. Lines of refugees were apparently heading towards Camp India, northwest of Nịhn Hoâ.

Nịhn Hoâ sat on the outskirts of Nha Trang Town. Its location made it a primary site for a refugee camp: out of sight of the populace of the provincial town, yet near enough to maintain and monitor. I distinctly remember my first view of Camp India. The sprawling 'tented city' appeared as if a blot on the landscape. The compound was situated off Route 3 the road to Bắn Mề Thưot. It was the biggest and most notorious camp in the area. It covered well over a square mile. The tents and other temporary shelters hardly had a footpath's width between them. The smell from the camp was oppressive, a manifestation of human suffering. There was no proper sanitation; disease was rife, particularly amongst the very old and young. Fatalities occurred on a weekly basis but got little airtime. The South Vietnamese Government was too concerned with propaganda reports on a victory that simply didn't exist.

Medicine was apparently in short supply, though we had heard a week before our arrival of boxes of medical supplies on the hospital ships in Cám Râhn Bay. The redundant vessels were waiting to weigh anchor for the return voyage to the 'States. The usual inane excuses followed, assertions that the drugs were inappropriate or that it would be logistically impracticable to transport supplies from the ships to the encampments.

The habitation embodied the inevitable cliques and ascendancies familiar to a conglomeration. Religious and ethnic groups; back market profiteers, drug dealers, pimps, moneylenders and punishment teams – the oppressors and the oppressed. We could see people queuing for food on a daily basis: those at the front received plenty, those at the rear the scraps. Women would only venture out of the camp in crowds. We'd see them stonewashing clothes on the banks of the tributaries adjoining the Nha Trang River.

There was a plethora of stories about women being rounded up by the SVA for questioning. Many were raped; the lucky ones lived to tell of their ordeal, not that anyone listened. Most would be found floating downriver weeks later, their bloated bodies too decomposed to glean forensic evidence.

The encampments were sustained by aid organisations. The Red Cross was the primary support group, with CAFOD, UNICEF, Christian Aid and the Franciscan Nuns supplementing their work. A number of Buddhist groups also provided relief, food and some medicine, but they had to operate separately due to the delicate politics of the region.

Two and Three Squads were designated a monitoring position on the periphery of the camp. We spent most of the day at the gates awaiting orders. None of us could work out why we'd been stationed at the compound. There were myriad stories of convoys of refugees being ambushed on Highway One and the surrounding roads.

Command had stationed One and Four Squads further north, somewhere off Highway One. Their task was to seek out the refugees and offer safe escort, if requested. By 15:30 it was apparent that no groupings could be found (though most had likely avoided detection).

At around 16:00 we noticed that there was more than the usual congregation of people gathering round the gates. By 16:30 we could see why. The camp supply lorries, an organized line of some twenty vehicles, were heading for the compound. Scraps would occasionally fall from the poorly stowed sacks and boxes. The refugees would take every opportunity to accrue extra vittles. We were fearful as the large Dodge trucks loomed. The crowd was disorderly. There were a number of children amongst them, some very small. The police appeared unconcerned; this was of no surprise, most of them considered the refugees to be 'dust people'. A number of young men jumped onto the back of some of the open trucks as they slowed before the gates. They began frantically throwing small sacks and boxes from the pile onto the road below. The people lining the way surged forward grabbing anything they could get their hands on. One or two police officers began blowing their whistles or yelling – the strategy was totally ineffective.

We, in the meantime, stood idly by waiting for instructions. None were forthcoming. We were thwarted by our enforced lack of response. Our frustration was exacerbated by the sight of some of the children falling in the crush. Those with caregivers were helped to their feet the others were simply left. The police continued to be inhibited. Some were even smiling; the odious pricks obviously found the sight of desperate people snatching at food parcels amusing.

Our frustration soon turned to open anger. "We can't just stand here doin' nothin'!" Lance Corporal McFall bellowed.

“Wait for orders!” Sergeant Edwards barked. “This isn’t our call; the police are overseeing the operation.”

Unfortunately, the police’s strategy consisted of none intervention; it was scandalous.

The trucks finally lumbered through the gates. Broken sacks and boxes littered the road in their wake. Some people began scooping up the broken biscuits, grains of rice and flour, indifferent to the dirt and dust. A few of the lads helped some of the people carry their bounty towards the gate; the Sergeant turned a blind eye. Meanwhile, Bronco, Giggsy, Macker and TC began helping some of the children; there was little they could do except direct them back towards the camp. I spotted a small Vietnamese boy sitting alone on the kerb crying. He’d scuffed his knees in the crush. He was no more than seven or eight years old. I went up to him: “Lại bé tré con ợn bài trí đìhn,” (*Come on little one, let’s get you back to the camp.*) I said.

The little boy stared up at me; his childish look a manifestation of innocence. He was gaunt, dreadfully undernourished. His tears had washed distinctive lines into his grubby little face. He was shaking with fear. “Lại bé tré con tói không đaư lơ,” (*Come on little one, I won’t hurt you.*) I said with a tender smile.

The little boy placed his tiny hand in mine. We slowly walked towards the gate. “Gia đìhn dia điểm,” (*Family, inside*?) I asked.

The boy shook his head. “Anh tria chi gái không,” (*Brother, sister, no*?) Again, the boy shook his head. I stopped and stooped in front of him. “Thừc hiền dể tím. Thừc hiên ban toy,” (*Who look after you; who’s your carer*?) I asked with continuing concern. The boy just stared at me, sobbing. He was likely an orphan – part of the Franciscan Nuns’ Collective.

The boy rubbed his stomach with his hand. “Đạ dây không án cơm,” (*Hungry, not eaten.*) He said, gesticulating hand to mouth.

“Thực phẩm dia điểm. Chắc chẳn thực phẩm trơng,” (*Food inside. Many food in camp now.*) I advised.

The little boy slowly shook his head whilst holding out his hand. “Không án cơm. Xin lương thưc mì đạ dây,” (*Not eaten. Please give food...hungry.*) He pleaded.

I looked into the boy’s face. His expression was piteous. I could clearly see the anguish in his eyes. The scenario gave true meaning to the metaphor, ‘Tugging at your heart strings’. I wanted to hold him in my arms, stroke his hair and comfort him, tell him that everything was going to be fine. I would have given anything to take him to the NAAFI for a double helping of nasi goreng.

“Thực phẩm dia điểm. Chắc chẳn só thưc phẩm trơng,” I repeated as we continued towards the site.

The child was silent as we entered the gates. He shuffled away as I let him go, his head bowed. My emotions were racing; I felt my eyes glazing over. The injustice, the inhumanity, the unbearable reality. I could contain myself no longer. "Bé tré con," (*Little one*!) I called out.

The boy spun round as I removed a vacuum packed meal from my webbing belt: "Cờ chứ một mính thời," (*Here, you take, for you only*.) The little boy grabbed the pack and scurried between the tents (likely looking for a safe place to eat his bonus).

I smiled as he disappeared. The pack was my evening meal. It mattered not, I could do without – he couldn't. I was in the throws of self-congratulation when Sergeant Edwards yelled at me. "Lance Corporal Morris, report to me, on the double!"

I doubled to where he was standing, a serious look on his face. He'd obviously seen me handing my ration pack to the boy.

"What the fuck do you think you're doing?" he barked. "You know the rules about handing out rations. Explain yourself."

"He was so hungry Sarge. It was pitiful; I only gave out a few bits."

"You're not supposed to give out anything! Why do think that is—?"

I was about to attempt an answer, but the question was clearly rhetorical.

"—How many ration packs have we presently got? 'round three each I'd reckon. That's forty-eight packs. What if we all handed them out? Forty-eight people would be happy. What about the forty-ninth? or the hundred and forty-ninth? What would we do for them? And what happens to us in the meantime? We go hungry, we get weak and when it comes to protecting these poor bastards from abuse we can't perform. Can't you see that?"

"Sarge," I replied knowing he was right but not liking it.

"Handing your rations to some half-starved urchin might make you feel good, but it's not a solution, the problem's bigger than that. What's more you're well aware of it! I expect better from you Lance Corporal Morris, you're an intelligent young man. Be advised, *you* are on a warning. There will not be a repeat of this, next time you'll go on report...now get out my sight!"

I rushed back to my position, my face red and my ears ringing. Lance Corporal McFall winked with a half-smile as I rejoined the squads. Though a small deed, it offered me comfort.

I'm not going to pretend I didn't know the rules. And it was true – my act of benevolence was a modest solution to a seemingly insurmountable problem. Maybe in some small way I had let the Platoon down, though it didn't feel that way. As for making myself feel better, so what? At that moment I didn't care. There was an inescapable fact: on that afternoon, at least one little Vietnamese boy did not go hungry.

20:30: Outskirts of Camp India.

For the fourth day in succession the expected influx of refugees did not materialise. One and Four Squads reported no extra movement on Highway One and there was clearly no activity around Camp India. Command called stand down at 20:45. A token force would be left overnight to police the perimeter. We wondered, as we packed our gear, who was going to draw the short straws. Buster put an end to our speculation five minutes later: “Lance Corporal Morris!” he hollered.

'Oh joy,' I thought, 'more fuckin’ lectures'—“Sarge.”

“I need a volunteer for a double shift, you’ve just volunteered. Check your equipment and team up with TC. Have you eaten?”

“Sarge...” I replied as I hauled up my gear, “I took a few bits from tomorrow’s pack.”

“Here…” Buster said as he placed a part-opened ration pack into my hand, “now hop-it!”

I waited until I had linked-up with Marine Clarke before checking my apparent benefaction. The contents, half a strip of turkey loaf, half a dozen cream crackers and four fig biscuits, were most welcome. Sergeant Edwards had given me a bollocking; a double shift and just a few items from his own ration pack.

23:00: Vừng Quệ Point, Nha Trang Beach, Tuesday 28 November.

We were on the last evening of five days off. We needed the break; we’d not had a consecutive run of more than a day and-a-half since August. Our brief Rest and Recuperation [R&R] had as usual gone far too quickly. I reflected on the past four days as the others chattered amongst themselves.

Most of us spent the first day chilling before sampling the delights of the provincial capital. Nha Trang Town was much the same as Sàigòn, though the Red Light District, with its lithe women gliding panther-like in their tight áo dài gowns, was less conspicuous. Illicit activities were, by all accounts, less tolerated in the predominantly Catholic community. We tried out a number of bars, nightclubs and shabiens. *Annam Nights*, a popular saloon on Tư Lừơ Street became our local. It contained the usual customers: journalists, attachés and official US personnel. One regular, a former War Correspondent who’d fallen out with his editor ’States-side spent most of his day sitting alone in a corner booth. He appeared to be in a constant stupor. He’d periodically feed the jukebox choosing the same two tracks: The Animals’ *House Of The Rising Sun* and Procol Harum’s *A Whiter Shade Of Pale*, with its distinctive ‘Air on a G String’ opening; the tracks were obviously of some significance. I once tried to engage him in conversation, but he was either too inebriated or too lethargic to respond.

Tommy and I visited Tháp Chầm [The Chầm Towers] two impressive Hindu structures on the western outskirts of Nha Trang. The Chầm had occupied the territory between the seventh and twelfth centuries when ethnic Vietnamese drove them out. We spent the day walking round Pó Nâgộr, an impressive complex surrounding the foot of the towers. The Hindus had intricately sculptured a collection of erotic gods and goddesses. Some had huge penises and open vaginas that emitted flowing water. I wondered how the historical structure had managed to escape the ravages of war. It was just as well – it would have been shameful to destroy such a splendid site.

Some of us considered undertaking a trip to Cám Râhn Bay or to the eastern slopes of the beautiful Nừí Co Tiến [Fairy Mountain]. Command advised we hold in place. Victor Charlie was active; they just about tolerated United Nations soldiers in uniform – in civilian clothes we would be simply viewed as 'Xâu ngớại' (*Unwelcome aliens.*)

We spent the following days in town. Jumper, JJ, Sugar, Speedy, Tommy and I sampled one of the local cinemas; *The Omega Man,* starring Charlton Heston was the main feature. The film had Vietnamese subtitles. Being a scholar of the language I couldn't help but try to follow the film by reading the fast flowing script. The soundtrack distracted my concentration. I intermittently covered my ears in a further attempt to test out my language skills. I noticed some of the lads gazing at me with bewilderment. I gave an embarrassed smile before aborting the experiment.

Twelve of us decided to check out Sông Lương Thực, a popular floating restaurant specialising in local cuisine: the crisp delicately spiced food was welcome after days of ration packs and canteen swill. The bill was even more welcome, less than sixty Đồng and ninety hào apiece (approximately five pounds sterling). Not a bad deal for a six-course meal and copious jugs of Tiger beer.

I shared my final day of R&R with eight of the lads on Nha Trang Beach. We'd decided on a barbecue at Vừng Qrệ Point, a secluded spot north of Nha Trang Bay. Our hastily arranged picnic turned into one of the best days I would have in the 'Nam. We jointly purchased ten boxes of San Miguel and Tiger beer, along with half a dozen chickens, a sack of assorted vegetables and a tub of Vietnamese marinade. Marine Miller brought along his newly acquired Sanyo radio cassette player. He said he'd found it in a box alongside the runway at Huê-Phu Baì Airport. Apparently, the box had some writing on it (**United States Army Surplus – Do Not Touch**). Dusty said he'd forgotten his glasses!

We built a large fire out of dried scrub, driftwood and other beach debris.

After marinating the chickens we oven foil wrapped them along with the vegetables and placed them in the embers to slowly cook. We spent the whole afternoon larking around. Jumper found a coconut shell washed up on the beach. We decided on a game of *murderball*, a combination of rugby and wrestling. The more intoxicated we became the more absurd we looked. It mattered not, the beach was deserted. It was incredible: miles of unspoiled golden sand, barren, except for some turtles, Tộnkinese hook crabs and nine drunken Bootnecks.

We tucked into our grub at sundown. The piping hot seasoned meat fell from the bone and the chicken-fat roasted vegetables melted in our mouths. We sounded like a herd of pigs chomping away around the fire – al fresco never seemed so good.

For some reason Sugar started giggling amid our feast. (He had a penchant for chortling for no apparent reason.) Soon, we were all rolling round in the sand in fits of laughter. We must have looked like a bunch of schoolboys on a venture outing.

Post meal, Bronco and Macker decided to have a pissing competition – who could write their name in the sand before emptying their bladders. Macker started complaining as soon as the steamy urine hit the ground: "Are aye, Bronco's not usin' capitals!"

The drunken bums ended up with half completed names and very wet feet.

After guzzling yet more ale we decide to go skinny-dipping. We'd been told umpteen times not to go swimming after consuming alcohol, or on a full stomach. We were oblivious to the advice as we stripped off and plunged into the warm South China Sea. Luckily, we escaped without harm, though Tommy suffered a few stings from a man-of-war jellyfish.

Our brief plunge was succeeded by yet another half-hearted attempt at murderball; this time we were all bollock-naked. What a sight: nine soaking wet drunken Bootnecks wrestling on the unspoilt beach. Jumper interrupted our shenanigans shouting that *Keep On Runnin'*, The Spencer Davies Group, was on the radio. He turned up the volume as we gathered round the fire striking up a drunken chorus, our damp sand rolled bodies dancing round the flames. The scene resembled something out of *Lord of the Flies*.

I collapsed onto a sandhill on the completion of our awful rendition. Dusty and JJ tried to rope me into further shenanigans. I was having none of it. I lay looking up at the stars, listening to my muckers larking around midst the sound of the thundering surf. Dinger, as usual, became emotional, bawling about missing his fiancée. Jumper tried offering him comfort by pouring even more beer down his throat.

Tommy dumped his large frame beside me. We talked for a short while before sitting in silence. We gazed at the crisscrossing lights from the fishing boats off Hộn Míeừ Island, twinkling beside the shimmering reflection of the haloed moon on the water. It looked so idyllic: unsullied, soothing, normal. The sound of rapid gunfire at our rear broke the calm. I turned to catch a glimpse of tracer shooting skyward; the armed conflict raged on. I felt as if I was sitting amid a schism: ahead, composure and peace, behind, calamity and disharmony. We had been on active duty for a little over a hundred days, already, it seemed like a thousand. All the same, I still enjoyed our five days off – it was a good break.

08:00: Highway One, Quang Ngaî Province, Friday 1 December.

Whilst in Vietnam we undertook any number of irregular duties, none more so than on a one day outing to Quang Ngaî. The Platoon boarded a Chinook at 06:30. We had no idea of our destination or mission. Lieutenant Derrick informed us we'd be briefed once we'd landed. We disembarked on the outskirts of Mờ Đưc, a town approximately 18 miles south of Quang Ngaî. Highway One ran through the centre of the modest district. On that day it was strewn with United States Army vehicles, sixty in total, seemingly abandoned in a line through the town. Jeeps and Armoured Personnel Carriers along with an assortment of Heavy Goods Vehicles. The convoy was en-route to the holding facility at Khânh Hoâ. The South Vietnamese drivers had apparently deserted the cortège after a dispute over pay. We learned sometime later that the workers had fled after Charlie had threatened to '...deal with them for being in cahoots with the enemy'. The absence of drivers left the Security Forces in a precarious position. Local Viet Cong Cadres were competing for aggregates – a rank of unguarded vehicles would be easy pickings.

It didn't take a genius to work out that we were to be given the task of completing the delivery to Khânh Hoâ. We speculated on how 32 men, a quarter of whom didn't hold driving licences, could manage to drive sixty vehicles a distance of 190 miles. Our speculation ended as we were joined by 2: Alpha 6 Platoon; they'd been bussed in from Chû Laị. The Security Forces were more than keen to clear the thoroughfare.

The two Platoons were designated tasks. Holders of HGV licences would drive the heavy trucks, the remainder driving the APCs and jeeps. It was becoming obvious as the assignments were handed out that there was a shortage of HGV drivers. Colour Sergeant Biffly, after asking me to confirm that I held a standard licence, directed me towards a large 12-wheel rigid: "Right young Morris, jump aboard that beast and start her up."

"But Colour Sergeant, I've never driven a—"

"Jump aboard now there's a good lad; the keys are in the ignition."

I jumped into the cab and checked the controls: the dashboard contained an array of switches, lights and buttons with no indicators. The steering wheel was huge and the gearstick adorned with more knobs than an erotic Hindu God. The metal-beast groaned and rumbled as the engine turned over. The cab was vibrating more than a Sàigòn massage parlour on a busy night. Colour Sergeant Biffly instructed me to follow a baton-controller ahead. He slowly walked alongside the cab as I slammed the first of the eight gears home. It was like shifting a dead weight. The gears crashed and clunked as I slowly moved off. My knuckles were white as I gripped the steering wheel. I'd moved less than 50 yards when the controller held up the baton to indicate halt.

Biffo opened the door: "Well done lad, you've now driven an HGV. Follow Lance Corporal Barilla in the truck ahead."

"But Colour Sarge, I—" It was useless, I'd been given the job and that was that!

By 10:15 most of the drivers had been allocated vehicles. Some of the jeeps were connected to HGVs by A-Bars. The APCs would lead and take up the rear of the convoy with the remaining jeeps acting as marshals. We all sat waiting for the signal to depart.

"**Move 'em out**!" Biffo yelled after blowing a whistle. Ricky took off following the train of vehicles. I followed, full of trepidation, struggling with the controls. The air in the cab was blue. If my truck had a personality it would've developed schizophrenia. I could hear thumping on the nearside of the cab as I slowly picked up speed. I unlocked the door to Marine Fox who duly jumped in: "What are you doin' up here?"

"Every tenth truck's gotta have a shotgun rider," Wolfie answered.

"Glad of the company."

Wolfie nervously watched me struggling with the controls as the convoy picked up further speed. "Gettin' the hang of it?" he enquired with a hopeful tone.

I gave an unconvincing nod as we progressed down the highway – it was going to be a long drive!

12:00: Highway One approximately 10 miles north of An Nhôn.

The convoy was in full flow. We moved at a steady pace along Highway One the vast An Loâ Valley on our right flank. I had managed to adapt to the controls by midday and was driving with more confidence. The inclusion of music helped. Wolfie discovered a 1970s 4-Track tape in the cab. It was crudely bolted to the underside of the dashboard. The machine had a tape jammed in its mechanism. He'd managed to get the motor working after some playful prodding. The solitary tape was a self-made compilation album of ’60s & ’70s music. The tracks included: David Bowie *Life On Mars*, Cream *I Feel Free*, Jefferson Airplane *White Rabbit*, Joni Mitchell *Big Yellow Taxi* and Scott McKenzie *San Francisco*. The cassette ran for well over an hour before the tape finally succumbed to the worn mechanism the sprockets grinding to a halt amid Smokey Robinson’s *The Tears Of A Clown*.

The monotony was occasionally broken by breathtaking scenery. The sporadically raised freeway cut through veritable oceans of rice paddies. There were moments when I felt as if we were gliding upon an enormous horizontal mirror.

There was to be no break for lunch. Our ration packs were passed into the cab by the speeding marshalling jeeps. Buster advised that we should be extra vigilant as we progressed through Bông Sơn towards a heavily contested bridge over the An Loâ River. We were entering Charlie Town (northern outskirts of Quì Nhôn). The yanks had given the name to the outlying districts of the provincial town after failing to secure any of the territory. Numerous American escorts had come to grief in the vicinity. Viet Cong guerrillas would hide in the undergrowth, often for days, to effect maximum stealth and surprise. Our vehicles were festooned with United Nations Flags. Unfortunately Charlie was prone to the occasional onset of colour blindness.

The National Liberation Front had taken great pleasure in taunting the yanks. Highway One was full of banners and road graffiti. We giggled at some of the writings:

VICTOR CHARLIE 1 - 0 UNCLE SAM; YANKEE DOODLE BUY A PONY,
RIDE IT HOME, GIDDY-UP!

We continued along the freeway the provincial town to the east. A collection of small villages straddled the Quì Nhôn intersection. The Viet Cong strongholds had quaint names: An Bốy Dả, Đặng Chị Khể, Lày Lợi Kỹ and Phức Mý Tưat (you had to be careful with your pronunciation of that one!).

Charlie Town was well behind us by 14:30. Once past Tựy Hoâ we’d be in Nha Trang Province, our destination less that 40 miles south. A Chinook buzzing the train of vehicles joined us at 15:00. Wolfie was half-asleep as the double rotor-thud interrupted the steady rumble of the truck. “What the fuck!” he said, bolting upright.

“Chinook…come to escort us in no doubt.”

“A Chinook, what’s the fuckin’ use of that? A Chinook’s not a gunship!”

“It’s probably just a deterrent,” I suggested, though I was unsure of the rationale. If Charlie wanted to have a go, he’d have a go!

A little while later we passed a line of refugees laboriously shuffling down the road laden with their belongings. “Look at those,” Wolfie said, “they're probably heading for Camp India. Poor bastards, they don't know what they're in for.”

I thought of the little Vietnamese boy in that beleaguered camp. Would he survive the war; would he survive in any case?

By 16:00 we were on the eastern outskirts of Nha Trang Town. To our right we could see the jagged silhouettes of the central massif, their inexorable ascent towards the Đac Lậc Plateau. Cotton wool mists hugged their peaks above the terraced plantations. The distinctive face of Nừí Co Tièn was closely followed by the columns of Tháp Chầm. Khânh Hoâ was less than 10 miles south by southeast. 'Cracked it!' I thought. Seems it's always the way: a chink, just when you'd convinced yourself you'd fastened it up.

There appeared to be clatter emanating from under the hood. I was hit by a sudden dread that we were about to breakdown. One dread was replaced by another at the realisation that the clamour was in fact rapid gunfire.

“**Charlie!**” Marine Fox screamed as he cocked his M16. “Where the fuck's it comin' from?”

I could no more answer the question as the reports of gunfire intensified. My anxiety was exacerbated by my inability to prime my weapon. It was laying behind me on a small shelf above my seat. “My rifle!” I shouted to Wolfie, “…cock my rifle!”

He grabbed my M16, hurriedly pulling on the cocking mechanism before placing it across my lap: “Weapon primed – safety on!”

The gunfire was accompanied by sporadic mortar fire, the unmistakable blunt detonation of 81mm tubes in the distance. I almost failed, in my elevated anxiety, to notice Ricky's truck come to a sudden halt. I caught the glare of his break lights just in time to avoid ramming his tailgate. I stalled the engine in my momentary alarm: “Oh fuck, not now!” I bellowed as I frantically turned the ignition switch. The engine fired just as Ricky was pulling away. I almost bent the gearstick as I slammed it home.

Meanwhile, the Chinook continued to fly the line, though with little effect. We must have travelled just over a mile when the gunfire suddenly abated. Five, ten, fifteen minutes passed – nothing. Wolfie, who had been silently staring out the window M16 gripped in his hands, broke the still: “Do you reckon that's it?”

“Seems to be. Were they shooting at us?”

“Hard to say, the volleys were echoing all over the place.”

We passed the sign for Khânh Hoâ 10 minutes later; the sign reduced our anxiety. We spotted another tented city, Camp Juliet, alongside the road. It looked and smelled exactly the same as Camp India.

The highway filtered towards the military compound at an intersection guarded by the SVA. The holding facility covered a massive area. It was ringed by a huge three-line fence patrolled by MPs with guard dogs. We were given a parking sector once through the gates. We passed row upon row of assorted vehicles before finding our sector. Once parked I handed the keys and logbook to an MP and we were off, heading for the main gate through the lines of military hardware.

Most of the lads were gathered around the entrance on our arrival. The conversation invariably revolved around the journey, with particular attention to the mêlée on the Khânh Hoâ bypass. It had become apparent that Viet Cong insurgents and the SVA were engaged in a fracas. We just so happened to interrupt the contest. Colour Sergeant Biffly congratulated us on delivering the vehicles in one piece. We were all pleased with ourselves; most of us had never been behind the wheel of a Heavy Goods Vehicle.

A Chinook arrived to collect 2: Alpha 6 Platoon for the flight to Chû Lại. It had been nice to make their acquaintance again. We bid them goodbye amid the usual ribbing. Meanwhile, some of the men had climbed on top of a Portakabin adjacent to the main gate. Marine Bernard shouted down to Wolfie and me: "Come up 'ere and take a dekko at this."

We clambered onto the roof to be greeted by an amazing sight. The compound was packed with military hardware, as far as the eye could see. Armoured Personnel Carriers, Jeeps and Troop Carriers. Amphibious Craft, Bailey Bridges, Cranes, Command Vehicles, Portable Generators and Water Bowsers. Howitzers, Half-tracks, Mine Layers, Mortars and M48 Tanks loaded onto enormous 16-wheel transporters. Portable Radar Trucks, Rocket Launchers and Triple-A Batteries. Lines of helicopters occupied a whole section: Chinooks, Hueys, Sikorskys and Siouxs. Row upon row – infinity in every direction within our vista.

"Holy shit!" Wolfie said, "…there's enough kick-shit here for half-a-dozen world wars."

We stood staring at the spectacle in semi-silence. An outgoing GI who had seen us climbing onto the roof joined us.

"Ain' it a sight," he said. "Goin to the junkyard most of it."

"Scrap," Corporal Farr enquired, "you mean scrap?"

"Yep! Oh some'll be goin back home and some'll be given to the South Vietnamese. But most'll just be cut up or dumped at sea."

"Dumped?" I said.

"Yep! Davy Jones's locker, too expensive to ship it all back to the 'States, and they daren't just leave it here. The South Vietnamese are too corrupt. They'd just peddle it to some other rogue state. Besides, none of us knows how long it'll take the commies to get here. Uncle Sam would be mighty pissed if Uncle Hồ got his hands on that lot, yes sir!"

"It's a military mausoleum," Corporal Lane muttered.

"Yeah..." Tommy added with a sardonic grin, "a *steel graveyard.*"

"It's a disgrace," I interjected, "obscene, beyond reproach—!"

I noticed some of lads looking at me.

"—How much do you reckon that lot's worth?"

"Hard to say," Bronco answered, "fifty, sixty million dollars maybe."

"Nah!" Bruiser cut in, "...no way."

"It won't be far off that," Tommy suggested. "So what's your point?"

"The refugees that's my point! The recent report on Radio Sàigòn, the one that said that the South Vietnamese Government would need twenty million dollars worth of US Aid to effectively deal with the escalating problem, twenty million dollars that Uncle Sam says he hasn't got. Now what do we hear; that around a third of the military hardware at Khânh Hoâ is gonna be dumped into the South China Sea. How much do you reckon that lot would fetch? twenty million dollars maybe. The whole thing sucks!"

I became aware that the GI was nervously staring at me, and lads at him: "Don't look at me buddy; I'm just a regular Joe who's eager to get-on home."

Tommy intervened: "It's an irony all right, a cruel one at that. But you know as well as I do, the money comes from different chests – the warmongers and the peace activists. Unfortunately, the hawks have got both sets of keys."

Sergeant Hoggs notified us that our transport had arrived. We bid the gregarious GI farewell. He half-smiled as we left, I think he felt a little embarrassed. We passed yet another convoy of vehicles destined for the facility on our way back to base. We later discovered that there were more steel graveyards at Bìen Hoâ and Chư Chì. One facility was three times the size of the compound at Khânh Hoâ. Absurdity upon absurdity.

23:30: UN Base Camp 3, Nịhn Hoâ.

I sat updating my journal whilst listening to Radio Sàigòn. It had been an eventful day. Our drive to Khânh Hoâ was different to say the least. As for the political situation, I simply had to contain my anger. I had to maintain my focus on future tasks.

Otis Redding's *(Sittin' On) The Dock Of The Bay* broke my cogitation. I sat back listening to the melodic piece. I'd always liked the track suddenly it had new significance. I thought of the roll-on, roll-off ships awaiting their condemned cargo at Nha Trang Docks. The ditching of millions of dollars worth of military hardware may've been obscene, but at least the weapons of destruction could no longer be used. For me, the news that the hospital ships in Cám Râhn Bay were finally weighing anchor was worse, particularly in the light of a final rejection by the administration to transport surplus medical supplies to the refugee camps. They rolled out the same excuse yet again '...logistically impracticable'. There was nothing impracticable about it; the supplies could've been transferred in less than a day. It didn't take a genius to work it out. All the halfwits had to do was fuel up some of the helicopters laying idle at Khânh Hoâ. Of course that would've taken political will and courage, concepts that were sadly lacking in South Vietnam.

22:00: Ả Choí, Nha Trang Province, Wednesday 6 December.

End of day one of a twelve-day reconnaissance of the Ả Choí Valley. It was good to get away from the mundane of roadblocks, checkpoints, overseeing almost none existent refugee movements and driving metal beasts to their demise.

Our new appointment was to monitor the interim ceasefire and record any violations. The Platoon had been split for the assignment. Three and Four Squads would progress through Chơn Biên concluding in the Thộc Điếm quarter; One and Two would move from the Shau Tiâ district concluding in the Tchựin rice fields. The National Liberation Front had been busy kicking arse. The Security Forces felt disaffected, they'd long been complaining about not being able to act against increased Viet Cong activity. The South Vietnamese Army were thwarted by their ineffectiveness. We'd obviously been sent in to prove a point – that the Viet Cong were the antagonists. We could've saved everybody a job: the NLF would not abate until they had won, and they were winning. Regardless, we would carry out our duties.

I lay my head to rest as the twilight slowly dimmed above the craggy mountains encircling the Ả Choí Valley: thoughts of our tasks, thoughts of home and thoughts of dreams to come. But there were to be no dreams – only nightmares.

SONGS FROM THE 'NAM

Nha Trang Days, Vừng Quệ Point
& Highway One

THE ANIMALS *House Of The Rising Sun; We Gotta Get Out Of This Place*

DAVID BOWIE *Life On Mars; Space Oddity*

CREAM *I Feel Free; World Of Pain*

JIM CROCE *Time In A Bottle*

THE SPENCER DAVIS GROUP *Keep On Runnin'*

THE HOLLIES *The Air That I Breathe; He Ain't Heavy He's My Brother; Bus Stop Wedding*

JEFFERSON AIRPLANE *White Rabbit; Volunteers*

SCOTT MCKENZIE *San Francisco (Be Sure To Wear Some Flowers In Your Hair)*

JONI MITCHELL *Big Yellow Taxi; Chelsea Morning*

PROCOL HARUM *A Whiter Shade Of Pale*

OTIS REDDING *(Sittin' On) The Dock Of The Bay*

SMOKEY ROBINSON & THE MIRACLES *The Tears Of A Clown*

THIN LIZZIE *Whisky In The Jar*

THUNDERCLAP NEWMAN *Something In The Air*

THE WALKER BROTHERS *Make It Easy On Yourself*

4: BAD DAY AT TCHỰIN LOY

They teach us how to drop napalm on Viet Cong villages
in patterns that will inflict maximum fatalities.
Yet our commanders refuse to let us write FUCK on the
side of the plane;
because they say it is obscene.

H Goresky

07:00: Ầ Choí, Nha Trang Province, 15 December 1972.

The day had started much the same as any other: up at 05:30, wash, a hastily consumed, and often half re-hydrated, C-Ration breakfast followed by the standard equipment check proceeding to our pre-mission briefing. Morning orientations invariably contained a reminder on elements familiar to peacekeeping duties. Regulation 6 subs. 1(a) to (g) '...to prevent the abuse and illegal killing of non-combatants and neutrals…' was the chosen rule of the day. We were oblivious, as we squatted on the rugged ground, of the manoeuvres developing in the nearby woods or of the drama that was about to unfold. By days' end we would learn with crystal clarity that prevention is dependant upon context. And that sometimes the struggle to come to terms with the unacceptable is the toughest battle that a soldier must learn to fight.

Headquarters had set the Detail's mission for the day. Our tasks were to carry out a close order reconnaissance of the Tchựin District. The locale incorporated a network of paddies staggered by three villages: Tchựin Điêt, Tchựin Khômn and Tchựin Loy, all VC strongholds. There had been a recent increase in guerrilla movements especially within the terrain interconnecting the villages. The Security Forces prolonged campaign of attempting to deprive Viet Cong hamlets of their recruits, supplies and shelter had long since failed; hence, the South Vietnamese Military had a particular enmity for the populace of Tchựin.

There were times during our Tour of Duty in that beautiful country that we had to remind ourselves that it was indeed at war with itself; such was the case on the morning of the fifteenth. The air was almost completely motionless, save for a gentle current that skimmed the paddies. Miniature rattan reeds swayed delicately in the breeze. This hardy vegetation cared nothing about politics; it would bend whichever way the wind cared to caress it. The rice pools, which seemed to extend beyond infinity itself, were reflecting a perfect image of the distant mountains. Bird song filled the air, as did the pungent smell of wild coriander as the leaves were sporadically cracked under foot. Annamese golden hornets danced above the half filled irrigation channels. We would occasionally see young Vietnamese couples chasing this innocuous wasp. The Viet Cong believed that if you could capture two mating hornets and hold them in the cups of your hands whilst thinking of your sweetheart, your love for each other would last forever. In the distance we could see the subtle silhouettes of men and women working the paddies. Children in their company were splashing and tossing the water in playful games. I remember viewing the scene with curiosity, wondering how long their parents or caregivers would tolerate the behaviour.

On that pleasant morning the harshness of war seemed as distant as the billowing cumulus that occasioned the cobalt skies. Every sight, sound, smell and feeling within my awareness filled me with an overwhelming sense of calm. But a cataclysmic event was about to shatter the tranquillity – an event that would have an inexorable effect on my young life.

11:30: Approximately 1 mile west by southwest of Tchựin Loy.

We had been advancing northeastward all morning. The extensive Tchựin rice fields were to the left of our position. The Sôn Kơi Woods, a remnant tropical rainforest running oblique the Ả Choí Valley, occupied our right flank. Sôn Kơi had escaped the ravages of the Agent Orange Defoliation Programme; hence, its terrain provided the perfect conditions required for ambuscade, a strategy Victor Charlie practised with notable effectiveness. Moreover, we were conscious that the VC had excavated a network of interconnecting tunnels throughout the woods leading to and from Tchựin Điêt in the south and Tchựin Loy to the northeast. The Detachment followed a typical infantry course between the fields and the treeline. We would not venture too far into the exposed paddies or through the dense undergrowth despite our impartial standing.

It was just before midday that we recorded the first volleys of automatic gunfire. A sudden flurry of echoes (source: Sôn Kơi Woods) hit us from the east provoking the teams to crouch in startled response.

“That’s Charlie!” Lieutenant Derrick said. “He’s come out to play.”

Sergeant Edwards issued orders in a semi-hushed voice: “Assume standby mode. Cock your weapons safety catches on. Align fingers with trigger guards – I don’t want any loose rounds going off!”

At that instant I remember feeling a sudden rush of excitement combined with an underlying anxiety; this dissonance made me feel decidedly uncomfortable. I also recall briefly glancing towards the paddies; the workers appeared to be unfazed by the commotion. Presumably, sporadic firefights had become second nature to them, though I noted that the children were less animated and closer to their caregivers.

Lieutenant Derrick ordered the Radio Operator, Marine Lyle, to scan all frequencies and called for the translators, Corporal Lane and myself, to monitor radio transmissions in an attempt to identify the warring parties. It was customary for two interpreters to attend broadcasts to lessen the likelihood of missing vital intelligence.

Bronco and I huddled close to the RT after donning multiple-line headsets. The frequencies scan initially revealed dead air, other than the sounds of some distant stations and a far-off clash too inaudible to identify.

Meanwhile the activity in the undergrowth appeared to be intensifying. The Detail had to remain at standby mode regardless. We were thwarted by the enforced lack of response. Nonetheless, we would not move up to investigate the skirmish until we were sure that we could, at least partially, identify the warring factions. This was essential, Viet Cong blocs were occasionally embroiled in inter-group fighting; this was no concern of ours. However, if the hostility involved an infiltrating North Vietnamese Army Unit and the SVA, or an ill disciplined American Infantry Unit seeking their final pound of flesh before retreating from Vietnam, then this would clearly constitute a breach of the interim ceasefire. Moreover, the SVA may have been defending themselves against a VC ambush. Conversely, an SVA Unit may have been probing well-established Viet Cong territory in a deliberate bid to provoke them into armed conflict. We were all too aware that the Security Forces were seeking to redress the balance after suffering heavy losses. It was an unequivocal reality: in the cruel and protracted war in Vietnam there were few innocents – save for the peasants who merely wanted to eke out a living and exercise their customs with at least a semblance of freedom and autonomy. Yet as in numerous preceding conflicts it was *they* who were suffering the most, a factor that was soon to be validated on that fateful day.

Sugar continued to delicately manipulate the frequency modulator in anticipation that Corporal Lane or I would intercept an inter-sectional transmission. We had to use every ounce of our resolve to remain focused on the task. The firefight ensuing within the woods continued to escalate. It was obvious that a major incident was developing. The rifle reports were becoming incessant and louder, an indication that the battle was closing on our location. As a precaution the squads regrouped to form a close-quarter stockade (a back-to-back defence strategy where the Detachment can monitor potential attack angles).

Lieutenant Derrick squatted alongside Bronco wearing an inquisitive, part anxious, expression: “Anything?”

“Nothing but dead air as yet Sir. A few live stations here and there but nothing of significance.”

The Lieutenant looked frustrated, he slowly shook his head: "Those bastards aren't stupid, they know we're here. They're trying not to give themselves away. Keep on sweeping the airwaves, they're gonna have to get into an inter-sectional dialogue at some time."

Almost precisely at that moment there was a burst of activity on a frequency that Sugar had moved through.

"Hold it!" Bronco said. "Did you get that?" he asked looking directly at me.

"Yeah and it was close."

"Go back a few clicks..." Bronco said to Sugar, "carry out a swing-scan. Dead slow now."

Marine Lyle complied, laboriously moving the dial over the frequency gauge as some of the lads looked on. Repeatedly, there was naught but dead air. Then abruptly, the stagnancy was broken. We'd intercepted a clearly identifiable communication – the elevated voice of a combatant issuing firing orders.

"**Contact!**" Bronco and I bellowed simultaneously.

The Lieutenant looked at us. "Are you sure?" he asked, seemingly desperate for an affirmative response.

"Positive," Bronco replied gaining a nod of approval from myself.

There was indeed no question that we'd intercepted a local interaction. During transmissions we could clearly hear the sound of gunfire in the background. The combatant, likely a senior officer with a South Vietnamese Army Unit, appeared to be talking to a support group positioned to his rear. His directives were unmistakable: "Nghe, bây giơ. Khẩm chuyển trền dia điểm. Phắt triển trền, phải trại. Nhanh lện," (*Hear now, priority. Assemble on my grid...close up on my flanks – move*!) He said, with more than a hint of urgency in his voice.

Confirmation that we had achieved contact sent a wave of excitement throughout the teams. Buster scanned the squads with an assertive look: "Steady now...stay cool."

Bronco and I continued to convey, all be it sparse, information on movements. We had also established that the skirmish involved an altercation with a Viet Cong element, a factor of no surprise. However, we were still lacking a vital piece of information: the precise location of the factions. Lieutenant Derrick asked Bronco if we could give him a grid (map reference).

He gave a negative response. Preceding and continuing transmissions, maybe with forethought, involved no cross-referencing of co-ordinates; this left the Detail in a precarious position. We were aware that warring parties were close – roughly east by northeast of our position – and that a South Vietnamese Army Unit was in pursuit of Viet Cong rebels, though, we could only estimate their positions and objectives.

Meanwhile, it was evident that the divisions were deploying serious weaponry within the combat zone. We could distinctly hear the discharge of mortar rockets, plus the reports of heavy machine-gun fire; this inevitably increased our anxiety and awareness.

Nevertheless, Sugar managed to maintain his wit: "I thought we were in the Tchụrin fields, not in the middle of the fuckin' OK Corral."

Lieutenant Derrick and Buster engaged in a discussion on possible strategies whilst scrutinising the Ordinance Survey Map [OSM]. There was a likelihood that Charlie would withdraw to the refuge of their nearest stronghold (Tchụrin Loy). However, in situations like these there was always an unpredictable element.

After some deliberation, Lieutenant Derrick determined that we should set a course for Tchụrin Loy. "I don't like working on assumptions," he said, "but we've got little choice."

Sergeant Edwards addressed the troop: "Assume spearhead configuration, objective Tchụrin Loy. Maintain squad formations. Move with stealth and at speed. Stay at close-quarters; don't get separated! Progress adjacent the treeline. Remember the primary directive…first we protect ourselves and each other."

The Detachment made formation and moved out closely following the mandate. As we departed I can recall being overcome by a feeling of foreboding: not because we were moving parallel to a live firefight or that we were pushing towards a Viet Cong stronghold. More, that we were moving towards the unknown.

12:10: Roughly 300 yards off the northwest perimeter, Tchụrin Loy.

The teams advanced rapidly on a northeastwardly objective with the aim of maintaining an array reciprocal to the firefight. We were mindful that the battling factions could break out of the woods at any time. We were also aware of the risks involved in nearing the uncovered terrain proximate to the village – we moved forwards with extreme caution.

Tchụrin Loy was less than a mile from our contact position. The squads, after a fleeting survey, took advantage of an elevated apex, which provided us with the benefit of cover and an almost panoramic view of the settlement. Lieutenant Derrick ordered the teams to spread out whilst Sergeant Edwards posted a lookout sentry, Marine Collins, with a pair of high-powered binoculars.

The Lieutenant also directed Bronco and I to stay close to the Radio Transmitter. After only a few minutes, and some mutterings as we attempted to settle on the rough ground, the squads established a covert observation post. From our apparent safe vantage we began to closely observe the treeline surrounding the southeastern perimeter of the village. If our theory was correct, Viet Cong guerrillas would carry out a withdrawal to the shelter of the commune.

During our observations the village provided us with a true picture of the communal life familiar to the Viet Cong. Tchụrin Loy – which had stood in the locale for over 600 years – was no different from any other hamlet in South Vietnam. It lay in a cutting fashioned by its creators to maximise the benefit of the open plains and woods (easy access to potentially lucrative earth and raw materials, plus shelter from the elements).

The village consisted of a cluster of bamboo and straw buildings suspended on short protruding stilts. These included a number of modestly sized huts, likely constituting the living quarters, randomly scattered throughout the settlement. And what appeared to be a community centre set in a central position. The commune also contained an abundance of work areas as well as a collection of communal stores constructed to stockpile rice and other provisions. A large livestock enclosure ran between the settlement and the woods along with a small area for growing a selection of alternative crops. A system of deep monsoon ditches, excavated to act as a flood barrier, encircled the locality.

The burial ground, offset from the main quarter, was of particular note. To the Viet Cong burial grounds were the most sacred of places. We had to adhere to a number of strict protocols during our Tour of Duty. Entering a Viet Cong burial ground in the absence of expressed permission was by far the most prominent. We would not venture onto the sacred soil even whilst carrying out a comprehensive search for weapons. (Not that the Viet Cong would even contemplate concealing firearms on consecrated earth; they may have been a cunning collective, but they would never insult their forefathers.)

It was apparent that some of the inhabitants had recently decorated a number of headstones within the grounds. In addition they had placed a large bamboo pole festooned with multi-coloured ribbons in a specific location, all indicators that a recent burial had taken place. The kinfolk and significant others of a departed soul would deposit adornments as an invitation to the spirits to welcome a cherished one into their protection. I can recall how striking the decorations looked as they fluttered in the breeze.

The commune was a bustle of activity. An assortment of inhabitants was gathered around workstations thrashing rice husks. Others were tending to the livestock. Alongside the community centre a small gathering of people were preparing the communal meal (during work hours all meals were consumed collectively, the resources being shared according to need). The midday sun was beginning to deliver its heat. This appeared to play no mind to the natives – to them hard labour in adverse conditions was a way of life.

Our location provided us with a clear vista of the Sôn Kơi treeline. Proximate to the footings we could observe smoke rising above the forest canopy – likely the after effect of spent mortar rounds – along with the occasional string of stray tracer fire. These were indicators that the battle was indeed driving towards the village. Meanwhile the inhabitants, as with their fellow workers in the fields, appeared to be unmoved by the advancing insurrection, though the mêlée appeared to be curtailing. The Detail had been in place for 10 minutes when we observed the insurgents retreating from Sôn Kơi.

"Guerrillas!" Marine Miller said, pointing towards the treeline.

"We've pinged them," the Sergeant returned.

The Lieutenant smirked: "Well I'll be dipped in shit if it ain't Victor Charlie, right on cue."

The whole Detachment was buzzing, satisfied that our predictions had been correct, at the sight of the rebels sporadically appearing from in-between the trees. Initially the insurgents emerged singularly, then in small groups. All were carrying an assortment of weaponry, ranging from Kalashnikov assault rifles to rocket propelled grenade launchers. Of particular note was the age variation of the revolutionaries. It was evident that the division was inclusive of a number of young boys. One was almost bent-double as he struggled to carry an AK47 and RPG launcher on his back. I can recall how tragically amusing this looked.

The appearance of the guerrillas, many of whom were likely inhabitants of the village, also had a notable effect upon the people within the settlement. Many had stopped what they were doing and were staring in the direction of the treeline. We could see one woman running towards them in a highly animated state, calling out and gesticulating.

"Can you get any of that?" Sergeant Edwards enquired glancing towards Bronco and I.

"Too far away, me and Bazzer would need to get in closer—"

"Forget it…" the Lieutenant replied whilst gently shaking his head, "too risky."

"I bet one of them's her old man," Sugar muttered. "She's probably pissed off with 'im cos he's spent all the family allowance on a box of fuckin' pineapples."

"Shut your fuckin' beer-hole!" Buster said above the chuckles, "and get both your lugholes plugged into that RT."

"Sarge," Sugar acknowledged as he manoeuvred the second earphone into place. As it transpired Sugar's timing was almost perfect. It became apparent that he'd re-established contact with the local broadcast. I could observe him placing his hands upon the earphones, likely to help him focus on the task. After a brief spell he turned towards Corporal Lane and me: "Bronco, Bazzer, transmissions!"

Bronco and I scrambled over to the RT and donned the multiple-line headsets. There was a broadcast and the source appeared to be commensurate with previous transmissions. We listened attentively to the intercourse ensuing between the transmitter and the receiving agents whilst Lieutenant Derrick observed. The broadcast was erratic and partially inaudible rendering the interpretation arduous.

"Anything to report?" the Lieutenant asked.

"I don't think the communications are inter-sectional," Bronco replied gaining a nod of agreement from Sugar and me.

"Who the hell are they talking to then, command, logistical support, a local battery; whom?"

I interjected: "There's a distinctive 'whirr' on the respondent's line and intermittent break-up."

The Lieutenant looked at the three of us. "Ground-to-air?" he enquired, a hint of puzzlement in his voice.

"That would be my guess," Bronco replied. "High speed, low flying aircraft receiving transmissions from dense woods, it adds up."

"An air strike…surely not. Any feedback at all?"

"Something about the identified foe driving north," I responded. "Plus the SVA Unit indicating that they were about to disengage and retreat deeper into the woods."

"I don't like this," the Lieutenant said a pensive look on his face, "I don't like this one bit. Stay tuned in, signal me if you manage to intercept any grid references."

Bronco and I complied with the directive whilst the rest of the Detail continued to monitor insurrectionary movements. At this juncture most of the militiamen had withdrawn from the woods. Some were posted close to the treeline, doubtless as a precaution against a counter attack by opposing forces, whilst others had made their way into the village. There was a notable increase of activity around the livestock enclosure. A number of children were tending the animals. One of them, a girl of no more than ten years of age, was attempting to haul a stubborn water buffalo closer to the village boundary presumably as a precaution against stray rounds. Unfortunately, the water buffalo was quite content to stay where it was. I noticed Bronco, who was also watching the scene, smiling sensitively to himself. The sight of this tiny waif hauling on the enormous ruminant enchanted us both.

Our attention was diverted away from the activities in the commune by an additional ground-to-air transmission. The transmitter, after confirming his group identification, made a request for a fire-mission (a concentrated attack on an identified grid). He began to reel off a series of co-ordinates, which Bronco and I recorded.

Marine Lyle alerted Lieutenant Derrick and Sergeant Edwards that we were about to identify a reference. They crawled over with the OSM as we separately completed the recordings: "Who were the interactions with?" the Lieutenant asked.

"Ground-to-air…" Bronco replied, "a clear request for a fire-mission."

"Any idea of the weaponry to be deployed?"

"No Sir, the respondent hasn't returned as yet."

"Alert me as soon as you pick up the response."

After crosschecking the co-ordinates we handed the figures (meridians, distance, angles and specific location) to Lieutenant Derrick and Sergeant Edwards who set to the task of transferring the data onto the Ordinance Survey Map. In the interim, it had become apparent that the gunfire below had completely abated. Nonetheless, the activity within the village was still at an elevated pitch. Doubtless they had experienced numerous close-sector firefights. They were taking no chances on the possibility of their adversaries returning with increased strength. They appeared to have completed transferring the data; both had a distinct look of trepidation. The Lieutenant looked at Bronco: "Crosscheck the co-ordinates," he said to a clear note of concern in his voice.

"We've cross-referenced them already Sir—"

"Do it again!"

Bronco and I compared data and conveyed the information back to him. Lieutenant Derrick re-surveyed the figures whilst checking the positions on the map. He looked at Bronco and me with an air of disbelief: "The grid…it's the village. The target for the fire-mission, its Tchựin Loy!"

A few seconds later the Radio Transmitter crackled-in; we instantaneously recognised the source of the broadcast as the responding agent. On this occasion the broadcast was audible indicating to our dismay that the aircraft was closer. The air-to-ground transmission opened with the pilot confirming the target-data, which Bronco and I checked to attain further verification. The pilot then issued a deployment confirmation that sent a shiver down my spine: "Chuyển đặt cừu thứ trên miền," (*Moving to place fire-line on target.*)

I looked at Bronco who appeared to be equally as stunned: "Did you get that? Did I hear him—?"

"Đặt cứu thứ trên miền," Bronco interrupted. "Place fire-line on target, that's what I got."

"Napalm! [Nape] ...that's napalm isn't it?"

"It was the last time I looked at the field manual."
We both became aware that Lieutenant Derrick and Buster were staring at us their expressions of disbelief ever increasing.
"Napalm!" Buster said, "…are you sure? Are you certain you've translated it right?"
"It can't be anything else Sir," Bronco replied. "No other armament's got that form of identification, in any language."
The information made its way down the line like wildfire, each marine as equally aghast as the next. The lads were muttering between themselves. I distinctly remember staring in a state of semi-shock at the activity within the settlement. Suddenly, the people became more noticeable: the VC guerrillas; the men and women young and old. And the children – the little girl and the water buffalo.
Marine Miller diverted my attention: "They can't nape a village!"
"Try telling that to the scumbags who ordered the air strike!" Bronco returned.
Unfortunately, as is often the case with those holding power, the depraved individuals responsible for ordering the fire-mission were not available to exhort.
As it stood Dusty was not alone in failing to comprehend the inevitability of what was about to transpire. I too, in my youthful naiveté, could not give credence to the concept of warplanes deploying napalm on a commune embodying non-combatants. I momentarily convinced myself that we had made a mistake despite the fact that I had jointly translated and conveyed information on the co-ordinates, and that the aircraft was destined for an alternative fire-mission. I reinforced my defensive construct with the notion that monstrous acts were things that happened in other places or on the silver screen, not before our very eyes. But this was no ITN News Report. No clapperboard was about to halt proceedings. There would be no intermission in this show. We were about to experience the cruel and cold reality of war. An unknown number of aircraft, each loaded with up to four 220-gallon pods of napalm, were on an inexorable trajectory for the village of Tchựin Loy.
Napalm is a veritably repulsive weapon. It consists of three elements: naphthalene, a dense highly combustible petroleum derivative; coconut palm oil, a viscous tallow with strong adhesive properties and white phosphorous. Napalm is deployed on specific targets for one reason – to annihilate every living organism in its path. Once released napalm bombs dispatch a terrifying inferno. The coagulate, which remains in a part fluid state throughout the initial flare, ignites at ground level creating an undulating fireball. Individuals caught within the epicentre, which burns at over one thousand degrees centigrade, are instantaneously vaporised. Those central-peripheral to the

detonation suffer any number of predominantly fatal injuries. These include severe blast wounds; extensive and enduring third degree burns (naphthalene and palm oil is designed to continue scorching the flesh long after initial contact) and suffocation due to the temporary vacuum caused by the firestorm. Those on the periphery of the burst suffer flash burns, which can result in blindness and extreme blistering to exposed skin. Napalm leaves few survivors in its wake. Those who do survive the initial explosion – unless subjected to immediate intensive medical care – suffer a slow and agonising death. If an individual were to compile a book of the evil that humankind has created, then napalm would surely be a prominent feature.

Lieutenant Derrick instructed Jumper to carry out a 360° scan: "Alert me at the sight of any aircraft no matter how innocuous it looks."

The Lieutenant, in an attempt to constrain the Security Forces, went on to instruct Marine Lyle to contact 'Supervisory Force Command on the priority channel.

"Do you think we'll be able to get them to abort the attack?" Buster asked hopefully.

"We may not have time, but if we can press Command into transmitting an all channels broadcast then the bastards might just back off."

Marine Lyle set about the task of contacting headquarters whilst Sergeant Edwards directed the squads to assemble and run through concealment drill (a pack formation intended to provide maximum cover given our exposed position).

The Detail, who by this time was in a state of high arousal, began listening attentively as Buster through the procedure.

"It's just like a close-quarter stockade, only cosier…" the Sergeant said, with a reassuring tone and smile that masked the underlying urgency. "…After covering all exposed skin we pull-in close to form a link, rows of five-to-six men, no more. Then we form a stack, part laying face down whilst pulling-in close, and up, on the troop in front. Remember we've likely got nape coming in so before you hit the dirt close your eyes tight and take a deep breath – and I mean fill your lungs! Do *not* breathe out or in again until I give—"

Buster had almost completed tutoring the Detachment when Jumper interrupted with the words that none of us wanted to hear: "Aircraft! Two F4s (Phantom Jets) bearing one four zero degrees. Approximately nine miles, objective, northerly, varying north by northeast."

"What?" Lieutenant Derrick said. "I don't believe it! …they're already on a swing trajectory. They must have been on a predetermined matrix; a calculated delay pattern." He asked Marine Collins for the aircraft's height and formation.

"Approximately two thousand feet, descending flight path...nose to wing configuration."

Lieutenant Derrick looked at Sergeant Edwards: "That confirms it, they're readying for a bombing run. Prepare for an air to ground attack!"

"Make formation…" Buster said, "wait for the cover-order before hitting the dirt!"

Prior to that moment I thought I understood the meaning of fear. Why should I not? I'd experienced fear on many occasions. My first fight in the playground; each time I stepped into the boxing ring; my maiden parachute jump and first excessive rock climb, and my first encounters on riot control in Northern Ireland. But I was to learn that the feelings associated with these things were nothing more than episodes of elevated anxiety – what I was experiencing was absolute *terror*! I was shaking so much that I had lost the dexterity in my hands. My breathing was so accelerated that my head began to spin. My heart was beating faster than an express train on a record run. The fear that I was experiencing was primal, a feature of the ultimate dread that lurks within the deepest recesses of our psychology, that uncharted territory where most of us would rather not venture.

The squads hastened to draw together. As we assembled I wondered whether the people in the village were aware that an air strike was imminent. It was highly doubtful; the Viet Cong were in possession of many things technology wasn't one of them. A fellow marine asked why we could not issue a warning to the inhabitants. Sergeant Edwards answered clearly: "Forget it, it's too late now, we protect ourselves and that's it!"

I could plainly hear the recital of a hopeful prayer: "*Holy Mary, Mother of God, do not desert us in this hour…*"

Though a confirmed non-believer somehow, at that time, I too held onto those words.

Jumper, who continued to stoically man his post binoculars firm against his eye sockets, interjected: "F4s, shift in status, they're turning inclining left."

"Vector?" Lieutenant Derrick enquired.

"Still banking...shit! new trajectory, west by northwest (on a direct flight path for the village and *our* position). Rapid descent—closing fast!"

"This is it!" Buster yelled, "…napalm incoming, pull-in tight!"

I linked-up, Dusty on my left side, Bronco on the other. I briefly glimpsed skyward where I could see the silhouettes of two Phantom Jets soaring towards us like birds of prey, visible wisps of smoke trailing their burners. Phantoms that had lost their cloaks; tangible apparitions, perceptible spectres about to spread their murderous fingers.

Marine Collins, who was still standing in a highly exposed position, was also surveying the jet aircraft.

"Jumper!" the Sergeant hollered, "get your fuckin' arse down here now!"

Jumper remained in place, as if hypnotised by the sight of the inbound jets. Bronco, tearing himself away from me, leapt up and hauled him to the ground. Both of them landed in a dusty heap beside me.

"**Cover!**" Buster roared just as Bronco and Jumper re-established the link.

The pack, each ensuring that we closed our eyes whilst taking a deep breath, nosedived to the ground. I've held human beings many times in my life: during affectionate hugs with family, friends and lovers; as a rugby player scrumming down and whilst manning the barricades in Belfast and Londonderry. But I had never held on to people more solidly. I remember squeezing Dusty and Bronco with so much force that I almost propelled the air from their lungs.

A split second after we hit the dirt there was a thunderous reverberation, obviously the surge of the F4s as they passed overhead, followed by a flash so intense that it penetrated through my eyelids. The illumination, a shade of bright orange that slowly faded to yellow, was accompanied by a blast and vibration so intense that it practically elevated us off the ground. This was succeeded by a blast of wind that ripped at the back of our flak jackets only to dissipate as quickly as it came. I could feel my heart pounding against my ribcage. I confess that my sole consideration was for *my* survival, nothing more.

The explosion was followed by a sustaining roar, assumed to be the firestorm, accompanied by a build up of heat, gradual at first, which crept over our backs in an increasing intensity as it rolled swiftly towards our legs. Then we could feel a squall of wind blowing back, moving from our feet upwards. This was clearly the back draft, the inrush of air that inevitably supervenes the blast vacuum.

A short time after the incident I remember reliving the primary phases of the bombing. The Detail was aware that an attack was imminent; hence we prepared ourselves accordingly. The inhabitants would've had virtually no indication that they were about to be hit, save for the sound of the incoming jets. This would've given them no time to take cover or hold their breaths. (Not that this would make any difference to those subjected to the epicentre.) I thought about the effects of napalm. The field manual stated that the blast vacuum and succeeding firestorm are so intense that they literally drag the air out of your lungs, deflating them like limp balloons. Regaining an immediate breathing pattern is almost impossible, especially for children; therefore, death by anoxia is inevitable.

The effect of burning napalm upon the body – particularly after what we'd witnessed in the aftermath of the bombing – was another matter. I simply didn't want to visit this area.

The enduring roar continued for what must have been at least a minute. By this time my desire to expel the noxious carbon dioxide was irresistible. The radiating heat upon our shoulders and backs was also increasing, a factor that exacerbated our discomfort. The roar lingered, the seconds ticked, the heat augmented; the craving to breathe out became overpowering. I felt like a condemned person locked in the gas chamber hopelessly holding that last inhalation in the knowledge that all that encircled me was deadly. One and three-quarter minutes, two minutes, how much longer! Just when I thought I couldn't take any more, Sergeant Edwards gave the signal that we'd all been waiting for—

"**Break cover!**" he bellowed in-between a fit of coughing.

The Detachment separated and lurched upward whilst exhaling and taking a much-needed intake of air. As we broke cover we were hit by a blast of heat that made us recoil. We must have taken all of 10 seconds to re-establish our alertness; such was the nature of our disorientation. Once we'd regained our composure we were confronted by a horrendous scene, a sight incomparable with any other monstrous act or human tribulation previously encountered.

The whole village was blazing, engulfed in a wall of flames that danced in every conceivable direction. The flames were generating a thick string of black smoke that rushed skyward as if to escape the heat at its tail. There was an overbearing smell of burnt napalm (napalm has a distinctive aroma akin to oxidised petroleum and heated coconut oil) accompanied by a fusion of scorched vegetation. The whole setting was shrouded in a dense shadow consequent of the smoke cloud that hovered overhead. I distinctly remember staring at the scene along with my compadrés in utter disbelief. I couldn't assimilate the actuality of what had come to pass, even in the face of the arena in which we were operating.

The whole Detail appeared to be dumbfounded; stunned into temporary catatonia. I can't recall the identity of the marine who initiated our awakening, though I can remember his cutting line: "The dirty bastards, they naped the place. Those dirty bastards!"

I turned to look at Bronco who was still focused on the deplorable spectacle. "Are you okay?" I said, unsure of what else to say or do.

"No, I mean yeah. Are you?"

"I think so…" I said in a nervous reply, "I just can't stop shaking."

Lieutenant Derrick began issuing orders: "Listen up, check yourselves over for any injuries. When you're done split up into your squads and await further instructions."

We checked ourselves and each other in a semi-hush. The fire had reduced to a partial smoulder by the time we'd finished. The pall of smoke had also moderately dispersed allowing shafts of light to illuminate the gloomy vista.

As this occurred we could see the full extent of the bombing. Nothing within the settlement was left standing or intact. There were no visible landmarks, identifiable shapes or distinctive lines; only an enormous blackened imprint containing a clump of small fires and smouldering areas. The curve of the Sôn Kơi treeline and the monsoon ditches that encircled the commune were the only visible evidence that anything had stood in the locale. Everything had been burned beyond recognition. I struggled to reconfigure a picture of the hamlet: the layout of the buildings; the community centre, workstations and livestock enclosure. Try as I may I could not reconstruct a laudable representation of what was, only three or so minutes before, the village of Tchựin Loy.

Then, in the midst of my attempt to come to terms with the situation, I was struck by an absolute reality. A commune is a construct beyond an assortment of buildings. Its very existence depends upon a conglomerate of people; the people are the village. The inhabitants, what of *them* within remnants of the blaze?

I hurriedly scanned the scene below in a hopeless attempt to see if I could identify signs of life. I momentarily examined the possibility that some of the inhabitants had made cover in the Sôn Kơi Woods, or had sought refuge in the myriad of tunnels under-running the commune. But, these thoughts were merely temporary fabrications. Feeble attempts to avoid an inescapable fact: that the air strike had incinerated, blasted or asphyxiated every man, woman and child within the settlement. Nobody could have survived the ferocity of such an attack. The foliage on the original Sôn Kơi treeline had been shattered into thousands of pieces. Anyone within the vicinity would have been peppered with red-hot splinters. What is more, the tunnels would have offered no protection against the firestorm; the air would have been sucked out suffocating all inside. The effects of napalm – hitherto understood within the abstract of military manuals – were now demonstrably evident. My initial elation at surviving the air strike was directly countered by the horror before my very eyes.

I was suddenly overcome with revulsion. I wanted to cry out, to release the irrepressible ache that had invaded my senses; the impact of the air strike was beginning to hit home.

Lieutenant Derrick issued instructions: "Squads! prepare to carry out a reconnaissance of the area. One Squad take the left flank round the village, Two Squad take the right. Squad Leaders, site one man at your rear. Move in groups of four. Look and listen for signs of life. Pay attention to the monsoon ditches, some people might have jumped into them for protection."

The Detachment, whose senses were still partially deadened, quickly grouped and proceeded in a link-echelon towards the boundary. We were all full of apprehension, it was clear that none of us were relishing the tasks ahead. As we moved towards the obliterated site the line of the fire-scar became identifiable. The fire-line stopped abruptly 80 yards short of our cover position.

"Fuck me, look at that," Marine Collins said. "If those bastards would have released their bombs a second later we'd have been barbecued!"

He was right. We could see just how close we were to the perimeter of the inferno. In addition, we observed a number of small flash ignitions on the periphery of the target; these quickly died out, likely because of high bedrock moisture levels. The inferno had also affected the burial ground: the burst and enduring heat had scorched the headstones and the bamboo poles containing the spiritual adornments were badly shrivelled and charred.

We were all fearful as we approached the position of what we were to be confronted with. I momentarily diverted my gaze away from the charred remnants of the settlement. Then, the discipline imbued into me as a Royal Marines Commando began to take over. Lieutenant Derrick and Sergeant Edwards had issued orders – I knew I had to follow them, regardless of my fears.

As we moved closer we could feel the heat radiating from the smouldering location. Moreover, we could hear the unmistakable sound of pyrotechnics sporadically exploding within the fire-scar. Smoke from the slowly burning clumps began to drift into our eyes making us wince with discomfort. A steady shower of minute debris and ash began to cover us. We had to briefly place our webbing scarves over our noses and mouths to avoid breathing the ashes.

One and Two Squads separated and proceeded in a flanking manoeuvre around the obliterated site. We made our way towards the Sôn Kơi treeline on the southeastern perimeter slowly advancing in teams of four. As we neared the village boundary it became evident that the water in the monsoon ditches had evaporated in the searing heat. Anybody seeking protection from this source would have been literally boiled alive.

As the team advanced we became acutely aware that we were in the vicinity of what used to be the livestock enclosure. We couldn't fail to note the smell of burning human flesh and animal carcasses. Marine Miller glanced at me, a look of pallor on his face: "This is fuckin' unreal."

I remember staring back at Dusty almost unable to respond. My mouth was dry and I felt unable to swallow. My stomach was churning resultant of the incessant smell of burning tissue. I couldn't hear the sound of my own footsteps. The palms of my hands were sticky, a condition that was seriously compromising my ability to maintain a grip on my M16.

Jumper, who was moving up immediately behind Bronco, Dusty and me,

suddenly stopped and called to us: "Wait up! …can you hear that?"
"Hear what?" Corporal Lane said.
"That noise…screaming, can't you hear it?"
Bronco was just about to suggest that he was hearing things when we also became aware of the distant sounds of anguish.
"Some of the villagers must still be alive," Bronco said. "Any idea where it's coming from?"
We were just about to respond in the negative when Jumper cried out, pointing in the direction of the rice paddies: "Oh fuck, look at that!"
We all turned and looked towards the southwest. There, we could see what must have been among 15 and 20 people running through the shallow water in an understandable state of distress towards the burnt out settlement.
"Oh no!" Bronco said, "…the workers we saw in the paddies, they're from Tchựin Loy!"
Within seconds the whole Detail became aware of the people advancing towards us. Lieutenant Derrick gave instructions: "Squads! Regroup; move down towards our former position. Squad Leaders, leave two men at our rear to continue the search."
The squads complied with the directive as the workers continued to run towards the obliterated commune. We hurriedly moved close to the line of the rice field reforming just behind our former position.
Corporal Farr called out to Lieutenant Derrick: "What the hell do we do now Sir?" The Lieutenant seemed to be transfixed by the scene, temporarily unable to grasp the inevitable – the wave of human agony that was about to confront us.
Sergeant Edwards approached and broke the deadlock: "I think we should unfurl the United Nations Flag and make ready the interpreters, don't you Sir?"
"What?" Lieutenant Derrick said breaking out of the trance. "Yeah...right. Get out the flag and form a partial blockade. These people are in a state of shock, they may try to move onto the fire-scar."
He was just finishing his directives when Lance Corporal Bell cautioned that one of the workers, a man approximately seventeen years of age, was armed with a Kalashnikov assault rifle. Lieutenant Derrick alerted the specialists in the squads: "Marksmen, get a clear sight on the Dink with the AK, if he moves to open fire, drop him! Sergeant, take up the rear. Translators, up front with me."
Bronco and I moved to a front position with the Lieutenant standing in a central status immediately behind. Meanwhile, I could see at least five M16s to our rear trained on the young man with the AK47.
Lieutenant Derrick instructed Bronco and me as the distraught villagers

advanced: "Back sling your rifles; assume a none aggressive stance. Corporal Lane, concentrate on the primary group. Give them a clear identification; emphasise our neutrality. Lance Corporal Morris, concentrate on the kid who's tooled-up; get him to drop the AK. Remember your training both of you. Establish clear non-threatening eye contact; use a calm but assertive voice, be aware of your body language."

We prepared for the onslaught of the villagers. As I looked at the anguish on the faces of the looming people I wondered how I would have coped with such a situation. I tried to imagine myself walking near my home: that place retaining all things dear to me: my loved ones, possessions, history; my very identity, only to see it blasted in a rolling fireball. How would I feel as I approached a concept that was once so complete, so secure, so much a part of *me* and see it in ruins? I quickly realised that I had to dismiss such thoughts; they would only encumber the tasks ahead.

Bronco began to focus on the group: "Nghe, nghe, ngừng lại. Không người Mỹ chiến sĩ dân tôc khắp thế giời," (*Attention, attention, hold. Not American soldiers, United Nations*!)

Meanwhile, I endeavoured to focus on the young man with the AK47. "Nghe ngừng bơ Kâlạsh nikóv ngay," (*Listen...halt and drop the Kalashnikov immediately*!) I shouted whilst seeking to establish firm eye contact. Initially, the young man continued to advance towards the Detail in a highly aroused state. He appeared to be taking no notice of my request. "Ngừng bơ Kâlạsh nikóv, ngay," I repeated in an assertive mode.

The man stopped abruptly and pointed the barrel of the AK47 in our direction screaming obscenities. I focused on the Kalashnikov. I could see from the position of the cocking mechanism that the breach contained a full metal jacket.

I suddenly felt exposed; the armed man was obviously in a state of shock, as a consequence, he was likely unstable. This probability only served to compound my apprehension. For the second time in less than 10 minutes I was overcome by a feeling of dread. I was already perspiring heavily; the bandanna on my head was soaking wet. Globules of salty sweat began to drop into my eyes making me blink with discomfort.

Bronco, who was still working on the main group, interrupted his task. He gave me an unmistakable side-glance: "Stay cool Bazzer, the lads are behind us, they've got it covered."

I also distinctly remember hearing Sergeant Edwards in the background conducting the snipers in a hushed voice: "Steady boys...stand fast on the trigger."

I partially regained my confidence and looked directly at the young man. I could see that he too was frightened (probably more frightened than me given the weight of firepower and that his village had just been destroyed). He was shaking violently and hyperventilating. His eyes were wide open as he nervously scanned me and the men to my rear.

"Nghe là toi," (*Listen to me.*) I said firmly whilst maintaining eye contact. "Chúng tôi chơng chơ, mà bắt đầu bơ Â-K, chơng ta là bắt đầu lý dờ cư bây giơ bơ Kâlạsh nikóv," (*We've no fight here, but if you don't drop the ÂK we may be forced to open fire, now drop the Kalashnikov!*)

The man gave me a hesitant look. He was clearly in a transient state uncertain of what to do next; the standoff had reached a critical point.

A fearful woman moving from my right towards the squads interrupted my focus on the armed man. The palms of her hands were pressed together in front of her face. (The Mahayana Buddhist sign for peace and harmony.) She was weeping and sobbing so much that she could hardly catch her breath. The woman pulled up in front of me and began to cry out between fits of howling: "Không không, xin đứng đaừ nó anh áy thộựi con trai," (*No, no, please don't hurt him; he's only a boy!*)

At that time I had to concentrate on splitting my gaze between the armed man and the distressed woman. I attempted above my nervousness to give the women a look of reassurance.

"Chơng tôi dùng gị dau nó chơng tôi thúc hiên an toàn," (*We don't want to hurt him; we make you safe.*) I said in a conciliatory tone. "Anh ây ngay bơ Kâlạsh nikóv," (*He must drop the Kalashnikov!*)

The woman gave me what appeared to be a look of mistrust. Like the armed man to her rear she seemed to be unsure of what to do, or of how to respond. This was understandable; to her we were just another collection of soldiers. American GIs, no friends of the Viet Cong, had occupied her country for over 9 years. Prior to this, the Japanese and French had terrorised her community. Oppression from men uniform was a regular occurrence. The United Nations Flag draped behind me meant little to this woman or her people.

I placed the palms of my hands together in the gesture of peace hoping that the two participants would accept our non-aggressive intentions. "Chơ phép cà doi vơi cho xin," (*Let us help you here, please.*) I said gently, being mindful of the menacing AK47.

The young man dropping the Kalashnikov and making his way towards the woman who turned to greet him unexpectedly broke the impasse. The angry young man suddenly looked like the *boy* he was. His eyes were welling-up. It was clear that he could no longer contain his stoicism. The woman embraced him as he approached. Both stood comforting each other on the edge of paddies.

There was a notable sigh of relief, not just from me, as Lieutenant Derrick ordered the snipers to stand down. Buster instructed Marine Jeffers to collect the AK47. Meanwhile, I joined Bronco still engaged in interactions with the main group.

Once my task was complete I had time to grasp the full magnitude of distress within the workers. They were in a line in front of the phalanx formed by the squads. Some of the people were standing; others were on their knees or squatting. There were approximately eight children of varying ages in the charge of caregivers.

The people were understandably traumatised. Most were weeping or sobbing heavily. Some appeared to be staring ahead in a continuing state of shock. Others were frantically enquiring between themselves about family or friends, likely asking if some of them had left the settlement or visited one of the neighbouring communities prior to the attack.

To the right of the gathering I could see a young pregnant woman on her knees wailing and rocking. An older woman was alongside trying to offer comfort. Marine Collins went over to the pregnant woman with his water bottle and offered a drink; the distressed woman turned her head away. Buster intervened: "She won't take a drink from you. Give the canteen to her companion; she'll accept a drink from her."

Jumper complied and indeed the woman did take a much-needed sip of water.

In the midst of this calamity Bronco, who on instructions had identified a senior member of the grouping, was trying to translate continuing directives from Lieutenant Derrick. He was experiencing great difficulty in gaining a coherent thread of interaction – such was the intensity of the peoples torment.

The senior member, a man of approximately 65 years of age, couldn't understand why the Detachment had set up a blockade to stop his people advancing towards the obliterated location. Bronco was desperately trying to translate often-complex words to the senior. I shifted alongside him and offered help via the translation manual.

Meanwhile, Marine Lyle, following an instruction to contact Command on the RT, called out that he'd established a line of communication. Lieutenant Derrick grabbed the handset and began talking to, what was likely, a senior officer at headquarters: "Be advised we have a major incident here…we need aid workers on site soonest. Also, I wish to report a clear violation of the interim ceasefire by the Security Forces. The village of—"

He stopped abruptly. It was obvious that the respondent had interrupted him. We could see a look of anger and frustration developing on his face as the IPSF representative talked to him. He attempted to interrupt the dispatch but to no avail. The one-way conversation concluded with the Lieutenant slamming the handset onto the cradle.

"—Those fucking arseholes! Sergeant Edwards, Red Cross workers from the bases at Lôc Nịnh and Đà Lắt are being alerted. In the meantime we'll continue to offer as much help as we can."

Buster gave the Lieutenant a thoughtful look: "We can't keep these people at bay much longer Sir; they want to check things out for themselves."

"There're unexploded pyrotechnics going off within the fire-scar! We've got a responsibility here—"

"I understand that Sir, but at the end of the day this is, or was, *their* village... I figure they've got a right."

Lieutenant Derrick stood contemplating. "Very well, instruct the men to allow an ordered line in-between the barricade. Meanwhile, get the squads to form a loop round the village boundary. We'll offer assistance if and when needed."

The Sergeant issued the information. The decision didn't come a minute too soon. Holding the inhabitants back from what was, quite rightly, their settlement was exacerbating their distress. Bronco and I explained our intentions to the senior representative and asked if he would help us maintain a semblance of order once we'd allowed the group through. The greying man, who maintained an air of calm and dignity throughout the whole ordeal, reluctantly agreed.

The squads separated and began to filter the people through. Corporal Lane and I stood each side offering guidance to the villagers: "Nghe, ngưng là khầm vưng không an toàn," (*Attention, be aware, area not safe*!)

The Detachment reformed, as the distressed workers broke free. Dusty, Jumper and I joined up and progressed on our former echelon (towards the southeastern perimeter). Bronco linked up with One Squad to ensure that translators were available on each side of the position, whilst Marine Lyle remained close to the Lieutenant with the Radio Transmitter.

We made way as the people began to move around the boundary. They appeared to be unsure of what to do next or where to turn. Many were pointing into the vicinity of the burnt out site in enduring cries of agony. Some began to cover their eyes and faces with their hands. Others fell onto their knees and prayed. A few attempted to venture onto the fire-scar but were driven back by ground-base heat. Meanwhile, a woman in her early twenties had gathered the children together in a position near the burial ground. The children were trembling in a huddle. The young woman was desperately trying to calm them. She appeared to be trying to sing Vietnamese lullabies whilst cradling and rocking two young ones in her arms. The spectacle of seeing already traumatised people trying to come to terms with the slaughter of their loved ones and the destruction of their commune was hard to take. "Offer assistance if and when needed," the Lieutenant said. 'What possible assistance could we offer these people?' I thought. I stood along with my fellow marines staring at the grief stricken inhabitants in a redundant poise. I felt as if a round peg on the planet of square holes; like a clown who had lost his mask in a ring void of props – I felt totally useless.

We moved silently along the perimeter trying our utmost not to interfere with the arrangements – for what they were worth amongst the aftermath of that man-made abomination – the remaining villagers were trying to make. It had been some 30 minutes since the attack. The smoke within the fire-scar was lessening revealing more than just smouldering clumps. The site was scattered with blackened and twisted bodies and the charred remnants of materials nearby. We were largely protected from the enormity of seeing the bodies close up due to our position on the perimeter. I can remember being thankful that I didn't have to venture onto the fire-scar to witness the carnage at close quarters.

It is somewhat of an irony that just when I was convincing myself I wouldn't have to deal with any more shocking revelations that I tripped on what I thought was a burnt log laying immediately in front of me. I remember staring at the object at my feet in a state of uncertainty. It must have taken all of five seconds before I realised that the blackened item was the charred body of an adult. The body was lying, feet first to my station, partially on its side. Its scorched arms were stretched out in a seemingly hopeless cry for assistance that would never arrive. The heat had welded the fingers together and the bones on the lower arms were visible through the shrivelled flesh. I couldn't tell if the body was of a man or a woman such was the intensity of the incineration. The searing napalm had literally bonded the clothing onto the skin charring the torso. The outline of the skull was visible; the skin on the face had almost been completely burnt off and the hair was singed into a blackened mat on the scalp. The individual's mouth was locked open, as if trapped in an eternal scream, revealing distinctive yellowed teeth. The enduring heat had reduced the lips back to the gum line and there was a darkened stump and empty recesses where the nose and eyes used to be. The heat had also burst the stomach open spilling the contents into a congealed pile over half of the empty cavity; the emanation of oxidised bile, part digested food and scorched flesh was oppressive.

I was overcome by a surge of nausea. I felt like emptying the contents of my stomach onto the charred ground. I turned away frantically grasping for my water bottle. My hands were shaking so much that I found myself wrestling with the stopper. I eventually released the top and tried to take a drink from the canteen. I tilted the bottle too much; such was the intensity of my clumsiness. The lukewarm water came gushing out over-filling my mouth. I briefly choked as the liquid puffed up my cheeks and pressed on my throat. The fluid came spewing back out in a cascade making me cough and gasp for air. I was aware by now that I was sobbing under my breath, hopelessly trying to hide my disturbance. I closed my eyes and desperately tried to conceive pleasant thoughts: cerise sunsets, warm summer meadows, cool clear waterfalls; beautiful Sàigòn bargirls with their sloe-eyes and jasmine fragrances.

I was stirred back to reality by a rattling sound. I observed that it was the top on my water bottle clattering against the neck of the canteen as my hand shook. 'No training manual, film or exercise could have prepared us for this,' I thought. This was experiential: raw, barbarous, gut wrenching, repugnant. Incomparable with even the worst of nightmares; a cavalcade of carnage deposited before our very eyes.

'Come-on…' I thought, 'get a grip; take a deep breath, it'll be over soon.'

I took a gentle sip from the canteen, poured the tepid water over my face and assuredly placed the top back on the bottle. I took a huge breath, gripped my rifle and with a look of fortitude turned back towards the carnage. As I regained my composure I caught Dusty and Jumper gazing in my direction. They were slightly in front of me. It was apparent they'd missed the body as they walked past. I noticed above my short-lived embarrassment that they too were staring at the hideous form. Jumper broke off and looked at me, his normally hardened face filled with anguish.

"Those poor bastards," he said his voice full of emotion.

Marine Miller, in the meantime, continued to stare at the charred remains.

"Come on boys," I said in a resolute voice, "let's move on."

Dusty, Jumper and I continued to move up on towards the vicinity of the livestock enclosure. As we advanced we couldn't fail to see the incinerated remains of animal carcasses. We observed a large water buffalo directly ahead of us. The half-cooked beast was laying belly down, its legs folded underneath. Wisps of acrid blue-black smoke were emanating from the carcass. Dusty stared at me noticing the look of perplexity on my face: "You okay mucker?"

"Is there a small body near that buffalo?" I enquired, unwilling to look for myself.

Dusty gingerly moved towards the steaming rump. "No," he replied, a look of nausea on his face, "there doesn't appear to be, why?"

"It's nothing. I don't suppose it matters, but there was a little girl, nine, ten tops, trying to pull a water buffalo towards the village boundary just before the attack—"

"I saw her, along with some other kids. The enclosure was full of them…"

Dusty broke off. An uneasy interlude followed, each of us waiting for the other to speak.

"It'll have been quick," Jumper, alleged with a look that contradicted his assertion, "...they wouldn't have felt anything. It'll have been over in a flash, yeah?"

"Yeah," Dusty replied unconvincingly, "it'll have been quick."

We continued to take a covert stance as the inhabitants went about their frenzied business. After some 45 minutes the heat within the fire-scar had ameliorated. There were no new reports of exploding rounds, hence, a few villagers ventured into the epicentre. Some of the inhabitants approached the incinerated corpses. They began to gently pick up the bodies, where they were able to without the corpse coming apart. It was evident that they were beginning the process of *passage*, the transfer of the Karma into the spiritual world.

Minutes later Corporal Farr, stationed on the perimeter proximate to the Sôn Kơi treeline, made a request for a translator. Two women were seemingly appealing for items. On my arrival it became evident that the women were asking for receptacles to carry or hold water. Doubtless they wanted the containers, along with fresh water, to wash the bodies of the dead. (Viet Cong passage rituals include ensuring their kinfolk are cleansed before being released into the care of their forefathers.) We westerners would largely see these practices as grotesque. The mere thought of washing a dead body would be eschewed by most, let alone cleansing a body that was twisted and charred, and whose flesh was likely to peel off as the kinfolk applied the damp cloth. Still, the Viet Cong had their ways. To them all heavenly bodies were sacred particularly their loved ones. Moreover, they were war hardened; they'd been in an armed struggle for 9000 days. To the Viet Cong death, violent or otherwise, was a way of life.

I conveyed the message to Sergeant Edwards who set about asking the men if they had any spare billycans. I can report that every marine dug into their webbing belts and began offering canteens to the women who gratefully took what they needed.

The people continued to move around the site: separating the charred bodies, trying to identify loved ones, sifting through the debris and offering each other solace. We, in the meantime, continued to stand back, surplus to requirement. Entrapped in a paradoxical situation – prepared to offer help yet not wanting to become involved; longing to offer condolences whilst deliberately avoiding eye contact; wanting to be gallant though fearful of the nausea and nightmares that adjoining the aftermath of carnage would inevitably bring.

During this time the two marines left behind to continue with the search for possible survivors returned with the news that all those subjected to the attack had perished. I swear there was a collective expression of relief. Who could blame us? What medical aid could we have administered to an individual with extensive and enduring third degree burns?

Marine Lyle interrupted our inactivity calling out to the Lieutenant whilst holding out the radiophone: "Sir, headquarters want to speak to you."

"Oh do they!" Lieutenant Derrick snapped, demonstrably scornful of the big-braids secluded in their far-off bunkers. He listened to the directives attentively, attempting yet again to intervene. He was clearly thwarted as he closed the broadcast: "Listen up…we've been given instructions to reposition; Red Cross workers incoming from Đà Lắt."

Buster gave the Lieutenant a cautionary look: "We can't just leave these people, they're highly vulnerable. What if the SVA return? You know what those bastards are like; they'll take great pleasure in finishing these people off."

"It's okay Sergeant, I've already thought of that. We'll withdraw slowly and leave a token force behind until the Red Cross workers have arrived. Those cowards won't try anything while we're still around."

"But Sir, Command—"

"Fuck Command…they're not here, we are!"

Sergeant Edwards directed Bronco and I to accompany Lieutenant Derrick and called the Squad Leaders to summons their men for muster. The Lieutenant instructed us to ask the senior, who by now was recognised as the Chû tuổi, to engage in a discussion on his peoples' immediate need. The honcho, who clearly did not wish to leave his people, grudgingly agreed. Lieutenant Derrick led the conversation. Bronco acted as the primary interpreter, myself acting as backup.

"Inform the honcho that we've been ordered to move out and that Red Cross workers are on their way from Đà Lắt. Also, inform him we'll be reporting the day's events to our seniors in the International Peacekeeping Supervisory Force. Add that he should be assured that we'll do our utmost to ensure that the culprits responsible for this monstrous act will be brought before the International War Crimes Tribunal."

Corporal Lane began to translate the message. However, the Chû tuổi appeared to be in an inert state. He had a desolate look on his face. His eyes were expressionless, as if an evil spirit had invaded his soul and doused the glow from within. Bronco struggled with the translation resultant of receiving no feedback.

Lieutenant Derrick intervened. "Leave it Corporal Lane; I'm sure it's just empty rhetoric." He pondered for a minute: "Tell him we're sorry."

Bronco gave the man a firm look: "Chơng tôi nổi bươn," (*We're so sorry.*)

It was true we were sorry. But whom were we really sorry for – this man and his people or ourselves'?

"Cám ơn," (*Thank you.*) The elder quietly replied.

The Lieutenant asked the elder if he and his people would like some protection. The Chû tuổi waved his hand (the Vietnamese gesticulation for 'forget it') whilst gently smiling… "Vài dồựng chí đén Tchựrin Điêt và Khômn. Sơ Việt Công chiến sĩ," (*Some comrades will be coming from Tchựrin Điêt and Khômn. There'll be Viet Cong rebels amongst them.*)

The honcho explained that he was needed by his people and gratefully requested our approval for him to rejoin his congregation. At that moment I felt a sombre ache. Here we were unwelcome aliens in his country, yet he was courteously beseeching *us* to release him. What a crazy mixed up world.

Lieutenant Derrick thanked the honcho for his time and gave a final offer of help. The village elder appreciatively declined and slowly turned away. The Lieutenant – who had a rudimentary grasp of Vietnamese – called out as he disengaged: "Đáo phât đối vơị liên hoựn," (*God bless you all.*)

The elder stopped and turned to face the three of us. He placed the palms of his hands in front of his face, closed his eyes and gently bowed his head. "Cấm chống bắn chân yên tĩnh," (*May no one tread on your dreams.*) He said. As the elder turned away I felt a total admiration for him. Through all of his and his peoples' adversity he still had the grace to offer us goodwill.

The Detachment gathered in the vicinity of the burial ground. As we came together Lance Corporal Bell covertly removed an instamatic camera from his flak jacket and took a picture of the obliterated spot. Bronco stared at him in amazement: "What the fuck are you doing?"

"Nobody will believe us," Dinger replied.

Sergeant Edwards issued movements: "Muscle-up your gear. Check your weapons are safe. Hold magazines in place until further instructions."

We moved out in a silent shuffle. To our left we could see the children, still being attended by the young caregiver. I momentarily gazed at them; they were outwardly calm but still quivering where they sat. Their incessant crying had reddened their little eyes. How painful to see these tiny waifs, their innocence violated by the evil men do. I had to bite my lip to stop myself crying.

As we evacuated the area I wanted for some unknown reason to glance back, to take one last look at the unbelievable spectacle. Something, however, stopped me. As if I didn't have the right; like looking back would have constituted an act of voyeurism. Besides, I needed no confirmation that a tragic event had taken place or that I was still alive. 'I've survived an air strike,' I recall thinking. But my joy was neutralised by a pervading void. Something inside me had died, though at that time, I was unsure of exactly what it was. Then, as we began to put distance between the carnage and ourselves, a feeling of remorse exacerbated my dissonance. I felt as if we were running from the scene of a crime; escaping from the inevitable tirade of questions that would follow this act of mass murder. I felt like an unwilling witness to a hundred executions in a state of kill-shock, unable to assimilate and accommodate the overflow of horror that had assaulted my senses. And so, we left the remnants of Tchựin Loy. We left the disturbing sights, the enduring cries of distress, and the smells: the emanation of scorched vegetation; the odour of burnt napalm; the reek of burning flesh. And the most repugnant smell of all – the stench of inhumanity!

21:30: UN Base Camp 4, Sơng Xuây.

Following the events of the day IPSF Command considered that it would not be prudent for the Detachment to remain in the Tchựin District. Control instructed us to expedite a course for the neutral UN Base at Sơng Xuây. Given the circumstances no helicopter transportation or personnel carriers were available; consequently, we had no option but to make the excursion on foot.

Sơng Xuây was some 25 miles south by southeast of Tchựin Loy. In order for us to reach our destination in good time we needed to walk at an extended pace throughout the rest of the day. As Royal Marine Commandos we were invariably at a peak of fitness. Nevertheless, on reaching our objective we were understandably fatigued. But it was the numbness of the psyche not the weariness in the limbs that was of particular heed. As members of the International Peacekeeping Supervisory Force the Commando carried the United Nations Peacekeeping emblem, which contained an axiom: '*If we cannot silence the guns, let not the guns silence us*'. The demeanour of the squads during the long trek to Sơng Xuây made a mockery of this tenet. The whole Detail appeared transfixed into a state of hush. The banter usually associated with a 'yomp' (rapid cross-country hike) was conspicuous by its absence; as if we were moving like ghosts through the landscape. Subsequent to this I created my own maxim: '*We may have left the horror of Tchựin Loy behind, but the horror has not left us*.'

A senior IPSF representative, who'd prepared a room for our reception, hosted our arrival at Base Camp 4. There was a well-provisioned spread of food and a crate of beer set central on a large conference table. The representative, who didn't have the courtesy to give us his name or speak to us directly, gestured that we should sit down and tuck in. Under normal circumstances Commandos would need no encouragement to attack a spread of vittles inclusive of free beer, especially after a 25 mile yomp. On the other hand, these were not normal circumstances; the events of the day had clearly moderated our appetites.

Lieutenant Derrick and the 'Supervisory Force representative engaged in a brief conversation. It was obvious we were being prepared for debrief. The representative departed leaving the Lieutenant to address us: "It's been a long walk here lads, we're all tired so let's get straight to business. You probably know that under usual circumstances IPSF Investigators would debrief us either separately or in groups. However, and don't ask me why, on this occasion they've elected to accept written statements on the events of the day. So, after you've had some tucker I want you to write a consecutive account of all movements and occurrences from 11:40 through to 1400 hours. Keep it brief and factual. Record only what you saw and heard. If you're unsure about something then leave it out. Don't embellish your accounts. Focus on the events that occurred, not what you *thought* was happening. Corporal Lane, Lance Corporal Morris, focus on the radio transmissions. Complete a detailed record in the Vietnamese text along with a précis in English."

The Lieutenant, wearing a thoughtful expression, broke off for a second: "I'm not sure how the IPSF are going to proceed with this one. They'll be sure to order an enquiry. However, I'm unsure whether we'll be called to give evidence. Until we know then be advised not to discuss the events of the day outside the Platoon. Our eye witness accounts may have a major effect on outcomes; let's not compromise that possibility with careless talk."

Lieutenant Derrick asked if we had any questions. The Detail failed to respond. We all appeared to be frozen into a state of silence, each submerged within our inner worlds.

"Very well…" the Lieutenant said, somewhat unconvincingly, "give your completed reports to Sergeant Edwards. Don't stay up too late, we've likely got a heavy day tomorrow. Muster at 0700 hours. Sergeant…" he called out making ready to leave, "you've got the Detachment."

Lieutenant Derrick prepared to leave. As he made his way towards the door Corporal Farr broke the stillness: "All bullshit, that's what it is!"

The Lieutenant turned sharply and looked at Tommy.

"Pipe down!" Buster snapped.

Lieutenant Derrick interjected: "No Sergeant, let him speak. Go on son, get it off your chest."

Tommy froze for a minute. I'm unsure whether it was with apprehension or that he was simply gathering his thoughts. Regardless, the whole Detail appeared to be gazing in his direction – as if desperate for somebody to help us escape our transient state.

"Come on…" Tommy said in a dismissive tone, "do you think any of us really believe that those gob-shites are going to take any notice of our accounts? We're not stupid. We all know the score. Oh we can be sure the big-braids will have their enquiry. They'll sit round the table wearing their usual dumb-arse expressions. Fingerin' through our reports, wringing their hands, tut-tutting, saying how shocked they are over the incident at Tchựin Loy. And then what? Enter the corrupt evil little bastards who run this Tinpot Dictatorship, brandishing the same old platitudes and tired excuses we've been listening to since the day we arrived. You'll know the script. The one that kicks off with an abject apology and winds up with an account of how the incident was the product of a tactical error due to poor intelligence, or the wrong grid reference being targeted. Or that all too familiar excuse, 'pilots discharging their bombs too late'! Whichever way it cuts the outcomes already been set. The fuckwit brigade will issue a statement full of the usual contrition while some big brass in Sàigòn will get his knuckles rapped. And what about the people who really matter, the peasants of Tchựin Loy? They'll be written off as casualties of war. The whole thing sucks. It's the same as it's always been, always will be!"

Lieutenant Derrick scanned the room. "Is that it?" he asked stopping to look directly at Corporal Farr, "quite a speech. So what now, do you want me to tell you that you're wrong? That the individuals responsible for that heinous act will be brought before the War Crimes Tribunal? Well I won't! Moreover, I wouldn't even if I could…"

He fell silent, thoughtful, whilst glancing round the table purposely halting his gaze to look at individuals and groups: "Seems to me like some of you fellows have forgotten who we are and why we're here. Well, let me refresh your memories. We are Royal Marine Commandos on active duty in a war zone, not politicians in the National Assembly. We are *peacekeepers*, not *peacemakers* and sometimes, as hard as it is, that means we've got to stand back and watch! Oh don't get me wrong; I'm not saying you're not entitled to your opinions. But you will be advised to keep them to yourselves! In this arena openly asserting your convictions serves only to compromise our neutrality, once that happens we'll find ourselves on the slippery slope towards taking sides—"

He broke off diverting his gaze away from us.

"—I know you're all hurting; you're not the only ones. There's no doubt, what we witnessed today was unacceptable. But sometimes the only way to deal with the unacceptable is to learn accept it. Some of you might be too young to understand that now, but you'll learn...just give it time. Meanwhile, at 0700 hours tomorrow morning I require you to be in a state of readiness! I need each and every one of you to maintain a clear focus on the tasks, whatever they may be. We can be sure that Command aren't going to leave us in Nha Trang. They'll have already determined a new assignment. I don't know where they're going to send us: Quì Nhôn, Quang Ngaî, Trệng Nhôy, maybe even back to Quang Trì for all I know, or care. We go where the powers that be send us and we do our duty. No more, no less. Ours is not to reason why, y'all know the rest. Our strengths have always been in our skills, our courage, our togetherness and our discipline! We hold on to these things then we cannot fail to do the job."

He reverted to a gentle tone: "I want every one of you ugly bastards on the plane back home with me in one piece, not laying in the cargo hold in body bags! We've lost enough men from this Platoon in that other shithole, Northern Ireland. No more…you hear me!"

"**Yes Sir!**" we replied simultaneously.

Lieutenant Derrick proceeded to walk slowly around the table on a direct route for Corporal Farr. He stopped briefly to pick up a beer can from the opened box. Tommy had a look of anxiety on his face as the Lieutenant approached. He halted in front of Tommy and handed him the can: "And that goes for you too shit-for-brains!"

Tommy took the can from him, as he did so there was a visible tear running down his cheek. Lieutenant Derrick put his hand on Tommy's head and softly rubbed his cropped hair. "I know son…" he said in a paternal manner, "I know."

Lieutenant Derrick disengaged and again made ready to leave: "Sergeant, you've got the Detachment."

Buster acknowledged his responsibilities as he accompanied the Lieutenant to the door. Before departing he turned to look at us: "Goodnight boys, see you in the morning."

We bid him goodnight and after picking at some food settled down to write our reports. Meanwhile, Bronco sensitively made his way over to Corporal Farr. "You okay mate?" he asked.

"Yeah..." Tommy nervously replied, "it all just got on top of me, you know."

I too wanted to speak to Tommy to give him a pat on the back. He was simply asserting what all of us were thinking and feeling. Life in Vietnam was cheap, particularly if you were a peasant. We had nothing but contempt for the despots in the National Assembly and the weak faceless bureaucrats in the IPSF.

As I began to gather my thoughts Marine Collins came over with a hopeful expression: "Bazzer, any chance of you giving me a hand with my report? You know what I'm like; I'm not very good at writing things down. I get all the words jumbled up."

Jumper wasn't the brightest light on the tree, but what he lacked in grey matter he made up for in sheer guts and determination. If your back were against the wall you'd want him there with you. He was one of the bravest marines I've ever had the privilege to fight alongside.

"Yeah, I'll help you, let me get mine done first okay?"

Jumper nodded as he sat next to me: "I'd like to get my hands on the bastards who ordered that strike. I'd rub their noses in it; give them a taste of nape, wouldn't you?"

I stopped writing: "No, I wouldn't."

"Why not?"

"Because if we did that we'd be no better. You can't fight fire with fire, napalm with napalm, it just reinforces the cycle of violence. Oh don't get me wrong; I've got as much aversion for those scumbags as you have. But there has to be another way. That's what the peace agreement is supposed to be about, an alternative model."

Jumper stared at me a look of puzzlement and agitation on his face: "You would say that. You probably got it from one of those books with the big words you read all the time—!"

"Steady on Jumper!" the Sergeant shouted from across the table looking directly at him. "He's not angry with you," he said glancing at me.

"I know," I quietly replied.

Jumper sat silently next to me as I continued writing my report. I thought it best to avoid contact with him for a while. Instead I gazed around the table at my comrades. I looked with curiosity at their young faces. Given the events of the day I wouldn't have expected them to have a look of contentment or to be relaxed. Nonetheless, I remember being stunned by their expressions. It was as if I was looking into dead eyes; like something had come along and sucked all the life, exuberance and vitality out of them. Most of the men were attempting to write their summaries in-between staring into space with blank faces, muttering to themselves. I shuddered at the realisation that I was probably looking at a mirror image. In 1972 the archetype of post supervision didn't include talking things through. Debriefing consisted of what did you do, see and hear? Not 'how do you feel?' (Although in retrospect I believe individuals should be left to work through their own emotions in the immediate aftermath of a traumatic experience.)

Jumper was trying to write a chronology of events. His account was indeed jumbled. (If I had known then what I am aware of now, I would have realised that he was dyslexic.) I felt sorry for him as he struggled with the words.

"Leave that Jumper..." I said taking the pencil from his hand, "I've nearly finished. When I'm done go through what you saw and I'll write it down for you."

"Thanks Bazzer. I wish I was smart; I hate being dumb."

I remember looking at Jumper as he stared introspectively at the half full beer can in his hand. On that evening, probably resultant of the tragic occurrences of the day, I somehow felt closer to my comrades. It was as if I could feel their pain, self-doubt and fears beside my own. As a Platoon we were already connected by common goals. On that occasion we appeared to be united by a harsh awareness: that the only certainty in life is change and that a large part of our existence is dependent upon elements that we have little or no control over. We were as fragile and vulnerable as any of our fellow humans – regardless of how dynamic we considered ourselves to be.

"Smart," I retorted, "like the studious politicians who countenanced the air strike. You can bet they'll have gone through the halls of academia, doesn't make them any less evil, might even make them more so. There's nothing special about being smart, but there's plenty special about being decent, generous and honourable and you've got those things in abundance."

Jumper cracked a smile apparently unsure of what to say. I could have informed him he needn't say anything, but somehow, I think he probably knew. There are times in relationships when more can be gleaned from silence than from a thousand words.

"Come on mucker…" I said, "let's get your statement done."

Once Jumper's report was complete Bronco and I set to crosschecking our summaries. I remember looking at him in bewilderment.

"What's up?" he enquired.

"You're going to think I'm crazy," I said in a cautious response, "but I've got this notion that I'm in some way answerable for the air strike because I translated and conveyed the information to the Detail."

"You too!"

Confirmation that Bronco had similar thoughts helped to validate my experience. Years later I'd discover that this phenomenon is quite common. Family members would frequently feel an irrational sense of responsibility for the loss of a loved one as they conveyed the bad news to relatives and friends.

The night dragged slowly once our duties were complete. Most of the lads had little time for idle chatter. Instead the men sat in silent isolation fingering through pictures of loved ones or re-reading letters from home, hoping to recapture the temporary magic that greets the receiver as the crisp paper slips from the envelope.

Bronco sat next to me staring at a crayon drawing sent by his seven-year-old daughter. I wondered if he too was thinking of the little girl with the water buffalo as he gazed at his daughter's creation: her childish appearance, her pigtails resting on her shoulders and her spindly legs. Doubtless, Bronco would have given anything on that evening for just one moment with his daughter. To have whispered playful sounds into her tiny ear; delighted in her smile; smelled her hair; hugged her warm figure and offered her his fatherly love and protection. But family and home seemed even more abstract on that reflective night, like concepts from another world. Precious gifts too far removed, yet near enough for the contagion of inhumanity to invade.

Sleep eluded us though this had little to do with the steamy barrack room. Intrusive representations of the days' events dominated our psyche. Images of the settlement: men, women and children going about their everyday business; the reverberation of the jet fighters; the thunder of napalm with its murderous aftermath; the charred bodies and screams of disbelief. Eyelids cannot block out images etched on the visual cortex. Earplugs bring no relief from screams taped on neurones that only brain death will erase. No incense can mask repugnant smells that have journeyed beyond the nasal passages.

Sleeplessness forced me outdoors, bedroll tucked underarm. I wanted to find some corner to nestle into to be alone with my thoughts. I was greeted by six of the lads sat round a Gaz lantern.

"Wot-ya Bazzer!" Corporal Lane called, "...come to join the legion of the insomniacs?"

"Something like that."

Jumper enquired if I'd like a beer, which I gratefully accepted as I settled next to my compadrés. Initially I felt uneasy joining the group. There didn't appear to be any particular topic of conversation, though certain things appeared to be taboo. I didn't want to do anything that would corrupt this unwritten agreement. Notwithstanding, a discussion eventually switched to the events of the day. Most of the men declared their hatred for the evil demagogues who'd targeted the settlement. It was obvious that the Security Forces wanted to punish the inhabitants of Tchựrin Loy for persistently humiliating them. Tchựrin Loy was to be an example to all the Viet Cong strongholds.

Regardless, this failed to satisfy questions that simply had no acceptable answers. Why an active village? Why innocent men, women and above all children? If the Security Forces were so determined to make an example why not empty the hamlet and simply raze it to the ground? (Not that this would be any more warranted.)

I remember sitting rather nervously listening to the conversation. It was well known that my belief system did not sit easy within the conservative establishment. There was little room in Her Majesty's Armed Forces for a radical socialist.

Marine Miller gave me an inquisitive look: "What do you reckon?"

"I don't know," I replied, "I'm not sure if I know anything right now."

"Come on! You're always going on about politics, power and all that shit. You must have a view so spill-it."

Dusty's rebuttal was more inquisitive than challenging. Nonetheless, he sat with the others awaiting a response. I recall secretly thinking of line from a

George Orwell novel '1984': '*...sometimes men do evil things, particularly when they can,*' but I thought it better to keep it to myself.

"Like I said, I don't know. Maybe it's best to just follow the Lieutenant's advice an' accept the whole thing, no matter how much it sucks."

"Bollocks! you don't believe that," Tommy said, as he handed me a rolled cigarette.

"Sorry friend, it's the best you're going to get," I said whilst reminding him that I was a non-smoker.

"That ain't your real answer..." Tommy replied continuing to offer me the lit cigarette, "just like this ain't no fuckin' Woodbine!"

The lads roared with laughter as I took the joint. I drew on the spliff as if it were a part of my last breath. Being a non-smoker the fumes hit my lungs with an unexpected jolt. The cannabis soon penetrated my system, first impairing my vision then ultimately my cognition. I suddenly found myself in a not too unpleasant haze unable to put my thoughts into a rational order. I stared curiously at my compadrés who appeared to be sat in a contradictory ring, '...the theatre of lost paradoxical souls,' I deduced. Each actor programmed to perform the same script. Conspicuous soldiers unseen on a dark battlefield flooded with light; catatonic men in a highly animated state; barren minds crammed with complex concepts; arid eyes emitting a deluge of tears; cold empty gazes full of empathy; unspoken words that deafen the senses. Let not our loved ones suffer this blissful torment they silently cried out, only we, alone, together. I suddenly felt at one with the Viet Cong who it was said dreamt of tigers and monkeys bearing messages of foreboding and goodwill. But napalm and phosphorous flames shatter all dreams; these demons bring only nightmares too thick for even the wisest of Charlie's Ancestors to forestall. In the midst of my psychedelic malaise I could hear Bronco calling out to me: "**Bazzer!** ...fuckin' hell buddy where've you been? You're well out of it."

"His head's probably on Jupiter again," Sugar said in a fit of ganja induced giggles.

"You think too much," Bronco said as he attempted to hand me the joint that had made its way round the semi-stoned band. "You wanna try switching off from time to time."

"I will..." I said, declining to indulge any further, "just as soon as I've found myself."

"I'm gonna find myself on R and R," Jumper said, "I'm gonna blow my fuckin' mind in Đà Nẵng, ain't nothing gonna—"

A flurry of distant gunfire interrupted him before he had a chance to finish. We instinctively turned in the direction of the rifle reports.

"Go on Charlie..." Dusty said, "up 'an-at-'em!"

"Somebody's gonna get their head's bent tonight," Sugar said.

"Let's hope it's the SVA," Marine Jeffers added, "Charlie deserves to score after Tchụin Loy."

Personally, I cared not. The firefight was just another skirmish. One more drama about to unfold; another set of co-ordinates to add to the pile, concrete beside the abstract of human misery that swamped that beautiful land.

After bidding the lads goodnight I gathered my bedroll and retired a few paces. Sleep, I thought, may not help me escape, but neither would the pitiful ramblings of men whose understanding of the world had just been shattered. I needed to wallow in my own sorrow and self-doubt regardless of how close I felt to my brothers.

Through my self imposed seclusion I realised just how much the tragic events of the day had challenged *my* understanding of human systems. The differing paradigms that underpin social and political justice; the meaning of fair play; the violation of the weak by the strong and the manipulation of the many by the few. I felt as if trapped in an inextricable maze of circular questions. Why did Command move us so quickly? What were the real reasons for our presence amid the conflict? Were we just convenient witnesses, a token force established to satisfy an immovable edict proclaimed by the United Nations? Endless questions with empty answers. For what must have been the umpteenth time that day reality hit home: I was 19 years old and I thought I knew it all, the truth was I knew nothing.

I tried to get some sleep, but the appalling images of the day invaded my psyche; persistent re-runs that added new depth to the meaning of psychological torment. The most disturbing representation of all was of the girl and the water buffalo, a mere child turned to ashes before the embers of her life had a chance to glow. Try as I may I couldn't erase her image from my mind. Seeing her so vividly before the air strike and facing the reality of her demise in the wake of napalm left me with an overwhelming feeling of grief. It was as if she were my own. As if I had a responsibility to protect her, shield her from evil that had inundated her village. Nothing made me hate the despots who indiscriminately wield their power for their own political ends more than the image of that innocent waif.

I wondered how long these images would be with me; would they still be there for the remainder of my Tour of Duty? The naiveté of youth, little did I know that not only would those things be with me for the remainder of my time in Vietnam – they would be with me for the rest of my life.

TORTURED DREAM

Tchựin Loy, Charlie boy, no more joy
Co-ordinates set, whoosh of the jet
Their just deserves they're gonna get!
Prime the bombs make it so
Blast the Cong scum & their water buffalo
Bone, hair, tit & testicles fly
Young people die, mothers cry
Can't block out the inner scream
Within a tortured dream.

Rifleman pray, shrapnel will stray
Shattered calm, smell of napalm
Hold your breath, feared of death
Fright frozen hearts longing to beat
Held fast in the searing heat
Twisted bodies burnt & sprawling
Teardrops splash on a crayon drawing
Foundationed, none more so obscene
Than this tortured dream.

Sàigòn bar, where we are
Laughing at fear, gimme a beer
Fuck the slope head, become a dope head
Rum & coke head
Block out the shit – just another hit
Painted smiles washed away by tears
Haggard faces that mask the years
Things aren't quite what they seem
In a tortured dream.

M16, RPG, AK47
Mess with me, I'll send you to heaven!
War hardened veteran lying to himself
Soft of heart & merciful soul
Packaged on the shelf
Cos you'll better know it
He ain't no poet
He's just a fucked-up marine
In a Tortured dream.

Lance Corporal Barry Morris
Nha Trang, December 1972.

5: A WALK THROUGH QUÌ NHÔN

The riflemen will wake & hold their breath
Though they may bleed,
They'll be proud a while of something death
Still seems to need.
L Simpson

13:00: UN Base Camp 4, Nha Trang Province, 25 December 1972.

Christmas Day – some Christmas! Yuletide was just about the last thing on our minds. It had been eleven days since the incident at Tchựin Loy; we were still battling with the consequences. We were all fractious and moody. Disputes that would normally be resolved went on for days; relationships were sorely tested. I found myself strangely detached, estranged from those whom I'd been close. I'd also lost my sense of humour. Black humour in particular was part of the way we functioned. Gallows humour acts as a relief as well as a display of profanity. Prior to December 15th I had never experienced a frontline tragedy. I quickly discovered a different view; I could find nothing humorous about the naping of a Viet Cong village.

We circumvented any reference to the incident. Anyone trying to broach the subject was given short shift; detachment and avoidance seemed to be the norm. Part of our condition had been exacerbated by empty promises. The Detail received no proper debrief, just a collection of questions followed by an undertaking that we'd be informed of developments – no information was forthcoming. It quickly became apparent that Command had no intention of providing feedback. They likely assumed that we'd put the affair behind us; move on. I'd have gladly washed my hands of the incident. Unfortunately my psychology had different ideas. The intrusive flashbacks continued, though they were becoming less frequent. I dreaded sleep; nocturnal periods contained a range of tormented dreams: fire, screaming, my own home being engulfed by flames. Daytime was no better. I suffered a number of mild anxiety attacks; it was as if the event was recurring. It was crazy, I couldn't identify the antecedent – there didn't appear to be any. The bouts would come out of the blue. I tried to replay the incident in an attempt to counteract the invasive sensations. In spite of this there were parts of the occurrence missing; massive gaps that I simply couldn't fill. The events seemed to have lost their chronological sequence; this bothered me. I was extraordinarily oversensitive; hypervigilant, restless and intolerant of other's foibles.

I had difficulty maintaining a focus on even basic tasks. I'd also lost interest in things hitherto important: local and world news including sports results from home. I had an overbearing feeling of a foreshortened future. Circular questions: would I make it out of 'Nam; would our luck run out; would I ever see my family again? Talking about my feelings may've helped, not that anyone wanted to listen. When I did manage to broach the subject I either dried up or deliberately changed the subject.

I was unaware that others in the Detail were feeling the same; they too were struggling, constantly battling with what feelings to demonstrate. Being joined by Three and Four Squads increased my ambivalence. They hadn't had it easy – they'd been involved in two firefights. In addition, they had to oversee the excavation of a mass grave in Thộc Điếm. The bodies had been beheaded to avoid identification. The shallow grave was inclusive of children, one newborn, the umbilical cord still attached to the tiny headless corpse. Nevertheless, they seemed less reticent, more willing to talk about their experiences whilst enquiring about ours. I clearly wasn't alone in not wanting to engage. Those who had witnessed the bombing did more listening than talking. Our reticence annoyed some from the other squads, but I think most understood.

I sat down to our Christmas dinner with thoughts of home. Christmas tree lights and gaudy Top of the Pops records; presents and selection boxes stacked high; freshly baked mince pies; sherry on Christmas morning and a pint in a warm pub on a cold dark winter's night. I thought of my early teenage years, my sister and I hanging up our stockings on Christmas Eve trying desperately to hold onto that magical feeling before succumbing to the stresses of adulthood.

There was a general feeling on the day that we somehow had to enjoy the festive season. The Beaujolais helped; an anonymous benefactor provided the sections with eight boxes. I felt a tad guilty sipping the ruby liquid. The benefactor was clearly the South Vietnamese Government – so much for neutrality.

The officers, as is the tradition in the British Forces, served the Christmas meal. Captain Page and the Lieutenants did the honours. The banter was abundant. Marine Lyle offered the Captain a crêpe party hat. He declined in his Oxbridge accent stating that he "...didn't want to ruffle his hair." He didn't have any hair!

"I'm not bald..." Captain Page said amid a tirade of ribbing, "I'm just suffering from a temporary loss of follicles."

"Sounds like he's 'ad a temporary loss of his fuckin' arsehole judgin' by the shit he's comin' out with," Sugar said amid a roar of laughter, the Captain laughing the loudest. The boys it seemed had at least temporarily returned to their facetious ways.

The IPSF in their generosity provided each of us with a small Christmas gift. I received a shoddy pen set likely made by cheap labour in Hong Kong or Taiwan. Marine Wood, a practising Methodist and the only member of the Platoon who abstained from alcohol, received a substandard hip flask. "Oh wot!" Woody said in his distinctive East London accent, "a far-kin 'ip flask! The only teetotaller in the section an' I get a far-kin' 'ip flask!"

Woody was also a confirmed virgin. He was "...saving himself for that special person with whom he'd seal his life." Members of the Platoon would go out of their way to tease him – though he was always up for it. We didn't want to miss another opportunity.

"It's alright Woody," Macker said, "you can fill it with *Cherry*-aid—"

"Yeah," Bronco cut in, "or *Virgin*-honeysuckle."

"'Ere y'are..." Wolfie enthused, "yer can swap with me if yer like. I've gotta shoe polishin' kit, with a tin of *Cherry*-blossom!"

Laughter filled the air the first time we'd really let go in nearly two weeks. Our after dinner activities revolved around additional alcohol. It was more than just a tonic; a way of blocking out the shit.

Macker, Tommy and I listened to the Six O'clock News on Radio Sàigòn. The Christmas spirit was clearly lacking in Washington – news of a massive bombing campaign against North Vietnam and purported Viet Cong positions in Laos and Cambodia. President Nixon was, yet again, trying to bomb the North Vietnamese back to the conference table. It was all hogwash: the yanks were simply gathering their last pounds of flesh before the inevitable withdrawal. Nobody seemed to question why squadrons of bombers and jets were laying tons of TNT, cluster bombs and napalm on non-combatant positions, particularly in light of the NVA and Viet Cong being constantly accused of failing to adhere to the interim ceasefire.

'Motown Magic', a regular two-hour evening slot, immediately followed the news. Unfortunately, somebody failed to tell the station that around a quarter of the back-to-back tracks had about as much connection to Motown as the Ku Klux Klan. Nonetheless, the tracks were wonderful. I sat listening to The Young Rascals singing *Groovin'*. It elicited memories of warm summer evenings on Plymouth Ho. Mandy Spruce, my first shag in the sand. I had a warm glow on my face. I wanted Macker or Tommy to ask what was tickling me, but they'd drifted into their own worlds.

I retired earlier than normal electing to scrutinize my journal. I stared at the dates on the countdown calendar. In 7 days it would be New Year. We'd be 19 weeks into our tour, 33 weeks away from the plane home and another 18 days away from the horror of Tchụin Loy.

*

21:30: Base Camp 5, Sơng Căn, Quì Nhôn Province, Tuesday 23 January.

Command had finally made a decision on our new district. Quì Nhôn didn't seem that much different from Nha Trang. Charlie Town had its reputation, but reputations were not an issue – we had our duties to carry out.

We'd just completed our third week of chaotic activity on the outskirts of Charlie Town; the Quì Nhôn districts had been active. We hardly had time to settle in one place when we'd be moved to another. Intelligence were either taking the mickey or taking every report seriously. There was activity: ambushes and minor firefights. Bombs in bars, hotels, shops and market places. Somebody had obviously failed to inform the warring factions that a full ceasefire was about to be endorsed. Talks at the Paris Peace Conference had gone deep into the previous night. Preceding talks had broken down. Mr Lế Đức Thơ, Hànội's chief negotiator commented '...the talks are the last chance of peace' and '...negotiators will not leave the table until a final agreement has been thrashed out'. We were all anxious to hear the outcome.

Lieutenant Derrick called for muster at 2130 hours. He had a serious expression as he removed an A4 sheet from a sealed dispatch folder: "Listen up boys, news hot off the press. The talks in Paris have concluded; we have a treaty. A full cessation of hostilities will take effect from 23:59 local time, Saturday 27th of January 1973. For our purposes the agreement has a code name, 'January Morning'. The concord incorporates a sixty day deadline for a pre-agreed number of US troops to be withdrawn and American Prisoners of War to be repatriated. In addition, a force of just over a thousand officers will arrive from West Germany, Hungary and Indonesia to oversee the implementation of the twelve-point plan. The advanced force will be joined by a permanent force mid February. Bottom line, everything up to now has been practice...this is for real."

The statement was followed by an uncanny silence. There was no cheering, clapping or whistling. Lance Corporal Bear glanced at Tommy: "Is that it?"

"Sounds like it. What did you expect, a fuckin' fanfare?"

"Nah..." Huggy replied with a perplexed look, "it's just; you know...I thought there'd be more. I thought, maybe—"

"What he means is he thought we'd be on a big bird home!" Bruiser cut in.

He was right, though Huggy wasn't the only one with a hopeful wish.

I lay on my bed looking at the clock tick round to 23:30. It had been a historical day. I felt it important to record my thoughts. Somehow I struggled. Maybe it was the anticlimax or an expectation that the 12-point concord was nought but hot air. Instead I read through the previous week's notes. New Year had largely been a non-event. A few of us had gathered in the mess room though we considered there was little to celebrate. World news had been interesting. Britain had finally become a full member of the EEC; in Manila, President Marcos, another dubious friend of Uncle Sam, extended his term of office indefinitely. President Richard Nixon had been sworn in for a second term of office and Yasser Arafat re-elected PLO Leader. And of particular note: January 22nd former President Lyndon B Johnson dies of a heart attack. There would be few tears shed in South Vietnam.

20:55: Xuần Tía Shau, Quì Nhôn Province, Tuesday 30 January.

We sat on the dry ground looking at the clear night sky. We'd been walking all day looking for possible movement of insurgents or army regulars. We were sixty-eight hours, fifty five minutes into the ceasefire – nothing. No artillery, mortar rounds or small arms fire. No apparent movement of guerrillas, no reported border crossings or skirmishes; just normality. 'Could it be?' I thought, '...Peace in Vietnam? The North Vietnamese satisfied with a pledge of future elections on unification; Charlie content with the promise of equality and land reform; the whole country at ease with the concord?' It was still early, we'd have to wait and see.

It was with an apparent quirk of fate that just when Macker, Tommy and I were talking about how the country might change that the skies lit up.

"Bloody Nora!" somebody hollered as we all bolted upright.

Artillery flew overhead as rapid small arms fire echoed in the distance: "Who's shootin' at who?" Marine Clarke enquired.

"Who gives a fuck as long as they're not shootin' at us!" Lance Corporal Jessop suggested.

"Ceasefire, what fuckin' ceasefire!" Jumper scornfully added.

"Okay calm down and take up your positions," Sergeant Edwards said as the mêlée intensified.

"This is too much like déjà vu," Tommy said, as we looked for movement in the dark expanse; the consolation that time was that the skirmish wasn't local. It was close, but likely not close enough to require our involvement.

Corporal Alan, designated Radio Operator, called to Bronco and I: "Come an' listen to this boys – the airways are buzzin'!"

We settled next to Nasher listening to the manic broadcasts part expectant of action. The clash appeared to be lessening; then suddenly, silence.

"That seems to be that," Buster said as the stillness continued. "Somebody's cracked seal; there'll be no fuckin' end to it now. We'd better double the watch tonight."

I escaped lookout duty, though it made little difference, I couldn't sleep. How naive to think the country would be at peace. The firefight was clearly a portent. Since being in Vietnam, 2: Bravo 6 Platoon had hiked some 200 miles – we still had many more to walk.

14:00: Quì Nhôn Town, Wednesday 14 February.

The Tết nguyên đán [New Year festival] was in full swing. It seemed somehow fitting, Valentines Day at home – Tết in 'Nam. The Lunar Festival had traditionally been associated with a temporary cessation of hostilities, though everyone was mindful of the 1968 Tết Offensive. 'Maybe the January Morning will make a difference,' I thought.

Tết lasts for 8 days, the first and last days being the most energetic. Half of us had been released for the day to savour the opening celebrations. The other half would be released for the closing ceremony. The town was alive with colour and noise. The end of the lunar year signalled a new character: Đin Đần-hớ (The year of the Tiger). The previous year's character, the Ox, would be returned to its forefathers. Paper effigies of Oxen and Tigers fluttered in the gentle air. The streets were adorned with Đông Hồ prints [Vietnamese folk sketches]. Zigzagging Dragons danced down the alleys to the beat of drums and cymbals, firecrackers exploding in the dragon's wake.

Everybody seemed happy. Children ran up us to pin small brightly coloured ribbons on our clothes. They wanted nothing in return, no money or sweets, just a smile.

A Folklore Theatre Group performed the Mûa rối nûóc [water puppet show] on a specially erected rostrum. The Mûa rối's uniqueness lies in its use of a water surface, the puppets being guided by puppeteers submerged in the water. The ông Tếu [buffoon joker] introduces the performances. Children excitedly gathered as the performance got under way. Sugar said that ông Tếu reminded him of President Nixon. Some of the English-speaking crowd laughed along with us.

People walked round wishing each other Chừc Mưng Nậm Môi (Happy New Year) and Yên tinh Khàp thế giời (calling their forefathers to grant world peace). We purchased some food from the street stalls. The vendors gave us extra portions after we'd paid; we were somewhat confused. A gregarious stallholder gave an explanation: "...generosity brings forth the greatest of rewards – especially during Tết."

We became acquainted with a party of Vietnamese Students eager to test out their language skills. A young enthusiastic man Ngờc Đớn Hầ, talked at length: "Good afternoon my Brit-ain friends. I like you and your speak... Your books are a most interesting read. I read much Dickens and Brontë. Many happy endings, not. Your stories have all many levels. Vietnamese fable straight though much philo-sophical..."

We couldn't stop him. We giggled along with his friends; they were all eager to talk. A stunning young woman Chựi Phận Hôy joined in: "I will visit your land and look at your cultures and many customs. I will enjoy to walk amongst your friendly peoples."

"You don't wanna go to some areas of Liverpool girl," Sugar said, "...not unless you wanna get your arse chalked—"

"Liver-pool, Beatle town!" the students enthusiastically cut in to roars of laughter.

We talked in-between eating imported kali for over an hour. Before we separated, Chựi Phận Hôy handed us a folded *Đông Hồ* print. I've no idea why we were so popular. They clearly enjoyed our presence – as we did theirs.

The celebrations went on deep into the night. Brightly coloured Vietnamese lanterns swung in the breeze. We could see the subtle beams from the orange and turquoise lamps in the clouds of smoke formed by the multiple band firecrackers dancing on the ground or wriggling on fire strings suspended from balconies. The crowd cheered loudly each time a curling haze ascended. The Vietnamese believed evil spirits to be trapped in the smoke.

The clock was quickly ticking round. We had strict instructions to be back at base by 2200 hours. Local rebels were still active – Command was taking no chances. We managed to witness a ritual before departing. Families would release miniature hot-air balloons into the night sky. Standard balloons were connected by thin wire to paper lanterns below. The concertina lanterns had a cardboard base covered with foil to accommodate a tea candle; the sight was striking. The delicate lanterns would be lit by the flickering light, as would the underside of the balloon. The youngest child would release the vessels, each family member making a silent wish to their forefathers.

We spotted a man in his late twenties. He had two small children with him. He smiled at us as his daughter released the balloon: "Chừc Mưng Nậm Môi," he said placing the palms of his hands together whilst slowly bowing.

We returned the salutation.

"Đần-hớ good omen," he said in broken English as his children watched the balloon slowly ascend. "Tiger strong, reli-able, will not back away. Many sign for cease fire...for peace." He closed his eyes tight, pressed the palms of his hands harder together and made his wish. It wouldn't have taken a genius to work out his request. It was self-evident: peace had eluded his country for over 9000 days. My heart sank as I looked at him. I was overcome with empathy. His hope was demonstrable: as if the Christmas wishes of a child; the hopes of a pregnant woman for a trouble free gestation; the lonely heart's wish for a Valentine's card; a yearning for the safe return of a loved one from a far off land. Heart felt, genuine, manifest – and so forlorn.

08:00: Qừan Đức, Quì Nhôn Province, Monday 26 February.

As mentioned hitherto, the massacre of non-combatants is a feature of armed conflict. The Americans have taken part in their fair share. The Téton Sioux massacre at Chakatta Falls South Dakota 1876, the 7th United States Cavalry led by Colonel Skimmerhorn running through men, women and children with bullet, lance and sabre. Some 92 years later Lieutenant James Calley would lead a company of the United States Infantry in the massacre of 567 Viet Cong men, women and children in the village of Mệ Laị. The slaughter included pregnant women; eggs turn to lice and lice multiply – another time, another country, the same principle.

Mệ Laị was the most publicised act of mass murder in the Vietnam War, but it was far from an isolated incident. Round-eyes had a shameful record in Vietnam. The French adopted a scorched earth policy throughout their administration. Villages that refused to follow the feudal system would have their livestock and supplies commandeered before being forced to watch their hamlet being razed to the ground. The French had a habit of corralling some of the inhabitants into the bamboo buildings, conveniently forgetting to release the unfortunates before the bonfire party. Non-compliant groups can be eradicated in many ways. Poisoning water or food supplies or through the deliberate proliferation of disease. Starvation is another tool though slow and difficult to maintain.

The Americans left a legacy of underhand ways of attempting to break the will of the opposition. Dropping cardboard barrels filled with crystals that produced a poisonous gas onto crops; impregnating rice and maize seeds with genetic mutations; lacing water supplies with chemicals that would induce severe vomiting and cause chronic diarrhoea. Dropping lines of antipersonnel mines into the rice paddies was a favourite ploy of the yanks, as was spraying the rice fields with oil. The covering would contaminate the water, burn the delicate plants and halt photosynthesis.

It was easy to see why the rice fields were a favourite target. The paddies were the lifeblood of the peasants, especially in the outlying districts. To the people of Vietnam the rice fields were as much a part of the landscape as the jagged mountains and palm trees. To us they were a miracle of civil engineering. The patchwork quilt paddies of Qừan Đức were no different from Shau Tiâ or Tchựin. The networks had been fashioned over hundreds of years. The waters of the rectangular pools were constantly replenished and siphoned via an elaborate system of paddle pumps, irrigation channels and sluices. The work was labour intensive. The often-unpredictable weather patterns dictated a constant watch: too much rain and the paddies would be swamped and even a short drought would dry out the fields shrivelling the delicate plants. Everybody pitched in, each task assigned according to strength and ability. Young men worked the foot driven paddle-pumps and undertook heavy chores. Women, including pregnant women, planted and picked the rice. Children tended the water buffalo; the more experienced men tilled the soil and maintained the cofferdams. The villagers depended on the yield for trade as well as food. The collectives worked like a well-oiled machine – it was a perfect example of Gestalt. The beauty and efficiency of the rice fields never failed to enthral me. I absorbed every detail, whether through my own observations or set lessons. But there were some lessons I could have done without.

10:30: Approximately 1 mile east by northeast of Lông Đáo.

We approached the paddies fronting the village of Lông Đáo with the same trepidation as any other Viet Cong stronghold. We'd spent the previous day carrying out checks in Đưng Rồí and Mịa Mây; the reception in each was cool though not openly hostile. We'd received reports of open violations of the ceasefire. Viet Cong insurgents had apparently been taking pot shots at the Security Forces. Our remit was to remind the people of the peace accord.

I remember that morning in particular. I had half a dozen painful mouth ulcers on the inside of my left cheek. The medics had given me some foul tasting mouth lozenges that turned the inside of my mouth black and had about as much effect as sucking Spangles.

We moved off a small back road towards the narrow paths cutting the paddies. I wasn't the only one wondering why we couldn't see the silhouettes of workers in the fields. It was mid-morning, the paddies would normally be full of men and women – there wasn't a soul in sight.

Lieutenant Derrick held up his hand to indicate halt: "What do you think Sergeant?"

"Not sure Sir…something's not right."

"I know," the Lieutenant said the men looking on. "Listen up boys, close up the formation and stay alert. I don't need to tell you what empty fields or empty anything indicates."

"Ambush?" Marine Vincent whispered from behind.

"Beats the shit out of me…" I replied shrugging my shoulders, "your guess is as good as mine."

We continued on our course each scanning the landscape as if deer looking out for danger. The continuing silence was overbearing; I suddenly found myself running my tongue across the stinging mouth ulcers. I don't know why; they hurt like hell. Maybe I needed to take my mind off the fact that something was clearly amiss.

We smelled the oil before we saw it; a foul stench invaded our nasal passages as we approached the cofferdams. The paddies were contaminated with a dense layer of Furnace Fuel Oil [FFO]. FFO was one process removed from crude. It is almost impossible to mop up; it can only be dispersed with specialist detergents that cause as much environmental damage as the oil. The thick black smear spread as far as our eyes could see. The FFO had covered even the tallest of rice grasses, their stalks bent over in submission.

"Those dirty bastards!" Sergeant Edwards said as we slowed by the pools.

"Hold up…" the Lieutenant said, "Marine Clarke, get up on Corporal Farr's shoulders, we need to get a blimp of this."

Tommy got down one on knee as TC prepared to mount his tall frame. TC was one of the lightest members of the Platoon. We had practised the drill many times before. TC would stand on Tommy's shoulders. Two men would stand each side with one at the rear to provide a supporting tripod. Corporal Farr was strong as an ox. Nevertheless, he still struggled up as TC gained his balance. Buster tossed Marine Clarke a pair of binoculars as Tommy gripped his ankles.

"What do you see?" Lieutenant Derrick said as TC continued to balance whilst looking through the eyeglasses.

"Oil…everywhere."

"What, on all the pools?"

"Yes Sir, the whole area looks like an empty car park."

"Okay son get down. Listen carefully y'all, we're likely gonna have one hell of a reception in Lông Đáo. Be on your guard, all of you."

"This oil isn't fresh…" Buster said as the Platoon reformed, "I reckon it's at least two days old."

"Yeah," Lieutenant Derrick replied as he scanned the field, "it was probably sprayed on by Dakotas."

We set a course for the village the reek from the FFO permeating the air.

We reached the perimeter of Lông Đáo in no time. Marine Cunliffe was on point, Bronco following close behind. The people were standing idle as we entered the hamlet. Cowboy held the United Nations Flag aloft as Bronco called our identification: "Nghe. Không người Mỹ chiến si dân tóc khắp thế giời," (*Attention, not American soldiers; United Nations*!)

The people of the collectives always seemed to have a look of defiance; the people of Lông Đáo displayed an immovable look of savageness – we were clearly not welcome.

We could see two young men openly carrying AK47s. "Keep your eye on those two…" the Lieutenant said to Sergeant Edwards, "and call up the translators."

Corporal Lane and I were already in the process of preparing to translate when a man in his early fifties pulled up: "No interpreter!" the man barked. "I speak English plenty good. If we must speak, speak your tongue!"

The man was clearly the Chû tuổi. He was by far the youngest we had encountered. The collective had likely suffered many losses, old as well as young. The elder could indeed speak English; it became evident during the preamble that he was an educated man.

Lieutenant Derrick opened with the usual information – our identification and designated assignments. It was easy to forget that we were visiting to remind the populace of the terms of the ceasefire; the context only temporarily changed our objective. The principal stared at him, silent and expressionless.

The Lieutenant broke from the customary protocol: "I see your paddies have been sprayed with oil."

"Very observant!" the elder replied.

"Would you like me to take a statement?"

The Chû tuổi gave a sardonic grin whilst slowly shaking his head: "Big planes come, buzz the fields early morning, still very dark. We run to the fields from our beds. Planes long gone, paddies full of oil. They came and went; not show their faces like the cowards they are!"

"Is there anything we can do for you; get for you?"

"What would we want from you? We not ask you come here!"

"I appreciate that Sir, but we can make a request for relief or arrange—"

"Cha-rity!" the elder cut in, "…you offer to arrange donation! What do you think you are, my representative?"

"No Sir. We've not come here to act for you, or dictate. We're simply carrying out our duties under the auspices, that is the banner, of the United Nations."

"Unite' Nation!" the elder said struggling to keep his voice under control. "I grow tired of speak with no result. Many come and tell of new beginnings yet we continue to suffer. Now *you* come say you can deal with these things. We not want you here; never have so—!"

The honcho gripped the hoe in his hand, his anger boiling. The inhabitants looked on, the majority understanding only the body language. All were silent, most staring impassively – the atmosphere was sinister.

"—You round-eyes, you come to my country, point your fingers, condemn our beliefs, rubbish our culture, try to change our values. What *you* know of values? You collect your gold, take from the earth without putting back, insult your forefathers, dishonour your families. You put your old in homes! What you here for now, to tell many bosses of a success in destroying my rice fields?"

"No Sir! we are neutral. We're here to support the peace accord—"

"Ha! Who you think you talk to, a fool? You Briton's friend of Nixon; as much in pocket as President Thiều! You come to tell me you are different? Not from where I stand. You same as those who bayonet our young and rape our women, burn our village and make our peoples walk to internment camp. And those who teach Thiều's many puppets how to oil our paddies. French, Ameri-can…round-eyes – just, like, **you!**"

The Lieutenant paused for an instant wanting to be sure that the elder had finished: "Sir, you can be sure that I will publish a comprehensive report on what we've seen here—"

"Report, ha! paper talk! You write report for Unite' Nation, not for me, not for my peoples."

Lieutenant Derrick yet again allowed a pause: "Sir…I have an obligation to remind you of the terms of the ceasefire—"

"Cease fire! Who want cease fire? those who lose! I have studied your proverbs, you Briton's say: '*If you cannot finish then you should take care not to start.*' Viet Cong did not start. Thiều's puppets kick us when we down, many time. Now they are floored we are to stop kicking. No cease fire! We not stop 'til they are buried – you put in your report!"

The Lieutenant was thoughtful; it was obvious he was getting nowhere. To have continued would have been fruitless: "No Sir, I will not put that in my report. But I will publish a testimony on the wanton destruction of your crops."

There was an unbearable period of silence, both men staring at each other. Lieutenant Derrick was a master of negotiation; I think the village elder could sense the fact. For just a moment the honcho lowered his gaze and gently nodded.

"Are you sure there isn't anything we can do for you?" the Lieutenant enquired.

"There is only one thing you can do," the elder replied, much quieter that time, "leave my commune; you are not welcome here."

Lieutenant Derrick attempted to hand the Chû tuổi a standard statement outlining the terms of January Morning. He refused to take it from his hand. He left the document on the ground and turned to join us: "Sergeant…move the men out."

We moved out on our former echelon still mindful of the two Kalashnikovs. Some of the inhabitants turned their backs as we walked past. One or two of the children spat at us. One line of spit landed squarely on Marine Collins' ear, the saliva dribbling off his earlobe. Jumper didn't flinch he just carried on walking.

"Bươn xẩự ông ấy," (*Nasty – evil persons*!) Some of the children hollered.

"Ngưng lai," (*Enough*!) The Chủ tuổi barked. The children quietened and turned their backs; the tone of his voice was sufficient.

Cowboy was muttering as we exited the village: "What a fuckin' bummer. We just can't win, damned if we do damned if we—"

"Plug that skull hole!" the Sergeant said without looking round.

I was reflective as we left the hamlet. We were professional soldiers. We'd been warned that our tasks would not be easy and largely thankless. Notwithstanding, after six months in the 'Nam I had grown fond of the Vietnamese. Most had been friendly; Lông Đáo was my first really negative experience. I tried hard to understand the honcho's attitude. Nevertheless, as we walked the path beside the vandalised paddies I couldn't help feeling hurt.

We progressed on a converse course occasionally staring at the black mass on the unmoving waters. We noticed a wading bird struggling in the oil. It was covered in FFO, unable to fly or move through the dense sludge. Nobody spoke; we just looked at the poor creature as we sauntered past hoping its struggle would soon end. Marine Lyle found a battery operated directional beacon on the edge of the field adjacent to the road; it was still bleeping. The culprits had likely laid four beacons in a square pattern enabling the aircraft to target a specific grid. Buster wrapped it in polythene ready for it to be presented as evidence.

Lieutenant Derrick called a five-minute halt once we'd cleared the area: "Okay listen up..." he said, as we squatted on the verge, "you'll know by now that we'll have to report our findings. I guess you'll also know that we'll get little or no feedback. Regardless, we move on. We've still got over half a dozen villages to visit and only a few days left to complete the task. In the meantime we'll contact the Red Cross; recommend a relief delivery to Lông Đáo, though they'll likely reject it—"

He was silent for a moment.

"—I'm sure you all got the drift of our conversation. Thing is, I seemed to suffer a temporary loss of hearing when the honcho was talking about the ceasefire. I don't suppose any of you fellows can help me out. Did anyone hear what he said?"

"No Sir," we answered sporadically.

"Well...that appears to be that. Sergeant, get this bunch of deaf reprobates back on the road."

The Detachment reformed, each sporting a grin. Lieutenant Derrick was a hard taskmaster. He despised sloppiness and was intolerant of anyone who failed to carry out instructions to the letter. He was also thoroughly human, a decent man who had the respect of every member of the Platoon.

We headed south by southwest towards our next objective. It may've been my imagination but I swear I could still smell the oil 3 miles down route. It would've made no difference whether I could smell it or not. The inexcusable act of sabotage was firmly etched on my mind. I wondered how the villagers would cope, and when they'd set to the task of ridding their fields of the rank substance. The oil would need to be skimmed off and disposed of, the water drained and replenished to rid the mud beds of the pollutant. The process may've involved a dozen cycles, months of toil. The paddies could take years to yield maximum productivity.

On further reflection I guess I could understand the elder's vexation, in spite of my anger. Nobody would be brought to book for the act of state vandalism. Corruption amongst independent investigators was extensive. Compensation, if awarded, would take years. The village would only be left with a few Đồng once the landowners; taxman and officials had taken their slice.

As we walked towards our next action I was reminded of yet another reality. Life is about perspectives. In the enormity of a hamlet robbed of its food and livelihood the discomfort of a few mouth ulcers seemed all so insignificant.

09:30: Outskirts of Phần Liứn Hơí, Quì Nhôn Province, Thursday 8 March.

The sun was shining in a cloudless azure sky. It was a perfect day, the sort you long for. Days at the seaside as a child; clear bright wedding days; brilliant one day cricket matches and warm barbeque evenings – glorious summers. It was not a day for an 18 mile yomp! The Platoon had linked up for an expedition from Phần Liứn Hơí to Thừ Tín via the Thuắt Lừơng fields and Đân Đơi Forest. The chosen route would cut at least 4 miles off our expedition though this was little comfort in the incessant heat and flies. The sun was relentless. When clear the vista shimmered – trees hovering above translucent images. The dynamic terrain made the excursion even more arduous. Elephant grass that towered above our shoulders and thin crusted quick sand that could swallow you in seconds.

Our entrance into the vast Đân Đơi Forest offered at least some relief. The trees provided a little protection from the sun, though the thick undergrowth was a nightmare to negotiate.

We'd been moving through the wood for an hour when we came across a large section of dead forest. The locale – a traditional hiding place of the Viet Cong – had been targeted for the Agent Orange Defoliation Programme. The DDT derivative had been indiscriminately sprayed over a vast area. The dead zone was spooky beyond belief. There was an unnatural silence; twisted leafless trees towered above barren ground. The once proud vegetation looked as if it had died in agony. Swathes of fungi dotted the area, the only living organism that would grow in the hideous contaminant. The deadly chemical would remain in the soil for generations poisoning almost anything that dared to anchor its roots. There were no crawling insects, small mammals or reptiles. It may've been my imagination, but I could swear that no birds flew overhead, though I would concur that this may've been clouded by stories of empty skies over the ash strewn fields surrounding Auschwitz. The lifeless ground crackled underfoot and clouds of dust billowed around our boots. The whole terrain was moribund, like something out of a '50s Science Fiction movie – a monochrome landscape on a lifeless planet.

We wondered why the whole forest had not been defoliated. We discovered sometime later that the mission was aborted due to increasing costs – typical!

Regardless, our return to an uncontaminated sector was a welcome relief. A steady walk towards our objective was followed by a brief break for lunch. Lance Corporal Jessop and Marine Vincent were nominated point, the remainder of the sections following in standard formation.

We were all looking forward to reaching our objective; the sooner we arrived the sooner we'd get settled. A five day police action was planned in the neighbourhoods encompassing Thừ Tín. Monitoring the Security Forces, checking movements, ensuring the general public were free to venture to the markets (it was rice yield time) and directing refugees if needed.

13:30: Đân Đơi Forest.

I drained the last of the lukewarm water from my canteen. I considered it safe enough. If all went to plan we'd be in Thừ Tín by 1500 hours. The wood was beginning to thin; peripheral trees are always weaker due to being exposed to the elements.

We could hear the sound of somebody advancing towards us. Colour Sergeant Biffly called a halt as Vinny hacked through the undergrowth with a look of nausea.

"What's up?" Biffo enquired.

"Me an' Jez, we, we…" he was struggling to get the words out, "back there about twenty yards…" he stopped amid a bout of coughing.

"Take your time…" Biffo said as our anxiety grew, "come on son, take deep breaths."

Vinny took a deep breath as Lieutenant Derrick came up from the rear: "Two bodies Colour Sarge, two bodies hanging from a tree. Naked, awful, fuckin' terrible—"

"Okay…where's Jez?"

"Still there, guarding the position."

The Lieutenant intervened: "Very well, we'll move in formation. Progress in stages and cover the flanks."

Biffo complied directing the rear and flank cover as Lieutenant Derrick took five of us towards the position. Sergeant Edwards, Cowboy, JJ, Wolfie and I cautiously pressed forward. We all spotted Lance Corporal Jessop through the undergrowth his ashen face staring at us.

"Holy Mother!" Buster said as we spotted the naked bodies of two young Vietnamese women hanging from a tree.

We stood staring at the horrendous sight as the remainder of the Platoon pulled up from the rear. One of the victims was facing us; the other had her back to us as her body slowly rotated counter clockwise. Both had distinctive red and black wheels across the front and backs of their legs and their buttocks – they'd obviously been extensively beaten.

Their hands, blown up black and blue, had been tied behind their backs with garrotte wire. The lips of their labia had been cut away as had their nipples, obviously taken as some perverse trophy. One had a distinct line of congealed blood running down her leg, likely the result of a multiple rape. Their faces looked distinctly different. One looked as if she was asleep; the back-knot from the noose had pushed her head to one side. Her neck may have broken, if so her death would likely have been quicker. The other victims face was distorted, her puffed up tongue was visible and her eyes wide as if trying to pop out of their sockets.

Their bodies had not been hanging for long. Their faces still had a flesh colour; extended suspension would've turned the skin a dark blood red. Swarms of flies buzzed around the corpses adding to the repulsive spectacle.

Lieutenant Derrick eventually broke an extended silence: "Colour Sergeant, establish a citadel. And post men at intervals in the surrounding area."

The men began to mutter as we set to our elected tasks: "Who the fuck would want to do something like that?" Marine Giggs said.

"Plenty in this godforsaken hole!" Buster answered.

Lieutenant Derrick ordered the Radio Operator, Marine Bernard, to send a priority message to the nearest Military Police Garrison. He had to walk some distance to attain a decent signal. The remainder in the meantime continued to stare.

Giggsy asked why we couldn't cut the bodies down and cover them with ponchos.

"What, and compromise forensic evidence," Colour Sergeant Biffly snarled, "if you can't stomach the sight then don't look!"

I'd have gladly adhered to Biffo's advice. Unfortunately I couldn't stop looking. I tried to divert my eyes away from the sickening scene, but I'd find myself looking again seconds later. The merest glimpse would result in further periods of staring. I wasn't the only one. Others gaped, each wearing the same look – bewilderment, fascination and horror.

After some frenzied activity we sat round on the dry forest floor; there was little to do but wait. Corporal Lane noticed some writing on a small piece of blood-spattered cardboard attached to the tied feet of one of the victims. CÔNG BỰỚN (*Cong scum*) it read. Bronco looked at me at the discovery. I could tell he was thinking the same: the only scum were the dirty bastards who carried out the perverse act.

Lance Corporal Barilla alerted that some children were moving through the wood towards our position. "Bronco," Sergeant Edwards said, "get out there and get rid of them; this is enough for us to take let alone little'ns."

We continued to sit in silence, locked, yet again, within our own thoughts.

Lance Corporal Jessop could no longer contain himself. He suddenly started to cry. Sergeant Edwards intervened: "Stop that blubberin' else I'll give you something to cry about!"

Speedy lightly rubbed Jez's head: "It's okay buddy."

I reached for my canteen in preparation to offer Jez a swig of water forgetting that it was empty.

We discovered sometime later why Lance Corporal Jessop broke down. His twin sister had been raped in 1969. "They never got the bastard," Jez told us. "My sis' changed after that. She used to be such a good kid. She became nasty, bitter and twisted."

We understood his reasons. Sergeant Edwards would've as well, but there'd been no time for pity or tears. There was only time to carry out our duties, for what they were worth.

15:05: Crime Scene Đân Đơi Forest.

The South Vietnamese Military Police arrived in comparatively good time. Bronco and I accompanied Lieutenant Derrick and Colour Sergeant Biffly to greet the party. The customary preamble was followed by the MPs inspecting the scene. One took photographs whilst another, myself acting as interpreter, asked Vinny and Jez about the finding.

After only ten minutes the MPs to our surprise cut the women's bodies down. They made no attempt to collect samples from the forest floor or from their bodies; they simply grabbed the limp corpses, the ropes still tightly attached, and tossed them into two body bags.

Lieutenant Derrick was concerned about the apparent lack of investigation. He called Bronco over to question the principal MP: "Ask him why he hasn't taken more forensic evidence?"

Bronco complied, the principal wearing an immutable grin.

"Không thức hiên cà bẳy giớ, vài Việt Công Chiến sĩ," (*No need, all finish now. Just Viet Cong guerrillas.*) The leader replied.

The Lieutenant slowly shook his head. He was far too experienced to become embroiled in an un-winnable argument. It was clear to us all that the Military Police were unconcerned about the identity of the culprits who committed the heinous acts. They may have already known of the incident and who the perpetrators were; they seemed to find our position relatively quickly.

We moved out on our former course; to remain would've been pointless. As we departed I heard the MPs joking amongst themselves, saying that the Cong bitches ought to think themselves lucky they had a good fucking before their necks were stretched.

I thought I couldn't have felt any more revulsion. The sound of men delighting in the torture and execution of two young women was insufferable. For a split second I wished I hadn't mastered the language. My contempt for the nauseating creeps was demonstrable. I glared at one of them; he stared back with a twisted smirk. It took all my resolve not to lash out with a tirade of abuse. My discipline, as always, took over.

The unrelenting sun hit us as we left the shelter of the woods. I reached for my canteen to take a swig of water – it was still empty of course. We walked in a steady silent line towards Thừ Tín wondering if anything else was about to attack our senses.

17:00: UN Base Camp 5, Sơng Căn.

A Chinook unexpectedly airlifted us back to base at 1600 hours. Command informed us that we would take up our instructions early morning. And that our police actions, mainly around the rice market, would be succeeded by a nightly airlift back to barracks. Something was brewing, probably between established Viet Cong paramilitary groups and the SVA. We were informed that the bodies of a number of suspected militiamen had been found. Most had their throats cut; some had been beaten to death. Victor Charlie was clearly out for revenge – a lot of arse was going to be kicked.

Nobody complained about the change of plans, or about the apparently futile 18 mile yomp. We had other things on our minds; the brutalising of two young women was difficult for even seasoned veterans to take.

The majority of the lads were quiet, immersed within their own thoughts. British men are notorious for not discussing their feelings; the men of 2: Bravo 6 was no different. We coped by engaging in occasional malarkey. Joking, ribbing each other or taking the piss out of the hierarchy. It worked for a short time, but the banter would often be replaced by extended silence. On that evening there was no banter – just silence.

I lay on my bed listening to 'Songs To Learn & Sing' on Sugar's radio: Gordon Lightfoot *If You Could Read My Mind*, followed by Leonard Cohen singing *Suzanne*. The melodious pieces were soothing. Unfortunately Sugar didn't seem to think so: "What's all that fuckin' warblin' about—?"

"Leave it Sugar; please," I said as he made to change the station.

He looked at me for a second: "Fuckin' Leonard Cohen makes me wanna cut me throat," he said, deciding to leave the channel.

Post evening meal I sat on the step leading to the dormitory in my boxer shorts. I'd decided to take in the warm evening air after enjoying an extra long shower. Corporal Farr joined me his towel wrapped around his waist: "You okay buddy—?"

I shrugged my shoulders.

"—There's still more good in the world than bad you know."

"I know…though at this moment I don't like being human. Do you ever cry in dreams?"

"No," Tommy replied with a chuckle.

"I do, its probably the only place I feel able. Sometimes I bawl, really let go. I remember the last time I cried. I was thirteen; a gang jumped me as I was coming home from school. I think the tears were more doubt and frustration than hurt. I thought I could defend myself against anything, anybody. It was a bit of a wake up call. I felt like crying after Tchụrin Loy and I've got close on other occasions, like today. Seeing Jez crying kinda gave me permission. Buster brought a swift end to that."

"Who said you have to shed tears to cry?" Tommy said to my interest. "We all weep; sometimes it's just not that obvious."

We sat for sometime in the warm evening air. The night was still; there was a pleasant smell of sandalwood that mingled with the remnants of perfumed soap. Fireflies sparked as they flitted across our view; there appeared to be more than usual. Some seemed to be temporarily suspended, as if dots in a joined up picture. Under normal circumstances I'd have remembered the evening as something magical. It would've been, apart from the fact that I couldn't remove the image of two hanging bodies from my mind.

21:00: Outskirts of Charlie Town, Friday 23 March.

End of day fourteen of a scatter patrol, we were all fatigued. The whole section had spent the last two weeks chasing shadows, shanks's pony our only mode of transport. I sat wondering why the ceasefire agreement carried the name January *Morning – mourning* would've been more apt. The killing continued, as much a free for all as ever. By March 17th 80% of US troops had left Vietnam; this had done nothing to decrease tensions. It was somewhat of an irony that Cambodian's repressive President Lồn Nôl had survived an assassination attempt on the same day. Brutal reprisals followed signalling yet another exodus of refugees from war torn Cambodia. Why hundreds of Khmer would want to move from one war ridden land to another was beyond us.

Debrief was succeeded by the news that we were to remain on patrol; there appeared to be no end, every day as if the last. Carbon copy orders: 'Set a course for Đừin Phộng to investigate further ceasefire violations; transfer 17 miles west by northwest to protect incoming refugees on Route 6; carry out an overnight expedition to Xừin Thuận to observe SVA checkpoints; relocate 14 miles to the outskirts of Charlie Town...' We predominantly walked by day. Most of the excursions were at a saunter with some at an extended pace. We had blisters on top of our blisters. Our boot leather groaned as much as we did.

By our 227th day in Vietnam we were well used to the consequences of war. Dead bodies in various states of rigor mortis or decay littered the highways, monsoon ditches and scrub. I never thought I'd get used to the stench of rotting corpses – it had become as if second nature. I'd developed a part-loss of affect. In the first instance this bothered me. I soon realised it was a necessary part of coping.

Our itinerary was handed out before stand down, further relocations to exotically named largely unknown venues. Our march was to continue, on and on: cutting through woods, yomping over fields, hiking down highways. Hour by hour, day-by-day, mile after mile: walking, walking, walking.

11:00: UN Base Camp 5, Sơng Căn, Wednesday 4 April.

We'd returned to base after further fruitless excursions through Quì Nhôn. Our final stint in Base 5 was accompanied by debriefings and equipment checks. Our minds were on other things. We were counting down to 8 days Rest and Recuperation at the United States Marines Recreational Facility, China Beach. We were all looking forward to the break. Numerous GIs had told us about the facility. Stories abounded of bright air conditioned Boâ Daí Villas fronted by rolling beaches with sand as white as snow. The resource contained 'eat 'til you burst' restaurants and duty free bars selling worldwide beers – eight Đổng feasts succeeded by mega piss-ups. The provision was located on the outskirts of Đà Nẵng, an extra bonus. The yanks considered Đà Nẵng the crème de la crème of South Vietnam – we'd do our utmost to test this out.

Our final debriefing was followed by our six monthly medical. We looked a motley crew lined up in our bare feet and boxer shorts. Routine checks were followed by a weigh in. I had a consistent weight of 150 lbs. I was shocked by the readout: 137 lbs – I had lost nearly a stone. I hardly recognised the skeletal figure in the full-length mirror. My collarbones, ribs and hipbones were protruding through tightly wrapped flesh. I'd also suffered significant muscle wastage and my stomach bowed inwards. The whole Platoon had suffered weight loss, a combined total of 590 lbs. We must have consumed around 4000 calories per day; we had clearly been burning more. Time off would be a chance for us to put back some flesh.

We were looking forward to relaxing. The recreational facility contained an extensive library and a complimentary 'Three-a-Day Movie Hall'. I thought, privately, that I'd do some reading and check out some of the films. I didn't want to see any movies featuring war, gratuitous violence, or anything that featured a hanging.

JANUARY MOURNING

Rifles cocked, breaches filled, trigger-fingers itch
Barrels glowing cold in the shadow of gun smoke
Deafening rounds slash the guileless quiet
Expected peace not shattered for not anticipated.

Tracer writes messages on disfigured skies
Clouds weep, torn apart forever separated
Healing wounds re-open
The cut too deep to remedy.

Tết tigers prowl eyes looking inward
Glowing balloons fade, wishes deflate
Oxen tell tales of woe
Their forefathers shunning their return.

Oil stained paddies reek
Rice never to look skyward
The children's hunger burns
The uncaring world turns.

Cloistered woods fail to hide mans evil deeds
Choked ground, choked lives
MPs taunt: warped values, twisted smiles
Fireflies gather to light the funeral pyre.

January mourning, perpetual grief
January evening the darkness of despair
The round-eyes deceit turns full circle
Never ending tragedies, the book unclosed.

No bells started ringing
No birds started singing
The people just kept on crying
Cos the guns just kept on firing.

Lance Corporal Barry Morris
Đà Nẵng, April 1973.

6: DARK DAYS – ILLUMINATED NIGHTS

Courage was mine & I had mystery
Wisdom was mine & I had mastery;
To miss the march of the retreating world
Into vain citadels that are not walled.

W Owen

19:00: UN Base Camp 8, Pleikû, Là Drang Valley, 16 April 1973.

Our period of Rest and Recuperation seemed to go quicker than a Phantom jet with its afterburners at full throttle. It seemed unreal, only 30 hours previously I was lounging on the balcony of my Boâ Daí villa with a cool glass of San Miguel, the condensate frosting the glass. Now I was covering my face with army-issue nightfighter cosmetic preparing for another patrol. The black paste smeared on my sweaty forehead. The humidity was unbearable; the erratic China Winds had turned yet again. The Detachment was fully loaded ready for a four-day reconnaissance of the main routes and byways connecting Pleikû, Xurin Đật and Kôntum. We were about to get back into the same old routine, though some things had changed. Our ration packs contained additions: double concentrate energy drinks, high-fat biscuits, book-size blocks of milk chocolate, vacuum sealed packs of diced fruit and foil wrapped slabs of lump cake. The Platoon had strict instructions to consume a minimum of 4600 calories per day. Command was evidently concerned about previous weight loss. A further reduction would clearly compromise our efficiency. I had only managed to put on a few pounds whilst on R&R, despite walking around as if I had a stomach like a barrage balloon full of concrete.

We'd also been issued with new high-resolution nightsights. The new model would make night images sharper though the attachment was more bulky and heavier.

My mind was still buzzing with thoughts of our period in Đà Nẳng. We'd tested out as many bars and nightclubs as possible given the brevity of our stay. I thought of some of the tracks I'd heard playing in the saloons along Đoc Mý Street – Bread, Jimmy Cliff, Neil Diamond, The Moody Blues, The Who. Wonderful music, good food; lazy days and sensuous nights.

We gathered at the gates wearing gloomy expressions; our leave was behind us, time to get back to work. Biffo called the advance: "Platoon, move out!"

"Follow the Yellow Brick Road, all paths lead home," Tommy said, as we disappeared into the night.

13:30: Sộc Trâng, Là Drang Valley, Sunday 22 April.

Post highway watch Command reassigned the Platoon to the flat iron plains of the Là Drang Valley. The United States 7th Cavalry had dubbed the gorge the 'valley of death'. We renamed it the 'valley of dullness' – our patrols were as prosaic as ever. Our briefing notes read, '...although there has been little apparent activity on the floor and surrounding slopes of the valley Command is still concerned that covert infiltration is occurring on a daily basis'. We had a sneaking suspicion Command was filling time. We were clearly not needed in Là Drang. The region seemed like a third world country within a third world country. Mechanisation was either unheard of or shunned. Ox driven carts largely transported goods and even medium sized towns seemed to have little electricity. The populace appeared to consider themselves detached from the conflict though it was difficult to see how against the backdrop of fierce battles in the mid to late '60s. The masses were as friendly as in most areas. Until our experience in Lông Đáo I thought this was due to our stance as United Nations troops. I was wrong; the welcoming of strangers was a long-standing feature of Vietnamese culture. This was certainly the case in the village of Sộc Trâng. The village elders and people willingly greeted us with trays of tea and rice cakes.

Lieutenant Derrick summoned me to act as the translator. The elders wanted their own interpreter to act on their behalf. A striking young woman joined us. She had long flowing hair parted at the side with an imitation silver comb. She wore a black silky top accentuated with white piping on the sleeves and collar, and traditional Vietnamese slacks.

The preambles ran the usual duration; introductions are important in Vietnamese culture. Once complete the elders explained about the problems they'd encountered with the South Vietnamese Army. Local units had been constantly terrorising their community accusing the inhabitants of harbouring NVA Regulars and Viet Cong militia. The honcho assured us that his village was neutral. He wanted to know if we could bring any influence to bear.

The conversation was at times convoluted. I found myself looking at the inhabitant's interpreter and smiling. At one stage the Lieutenant gave me a fierce look. The one-hour conversation adjourned with a promise that we'd provide central office with a detailed report. It was hard to see if the elders believed our assurance. I couldn't blame them; we would have little to no influence anyway. The Detail slowly regrouped once we'd completed our tasks. We were in no rush; the inhabitants wanted to be friendly – we wanted to respond. This suited me; I wanted to have a chance to talk to my fellow translator.

She gently swept her hair from her shoulders as we slowly walked alongside

each other. "Your master of Vietnamese very good," she said.
"Thank you, though I'm not sure, I sometimes struggle with the tones. I once asked for a plate of pigs' ears when I wanted prawn crackers." We both giggled. "Your English is good also."
"No, not can understand your grammar, very com-plex. I sorry, not catch tên (*name*) at opening."
"Barry," I said with a smile.
"Bảr-rý," she deliberately repeated. "Nice name – I am Lứin Bận Dưìn."
"It rhymes," I said enthusiastically. ('What am I saying?' I thought as she gave me a vacant look, 'there's no such thing as a rhyme in Vietnamese.')
"Bảr-rý is bố tên," (*fathers name*?) She eagerly asked.
"No, English don't automatically name a boy after their father."
"Ông ngoại," (*Grandfather*?) She enquired looking perplexed.
"No, different customs, different…erm, văn hóa, (*culture*.) Not disrespectful not to name children after immediate family, though my middle name is that of my ông ngoại."
Lứin looked even more confused. This was understandable; in her culture a male's middle name is that of their mother.
"You been many country on your travel?" Lứin asked.
"Yeah, we've been 'round."
"I would like to travel one day. I would go to Britain and the Viking lands. And I would go to the northern lands of the many snows to see pen-gùins and polar bears."
"You'd need to go to the southern hemisphere to see penguins…there aren't any in the Arctic."
"I did not know that," Lứin responded with a serious look.
"It's okay it's just me being a điđị mơa (*smart arse*). Have you lived here all your life?"
"No, I am coming originally from Đà Nẳng…" She saw me grin. "What is smile, you know Đà Nẳng?"
"Oh yeah, I know it. China Beach, Marble Mountain and the nightlife, did we have us some time in Đà Nẳng! Is that where you learned to speak English?"
"Yes, in Christian school, then at the adult peoples' college. Had to leave; had to come live with grandparent."
"Your mother, father—?"
"My father he die in fighting. Mother soon follow; she very sick."
"Brothers, sisters?"
"One brother only, he away now, fighting."
"Army? is he in the army?"
"No, he just away, fighting."

I knew the faction to whom she was referring. She couldn't utter the words, she daren't. She had no idea I wouldn't grass – on her or her brother.

"You Brit-ains," she said, after a brief silence, "you win your war against, how you say nâh, nát—"

"Nazis."

"Yes, nát-xếs."

"We didn't beat them alone. We were part of a bigger force: the resistance in occupied countries, the Russians and the Americans."

"You be happy to fight with American?"

I had to consider for a second. "I don't like what they've done here, but they helped us fight against the evil of Hitler. They lost a lot of young men: on the beaches of France; in the air over Europe and on the road to Berlin. Nobody could deny that."

"You beat người Nhật Bản (*Japanese*) also. Nhật Bản come my country, very cruel."

"I think maybe round-eyes have been cruel also."

She stopped and gave me a gentle look: "You are not cruel; you have kind face."

"Thank you," I returned, with a thousand-watt smile. My hormones were sparking. The electricity between us could've lit the village.

"How old you are?" she asked returning the smile, "…I am nineteen years only."

"I'm nineteen also, twenty in June."

"I twenty in June, on day twenty-four—"

"The twenty-fourth of June!" I said in amazement, "…that's my birthday, the same day!"

"Our spirits journeyed on the same time, different side of world."

"We Britons would call that coincidence. Good omen."

"Not so," she said to my surprise. "Coin need two faces so when coin fall not same side show each time."

"Opposites attract. So, have you got a boyfriend?"

"No," she said putting her head down, "can not find."

"Well, all I can say is the boys in these parts must be blind; you're beautiful."

"Am not so," she said, with a bashfulness I'd not seen in a long time.

"Detail to muster!" Sergeant Edwards called out.

We both stopped walking. I found myself suddenly lost for words. Lứin broke the silence: "It has been much pleasure to talk with you."

"Yeah, it's been nice—"

"Bazzer!" Corporal Lane yelled, "…come on son."

"I've got to go now."

“Oh, never mind. I will light incense; make many wish for your home return to be safe.”

“Thank you and I’ll wish that maybe one day you can travel. Visit my country and go to the land of northern snows, talk with Inuits. And if you see any penguins be sure to let me know.”

We both laughed. I bid Lứin goodbye wishing we could’ve had longer.

I joined the men most of whom were sniggering.

“You cockhappy little bastard!” Wolfie said.

“It wasn’t like that—”

“Oh right, so what’s that bulgin’ in your keks a six inch fuck-stick!”

We moved out towards our next objective. Some of the children walked beside us carrying sticks at slope-arms on their shoulders, imitating marching soldiers. We mimicked them laughing as we left. I looked for Lứin. I spotted her walking towards what was likely her living quarters. She turned and waved. I nodded with a smile. How different from our exit from Lông Đáo.

Three weeks after leaving Sộc Trâng we were privy to an IPSF report stating that the SVA had entered the commune in the middle of the night arresting 14 young men. The report concluded that 5 of the men had failed to return. The SVA swore they released all of the subjects after questioning. I thought of Lứin Bận Dưìn; there were other members of her extended family in the village. In most countries the disappearance of 5 men from one community would be a major news item. In Vietnam it was just another week in a senseless war.

06:00: Qưan Đrín, Là Drang Valley, Wednesday 25 April.

I was coming to the end of the morning watch. The lads had risen; we’d breakfasted and received details on our mission. It had been a slow lookout, like most. I was in the midst of packing my gear ready to break camp when the sun poked its head above the eastern massif. It seemed to stop two-thirds of the way, the dense atmosphere momentarily splitting the crimson sphere. The two segments hovered before rejoining, the sun floodlighting the valley as it arced westward.

Buster snapped me out of my trance: “I don’t know where you drift off to young man but it’s time to get on back here…now hustle up!”

The Detail advanced on a north by northwest echelon towards the Phừan Đóc Plains. We’d received information that erstwhile Viet Cong Cadres had reformed. Victor Charlie had a habit of disappearing without trace only to reappear days or weeks later with increased strength. They would leave little parcels behind as a reminder that they could still kick arse. Their favourite calling cards would be, often in the guise of, homemade antipersonnel mines.

There were two types: a pressure–activated device, which would detonate on immediate load, and a pressure–release design, which would not prime until the spring-pin had completed a downward and upward motion. The problem with the homemade devices was that you didn't know if they were real or duds. Rebels would often place a mixture in a given locale. If somebody stepped on a dud, word would get round that the purportedly mined area was bogus. Days later a victim would have a leg or foot blown off striking new fear into local communities.

We'd been forewarned that the locale was strewn with antipersonnel mines. We could do little but stick to regular paths. Sometimes this was either impractical or equally as dangerous. Insurgents would often choose familiar routes to lay ambush. As with most hazards you had to just put the possibility of falling victim to the back of your mind. Instead, I once again found myself playing the songs enjoyed on R&R. In the vastness of the Là Drang Valley, China Beach seemed oh so far away.

14:30: The Phừan Đóc Plains.

Sergeant Edwards checked our recon' position. The halt was a welcome break, the China Winds were still playing games; there wasn't a breath of air. Bronco and JJ were on point. Tommy led the mid-group with Dinger taking up the rear. Phừan Đóc was battle scarred. The natives said that the rust-red soil was resultant of rivers of blood. In '65 the 7th US Cavalry lost more men in one skirmish than at the battle of *Little Big Horn*.

We negotiated the weed-strewn remnants of bomb and mortar craters with the usual caution. I didn't see Marine Miller stop, but I did hear him call out: "Oh fuck! I think I've stepped on a mine!"

"What?" Buster said, "okay everybody freeze! Are you sure it's a mine?"

"It can't be anything else," Dusty replied as we nervously looked upon our own feet clamped to the ground. "There was a load click. I can feel the plate under my foot."

"Okay Dusty stay perfectly motionless," Buster advised. "Sugar get on the RT, convey our position and predicament. Make a priority request for Weapons' Specialists—"

"Maybe it's a dud Sarge," Marine Miller nervously cut in.

"And maybe it's a pressure–release mine! You don't want to check it out. If it's not a dud you'll lose your foot the minute you take the load off – if you're lucky! Now you make like a statue. The rest of you, slowly stoop and offload your gear behind you."

We nervously complied as Sugar contacted the engineers based at Bịnh Đính. Buster offered specific words of encouragement and advice to Dusty.

He told him to slowly lower his bergen behind him and to assume a boxer's stance to spread the load.

Sergeant Edwards briefed us: "Listen carefully, no sudden movements. If we come under fire we'll fight in place. If we have to retreat we'll move on our former course, if possible. Let's hope we won't have to run a catch twenty-two."

The whole Detail was in a precarious position; the landscape was like a billiard table. A sniper would've had a field day, literally. I tried to put the prospect of having to fight out of my mind. We were spread on a regular central line with support. Dusty was eight o'clock to my position. Jumper was immediately behind me. Bronco and JJ were on the same line as Dusty. The only factor that lessened our collective problem was Marine Miller's dilemma. He stood in silence a persistent look of dread cut into his face. I couldn't decide whether I felt frightened for him or for myself; probably both. I looked at the rough ground that surrounded me. I could've been inches from an antipersonnel mine. Some devices had hair triggers. 'Freeze', the Sergeant had said – none of us needed to be prompted. I was as solid as a stalagmite and as quiet as a church mouse.

The sun beat down, the clock ticked. We looked at the empty fields that encircled us, waiting for the engineers to arrive.

16:00: Cessation point.

An hour and a half had passed since our enforced halt. Marine Miller's foot was still firmly positioned on the pressure–plate. We spent our time shouting encouragement to him. Marine Lyle said he wished he could get the bastards who had laid the devices. He would make them play blind hopscotch in the field. Dusty's spirit was initially high, but time was moving on. The engineers couldn't give an ETA.

Dusty reached for his canteen, it slipped from his hand as he was bringing it up to his lips bouncing on the ground, the precious water spewing from the open canister.

"My canteen! I've dropped my canteen!" he screamed the distress in his voice palpable.

"It's okay son calm down now," Sergeant Edwards said. "Can you reach it?"

"No, I don't wanna chance it; it's too far to my right—"

"He can have mine," Marine Collins cut in, "I'm not far from him."

"You stay exactly where you are!" Buster said. He was suddenly deep in thought.

I focused on Dusty. He was shaking, the stress on his face ever-growing. It was pitiful – I felt for him as he stood in the blistering heat.

"Jumper," Buster called over, "do you reckon you could crawl over to him using your bayonet as a prod?"

"I think so—"

"Don't think so boy! Can ya or can't ya?"

"Yeah Sarge, I can. I can do it!"

Buster took him through the drill. Crawling on your hands and knees prodding the ground at a 45° angle with your bayonet was a last resort. There was no guarantee you'd find a device. In addition, your bayonet could trigger a mine blowing off your hand whilst sending red-hot shards into your face.

Jumper set off. He was approximately 12 yards from Dusty's position. His progress was painfully slow. He used a variety of small items to trace his path. He had completed about half the distance when he stopped his bayonet at a 45° angle in the ground: "Oh fuck I got one!"

"Are you sure?" Buster enquired.

"Yeah, a definite obstruction."

"Okay mark it, and give it a wide berth. Listen y'all that confirms the worst."

Jumper continued on his perilous course, droplets of sweat dripping from his forehead.

"Made it!" he said, placing himself alongside Marine Miller on one knee. We cheered as Jumper handed Dusty his canteen.

"Okay you lot keep it down!" Buster said. "Well done Jumper; stay with him a while."

Jumper nodded as Dusty sipped water from the canteen.

"Thanks buddy," Dusty said, "I owe ya."

Marine Collins offered his shoulder. "Lean on me," he said, "...put your hand on my shoulder."

Dusty complied, partially taking the pressure off his legs and lower back.

"Lean on me," Jumper said. I thought of the line from the song: '...*we all need somebody to lean on.*' On that afternoon I realised exactly what that meant.

17:00.

Two and a half hours, still no sign of the weapons' specialists; we were all concerned. Dusty was beginning to tremble slowly rocking to and fro. He'd been muttering and singing under his breath for sometime. Jumper too was uncomfortable. He had to transfer his weight from one knee to the next to continue offering prop-support; the Sergeant was concerned for both. He judged that Marine Cunliffe was the nearest to them. He could've ordered him to relieve Jumper but he chose to ask first. Cowboy responded without a moment's hesitation.

I felt guilty as Cowboy nervously crawled towards the position. We'd all managed to sit down. I'd put my towel over my damp bandana to shade my head and neck from the sun. Dusty, on the other hand, was still standing. The intolerable stress would've sapped his energy let alone having to maintain pressure on the plate. Our fear was that he'd become delirious or pass out. Given the situation the antipersonnel mine would've injured two men.

Cowboy adroitly moved closer slowly prodding the soil with his bayonet. We were all holding our breaths. A distant hum interrupted our attention. We looked in hope in the direction of the far-off sound.

"Chopper…" Lance Corporal Bell said, "is that a chopper?"

"You bet!" JJ said. "Wasp helicopter inbound east by southeast."

"Engineers!" the Sergeant said, "…at last."

"Can you hear that Dusty?" Sugar excitedly asked. "Can you hear that beautiful sound?"

"Yeah…" Marine Miller replied his voice tinged with emotion.

We were all nervously laughing as the chopper glided in; the gloom had suddenly lifted. I looked at Dusty; his eyes were closed. Jumper, still stoically down on one knee, gripped Dusty's leg: "We'll get ya back in one piece mucker," he said, "we'll get ya back!"

Buster set off a smoke flare as the Wasp approached. The 'copter hovered, roughly 250 yards from our position, feet from the ground. Three Bomb Disposal experts jumped out each holding long aluminium probes. The specialists had an array of instruments attached to tool belts. They were heavily clad in blast proof waist jackets and their reinforced helmets were inclusive of shatterproof visors. The experts checked their immediate area as the chopper circled above; they were obviously clearing a landing zone.

Sergeant Edwards instructed Marine Collins to retire to his former position and Cowboy to abort the relief as the Wasp landed. Jumper toed the path he'd laid as if a tightrope walker.

The Royal Canadian Weapons' Specialists seemed to take an age reaching Dusty's location. They crawled in a parallel line towards us, deliberately stabbing the ground with their long probes. They stopped at intervals to lay markers; yellow triangles and red flags. It didn't take a mastermind to work out that the flags indicated a hazard. By half way we could count a total of five red pennants.

"Blimey!" Vinny said as the specialists passed him, "…the fuckin' fields full of them."

We were all silent as the crew crawled the last couple of yards, a total of seven red flags in the ground. We'd obviously walked into a heavily mined area. I wondered how we'd managed to advance so far without triggering a device. Focusing on Dusty, his foot depressing the pressure-plate reminded me that one of us had partially activated a fuse.

The specialists set to laying out their equipment once they'd reached Dusty. We watched in fascination as two of the crew manoeuvred into position. One used a sharp horn-knife to slice along the seam that joins the upper layer of the boot to the sole. He carefully removed the laced top advising Dusty to maintain pressure on the sole. The other crewmember slid an 18-by-2 inch steel plate between the underside of Dusty's foot and the sole. The metal was smeared with Vaseline to aid movement. Once through the oblong plate was secured to the ground by two corkscrew pins, hence providing constant load on the mine. We assumed that all Dusty would have to do was step off and back away from the device – it wasn't that simple. There was no guarantee that the load provided by the steel plate was enough. The firing pin may've already partially travelled upwards. A small amount of play could've primed the weapon. Instead, the specialists took him through an escape drill. We couldn't hear the instructions. Dusty listened attentively to the specialists who withdrew backwards, dragging his bergen with them, once they had completed the brief.

Marine Miller stood for a moment collecting his thoughts. I couldn't imagine what he was going through. The mine would've remained inert all the time he held in place; this was obviously impractical. The silence was unbearable. Dusty seemed to be frozen, then, he began slowly falling backwards his arms outstretched. His falling frame gathered momentum. He pulled both his knees towards his chest as he plummeted down, rolling into a tight ball on his back, his frame slowly rocking back and forth. The two engineers, who'd been lying face-down behind him, rushed to his position and unceremoniously dragged him from the hazard: "Clear!" they both bellowed.

"**Yes!**" we collectively cried out, Jumper punching the air with his fist.

"Okay keep calm now!" Buster said.

Sergeant Edwards had the same smile on his face as the rest of us as Dusty picked himself up. He stumbled around in a safe area; his right leg was obviously dead. He didn't know whether to laugh or cry – I think he did both.

Some five minutes later the remaining crewman reached Bronco and JJ still dutifully on point. A total of eleven antipersonnel mines had been located including Dusty's death trap and the device that Jumper found. We looked at the winding course behind us. The yellow markers resembled a slalom planned by a chronic dope head. The indicators still presented as if twinkling beacons of pure gold; they were no less valuable.

Buster determined a rallying point, which we carefully made our way towards. Once regrouped we slowly retreated from the lethal minefield. Dusty was hobbling on one booted foot. We wondered how he was going to make it back to the C-P. The engineers ameliorated his problem when they produced a sack full of second-hand boots. We ribbed him unmercifully as he tried on a selection of musty footwear. He settled for a battered GI issue that looked as if it had been on the foot of a partially sighted man who'd spent his entire life kicking half-bricks down narrow alleys.

We bid the Canucks goodbye after thanking them. Command aborted our mission redirecting us back towards Quran Đrín. I'd never known us to be so closely grouped. We looked at the terrain ahead trying, unsurprisingly without success, to tread ground we'd already covered.

Marine Miller walked behind me – he was understandably hushed. We all wanted to offer him congratulations. I held back allowing him to catch up with me: "That was close. You okay?"

"Yeah," he responded in a nonchalant manner, "it's no sweat."

I gazed at him. He didn't seem any different, except for a slight look of tiredness. I grabbed his left wrist with my hand: "See you later."

I was about to pull my hand away when Dusty placed his free hand on mine in a vice-like grip. He didn't give me eye contact; he didn't need to. I smiled, a smile he was aware of, a smile that said, '…its okay, I understand.'

Men don't wilt, especially Royal Marines – at least not on the outside.

18:50: Phừan Đóc Plains.

The Detachment stepped out towards Quran Đrín: 14 Royal Marines, 28 legs and feet intact. Approximately 15 minutes after we'd cleared the area we heard a distant explosion at our rear.

"They've pulled the pins…" Sergeant Edwards said as we all looked back, "the mine was live."

"You lucky bastard!" Cowboy said, slapping Dusty on the back.

We moved out of cover onto a metal road, relieved to be away from the bracken below our feet. The possibility of falling victim to ambuscade was a chance we'd have to take. We were all in high spirits as we neared our objective. As the lads conversed, I gazed at the sun as it slowly dipped below the jagged line of the western mountains. Some 13 hours previously I had watched a spectacular sunrise, the sunset was equally as beautiful. As the giant shimmering sphere disappeared sucking the light and heat in its wake I was hit by a thought: 'if the sunset looked beautiful to me, how must it have looked to Royal Marine Greg Miller.'

*

19:30: UN Base Camp 8, Pleikû, Friday 27 April.

We sat on our rattan chairs awaiting our hastily arranged open-air movie. Lance Corporal Barilla had managed to persuade an outgoing Quartermaster to lend us a dilapidated open-reel projector along with a bootleg copy of Stanley Kubrick's *A Clockwork Orange*. The evening was warm and clear. We could see the strobe lights of jet aircraft high above crisscrossing the dark sky. I wondered if they were passenger liners or B52 Bombers outbound or returning from further missions over Southern Laos or Eastern Cambodia.

The start of the film diverted my attention. The projector rumbled and clicked as it rotated – it sounded like a shagged out air compressor that had lost its retaining bolts. The temporary screen was fashioned from the side of a 16-wheel troop carrier. Bronco and Nasher had whitewashed one side of the army-green canvas in the afternoon. It was initially difficult to make out the images on the ribs and wavy canvas. The sound quality from the box-speaker was dreadful, a pity since pieces from Beethoven, Elgar and Rossini were included in the soundtrack. Tiny insects and huge moths performed figure of eight patterns in the projectors' beam. The flickering ray was the only light for miles, excluding the dim lights in the former US Cavalry Garrison. I'd loved to have had an aerial view of the show. Distant gunfire cracked in the middle of the disturbing rape scene; nobody flinched. Rifle and machine-gun reports had become habitual.

The movie had taken our minds off the fact that we were awaiting new instructions. Lieutenant Derrick took the final spool change as an opportunity to inform us that we'd be moving to Trệng Nhôy at 0600 hours. Post briefing it was difficult to concentrate on the last section.

As it transpired the smoking projector only just made it to the credits.

I tried to engage Bronco and Tommy in a discussion about the film; they were too busy packing their gear for our reassignment. Instead, I recorded my thoughts in my journal. I'd already read Anthony Burgess's book. I couldn't understand the furore surrounding the release, and Kubrick's ultimate withdrawal of the film in the UK. Granted, the film was violent and the perpetrators in the rape scene displayed a definitive absence of feeling. Nevertheless, in my view *A Clockwork Orange* was no worse than any other early '70s genre. On the contrary it had honesty about it: the group brutality of men striving for power; the honesty of the penal system contra the dishonesty of the sociologists and aversion therapists interested only in furthering their importance and self-satisfaction. And the consequences of brainwashing a habitual thug into passivity only to release him, without support, into a cruel society: the crimes of the individual – the crimes of the system.

I remember reading a piece from the Mary Whitehouse brigade suggesting that the film was a product of misguided values and ungodly morals; bullshit! At the release of the film there were a total of 14-armed conflicts of varying degrees raging around the world. Whitehouse and her cronies apparently had no comment. I wrote about my feelings in bold letters, an indication that I felt angry—

'...Whilst in Vietnam I've witnessed the proliferation of a bloody civil war. A conflict in which children die from curable childhood diseases whilst millions of dollars of military hardware is dumped in the South China Sea. A fractured society where street children are treated like vermin and boys forcibly recruited as child soldiers. A region where refugees are used as political pawns and women systematically raped and abused without redress. A devastated country where promises are made and constantly broken. An arena where hundreds of non-combatants are murdered on a weekly basis... If individuals or groups want to get passionate about something, then let them get passionate about the brutality that is an everyday reality for millions of people in at least 14 countries, not something that is a product of celluloid!'

22:00: UN Base Camp 9, Phờn Xurýen, Trệng Nhôy, Sunday 6 May.

The Platoon settled earlier than normal, we all needed a good night's sleep. Our annual shakedown was scheduled for the following day. None of us looked forward to shakedown, in spite of being pulled from the dullness of police actions. I knew I'd have difficulty sleeping despite being worn-out. I lay on my bed propped against the headboard. The evening was steamy. My mosquito net had more holes in it than a colander; I really would have trouble sleeping. I perused the scribble in my journal. Our arrival in Trệng Nhôy was followed by an eventful 9 days. We spent the first two days dodging sniper fire. The residing militia was probably testing our metal. We found that highly amusing – if they really wanted to test us out why didn't they take us on squad-on-squad.

World news was as interesting as ever: April 29th growing anger in Israel at the disclosure that Archbishop Roncalli, later Pope John XXIII, had prior information about the holocaust, information that the Vatican conveniently buried. As a lapsed catholic I thought I couldn't have any more contempt for the corrupt and outdated institution.

Meanwhile in London, concerns that the dispute over fishing rights around the Icelandic coast is spiralling out of control after an Icelandic gunboat opens fire on British trawlers. The Shadow Foreign Secretary remarks that the dispute is turning into a *Cod War*.

On the 30th a White House Spokesman announces the resignation of four of

President Nixon's top aides in the spreading Watergate scandal. Bob Cramer of *The New York Times* wrote, '...the bloodhounds are sniffing, the vultures are circling... Nixon will fall!'

The following day Radio Sàigòn announced the stepping up of bombing raids – resumed on April 1st – against NVA positions along the Hồ Chí Minh Trail. Corporal Farr said that the yanks had obviously forgotten that April fools lasts for one day.

On May 1st Four Squad almost had a belated April fool of their own. One of them activated the tripwire of a claymore in the Pắk Quơ Woods. The lone team hit the ground faster than a meteor only to discover that the device had not primed. They almost made a fatal error rising from their positions instead of crawling from the immediate area. The claymore, likely set on a delayed fuse, exploded, the deadly shrapnel slicing through the dense undergrowth. Mercifully they escaped unharmed. It was a stark lesson – they'd not forget withdrawal drill in a hurry.

Wednesday the 2nd was memorable. We experienced our first really serious firefight. We were not the targets. As many times before we were simply caught in the middle of a fracas; this made no difference as the tracer soared above our prostrate bodies. We were pinned down for almost two hours, eventually electing to fight our way out. We were buzzing on our return to base. We thought we'd all escaped without harm. Incredibly, Lance Corporal Barilla found a bullet lodged in his hip after he'd stripped off in preparation for a shower. He said he thought the pain was from lying on the rough ground.

The following evening, Marines Gipsy and Woods discovered a mixed race baby (approximately two months old) wrapped in a Khmer scarf just outside the gates. The child was likely the offspring of a GI. Viet Cong communities in particular would ostracise any women who fraternised with a sworn enemy. The whole corps spent the evening cooing over the tiny boy. Nuns from the Order of Sister Thérèse eventually collected the baby. Tinker and Woody wondered if they could get the tiny boy named after them; no such customs or possibilities existed in South Vietnam.

On Friday the 4th Marine Taylor was airlifted to a US Mobile Army Surgical Hospital south of Kôntum suffering from a burst appendix. He had been grumbling about lower abdominal pain for days. Biffo told him to stop bellyaching and get to the sickbay. Buck doubled up in agony amid seeking advice from the medics. He was lucky; the minimally staffed field hospital was days away from a final evacuation.

On Saturday the 5th a bunch of us gathered round JJ's transistor radio to listen to the FA Cup Final on the BBC World Service: Second division Sunderland against the might of Don Revie's Leeds United. It was arduous listening to the faint signal. The broadcast kept on fading, often at important moments. Unfortunately for us the signal almost completely dissipated minutes before the final whistle, returning just in time for us to hear the excited commentator saying that Sunderland had done the impossible, beating Leeds United by one goal to nil. The two Leeds supporters in the Platoon were inconsolable.

The misery of a couple of football supporters coming to terms with an FA Cup Final defeat was nothing compared to the sad news that greeted Marine Rippley. He learned that his father had died of a heart attack. Blue was a late replacement. It was only three days after his eighteenth birthday when we set off for Vietnam. Blue lacked confidence. For a Royal Marine he was unusually introvert. He tried to emulate people in an apparent attempt to mould his personality. There was something tormented about him. He was a good enough soldier, but he somehow found it difficult to fit in. He once tried to attach himself to me but I found a way of eschewing his advances. I remember feeling sorry about that. Truth is I was too concerned about peer group attitudes. Some thought that Blue was weird; he wasn't of course, he was just different. His struggle would continue for a further three years coming to a tragic end in a high-speed motorbike accident that somehow smacked of suicide. I remember feeling sad at the news of his fate. I thought of how I'd felt sorry for him. Some years later I would be forced to reflect with greater honesty. My contemplation fostered a cruel certainty. I never really felt sorry for him, I only felt sorry for myself.

06:30: UN Base Camp 9, Phờn Xuýen, Monday 7 May.

The Platoons mustered at the gates in preparation for our shakedown. We'd been joined by 2: Delta 6 Platoon for our annual 'brutal'. The start of the workout was always the worst. You knew you had a whole day of pain ahead. The Royal Marines Endurance Test contained no half measures. The Physical Training Instructors [PTIs] divided the combined sections into three teams of twenty. If you failed individually you had to do the whole thing again eight days later. If more than four from a troop failed the whole team would have to retake. More than a quarter of the combined teams failing would constitute a total retake. Failure to complete the task on a retake would result in immediate dismissal from the Cadre. The penalties were one hell of an incentive – failure was not an option.

We set off, a time lapse between the teams, for our first discipline: a 5 mile run carrying a 50 lb pack towards the banks of the Trá Khưc River. It was still early morning though the sun was already beginning to deliver its heat; it was going to be a long workout.

07:10: Banks of the Trá Khưc River, Trệng Nhôy.

I was already drenched in sweat as we neared the banks of the river. I wasn't looking forward to the 1 mile swim. Running was my strong point; I was an average swimmer at best. We plunged into the river after stripping down to our trunks. The fast running water was surprisingly cold. Thankfully, the Physical Training Instructors had set the course downstream. Even so, I still struggled with the initial quarter-mile. Some of the others helped: JJ and Vinny were strong swimmers; they could've taken off and left me in their wake. The task however was a team event. They gave me encouragement; I would return the favour, if needed, later. The swim was over surprisingly quickly. We scurried up the bank to collect our clothes – which had been transported downriver – as a closely-knit group. We were all pretty pleased with ourselves as we ripped our trunks off and started throwing on our combat fatigues. We could hear a commotion from the other bank as we dressed. We quickly discovered it was a bunch of women stonewashing clothes. We waved to them as they whistled and giggled.

"Fuck me, I feel like a flasher!" Sugar said.

"You are a flasher…" Corporal Farr returned, "now belt up, buckle up and fuckin' move!"

The 5 mile run back to base was excruciating. It was virtually up hill all the way. My legs already felt heavy and the straps on my pack were beginning to chafe. I cursed myself for not checking the adjustments on the fastenings. On our return I got Tommy to rub a liberal layer of Vaseline on the chafed areas before undertaking our next discipline.

A hot mug of tea and slice of lump cake was swiftly followed by our call to the gymnasium. We were to experience the delights of a 60 minute beasting, a non-stop circuit incorporating grid-sprints, pull-ups, push-ups, sit-ups, bar curls, squat-thrusts, bench jumps and fireman's lifts over undulating ramps. By halfway into the circuit we were all gulping in buckets of air. This made no mind to the PTIs – they were merciless. One kept ordering me to restart a high knee exercise because I failed to touch the yardstick at each elevation. Cursing the sadistic bastard under my breath helped. The beasting was succeeded by 2 circuits of a Tarzan Assault Course; the double fifty-foot rope climb and quarter-mile mud run had never seemed so difficult.

A hastily scoffed lunch of acacia honey on cornbread and soft fruit was followed by muster for the 30 mile yomp, the last and worst leg. Captain Page briefed us as we hauled our fully loaded bergens onto our backs: "Okay boys, now for the pleasure of a little saunter across the rolling countryside of South Vietnam—"

"Boo…" We all heckled.

"—Now then ladies, you all know by now that we'll be competing against the clock. Now I know your delicate little feet are probably aching and your faint hearts and pussy-deprived dicks yearning for a long slow screw. Well tough fuckin' shit! We gotta a thirty-mile forced march and that's the end of it. Any of you little fairies got any complaints?"

"Yes Sir," Sugar said, "…'ow cum the brutal never includes dick exercise?"

"Marine Lyle…" the Captain answered pretending to be serious, "you can pull your plonker to your hearts content once we've completed the yomp—"

"He wants you to pull it!" somebody exclaimed amid roars of laughter.

The Captain, laughing along with us, handed over to Colour Sergeant Biffly: "Teams!" he shouted bringing an end to our chortling. "Saddle up, move on out!"

"Good luck boys!" The PTIs hollered as the three teams set off, a time lapse between each, for our excursion. We synchronised our timepieces, pulled our bergens close and high and trundled out – 30 miles and counting.

14:30: The Thrức Nhậ Qưi slopes.

We were well into our stride by the 10 mile marker. Morale in our team was high; we all felt strong. The conditions could've been more favourable. On the very day we needed an overcast sky the sun was a demon, what we'd have done for an intermittent shower. The PTIs occasionally drove beside us offering water and glucose tablets; their input was essential. We'd walked miles during our tour, but none of our excursions had been against the clock or following a morning of beasting.

We had to keep on reminding ourselves that we were still on active duty. Charlie was in the undergrowth; they cared nothing about our rituals. We took turns in walking the flanks, keeping our eyes open for danger. The members of One and Two Squads had the added burden of worrying about antipersonnel mines; the heinous devices were far from unique to Là Drang. I kept imagining that disturbances in the ground ahead were due to fresh deposits; they were largely due to moles. Sugar kept us entertained as normal. His jokes and anecdotes helped break the monotony.

Lance Corporal Jessop alerted us that Red Troop, who had set off before us, were just ahead. We were in the throws of self-congratulation when a marshalling jeep pulled alongside. "Listen up!" a PTI hollered, "…the groups are falling behind schedule – open the pace!"

From elation to despair in a spilt second.

The sun peeked from behind a lone cloud as we extended the pace. Minutes before the undulating landscape looked beautiful, at that moment it looked like a multiple Tarzan Assault Course.

20:00: Approximately 2 miles from Base Camp 9.

As a Royal Marine you learn how to switch to autopilot. You learn how to block out the pain; focus on an objective with an unyielding determination. There had never been more of a need to put our heads down and slog than on that occasion. The ravages of nine months of a Tour of Duty had finally caught up with us. I felt like I was in purgatory. My lower back ached and my legs felt like lumps of clay; there was enough lactic acid in my muscles to fill a vat. There was no chat or banter between us, just hard labour. We were so engrossed in the yomp that we failed to see the lights of the UN Garrison in the distance. Cowboy was the first to spot them: "Home boys, its home...a mile and a bit ahead!"

The sight of the base gave us new impetus. Red Troop had just arrived; they clapped us at the gates as we struggled through. We dumped our bergens on the ground and collapsed in a heap. I lay next to my compadrés staring at the dark sky. I was just gathering my thoughts when we were alerted that Green Troop was approaching the gates. We all lined the entrance clapping and cheering as the last troop trundled through. The teams had completed the task with over forty minutes to spare.

The PTIs handed out space blankets and we were each awarded a bottle of San Miguel. Jumper swigged his; I sipped mine. Captain Page debriefed us; we'd passed of course. There was no self-congratulation or applause, just silent relief and reflection. I sat on the ground leaning against my bergen, the space blanket round my shoulders. The heavens suddenly opened up in a sledgehammer downpour; the China Winds had finally done a U turn. The shower would be a portent of things to come. A fresh police action was planned for the following day. At that time I cared not. I sat on the ground amid the bouncing raindrops. I felt as if the warm droplets and cool beer were cleansing my soul. I was fooling myself of course. There were still three months of our tour to go, plenty more time to be infected by the continuing poison of war.

09:00: South Vietnamese—Cambodian border, Tuesday 15 May.

The eighth day of another mind-numbing patrol. Every police action had its similarities and differences. Moving through ghost-mists chasing shadows was the biggest similarity. The environments on the other hand were subtly different. We could never actually establish if Trệng Nhôy was a district, a province or just a figment of somebody's imagination. It ran the Cambodian border seemingly disappearing in the tributaries of the Mêkong River.

It was by far the most mountainous region we'd patrolled. Thick sprawling jungle also covered the area. What was a botanists' paradise was a pathfinder's hellhole. The thick vegetation was a nightmare to negotiate. Indigenous plants sprung in every conceivable direction. The thinner varieties were often harder to cut through than the broader assortments. Our machetes would be dulled in hours. We were convinced that the bamboo was impregnated with wire. There was a multitude of foliage: brightly coloured orchids pushing their way through uninspiring vegetation; slender fairy-leaf shrubbery beside cabbage-green docks with leaves the size of hammocks; multi-tentacle spider plants and rapidly creeping bindweed that would curl round your foot should you stand long enough.

The jungle was inclusive of any manner of exotic creatures: scorpions and multi-coloured snakes of various sizes. There was a general rule: the brighter the colours the more deadly the creature. Some of the colours and designs were indeed striking, though we didn't hang around to take a second look.

The vicinity was inundated with hemipterous insects. Creatures that would attack your flesh in any number of ways: burrowing, biting, injecting their eggs or seemingly assaulting your flesh for the sheer hell of it. Toileting or bathing, for what it was worth, was a finite operation. You dare not leave delicate flesh exposed for too long; bites and stings were bad enough on tough areas of skin. The mosquito was by far the most detested insect. We were unaware pre-briefings of the variations of the genus. There was no defence against the irritating little bastards. 'Squito repellent was largely ineffective. It reeked, stained your clothes and often caused skin complaints. You had two choices once confronted: cover yourself and bake in the searing heat or leave gaps to effect some ventilation and be eaten alive – the ultimate Hobson's choice. Night time was the worst: swarms of mosquitoes would descend, buzzing, crawling, biting; a never-ending torment.

The myriad crawling creatures were no less innocuous: tiny worms that would crawl into orifices; red and black ants with crocodile jaws; grappling hook leeches with insatiable appetites and wax eating beetles trying to set up home in your lug holes. We had strict instructions not to place our bare feet on the forest floor, to do so would leave you open to infestation by the 'gudgery', a small silver worm that would burrow into your skin. If infected your foot would swell up like a balloon, your skin splitting and toenails turning black.

The unpredictable environment presented us with frequent challenges: hidden ravines with frightening drops; decaying tree limbs thundering to the ground; emerald flora with pinprick leaves and barbed stems fortified with contact poison that would induce spot blisters and acute delirium. One night we made camp approximately 15 yards from a fast running stream. It rained throughout the night. We could hear the flow from the stream becoming louder. Chopper woke us two hours before sunrise shouting that we should "...gear-up and move, on the double!" It was just as well, some ten minutes later the stream had swollen to a rapidly running river. The roar was deafening and the speed frightening. The Detail would've been washed away in seconds. We passed through the same locale days later; the waterway had reduced back to a gentle stream. We'd been warned that the environment was erratic and hazardous. After our experience by the stream we took greater heed of the advice.

Trying to deal with our environment was nothing compared to attempting to deal with our objectives. Command had sent us to the quarter to monitor border activities – whatever they were supposed to be. We had been informed that Khmer Rouge separatists and North Vietnamese Regulars had been crisscrossing the border for a number of weeks. Initially we could find no evidence, yet there was a strange feeling that movements were taking place. Our feelings were eventually reinforced by chance finds. The remnants of campfires alongside the residue of human habitation; occasional dugouts and logged bunkers fronted by spent rounds. Paramilitary cells were in the area all right, but where?

20:30: Eastern reaches of Plềi Ví, Trệng Nhôy, Thursday 17 May.

It was raining again! I'd never known rain like it: vertical rain, horizontal, diagonal and swirling rain. Warm rain, freezing rain; rain that would be accompanied by stinging hail stones. Acid rain, alkaline rain; rain that had a pungent smell and strange bittersweet taste. Staying dry for a concerted period was all but impossible. Our waterproofs offered little protection. If not soaked by the rain you'd be drenched in sweat. Our soaking wet clothes would stick to our skin. Undressing was a hoot, like trying to unwrap a tacky toffee.

Some days we could manage to part dry our clothes, only for them to be soaked again in a three-minute downpour. The only option was to accept the inevitable – get used to our saturated existence.

The monsoon was relentless. The pattern always seemed the same: black thunderclouds would augment rising through the stratosphere faster than a Saturn Rocket. A cloak-like gloom would envelope the whole area, often making it seem as dark as night. Sledgehammer downpours would replace a spooky silence. Rain, semi-swamp, ghost shrouded mists followed by swarms of mosquitoes hammered into submission by further downpours: a perpetual script, the writer's pen caught in an irresistible groove.

The wet monsoon was supposed to be accompanied by lower temperatures; somebody forgot to tell the sun to pack its bags. Blazing sunshine would succeed the rainfall. The result was predictable; the whole forest would become a giant al fresco sauna the steam slowly rising like an ascending fogbank.

The occasional hail was even worse. Being caught in a downpour under the forest canopy was a nightmare. Some of the stones were the size of goofballs. The stones would sometimes ricochet off the trees; it was like trying to dodge .50 calibre bullets on a practice range. One day we were caught in the open during the worst hailstorm I've ever encountered. The tiny stones pelted us relentlessly. We ended up gathering in a scrum-like circle whilst squatting on the ground. The pebbledash storm intensified, the hail bouncing on our helmets; it sounded like a battalion of army ants performing a manic clog dance on a tin roof.

The previous forty-eight hours had been particularly bad. Being informed that our survey was to continue dampened our already soaked spirits even further. We were due to return headquarters. Intelligence had apparently narrowed the border crossings down to one sector, *our* sector. They could've fooled us – all we could see and hear was each other and the unremitting rain.

I decided to put my annoyance to one side as I cleared my bivouac to settle for the night. I had enough to worry about. I'd drawn the short straw for the early morning watch. I wrapped myself up in my damp poncho and prepared for dreams of walking the streets of Atlantis.

22:00: 2: Bravo 6 bivouac.

Waiting for something to happen is a constant feature of peacekeeping. I had no idea prior to our tour how exhausting waiting for action can be. You are hoodwinked into a false sense of security: 'nothing has happened, ergo, nothing will happen.' The underlying stress was emotionally draining. I never *really* slept on patrol. It didn't matter how tired I was; I dozed at best. I was somewhere between sleep and slumber when the first illumination rounds were thrust skyward. I bolted upright at the distinct dull thud from distant mortars.

"Thompson Flares…" somebody half-whispered, "glowing in the west."

I threw off my sodden covers and grabbed my M16, as I looked westward. We'd bivouacked in a clearing roughly 3 miles from the Cambodian border; hence we had a clear view of the expanse. It had stopped raining, the sky was clear. We could see three illumination rounds slowly floating to earth about a mile and a half ahead.

"Who's probing who?" somebody asked.

"That'll be the SVA lookin' for infiltrators," Biffo suggested. "We'd better double the lookout – something's goin' down."

I found myself mesmerized by the slowly descending flares. They lit up the immediate vicinity. The flickering phosphorous rounds producing jagged shadows immediately below. The rounds slowly faded only to be rapidly replaced. The sudden flash of bright light woke some of the animals in the surrounding bush. Many started screeching, squawking and calling out, momentarily confused by the unexpected onset of daybreak. Distant gunfire accompanied the premature morning chorus.

"Here we go!" Colour Sergeant Biffly said, "...stay alert y'all. Be on the lookout for movement."

The barrage of illumination rounds continued. Some of the rounds drifted our way, the tiny parachutes visible above the burning phosphorous. Lines of smoke trailed the flares, looking like snakes on an enormous snakes and ladders board. What or who the unit responsible for the light show was looking for was beyond us. The individuals propelling the rounds were either inexperienced or downright stupid. A first year infantryman would tell you that you should limit firing rounds from one position to avoid detection; the element couldn't have made themselves any more conspicuous.

The whole Platoon was keyed up part expectant of action. Our enthusiasm was thwarted when the rounds suddenly stopped. Nonetheless, we couldn't stand down. There was definite activity – someone or something was heading our way.

03:00: South Vietnamese—Cambodian border, Friday 18 May.

Command instructed us to covertly check out the border activity. We hastily broke camp and moved westward from our exposed position back towards thick jungle. The rounds repeated with intermittent breaks. We were all excited as we advanced towards the engagement – for what it was worth. We were convinced that the corps was shooting at illuminated silhouettes in the darkness; their action lacked coherence. We stopped in a dense area of tropical forest. The gentle westerly breeze pushed the illuminations nearer to our position. Lieutenant Derrick was hit by a realisation: that *we* could be mistaken for an infiltrating faction. He ordered a halt and the setting up of a three-line citadel.

Most of the lads settled once the citadel had been established. I sat alongside TC and Wolfie looking and listening for movement. The illumination rounds kicked off yet again. The flares hovered above the canopy; the blanched swinging light produced weird shadows swaying back and forth. It resembled the closing scene from Hitchcock's *Psycho*, the lone light bulb swinging across the dark room as Bates slashed at his last victim.

It's amazing what you can imagine when sat in the silence of the jungle, things clearly not feasible: the sounds of insects copulating, worms tunnelling and plants growing. The slightest snap of a twig or rustling bush would initiate a startled response. The combination of, often spooky, sounds and incandescent lights scattering toothed beams and swinging shades between the trees and across the forest floor was chilling. None of the troop slept; for once I was pleased to be on guard.

The probing ceased just before daybreak. Black clouds rushing in from the east succeeded sunrise. We set off in the gloom – the dejected chasing the indeterminate.

14:00: The Chơui Bậnár paths.

We were slowly moving north by northwest back towards the Plềi Ví reaches. Yet another al fresco sauna had replaced the deafening booms of thunder and machine-gun downpours. It had been some ten minutes since we'd heard a commotion ahead; automatic gunfire accompanied by RPG reports. We were close to a sortie – closer than we'd been since our transfer. I considered it a cruel twist of fate that I was on point at the very time we were nearing an action. Marine Wood was close behind as we crept along a dirt road that had all but disappeared in the deluges. The layers of mist shrouded our advance. Unfortunately the haze also hid any potential hazards.

My mouth was dry as we hugged a line of wild hedges running beside a small wooded area. There was something unusual about the density of the fog. Woody and I realised it was smog resultant of recent gunfire. Spent 7.62 rounds littered the ground. I held up my fisted hand to indicate a hazard.

"What do you see?" Colour Sergeant Biffly enquired in a hushed voice.

"The ground's covered with spent thirty calibre rounds; there's been definite activity."

Biffo instructed me to hold in place whilst the reminder of the Detachment moved up. I picked up one of the cartridges; it was still warm. "Oh fuck!" I whispered, "…they really were just here."

"I know," Woody replied looking behind me. "Take a dekko at the ground."

I spun round to see a distinct line of blood amid the damp soil and bracken. The scarlet droplets zigzagged through a space in the hedge: "Somebody's been wounded—"

"That's more than just wounded judgin' by the amount of blood," Buster cut in. "Corporal Lane, take young Morris and Woods through that gap; no more than a hundred yards. Report your findings back to the position."

We looked at each other as we prepared to advance. Bronco winked at me. Woody mirrored my expression, a clear look of apprehension. We crept through the medium undergrowth: myself on point, Bronco and Woody closely following. The trail of blood was splattered on the leaves of low shrubbery; the victim had either made an escape or been dragged through the undergrowth by fellow guerrillas. I took a deep breath as we pressed forward. I wasn't apprehensive about the possibility of discovering a body. After six months of war I was death-hardened. It was confronting an injured man, desperate and in pain that I was concerned about. A wounded animal is always more dangerous; Homo sapiens are no different.

"Anything?" Corporal Lane enquired.

"No," I whispered, "the trail's thinning—"

"Hold up…look what I found," Woody said, clutching a Khmer blood band.

"Khmer Rouge!" Bronco said. "At least we've identified one of the groups."

The Khmer blood band was the mark of a breakaway KR faction. The rebels would swear an oath before each drawing blood, which would be pooled in a container. Khmer scarves would then be soaked in the cocktail. Once dried out the scarves would be cut into strips and used as headbands. The representation was a show of defiance and brotherhood: we are not afraid to bleed; we are not afraid to die. In most instances they were faithful assertions.

The trail, luckily, went cold. Bronco decided that we should turn back. We rejoined the Detail relieved to be out of the woodland. Lieutenant Derrick was receiving further instructions on the RT as the lads sat loafing round. After a brief consultation Biffo and Buster called the move on. One more day of futile patrols; another night of illumination rounds. The skies opened up with the delights of another hailstorm. The stones bombarded our miserable forms as we rolled along seemingly without end.

14:30: UN Base Camp 9, Phờn Xượ́en, Monday 21 May.

Our second day of a four-day stint in Base 9 – bliss! The Platoon sat in the briefing room receiving yet more inconsequential lectures. We were clearly filling time. None of us were bothered – we were out of the jungle and in the dry.

We had spent our first day trying to wash our damp, filthy fatigues. We all rushed to the ablutions keen to launder our gear. We stood bollock-naked dumping our clothes in and out of the stone sinks. There was no soap powder left in the NAAFI or our lockers. We had to resort to using navy-issue carbolic soap. The beige foul smelling blocks were useless they hardly produced any suds. My fatigues remained soiled no matter how many times I washed them. The steaming bathhouse smelled like a Chinese dhobi-den; what we'd have done for a jumbo box of Fairy. I checked myself over prior to a shower. I resembled something that belonged on a quarantine ward. I was covered from head to toe with scratches, rashes, bites and stings. We still had to shave on patrol, despite running out of fresh razorblades. My phizog was horrendous, it looked like a spot-welders' bench. My physical appearance was nothing compared to my innards. Our continual C-Ration diets had given us all constipation. The medics gave each of us a measure of syrup of figs in conjunction with Ex-Lax tablets. We were unsure if we should've been given the double-dose. As it transpired we spent the whole of Monday morning with our arses firmly pressed on bog seats. We were crapping more than a herd of water buffalos with ruminant dysentery.

I'd lost all interest in the lecture. A United States Intelligence Official gave us a talk on the historical context of boundary disputes. It was beyond me why we were being lectured on the minutiae surrounding long-standing power struggles. The word *ceasefire* didn't seem to be in his vocabulary. I struggled to keep awake amidst his monotone presentation. I wasn't the only one; Jez and Vinny were already fast asleep. I'd have gladly joined them. I tried closing one eyelid at a time; it didn't work. A heading on the regional map displayed on the overhead screen caught my interest: 'War Zone C3'. I giggled under my breath.

"What are you sniggerin' at?" Tommy whispered.

"Irony, we're supposed to be in the middle of a fuckin' ceasefire yet they're still referring to sectors as war zones!"

That evening we all had difficulty sleeping. We could hear the border section being hammered with bombs, likely from B52s based in Thailand. We were aware that the South Vietnamese Government had requested air strikes. I wondered why the intelligence official had not mentioned how bombers based in unrelated countries could continue to indiscriminately bomb areas containing non-combatants.

The bombing continued deep into the morning. The booms were so intense we could feel tremors resonating through our beds. I got up at around four o'clock to take a leak. A number of beds in the dormitory were empty. I sauntered outside to find four of the lads sitting on the step looking southeasterly. The horizon was alight with distant flashes accompanied by rumbles.

"Now that's what I call fireworks!" Giggsy said.

"I wouldn't like to be under that lot," Wolfie added.

"Let's hope they've completed the mission by the time we go back out," I said. "I don't trust those incompetent bastards."

I returned to my bed wondering if I'd be able to get back to sleep. The bombing continued. I could see the outlines of the narrow windows in flashes of light on the walls – the ceasefire was clearly in full swing.

I did manage some sleep. My slumber was accompanied by dreams of lying on a pulsating bed in a massage parlour with brightly coloured lights flitting across lacklustre walls. Someone or something was lying on top of me. I wouldn't have objected if it was an alluring bargirl. Unfortunately, it was something resembling a B52 Bomber.

17:00: South Vietnamese—Cambodian border, Thursday 31 May.

Our eighth day of more ineffective patrols. We'd returned to the bush to the aftermath of the incessant bombing. Parts of the terrain looked like a moonscape. Enormous craters surrounded by smouldering earth. The barrage had dislodged millions of fire ants from their nests. One area looked like a moving ginger carpet. We tightened the putties on our trouser bottoms in an attempt to keep the vicious insects from crawling up our legs. It was useless; we spent the afternoon dancing round whilst beating ten bells of shit out of our camo' trousers.

Corporal Biggs suffered a snakebite on his calf on our second day. Medical Attendant Hughes ripped the back of his combat trousers and immediately set to sucking out any potential poison. Ronnie was understandably in a state of panic. Marine Cunliffe called out that he'd trapped the scaly reptile under his foot. We looked to see him standing on the three-foot snake, its head a few inches from his boot. The limbless creature was struggling to break free, its body wriggling and tongue probing the air.

"Get the manual and check it out," Lieutenant Derrick said to Sergeant Edwards.

Buster complied, Corporal Lane accompanying him as he stooped down. He turned the pages as Yozzer continued dispensing care to Ronnie. He settled on a page. "Can you confirm a yellow spot on top of its head fronted by a small violet diamond?" he asked Bronco.

"Confirmed."

"Relax, its not poisonous. It's called a choịquar, indigenous to Indo-China. It's got a vicious bite 'tis all—"

"Don't I know it!" Corporal Biggs said. "Are you sure that's the snake?"

"It can't be any other," the Lieutenant said, "not unless you can see anything else crawling around. Administer an antidote anyway."

"I'm on to it Sir," the Doc' responded.

"What shall I do with it Sir?" Cowboy enquired, holding his menacing machete in his hand.

Lieutenant Derrick was thoughtful for a second: "Let it go."

Cowboy lifted his boot and stepped back. We watched as the choịquar slithered away. I was glad we set it free. It meant no harm – it was just trying to defend itself.

On the night of the 26th we established our first contact: a close-order line of

North Vietnamese troops, possibly up to a company, slowly walking on the periphery of the jungle. We followed the task force through our nightsights. At one stage we were less than a quarter mile from them. I could see their AK47s and the distinctive red stars on their 1950s helmets. We recorded their movements, no more. The following night the illumination rounds restarted. The SVA were likely in hot pursuit. On that occasion the rounds were being fired from different sources. At one stage the whole area was lit up as if daylight.

"This place has got more fuckin' illuminations than Blackpool," Lance Corporal Jessop said as we sat gazing at the glowing rounds.

A South Vietnamese Army Unit approached us on the following day. The unit was carrying mortar tubes; they were clearly part of the light show. I acted as interpreter as a Captain asked the Lieutenant if we'd witnessed any NVA or KR activity.

Lieutenant Derrick explained that we were not at liberty to divulge movements, only to report our findings to IPSF Command.

The Captain became frustrated as he continued to press for information. The Lieutenant remained deadpan. Indeed at one stage he instructed me to remind the Vietnamese officer of the terms of January Morning.

The Captain gave up muttering expletives as he withdrew to his men.

"What did he say young Morris?" Lieutenant Derrick enquired.

"Something about you being the product of a questionable relationship between your mother and father Sir."

"Charming!"

The boys were in fine form as the SVA Unit set off; they knew we held them in contempt. Both were covertly throwing insults. Marine Lyle had other ideas. He wasn't content with muttering. He stood shouting in laborious English whilst mimicking semaphore: "You are a bunch of skunk-fucks. The spirit of Hồ Chí Minh he sneaky-upy and bone your arses! Your Captain is a cunt-weasel—"

"That's enough Lyle!" Biffo hollered as we sniggered.

Thursday the 29th turned into the most hectic day and night we had experienced since moving to the province. Command directed us from one position to another in further pursuit of ghost-shadows. There didn't appear to be any rhyme or reason to our tasks. Our pointless trek included a treacherous river crossing using guide ropes. Some of the lads lost their footing. We found ourselves battling against the torrent desperately trying to help our fallen comrades.

We were exhausted by nightfall; this made no difference to Control. They contacted the Platoon for the umpteenth time with new instructions. The Lieutenant rarely lost his temper – he was as cool as an Eskimo working in a freezer store. By our 19th day of chasing amorphous shapes during the darkness of the day, and blanched apparitions in the incandescent flashes of the night, he was as thoroughly pissed off as the rest of us. Command ordering the Detachment to swing southwesterly, yet again, was the last straw. "Christ, this is futile..." the Lieutenant, snarled slamming the receiver onto the cradle, "how the hell are four sections of twenty-nine men supposed to cover an expanse this extensive? Who gives a shit about border crossings anyway!"

We stood looking at Lieutenant Derrick in the torrential rain. We were taken aback by his outburst. Biffo winked at him and asked if he should get the teams moving.

I smiled to myself as we moved out. I'd wondered if the Lieutenant held the same beliefs as us all; he likely did. Fact is none of us could work out exactly what we were meant to be doing. If the North and South Vietnamese Armies, and the Viet Cong and Khmer Rouge wanted to have a barney on the border then let them. As long as none combatants were not being targeted we cared not.

The mundane continued: black clouds, torrential rain, Thompson Flares, bites and stings; misery. I found little to write about in my journal. That was until Jumper made a cursory remark: "It's weird, this place," he said with a thoughtful expression, "...with all these clouds and illumination rounds it seems like the days are darker than the nights."

I reflected for second before recording his notion in my journal, amending his statement—

'...Nothing new in this place, just the same old routine. Hacking through jungle, striking the numbers from the calendar: counting down the dark days and illuminated nights.'

14:00: Chinook outbound War Zone C5, Thursday 7 June.

The Chinook slashed its way through the low cloud. The ride was bumpier than normal. The Platoon was tense and introspective as the chopper bounced the eddies. The austere cabin gave little to focus on, apart from each other. Being unsure of our new objectives didn't help. Command in their infinite wisdom had withheld information. We'd be given our instructions once in place. It seemed a pretty good bet we would be monitoring Khmer Rouge movements. The KR were becoming bolder, crossing the Cambodian border during daylight hours to challenge hidden North Vietnamese infiltrators. The sensitive politics of the region dictated that we could not be imbued with information, at least that's what Command told us. I wouldn't have had a problem with the policy; save for an inclination that control was persistently feeding us a line of hogwash. We were already aware that border activity in the southeast had augmented since the relentless carpet-bombing of the northeastern sector; this did nothing to assuage our anxieties.

None of us looked forward to fresh assignments, particularly in new sectors. Becoming familiar with a locale increased confidence. Apprehension was a natural element of armed conflict. Jangled nerves played havoc with the emotions. Often, experience didn't equal anticipation. I have never been a believer in premonition. In my view extra sensory perceptions have more to do with mythology and a trick of psychology rather than a natural gift. Even so, I felt unusually uneasy. The empty pit in my stomach had suddenly become bottomless. I was fidgeting more than usual and my left foot had apparently developed a mind of its own tapping out Morse code on the cabin floor.

I did my best to dismiss my feelings, the customary strategies: thinking of the numerous drills that reinforce our function as an élite unit and that we'd completed two-thirds of our tour relatively unscathed, but the spooky unease continued.

Marine Collins was blowing enormous bubbles out of disgusting pink bubblegum. A balloon sized bubble burst spattering over his face. The lads chuckled as Jumper peeled the sticky film from his skin.

"You'd be better off blowin' bubbles out of yer fuckin' arsehole," Marine Wood suggested.

"Who asked you twat-hooks!" Jumper retorted whilst shoving the stringing gum back into his mouth.

The temporary lift in mood eased my anxiety. That was until the magazine dropped from my M16. I struggled to get the loaded jacket back into the slot realising that the lock-tab had jammed in the withdrawal position.

"What's the trouble?" Biffo enquired.

"Don't know Colour Sergeant, the damn thing just popped out. I can't get it back in again."

"You'd better get that stripped down as soon as we've landed; get it back on line. We don't know what's going to be waiting for us."

I sat with my magazine in one hand, my rifle in the other hit yet again by a feeling of foreboding. Irrational as it seemed, I was convinced that something was going to drop on me from a great height.

SONGS FROM THE 'NAM
China Beach, Đà Nẵng Nights
& Radio Sàigòn

BREAD *Everything I Own; Too Much Love*

THE BEATLES *Here Comes The Sun; Magical Mystery Tour; Something*

JIMMY CLIFF *Wonderful World Beautiful People*

CHRISTIE *Yellow River*

LEONARD COHEN *Suzanne*

ROGER DALTREY *Just A Boy*

NEIL DIAMOND *Cracklin' Rosie; I Am I Said; Stones*

BOB DYLAN *A Hard Rain's A-Gonna Fall; I Want You; Lay Lady Lay*

BOBBY GOLDSBORO' *The First Time*

GORDON LIGHTFOOT *If You Could Read My Mind; Sundown*

PAUL McCARTNEY *C Moon*

THE MOODY BLUES *Lost In A Lost World; When You're A Free Man*

KENNY ROGERS *Ruby*

CARLY SIMON *You're So Vain*

ROD STEWART *Maggie May; Mandolin Wind; Reason To Believe*

THE WHO *My Generation; Pinball Wizard; Won't Get Fooled Again*

THE YOUNG RASCALS *Groovin'*

7: SHADOWDANCING

We had no cameras, to shoot the landscape,
We passed the hash pipe & played our Doors tapes,
And it was dark, so dark at night,
That we held on to each other, like brother to brother
And we promised our mothers we'd write…

Billy Joel

19:00: Two miles east of the Cambodian border, Trệng Nhôy, 19 June 1973.

We had been hacking our way through the thick jungle undergrowth all day. The abundant forest canopy had long since smothered the sun's rays hampering our progress even further. At 19:15 Lieutenant Derrick ordered the Platoon to bivouac for the night. The call to discontinue didn't come a minute too soon. The Detachment was exhausted. We were on day five of a fourteen-day mission to covertly observe border activities. The IPSF had assigned 2: Bravo 6 Platoon the task of monitoring the movement of Khmer Rouge revolutionaries. Intelligence suggested that Khmer Rouge insurgents had been involved in border skirmishes with North Vietnamese Army Units, long established Viet Cong elements and Specialist Montagnard Forces; this was no surprise. The boundary regions had a long history of turmoil. The geographical area was of strategic significance to all warring factions. The pivotal towns of Neặk Lượng (Cambodia), and Lắk (Vietnam) lay to the west and east of the sector with the key town of Lôc Nịnh to the south. United States Forces had been involved in numerous territorial battles throughout the confrontation. The Khmer Rouge and NLF had been contesting the area since the US withdrawal.

Colour Sergeant Biffly gave the standard daily debrief, which included a reminder on the importance of daily 'prophylaxis' (prevention against diseases). The practices were essential due to the dangers of the exotic sounding disorders familiar to the region. There was one prophylaxis routine that required no prompts, the routine to guard against Malaria or more precisely, Malaria: Malignant Tertian Strain-7 [M: MTS-7 or Strain-7]. The Platoon had previously received specific instructions on the indigenous variety from an expert in tropical medicine. The strain was a highly virulent plasmodium (parasitic protozoan) that manifested itself every seven years. It dwelled in the mud-tracts of Eastern Cambodia. Once out of dormancy it would attach itself to the more prevalent single and multiple strand plasmodiums common to the territory. The last manifestation occurred in

1966, it didn't take a mathematician to work out that was seven years ago. We had been instructed to double up on Mefloquine and Cholorquine tablets and on the use of mosquito repellent. It was well known that common malaria would put you on your back, but M: MTS-7, unless treated with expedience, would put you on your back for good. There was a plethora of well-known stories surrounding the condition including the demise of a Detachment of US Rangers who had crossed the Cambodian border in '66. A search party discovered their bloated bodies after they'd failed to return from the clandestine mission. The whole Detail went down with the strain but had dehydrated and lapsed into coma before they could reach the safety of Vietnam. Strain-7 elicited almost as much dread amongst the Platoon as being trapped in the middle of a firefight between Khmer Rouge and Viet Cong guerrillas.

The Platoon, subsequent to detailing perimeter sentries and setting tripflares, bivouacked at 2200 hours. It was an unusually dry and clear evening for the height of the wet season. The monsoon had recently veered south easterly bringing temporary relief from the heavy rainfall in conjunction with slightly higher night time temperatures.

Nonetheless, I felt unusually clammy for the time of year. I also had a sudden loss of appetite and felt more fatigued than usual. I decided as I lay listening to the distant rumbles of thunder that all I needed was a good night's sleep, unknowing, that something adverse had entered my system, something that would threaten my very existence.

05:30: South Vietnamese—Cambodian border, Wednesday 20 June.

The gargoyles had me surrounded: triple headed horned basilisks adorned with Khmer blood bands; firefly eyes and flame-lined mouths drooling in anticipation of the kill. Phantoms laden with napalm hover in crimson skies. Obliterated hamlets litter the scarred landscape, their inhabitants' legs aloft as if exterminated cockroaches. Mouths wide with silent screams; blackened forms shifting as if ghosts, their charred flesh descending the steaming ash 'neath their tortured bodies. They're closing in now. I cry out: "No, get away from me it wasn't my fault. I couldn't stop it!"

I awoke in a frenzy my breathing elevated and heart pounding. I was drenched in sweat yet shivering as if a man trapped in a deep-freeze. I had not had a comfortable night. My daybreak nightmare was a conclusion in a night of bad dreams. The unrelenting thunder didn't help. To soldiers on frontline duty, thunder is always unwelcome; its sound is too alike distant artillery. My nocturnal thrashing had discarded my covers exposing my body to any manner of hemipterous insects.

Regardless, I lay staring at the ragged shapes etched in the morning sky amidst the forest canopy. I felt decidedly unwell. My legs felt heavy and unresponsive. I had a burning sensation in my bladder along with chronic stomach cramps and a raging thirst. My head was thumping, my neck stiff and my joints sore.

The dawn chorus was in full swing: Annamese bullfrogs, chitchats, macaws, manikins, jade monkeys and tamarins confirming their territorial rights or gathering their bands'. I had learned to live with the morning din during successive patrols – on that morning it was anything but habitual.

It took every ounce of my resolve to rise from my bivouac. My head was swimming and my stomach churning as I laboriously checked my boots for black or amber scorpions. The term 'weak as a kitten' didn't do justice to my predicament as I leaned on a nearby termite mound to take a leak. Passing water didn't help, I felt like I was urinating passed white-hot needles. My urine was as dark as stewed tea and had pungent aroma akin to ammonia and strychnine.

Marine Collins was sitting near my bivouac on my return. He was wrapped in his poncho and had a look of death. "You too?" he enquired.

"Yeah…me too what?" I followed as I dumped my clammy body beside him.

"Pissing passed razor blades, I heard you cursing behind the mound."

"Something like that. You look like I feel."

"I've been up since four," Jumper grumbled, "had a bad attack of night terrors. Speedy and JJ aren't too good either."

Sergeant Edwards interrupted us. "Keep the noise down you two," he said in an assertive whisper. "You're gonna alert every fuckin' guerrilla in the bush. What are you doing out your bivouacs?"

"I...we, feel like shit," Jumper replied.

"Okay," Buster said with an increasing look of concern, "get back to your bedrolls. Moose is on his way round."

"What do you mean Sarge 'on his way round'?"

"You're not the only ones that are going down with something. Now get in your bivouacs and wait for Moose. And try not to go to sleep, got it."

Jumper painfully shuffled away as I crawled onto my damp bedroll. I felt like I was in purgatory. There was a continuous ringing in my ears. I was intermittently overcome by waves of nausea accompanied by hot-sweats and shivers. I had an insatiable thirst yet a dread of water. I began to hallucinate: demonic forms and cadavers dancing in menacing configurations; day-glo crabs and triple-headed scorpions crawling over my torso, feasting on my flesh. I tried desperately to hold onto reality, to stay alert, 'I've got to keep awake,' I told myself, 'I must stay awake, I must...'

"**Bazzer, wake-up!**" the seemingly distant voice bellowed, "...Lance Corporal Morris, up! Come on son, up!"

I awoke to Buster pulling me up to a sitting position. Corporal Lane was stooping beside me with Moose kneeling at my feet, medical bag in hand.

"I wanna see your eyeballs soldier!" Buster said as Bronco gently poured water over my head. I remember panicking, wondering why these cruel individuals wanted to hurt me. Why didn't they just let me sleep?

"Leave me alone," I said in a languid state. "I haven't done anything, I just wanna—"

Buster offering a water canteen to my mouth interrupted me: "No!" I cried out as Bronco held my delicate head. It was useless; I was so weak I had no choice but to swallow the water trickling into my mouth.

"You've gotta take fluids," the Sergeant said, "you're burning up."

Bronco and Moose offered words of encouragement as I drank the tepid liquid. I slowly began to regain some sense of normality.

"I don't know," Bronco murmured with a grin. "Some people will do anything to get out the bush."

"I'm cold," I responded desperately trying to raise a smile. Bronco put some covers over my shoulders as Buster moved on.

The Doc' began checking me over: "Have you got stomach cramps, a headache and the shivers? Are you having difficulty passing water?"

"Yeah, all those things, is it strain-seven Doc'?"

"We don't know yet, it could be common malaria or a dose of river fever."

"Don't fuck with me Doc', I've had river fever it's nothing like this!"

"Okay," he said offering me more water, "it doesn't look good, but we're gonna get you all priority treatment. We've contacted the Medical Corps; they're sending two Medevac birds [casualty evacuation helicopters] ...to fly you and the others to the Ran'," (Rậnlạntoì: United States Marine Corps Hospital, Lôc Nịnh.)

"Who are the others?" I asked Bronco.

"Speedy, JJ, Dusty, Sugar, Dinger, Tommy and you already know about Jumper. Don't fret, y'all gonna be fine."

In the distance I could hear the unmistakable pitch of two Bell Huey helicopters. The Huey's motor and rotors have a distinguishable hum and chop – dull and cutting at the same time. The closer a Huey got to you the greater the resonance, eventually entering your senses through your skull rather than your ears.

Marine Clarke called over: "Birds on the way."

"I hear them," I replied trying to hide my obvious relief.

Buster came back over: "Medevac inbound, we've located a clearing fifty yards back, smoke-target imminent. Are you able to walk?"

"I'll try," I said as Bronco helped me up. I propped myself against him arm on shoulder and began to painfully shuffle towards the clearing. My legs were totally unresponsive. The irregular forest floor hindered our progress even further. Bronco called for TC to give him a hand. My buddies hastily carried me towards the clearing, which was nothing more than a modest gap in the thick canopy. I wondered in my heightened anxiety if the helicopters would have enough clearance. I needn't have bothered, the pilot placed the lead 'copter on the ground with absolute proficiency. We were generally critical of the US Forces in Vietnam; how could we not be? Charlie had kicked their arses from Quang Trì to Cấ Maừ. There was one exception: their 'chopper pilots'. We had no doubts about their skills; they could balance the skid of a Huey on a pinhead in zero visibility – they were all Aces.

Bronco and TC laid me alongside Corporal Speed and Marine Collins whilst the others loaded Dusty, Sugar, JJ, Dinger and Tommy aboard the lead Huey. Once laden the chopper thundered skyward scattering any manner of debris through the swirling downdraft.

The second helicopter swooped down with perfect timing landing almost exactly in the same place. Jumper and Speedy were swiftly taken aboard leaving Corporal Lane stooping beside me. Bronco gave me a reassuring smile. "Come on mucker," he said hauling me up to a piggyback. It took every ounce of effort to grip his strong frame as he lumbered towards the pulsing 'copter. My legs felt like lead in the cups of his hands. My neck felt so weak that I had to rest my forehead on his left shoulder. He adroitly spun round as we reached the gale-sucking portal of the chopper and gently placed my posterior on the floor of the seat-less cabin. The US Aircrew Paramedic [ACP] pulled in my legs whilst fastening my safety belt.

Jumper and Speedy were already strapped in as Bronco threw his arms round the top of my shoulders pulling my head towards him. "Y'all come back to us now, ya hear!" he hollered above the reverberation of the spinning rotors. I grabbed his left hand as he began to move away; though weak I still held it tight. Bronco gave me a further reassuring hug before letting go to give the Huey take-off clearance.

I stared out at the remainder of my compadrés, lined up, thumbs high. It was hard to leave my brothers-in-arms. We'd not been separated in our ten months in the 'Nam. I could clearly see their faces smiling mid the fluttering ragged tails of their bandannas. I nervously glanced at Jumper and Speedy as the pilot throttled up for confirmation I was not alone. The Huey vibrated as it began its ascent; it took-off so fast that I felt as if my stomach and burning bladder were going to be left behind. I winced with pain as the chopper rapidly gained height leaving the steaming canopy in its wake. Casualty evacuation helicopters had no passenger cab doors, ergo their occupants were fully exposed to the elements. The ride was a tour-de-force at the best of times; whilst ailing it was a downright nightmare!

The Bell Huey was the indisputable warhorse and workhorse of the US Forces in Vietnam. Ours had undoubtedly seen better days. It shook, groaned and rattled with every pitch and yaw. The internal fabric was threadbare. The metal frames contained layers of chipped army-green paint and there was a musty smell that mingled with the aviation fuel and heavily oxidised electrical circuits. The cab had an arrangement of bars and clips, likely placed to accommodate drip lines, and an obsolete oxygen manifold. There was a collection of US Marine Corps helmets permanently strapped to webbing on the forward bulkhead. Each, as the custom amongst the yanks in the 'Nam, had a personalised note scribed on the canvas camouflage cover. I strained to make out some of the graffiti:

KILL JUNKIE; DODGIN' DEATH-SPOOKIN' CHARLIE; HELL CAN WAIT; NATURAL BORN SINNER; CAN'T BUY ME HATE; COLOR ME DEAD.

The ACP, who had iced blue-grey eyes and several front teeth missing, was gazing at me with a deranged expression: "Souvenirs!" he cried out amid hysterical laughter, "…them lids be from boys who didn't make it. It's a fair catch; they won't be needin' 'em no more—!"

He paused briefly, likely due to the look of disapproval on my face.

"—You ought to think yourself lucky motherfucker. Some birds got that many lids on board they can't take-off!"

I disengaged his widely staring eyes and slowly shook my head, more out of pity than disgust; he'd obviously been in Vietnam too long.

I looked briefly at my comrades. Marine Collins was curled up on the floor alongside me occasionally crying out. I thought I heard him cry out for his mother, though I couldn't be sure. Either way I kept the possibility to myself. I gently rubbed his head in an attempt to offer him some comfort, not realising that I was also trying to comfort myself. Corporal Speed, who was as white as a ghost and drenched in sweat, was sitting against the forward bulkhead. He appeared to be praying whilst gripping a crucifix attached to his dog tags. I wasn't aware he was a practising Christian, he may not have been, but at that moment, he was praying hard.

I sensed the onset of another wave of delirium: flashes before my eyes, ringing in my ears – fleeting confusion and disorientation. I leaned part out of the cabin in an attempt to get a blast of air across my face. Just as I did the Huey lurched violently to port, then starboard in a continuing series of severe manoeuvres. I cried out as the safety line cut into my waist constricting my already fragile guts.

The Paramedic, who could clearly see the distress on my face, whooped excitedly amid the wildly alternating swings: "Yee-ha! ride 'em cowboy! Y'all better get used to it buddy, we're gonna be zigzaggin' all the way to the Ran'. It's crawlin' with Viet Cong guerrillas down there; they'd knock us out the sky quicker than you could say Uncle Hồ. Don't you worry none, y'all soon be in pussy heaven. White sheets, soft pillows and horny wet bitches!"

I gazed out of the cab at the rushing canopy below in a grave attempt to fight off the hallucinations. I could see the shadow of the helicopter moving laterally to our status, dancing in a succession of rapid movements across the treetops and along the undulating terraces. It appeared as if an aberration on the hillside, our contours eclipsed within the slender body. I struggled, caught in the transient world between consciousness and delirium, to make out the ghost-like frame. I deduced, in a fleeting grasp of part-reality, that the silhouette was of a dragonfly in flight imitating our every manoeuvre in perfect harmony. I was spellbound by its gracefulness. I further caught a glimpse of the lead Huey's tail as it zigzagged ahead. The whole spectacle appeared as if some elaborate choreography.

I couldn't decide which was worse as the Huey continued on its turbulent course, the enduring ague or the inexorable onset of airsickness. I couldn't get comfortable no matter which way I shifted, and the persistent report from the rotors was drumming into my brain. I felt as if a slain warrior en-route to Valhalla!

The thick canopy eventually gave way to consistent open terraces and bamboo huts. We were clearly approaching the outskirts of Lôc Nịnh. The pitch of the motor changed as the Huey glided above the furrowed roofs of the town.

"Target one-decimal mile!" the pilot called out to my obvious relief.

Within minutes the Huey banked to port and slowed to a hover above the hospital.

Rậnlạntoì, named after a 6th Century Nguyển philosopher, was positioned on the edge of the largely deserted Marine Garrison. The compound was ringed with a double line razor wire fence containing enough steel to make a full-scale replica of the Titanic. The 1920s building was constructed in typical French Colonial style. Its three-storey 'H' Block, characterised by narrow shutter-lined windows and balustrade balconies, seemed more in keeping with the sleepy Avenues of Baton Rouge than the one-storey buildings and lavish pagodas of Lôc Nịnh. The structure was wrapped in a range of climbing and overhanging plants that fluttered wildly in the wake of the choppers' downdraft. The pilot patiently hovered our Huey as the lead 'copter landed with military exactness on the helicopter pad stationed on the roof. I could clearly see the activity below. The lead Huey was surrounded by ant-like figures frantically hauling the occupants out of the cab onto waiting gurneys.

"We're going in," the pilot said as the lead helicopter took-off.

We banked and descended at a frightening rate pulling up onto the heli-pad. An army of medics ringed the Huey as the Aircrew Paramedic unbuckled my harness. The medics unceremoniously lifted the three of us onto individual gurneys, which they wheeled towards the roof lift. The gust from the chopper quickly dissipated as the open lift rumbled down the shaft. The medics didn't stand on formality; they pulled our boots and fatigues off in an almost perfect drill leaving the three of us prostrate in nought but boxer shorts. One of the crew removed my dog tags and proceeded to wrap them around my left ankle before securing them with a strip of Band Aid.

The lumbering lift seemed to take an age reaching its destination. I could still feel the vibration from the Huey resonating through the gurney against my shoulder blades, or was the vibration from the elevator? My confusion was exacerbated by a continuing afternoise, combined with the medics' constant babbling. Were they asking me questions or talking amongst themselves? Why were lights flashing in my eyes? Why did I feel as if I was still flying when I was in actuality descending a seemingly bottomless pit?

I suddenly found myself being raced down a narrow windowless corridor resembling something out of *The Twilight Zone* towards a reception area filled with echoes. I'm convinced I could hear screaming. Maybe the walls contained memories of multiple amputees', their tormented journey towards a final separation from limbs that once carried them through childhood games.

A blanched fluorescent light that filled a stark room replaced the dimness. A male nurse started to ask a tirade of questions after examining my dog tags.

"Name, Rank, Number and Religion?" he asked, without giving eye contact.

"Morris, Barry. Royal Marine Lance Corporal, RM: 112463. Atheist," I answered flinching in the torrent of bright light.

"It says Roman Catholic on your dog tag—"

"I don't give a fuck what it says, I'm an Atheist; I don't want any Priest hovering round me!"

"Fair enough buddy. You got any allergies?"

"Yeah, fuckin' mosquitoes!"

I couldn't decide if I felt relieved at being in hospital or frightened by the prospect of what was to come in the bustle of triage. My anxiety was reinforced by the approach of a female nurse, who looked more like an East German hammer thrower than a medic, with a probe on the end of spiralling wire. "I'm gonna have to stick this up your ass fella, nothin' personal," she said, rolling me onto my side before forcing the probe into the delicate flesh of my rectum. "This boy's temperature's a racin'..." she called as she observed the readout on the digital gauge hanging from a stainless steel hook, "a hundred-and-four an' risin'!"

"Give him a spell in the tub," a voice shouted amid medical staff calling out the temperatures of the other lads scattered throughout the sterile chamber.

'What's a spell in the tub?' I thought as the nurse removed the probe. I was soon to find out as a gang of medics surrounded my position and rolled me onto a rubber mat. They carried me into a tiled room where I could hear running water.

"Listen up buddy..." a male nurse who I could not see said, "we're gonna have to dump you in an Ice bath, do-ya-hear?"

I was about to tell him to 'fry his arse' when the personnel lowered me into a stainless steel bath.

"Holy fuckin' shit!" I cried out in a high pitch voice as I was engulfed by numbingly cold water. I struggled in the chill to establish a steady breathing pattern. I felt as if surrounded by a thousand daggers. I began to shiver uncontrollably and in a recoil reaction attempted to exit the steel tub; the staff were having none of it.

"Come on babe take slow deep breaths now," a nurse in a polythene apron said.

'You take fuckin' deep breaths!' I felt like screaming, but my vocal cords had apparently imploded.

The nurse added to my torment by pouring the freezing water over my head: "We gotta get your temperature down. Come on cobber, talk to me, what's ya name? Where ya from?"

I wanted to cry out in anguish as the icy soak penetrated my bones, yet I felt compelled to answer her questions.

"Barry..." I said as my teeth clattered, "I'm from Liverpool."

"Oh what! My sister lives just outside Liverpool, New South Wales that is."

I was aware that I'd stopped shivering. I'd also regained a steady breathing pattern. I had either run out of energy or simply become used to the cold, or did the nurse's soothing words divert my attention?

"What's an Aussie doing in this shit hole?" I asked.

"Workin' my ticket; it's as good a place as any. Come to think of it what's a bunch of Poms doing out here—?"

I was about to answer when I was yanked from the tub as unceremoniously as I was dumped.

"Catch ya later mate," the Aussie nurse said as I was hauled back to triage.

The temperature probe was again rammed into my rectum as I was slid back onto the gurney and wrapped in a towel.

"I'm gonna leave ya here a whiles," the hammer throwing nurse said with a smile that belied her appearance, "y'all be okay."

The bleached rays from the fluorescent tubes hurt my eyes. Blocking out the light was no relief, I felt as if in an uncontrollable spin each time I closed them. The resounding noise added to my misery. The room was buzzing: talking, shouting, cursing and praying. The clatter resembled a weapon emplacement before an assault on a barricade. I heard a warning bleep ring out in the clamour. I strained to see if it was the alarm on my digital readout. It appeared to be Jumper's. I vaguely caught the sound of his voice as the triage team carted him off to the wet room. Something about him, "…ripping off peoples heads and shoving them up their fucking arseholes!"

I spent the remaining forty minutes drifting in-and-out of consciousness. Somewhere along the line a medic inserted a cannula in my left arm and connected it to an intravenous drip. My body was so numb I failed to flinch as the needle penetrated. I could hear Lance Corporal Bell on an adjacent gurney rambling about somebody snatching his rifle. I tried to offer comfort but to no avail; he was clearly hallucinating.

The crew placed Dinger, Sugar, Tommy and me in a lift informing us we were to be taken onto a ward. We were all in a pitiful state. Tommy asked about the others; an attendant said some of the lads had already been taken up and the others would follow. I'm sure we all felt the same as our gurneys were wheeled down the colourless corridors. We didn't want to be separated. We needed the mutual reassurance each of us offered.

I fought to stay awake as hushed voices surrounded me. I vaguely remember being lifted onto a bed, my eyelids rolling ever down. 'I have to stay awake,' I thought, 'I've got to wait for the others.' The room turned, my eyelids acquiesced, my body descended, slowly spinning into an abyss.

I awoke in a state of bewilderment. It must have taken all of 5 minutes to focus or recognise any objects within my environment. I knew I was in hospital – the drama preceding my predicament was hard to forget. I lay on my back staring at the elaborate ceiling aloft, its jagged cornice resembling inverted steps in the sky. I could see the transparent drip bag suspended from the metal 'T' frame, its clear fluid slowly dripping in the reservoir. I had the mother of all hangovers and a highly unpleasant aftertaste in my parched mouth. I shifted in an attempt to acquire some comfort in my perceptively concrete padded bed, but decided against the strategy after being hit by a wave of nausea. I lay perfectly motionless trying to discern aspects of my surroundings. All was silent, except for the faint sound of music. The melodic orchestral piece was too inaudible to identify. Nevertheless, it soothed my immediate anxiety.

The silhouette of a nurse moving slowly towards my bed caught my attention. I briefly closed my eyes pretending to be asleep. I don't know why, maybe I thought I was expected to still be in stupor. The staff nurse slowly raised my wrist to check my pulse. She had an unusual face: chiselled out cheekbones and hard mouth below strikingly gentle eyes. A strange incongruity; plain but pretty at the same time. Her ebony complexion looked striking contra to her starched white uniform. She had short curly hair cut close to head. Her hands looked work hardened, though her slender fingers had a gentle touch. She looked down at me with a broad smile: "You with us now?"

"Think so..." I replied in a drowsy voice that was hardly recognisable, "I feel like I've been hit by a train."

"Figures, you got Malaria."

"Strain-seven?"

"That be the bitch."

"What time is it?"

"Time ain' your concern presently," she said in a distinct southern states accent. "Let time be, it'll still be there when you next need to chase it."

"Are the other boys okay?"

"They're fine, nursin' sore heads like you."

"They haven't separated us have they? I want to stay—"

"Don't you worry none...y'all together."

The staff nurse removed a thermometer from a container pinned to the bedside.

"You're not gonna stick that up my arse are you?" I enquired remembering the painful anal probe whilst in triage.

"Not unless those bugs have moved your asshole to below your nose!" she said whilst popping the glass tube in my gaping mouth. She pulled back the bedclothes after reading the thermometer and gently pressed me in the area of my bladder. I winced with discomfort. "Sorry honey, I needed to check your bladder. It's distended, you're gonna have to pass water."

"I'm not sure if I can—"

"You're gonna have to! I don't wanna have to catheterise you."

"What does that mean?"

"You don't wanna know. Come-on honey..." she said, handing me a disposable bottle, "I'll be back directly."

I managed, after three aborted attempts, to take a much needed pee. The discomfort of the hot pungent liquid was less uninviting than the thought of having a tube rammed up my wedding tackle. The staff nurse returned to collect the brimming carafe-like container and then seemed to be on her way without a bye or leave. She stopped at the end of the bed and slowly turned her head. "You can go back to pretending to be asleep now," she whispered with a smile.

I returned the smile as she moved gracefully across the ward. I suddenly felt a little less uncomfortable. I felt I was in safe hands; in the hands of somebody kind who, even for an instant, made me feel at ease. I lay my head on my pillow with a wish that I would get better acquainted with her. Within a very short time I no longer needed to pretend to be asleep.

06:45: Ward 6, Rậnlạntoì, US Marine Corps Hospital, Thursday 21 June.

I've had the misfortune of spending time in a number of hospitals around the world. Freedom Fields, New York with a switchblade knife wound in my lower abdomen, the legacy of a barroom brawl in Brooklyn. Trondheim General, Norway after a badly timed parachute jump onto an icefield put me and four members of the section in an orthopaedic ward. And BMH Hong Kong with delayed concussion and double vision after one of the toughest fights I've ever had in the boxing ring. Without exception, every morning routine has been the same – lights on at 06:45, hastily applied meds followed by breakfast at a time when the last thing you wanted to do was eat.

I quickly discovered in the morning clamour that Rậnlạntoì was no different. I was woken by the clatter of mess tins and the whoosh of heavy blinds being raised. I scanned the enormous twenty-bed ward; all beds vacant save for the eight members of 2: Bravo 6 Platoon. Sugar was to my right, still asleep, with Tommy, Dinger and JJ in the three beds to my left. Jumper, Speedy and Dusty occupied the three beds immediately facing us. I had a restless night, transitory periods of being half awake trying to make out the shapes, shadows and sounds that surrounded me. I vaguely recall one of the lads crying out in the night and another being violently sick.

A small Hispanic nurse approached: "Would you like any breakfast?"

"I don't think I'll be able to keep anything down."

"How about some juice or warm milk?"

"I'll try," I said, knowing there was little chance I'd even attempt to take anything into my fragile body. I spent the whole morning trying to adapt to my condition. I couldn't determine which of the erratic cycles was worse, the spasmodic shivers or burning sweats. Either way, if I stayed relatively motionless I just about managed to maintain some semblance of comfort. I still had a raging thirst, though the hydrophobia had thankfully subsided and the medication was beginning to ease my pain. I also experienced a series of episodic flashbacks a factor that caused me some consternation, unaware that the phenomenon was a necessity, a way of helping me come to terms with the previous days' events. Lunch remained as untouched as breakfast and other than some salutations to the lads whom it appeared were feeling just as sorry for themselves, I stayed relatively quiet.

I dozed until the rota change at 14:00, another collection of new faces, save for the black nurse from the previous night. I surveyed her, trying not to make it obvious I was looking, as she walked up and down the ward. I scanned her identification tag as she came over, 'Staff Nurse B Ebotée', it read.
"How are you today?" she asked.
"Lousy," I nervously replied, "my sheets are soaking wet."
"I'll get them changed for you. I see from your chart that you haven't eaten," she said whilst regulating the valve on my drip line.
"I've got no appetite."
"You've gotta eat. You need to keep up your strength to fight those bugs."
"Oh yeah..." I said with a grin, "so they won't move my arsehole to below my nose."
"Right-on!" she replied, smiling back. "They'll move a lot more if'n you don't take some sustenance."
"I'm nauseous and I've got a taste in my mouth like rotten eggs."
"That'll be the quinine sulphate," she said, adjusting my pillows. "I'll get some magnesia to settle your stomach."
I got a closer look at her as she stood aside my bed. I guessed she must have been in her mid-thirties. Nevertheless, her skin was still taught and as smooth and shiny as a fresh aubergine. There were a few visible wisps of grey around her temple, a feature she apparently had no intention of trying to hide. Her voice was particularly distinct, as clear as spring water and crisp as Kentucky fried chicken. I could've listened to her talking all day.
I had my first chance since the onset of the ailment to talk to the lads. Jumper was as resilient as always and Sugar managed to maintain his usual flow of humour. Marine Jeffers gave us cause for concern. He seemed to be in a constant slumber. He'd apparently had a convulsion in triage. Nursing staff spent the whole morning monitoring him. Tommy had a look of death whilst Dinger, Speedy and Dusty spent the majority of time sleeping. None of us were in the mood for conversation, yet I felt it important to communicate. We felt vulnerable in our new environment. We needed to talk to reinforce our fellowship, confirm that we were still part of a unit. Tommy, as always, seemed alert despite his pallor.
"You okay?" I enquired.
"I've had better days. What the fuck was all that about in triage?" he asked referring to the ice-plunge we'd received.
"They had to get our temperatures down," I replied, though I guess his question was rhetorical.
"Nearly gave me a fuckin' heart attack!"
"I woke up with three Adam's apples," Sugar cut in, "had to swallow hard

to get me balls' back in me sack!"

The three of us laughed though not without some discomfort.

A Senior Doctor carried out an extraordinary ward round at 16:00. He reminded us that we were still on duty whilst on the ward and asked for a Platoon spokesman. Corporal Farr, a veteran of conflicts in Cyprus, Aden and Northern Ireland, acted as the natural choice. Tommy was one of the most popular members of the Platoon. He was a particular soul mate of mine. The two of us would often sit up until the early hours talking about any number of topics. Some of the lads nicknamed us *The Professors.* Personally I found that flattering.

At around 17:00 staff started asking if we could manage an evening meal. Staff Nurse Ebotée strolled over to my bed: "How about you honey, could I persuade you try something light?"

"Like what?"

"Some toasted rye maybe with a thin layer of peanut butter and some soft fruit?"

Her voice was so anodyne it was hard for me to refuse. "Okay…can you take my dog tags from around my ankle?" I continued, hoping that I could get her into a conversation.

"Sure," she replied, gently raising the covers to expose my left leg.

"How come they strap the tags on there anyway?"

"Easy identification in the morgue," she whispered, "the creeps down there are only interested lookin' at your feet."

"Very comforting," I said as she removed the tape and hung my tags' on the bedrail.

"How long have you been here?"

"Since 'sixty-eight, arrived at the beginning of the Tết Offensive. Walked straight from the plane into triage; didn't even get me time to unpack."

"Blimey, that must have been a barrel of laughs."

"It was one hell of an initiation I don't mind tellin' you. Medevacs were hoverin' like bees waitin' to get into a hive. We all ended up on double shifts. There were that many injured we ran out of blood. The morgue couldn't take all the dead; they ended up laying the body bags on the grass outside. You could see them from the balcony, looked like dominoes in a row."

"Shit and I thought *we* had it bad."

"Everyone got it bad out here honey," she said, moving on to Tommy.

Her promise of a light meal transpired and it was most welcome. By late afternoon the shivers and sweats had largely abated though we all remained fragile. Lance Corporal Bell asked one of the staff if we could get out of bed. She gave him a swift response: "Honey, if you put your feet on the floor your nose will surely follow…give it time, huh."

The early evening light quickly faded; the onset of night seemed somewhat strange. 'Where had the day gone?' I thought. Come to think of it, where had the last two days gone? Staff Nurse Ebotée noticed my perplexed expression: "You okay honey?"

"Yeah..." I replied nonchalantly, "just tryin' to get used to our new routines."

"I've bin tryin' to make out your accent, kinda familiar."

"I'm from Liverpool, what about you, where you from?"

"Birming-ham," she replied, a deliberate break in the intonation, "that be the one in Alabamie [Alabama] not little ol' England."

"Ebotée?" I said gesticulating towards her nametag, "...that's not southern states."

"West African, Leonard be my christened name. I changed it after searchin' my roots."

"What's the *B* stand for?"

"Billie."

"Don't tell me your parents named you after Billie Holiday?"

"Nope, my Aunt Billie. She was a Civil Rights activist; got killed in the disturbances of 'thirty-six, least-wise that's what the big-dicks in City Hall called them. We be sayin' they be justifiable demonstrations against the Colour Bar."

"It's better now though isn't it?"

"Is it..." she responded with a hint of anger that wasn't aimed at me, "so how come after nine years of exemplary service in the Medical Corps I'm still only a Staff Nurse?"

"I'm sorry," I said avoiding eye contact.

"Why? ain' your fault, seems to me there ain' a racist bone in your body."

"I should hope not, how can you tell?"

"You can see it in your eyes; hear it in your voice. When you be black in Alabamie you get to learn these things."

"There are plenty of racists and xenophobes in my country too you know."

"Oh yeah, so how many niggers bin lynched 'round your parts of late?"

"None," I replied, feeling a tad regretful that I'd continued the topic.

"I've bin 'round yo' liddle ol' island," she said with a broad grin. "I likes England, people seem less hostile, though I knows you got yo' dinkberries, every place has."

"Did you visit Liverpool?"

"Sure, alongs with Manchester, Yoke (York) and Birmingham. Had to go there, see what the other town was like."

"And?"

"It was big. They were all big an' real friendly."

"What were you doing in England?"
"Just travellin', though I visited Liverpool to see where my Ancestors landed."
"In a slave ship!"
"There you go again," Billie, said gently touching my arm, "sayin' things like it's yo' fault. Yeah, in a slave ship on route to the plantations. I visited your Cunard buildings, got a look at some ol' shippin' registers. The gal in the office was real nice. Dressed up like yo' Twiggy but a bit big if the truth be told. She made a pot of tea an' we got talkin'. I couldn't figure out how comes this white lady was bein' so nice after I'd just met her an' all, but that's the way you people be. Reckons I'm gonna like havin' you boys on this ward."
"The shipping manifests..." I called out as she moved towards the office, "did you find what you were looking for?"
"No, the boat owners weren't interested in slave's names. The inventories just recorded numbers: those boarded on sailin', those fit for market, those dead or dyin' an' the likes. But I knows they were on one of the ships. Don't ask me how, I just gotta a feelin'."
I smiled to myself as she walked down the ward. It felt good talking to her. I felt as if I'd known her for sometime; that was likely due to her charisma. She had natural warmth about her, a way of making you feel comfortable. She said she'd "...enjoy having us on the ward." I had a feeling I was going to enjoy being on her ward, regardless of the fact that I still felt like shit.

Prior to the 22:00 roster change, nursing staff walked around asking us if there was anything we needed. Most of the men asked for some toiletries and stationery to write home. Sugar asked for a crate of Bud' and got short shift, whilst Tommy asked if we could have a change of underwear.
"That's what I like to see a nice smile," Billie said as she drew near.
"That's cos you've come up to my bed."
"Put yo' silver tongue away! Anything you need afore I go?"
"You could get me some writing paper and a pencil if you'd be so kind."
"You wanna write home?"
"Maybe later, truth is I've been writing a journal since I've been in the 'Nam. I wanna keep it up, record as much as I can."
"Sheeit, you really writin' about your time out here?"
"I'm trying; problem is there isn't always a lot to write about. Most days are pretty monotonous. We can go weeks without any action then, suddenly, all hell breaks loose. Most of the time I just write my thoughts."
Billie looked thoughtful for a second, kind of half interested, half confused: "You can still write home...ain' you gotta girl?"

“Did have, it wasn’t anything big. We both kinda stopped writing.”

“Best way – ain’ no girl in her right mind should keep it on with a boy in the ’Nam, best forget him. If he makes it on home, y’all can pick it up again. If he don’t, it don’t make no mind cos he’s already done gone.”

“Sounds a bit harsh.”

“Everythin’ harsh in this place, y’all should know that. Here you keep your cards packed tight in the box. Y’all don’t smile lessen you bin smiled too. You agree with whatever hue and cry be in favour an’ be silent when silence tells you it be time. An’ if you gonna cry, best does your cryin’ in the rain.”

“Sounds a bit like another place we’ve toured.”

“Ireland?”

“Right, how did you guess?”

“I listen to the news don’t-ya-know. I bin followin’ those troubles on over there. Seems kinda sad people not bein’ able to see eye-to-eye over religion. War’s always bad, but civil war that kinda seems worse. Brothers an’ sisters fightin’ their kind don’t seem just.”

“It’s not just about religion; it’s a wee bit more complex than that though I know what you mean. Fact is most of the folk over there are decent, kinda like this place.”

“Seems to me it’s always the decent folk that suffer.”

“Ain’t that the truth!”

“I’ll see what I can do ’bout gettin’ you a pad. An’ we’ll get y’all some tooth-wash an’ soap, seein’ as you guys only arrived in the skin that wraps your bones.”

Billie checked Jumper, JJ and Dusty before scurrying off, eager to complete her tasks before going off duty no doubt. Some twenty minutes later she walked over to my bed concealing something under her cape. She glanced towards the office to check that no one was looking before slipping a large flat object under the bedclothes. “Don’t be conspicuous with it now…” she whispered, “we’re not supposed to hand out supplies.”

I thanked her, without knowing what it was she slipped under my covers, as she retired for the night. Once all had settled, I secretly examined my newly acquired bounty: a large A4 notebook with *Property of the United States Government*, printed on its rear. 'Oh yeah,' I thought as I prepared to record a chronology of the recent dramatic events. 'I'm going to enjoy writing on this!'

Friday 22 June.

I woke up after a surprisingly good nights sleep. My appetite was slowly coming back and I was beginning to feel a bit more human. After breakfast staff issued us each with a polythene bag containing three pairs of boxer shorts and a range of toiletries, as well as a large bar of chocolate, a packet of mints, a bottle of orange squash and a miniature Gideon's Bible. I eventually used mine to prop up one of the uneven legs on my bed – come in really handy. Staff carried out blood and urine tests after ward round and extracted our intravenous drips; from then on medication was oral.

We soon became acquainted with staff. They worked a three sectioned, eight-hour alternating shift pattern. Five days on, two days off. The primary shift consisted of Nurse Gerrard [Phillipa] a tall strawberry blond with a thick Wisconsin accent. Nurse Richie [Molly] a bubbly woman who seemed to be forever smiling (if anyone could brighten up your day it was Molly) and Ward Orderly Leigh [Chauncey] a thickset black man from Chorlton, Louisiana. Chauncey was as strong as an ox and always on the make. He would tiptoe round asking us in a hushed voice if there was anything we needed. He reckoned he could lay his hands on anything from top quality Moroccan hashish (though why anyone would want to purchase this in a place abundant with cannabis was beyond us) to newspaper wrapped fish and chips. Once past Chauncey's façade we found him to be one of the nicest guys we'd come across in Charlieville.

Sister Calley [Vinegar tits] was the Governor, with Staff Nurse Ebotée acting as Deputy. Vinegar was a fierce woman who, rumour had it, was thrown out of the Gestapo for cruelty. She was a true-grit Republican who ruled the ward with an iron fist. The term 'autocratic' didn't do justice to her modus operandi. She totally lacked charisma and seemed to be devoid of humanity. The staff, understandably, appeared to be in awe of her, though their deference was more to do with a need to get by rather than a motivated loyalty. It was apparent that Vinegar expected her patients to kowtow to her unequivocal authority. She once admonished Sugar for cursing demanding that he, "...modify his language while on *her* ward." He apologised profusely promising to pronounce fuck with a 'ph' and cunt with a 'k'.

Billie's approach to staff if or when Vinegar was off ward was totally different. Staff were more relaxed and appeared to be more industrious. Chauncey in particular was happier when Vinegar wasn't in-situ, as on the 22nd. Around mid afternoon Billie asked Chauncey to begin securing the outer shutters.

"What's up?" Speedy asked him as he began manhandling the louvered coverings.

"Ain' you bin listening to the news? There's a typhoon a brewin', big swirlin' bitch comin' in from the South China Sea. Y'all better tuck yo'selves in the-night, we all in for a bumpy ride, hot damn!"

We had reservations about whether the building would stand up to a typhoon. If the external fabric was anything like the internal fittings and decoration then we would be in for more than just a bumpy ride. The former Jewel in the Crown of French Indo-Chinese Medical Institutions was badly run down. The whole building reeked of disinfectant, likely applied to mask the smells emanating from the poorly serviced drains and rampant dry rot. Ceiling fans hung motionless alongside dimly lit globes. The elaborate teak and ash floors hadn't seen a lick of varnish since the '60s and the baroque arch supports had long lost their palatial appearance. There were large gaps in the sash window frames covered with woefully inadequate ducting tape. The walls were heavily stained with mouldy damp patches and the electrical circuits sparked every time a breaker was closed. We were inspired by the total professionalism and dedication of the nursing staff. The building, on the other hand, left a lot to be desired.

Late afternoon Staff Nurse Ebotée sauntered round asking the boys if we would like some books to read. She began to compile a list. Jumper appealed for comics. Dinger, JJ and Speedy asked if she could get hold of some shitkickers (western adventures). Tommy said anything but a war story whilst Sugar, with his usual wry grin, said the only thing he could read was the names of the pussy in *Playboy* magazine.

"How about you," Billie asked, seemingly awaiting another wisecrack.

"He'll want one of those big fuck off 'ardbacks that no-one else can read without a dictionary," Sugar chortled.

"Shit-in-it you," I said, "be content with your tits and fanny. I don't suppose you could get me any science fiction; Asimov, Simak or the like?"

"We can try. Would *sir* like anything else if they don't be to hand?" she responded in a jocular manner.

"Well now..." I said, joining in the fun, "I don't suppose *madam* could acquire anything by Orwell, Wallace Stevens, Steinbeck or Chomsky—"

"Chomsky! sheeit, you won't finds any Chomsky round here. He's too socially minded for the rednecks in this little ole cow town; Steinbeck likewise."

"That's a pity; dad gave me *The Grapes of Wrath* [John Steinbeck] to read when I was about twelve. He asked what I thought after I'd read it. Trouble is it didn't really impact on me. My dad said I'd probably understand its significance when I was a bit older. I've been planning to re-read it ever since."

"No offence honey, but I think yo' daddy be meanin' you'd understand it more when you be quite a bit older."

"I'm nearly twenty—!"

"Well now don't that make you the ole bird-dog in the bush!" Billie chortled.

Billie never found any Steinbeck or Chomsky. Nonetheless, she managed to acquire Clifford Simak's *Ring Around the Sun.* I'd read it before but didn't have the heart to tell her, particularly since she'd gone to so much trouble.

Prior to tea Billie come up to my bed carrying a kidney bowl. She had a half serious, half empathetic look on her face: "Your blood counts way down honey."

"So," I said, observing the translucent syringe containing a molasses-like liquid.

"So you're gonna have to take a course of iron."

"Wonderful!" I muttered, rolling onto my side in preparation for the injection.

"You've got 'O' Negative did you know that?" she said, scrutinising the contents of the syringe.

"Yeah and I know it's rare."

"It's also prone to anaemia, particularly since you got those parasites eatin' away at your red blood cells. Don't you trouble now…" Billie said as she prepared a swab, "I'll be gentle."

Something told me she would be gentle, though I would concur this may've had something to do with the fact that I was sweet on her.

"Good grief," she said as she ran the damp swab over my left buttock, "you got no ass! just bone. Don't you eat?"

"Like a horse," I said with a forced enthusiasm.

"We gals gotta sayin' for guys like you," she said as she expertly threw the needle into my flesh, "lucky son-bitch!" Billie was gentle, or as gentle as you can be injecting the syrup-like fluid.

"How many more of those have I got to look forward to?"

"Not many. You're young and strong, shouldn't take a whiles."

Dinger and JJ's haemoglobin levels also gave cause for concern, though JJ escaped with nothing more than a course of tablets.

It must have been obvious as the evening rolled on that I fancied Billie. It would've taken a blind man not to notice me eyeing her as she went about her duties. I wasn't the only one that took a fancy to one of the nurses. All the lads had their favourites. Corporal Speed was plainly sweet on Molly; he used to beam at her presence. Sugar, Jumper and JJ used to leer at Phillipa as she walked down the ward. I couldn't blame them; she had legs up to her armpits and brown eyes the size of saucers. The three of them would gesticulate to each other as she swept passed, the usual vulgar stuff. Sugar's face was a picture one morning. Phillipa approached him with a large bowl and sponge in preparation to give him a bed bath. He sat in bed with his mouth gaping; for once it appeared he had nothing to say!

*

The rain lashed against the rattling shutters, a precursor to the typhoon due at midnight. The wind whistled through cracks in the crumbling mortar inexorably stubborn in its fight against gravity. One of the redundant ceiling fans tortuously rotated, feathered by air venting the deckhead void. Its worn bearings groaned – a swansong for the once proud building. The lights occasionally dimmed changing the craggy shadows on the flaking walls, a grotesque picture show with quadraphonic sound effects. The wild foliage that hugged the structure amplified the intermittent gusts evoking memories of the firestorm witnessed in Nha Trang. It was not a night to be out in the bush. I didn't envy the guys out on patrol. I felt safe, cocooned, even in that perceivably fragile structure.

Nursing staff came round with supper at 21:00, the normal vittles – tea and Maryland cookies. The Americans had the technology to send men to the moon, but they couldn't make a decent pot of tea to save their lives. Billie's joyful face made up for the foul tasting beverage. I'd convinced myself that she had manipulated the sequence to ensure she delivered my tray last. "Wind's getting' up an' this ain' a half of it yet," she said placing the tray on my swing-table.

"Have you experienced many typhoons since being here?"

"Couple…real bad one in 'seventy. A lot of people from the town got injured. We took some in, broke the rules. Charlie must-a been amongst 'em, but we got away with it. I see you've started your book," she said, observing *Ring Around the Sun* laying pages down on my bedside table.

"Yeah…" I said, still unable to tell her I'd already read it.

"I can't make head-nor-tail out'a those sci-fi books. What you get from them?"

"They're different, they stretch my imagination. Everyone can picture a cow town in a shitkicker, or a sun bleached fort in a Beau Geste novel. And anyone who's been in love can connect with a romantic novella. But science fiction that's totally different. When I read Asimov and Simak I just float onto another sphere. There's something magic about forming new concepts in your mind's eye. Something challenging, unique and distinct in every chapter. Take Simak's *Ring Around the Sun*, he postulates that there's a parallel galaxy, a mirror image of our own embodying billions of stars along with pulsars and quasars. And coequal solar systems possessing advanced beings, maybe even mirror images of ourselves."

"Sheeit!" Billie said picking up the book and observing that I'd thumbed through less than twelve pages, "…you got all that from just readin' a few pages?"

'Oh shit!' I thought. "No…" I responded deploying that uniquely male strategy 'the thoughtful delay whilst you devise a convincing lie', "I kinda know the story from—"

It was useless. Billie's almost straight smile and half frown said it all. "Why didn't you tell me you'd read it," she said, playfully slapping my leg with the book.

"I didn't wanna bother you. You seemed to go to so much trouble getting hold of it."

"There's plenty of books downstairs. It so happens I'm lookin' for some readin' for my two days off. What else would you like?"

I was thoughtful a moment, trawling through editions digested and to be read.

"There is a book, it's a while since I set eyes on it," I said to Billie's obvious interest, "its entitled *The Outer Edge*, a story about the crew of a supply vessel blown to the other side of the galaxy after our sun self-destructs in a colossal supernova. It chronicles the crews' struggle to survive; trying to come to terms with the obliteration of earth and adapt to a future as nomads. Their desperate search for a desert island planet. Negotiating the Pleiades cluster and spiralling the perilous Crab Nebula, a giant remnant supernova dust-cloud with its distinctive pulsar flashing at thirty times per second, red, to orange, to yellow, to green, to blue. A constant beacon twinkling amid the embrace of the nebula, beautiful and dangerous at the same time. The crews' exploration of Baharé, a planet abounding with precious minerals. Mountains of gold and platinum, valueless in the absence of a market. A world with luminous turquoise rain clouds the size of Lake Michigan. Where every sunset is preceded by horizon wrapped rainbows, each coloured strip a thousand earth-miles high. A land where multi-coloured interactive flora flourish all year round – trees that sing as if landlocked whales. A planet with an eco-system so finely balanced that all pollutants are instantaneously neutralised and all bacteria benign, some are even intelligent. The groups' encounters with the Dakâhran; beings so harmonious that concepts such as oppression, malevolence and conflict belong only in ancient books, and so advanced they communicate via thought. A race that uses technology only for the greater good and their continuing survival."

"How does it end?" she asked with the eagerness of a child awaiting the conclusion of a bedtime story.

"The crew perish; unfit to exist amongst such progressive entities. They simply couldn't contain their negative human attributes. Intolerance, mistrust, greed, jealousy, arrogance; the need to master and control others. The Dakâhran ostracised them, left them to their demise."

"I can look out for it," she said, forever accommodating. "What's it called again?"

I suddenly felt guilty and a little conceited: "You won't find it; its writer's

unknown. Its not even in print, just scribbled onto pages stacked in a box."
Billie looked at me, unsure at first: "Sheeit! you made all that up?"
"Yeah…completed it a while back. Started writing it at school, during history lessons mostly, never saw the need to learn about who'd been fucking who in the Royal household. One of the teachers caught me writing a chapter once. Made me rip it up and throw it in the bin. Didn't he look the arsehole trying to drive home in a car with two flat tyres!"
"Oh mama!" she giggled, "…I guess its different strokes an' all, though I reckons that sci-fi's too much like tryin' to assimilate the encyclopaedia of tropical diseases. I likes to relax when I read."
"I bet you like all that romantic shit don't you?"
"Do not! Though I won't deny I likes a story where people use their love to win the day. Love's one of the greatest gifts a person can give."
"I won't deny that though you don't see a lot of it round this place."
"Its there, if you look hard enough."
"Pity you have to look."
Billie looked pensive for a second: "*Pity not the land where you have to search for love, pity the land that has no love*," she said, staring as if into a void.
"Martin Luther King," I followed, recognising the maxim from a speech delivered during the '63 Civil Rights disturbances.
"Right-on! You ain' as dumb as you look."
"I resemble that remark…" I returned laughing with her.
The time as always swiftly rolled on. I was conscious that Billie had to take care not to leave herself open to accusations of favouritism. She moved on, assuring me she would find another book for me to read. She suggested, in the meantime, I carried on '…ridin' them rings 'round the sun.' "You never know," she whispered before departing, "you might just bump into the crew of the ship searchin' for their new home on the *other side*!"
I lay in the dark at lights out listening to the wind intensifying. Some of the shutters began to clatter. I hoped that the gale wouldn't keep me awake. Somewhere between worrying about the cyclone and thinking of how nice it would be to have a candlelit dinner with Billie, I fell to sleep.

Saturday 23 June.

The typhoon never came our way, except for sustaining peripheral winds and squally showers. Chauncey, after bidding us all "Good mornin'," opened the shutters and windows letting in welcome rays of sunlight and much needed fresh air.
By day three we were accustomed to the ward's routine: 06:00 shift change,

breakfast 07:00, swiftly followed by the Việt Kieư cleaners. We were amazed how they managed to keep the ward so clean with their bamboo and straw brooms and Tộnkin sponges. The linen trolley squeaked its way down the central isle at 09:00. The immaculate blue-white sheets, each folded into uniform triangles, bristled with static as the auxiliaries remade the beds with military speed and precision.

Doctors' rounds, for what they were worth, were at 10:00. We found the ritual highly amusing. Vinegar would walk in-step alongside the practitioner with the duty staff nurse walking in step behind. All questions and answers were addressed through the sister. If she couldn't give an answer she would turn to staff and bark orders to, "...collate the information and report back to me at once!" The remaining changes were at 14:00 and 22:00, though the interchanging rotas left us baffled.

Mealtimes were a hoot. We would be given a daily choice of Vietnamese or American cuisine. Notwithstanding, we'd receive the same American hash every day. Chipped beef and burgers that smelled like horseshit; reconstituted egg and mashed potatoes that had a texture like latex and tasted like Pollyfiller. Sugar reckoned the pizzas were made out of discarded Frisbees and the Danish pastries out of corrugated cardboard, and he was convinced that some twat had stolen all the waffles and replaced them with manhole covers.

Sugar – unable to take the swill any more – asked Phillipa if there was any chance of a 'carry out'.

"What!" a bemused Phillipa said, "you hate this place so much you tired of livin'?"

"Nah..." a somewhat baffled Sugar answered, "it's just the chow, its crap!"

"That's no reason to wanna die!" Phillipa said confusing him even further.

"I think in these parts a carry out means leaving in a body bag," I cut in.

"Nah, not that, I mean a *carry out*, yer know – a Chinky or an Indian or a big fuck off pizza!" (Fuck pronounced with a 'ph' of course.)

"This is Lôc Nịnh not Long Island," Phillipa chuckled, "y'all won't find any Italiano outside those gates a-yonder."

The ward was always ringing with laughter and it wasn't just Sugar who provided the entertainment. Marine Miller was dozing post breakfast when Staff Nurse Ebotée unceremoniously pulled back the covers in preparation for a bed bath. Unfortunately, he was sporting a 'morning glory': "Woo'ee!" she cried out, "ain't you got a sack full o' beans. How come you packin' a pistol, you got dirty thoughts or you just glad to see me?"

Billie hollered down the ward to Nurse Richie amid a chorus of hysterical laughter: "Molly! you still puttin' that stuff in these boys drinks?"

"Sure am!" Molly returned.

"Well judgin' by the lead in this boy's barrel it ain't workin'!"

Dusty desperately tried to hide his obvious embarrassment. Unfortunately he had seven members of 2: Bravo 6 Platoon to contend with as well as the nursing staff.

"Fuck me!" Sugar roared. "Who's as hard as a chocolate frog? Who can only turn over on his back in bed?"

"You dirty little bastard..." Speedy joined in, "pitching a pork-pole tent in the middle of the fuckin' mornin'!"

"Oh lord…" Billie chortled looking at Dusty, "ain't you a pretty picture; yo' face is as red as a mosquito's belly after a good feed. I shouldn't worry none, ain' nothin' a gal likes better than a good stiffy!"

Post lunch, Billie asked us if we would like a movie? We were taken aback, we all though she was joshing: "What's this?" she asked after her question was greeted with stunned silence. "You boys like your own company that much?"

"**No!**" we all responded.

"Can we really have a film?" Marine Jeffers asked.

"Well didn't I say!" Billie cried out in her usual jocose tone. "What kinda movie would you boys be likin', as if I needed to ask!"

"Linda Lovelace does Bravo Platoon!" Lance Corporal Bell acclaimed amid cries of laughter.

"Yeah," Sugar joined in, "followed by 'Bravo Platoon does Charlieville,' a raunchy tale about the meanest bunch of motherfuckin' pussy-lickin' twats in Southeast Asia. Produced and Directed by Her-re Cunt...with a K!"

Staff Nurse Ebotée stood in the middle of the ward, arms folded, a droll look of disapproval on her face. "Molly!" she hollered desperately trying to keep a straight face whilst playfully tapping her foot on the floor.

"Yeah," Molly replied standing beside Phillipa, both with a likewise look.

"You sure yo' puttin' that stuff in these boys drinks?"

"Yes ma'am…" Molly said slowly scanning our faces, "I can double the dose if it be in the interest of some order on this ward."

"Are-aye," Sugar groaned, "don't do that, we need the lead in our pencils."

"Honey you can have as much lead in yo' pencil as you want…" Billie said, "as long as you don't do any *handwriting* while you're on this ward!"

They must have heard the resulting laughter in Eastern Cambodia. Everyone was splitting their sides. Sister Calley brought an abrupt end to the jesting.

"Staff Nurse Ebotée!" she called out from the office.

"Yes ma'am," Billie replied a noticeable uneasiness in her voice.

"Have you finished the drugs inventory yet?"

"Er, no ma'am, I'm addressin' it shortly."

"Well best you do, lessen you want a stay behind!"

“Yes ma’am,” Billie said as Molly and Phillipa hastily returned to stripping and remaking the twelve empty beds.

“Fuckin’ ’ell,” Sugar said, “that’s gotta be the ugliest thing with a pulse I’ve ever ’ad the misfortune to meet. How cum she always looks like someone’s been choppin’ wood on ’er face?”

“That bitch’s got nipple clamps permanently sewn into her bra,” JJ added. “Some twat ought-a plug them in!”

The lads chuckled as usual, but I was too focused on Billie. She had a part incensed, part hurt look on her face. I felt for her.

“Vinegar really doesn’t like you does she?” I whispered as she breezed past.

“She don’t like herself,” Billie murmured whilst stopping briefly. “A person who don’t like themselves don’t like nobody. Don’t worry yo’ pretty little head, is-all fine.”

With that, she stoically carried on with her duties: "...is-all fine," Billie said, but deep inside I knew that it wasn’t.

We finally got round to choosing a film *Midnight Cowboy*, starring Jon Voight and Dustin Hoffman gained the consensus. We were all looking forward to the movie; it would be a break from the boredom. There was little to do on the ward except read, play cards, doze or listen to Radio Ran’ on the bed-station earphones. The hospital station only had one regular Disc Jockey: BJ Benson, a burnt out former frontline Combat Marine whose manic presentation gave you the impression that he was as permanently on drugs as he was On Air. BJ was desperately trying to hold onto the last vestiges of US Forces in the ’Nam. He’d talk at breakneck speed about halcyon Khề Sahn days and dope crazed Sàigòn nights. He had one foot in the grave (ostensibly because he only had one leg) and his head firmly placed in the smoke-filled skies over war-torn Quang Trì.

BJ’s saving grace was his impeccable selection of music: Aretha Franklin, Bob Dylan, Creedence Clearwater Revival, James Taylor, Joan Baez, The Mama’s *&* The Papa’s, Simon *&* Garfunkel, Neil Young. BJ used to switch to Radio Sàigòn, every hour on the hour, for up to date news reports. Summaries of continuing fighting in, Bịnh Đính, Mý Khề Tội, Pớlị Klằng, Kôntum, Phân Thiệt and Đọng Hầ Province. Stories of Viet Cong villages being razed to the ground by SVA Regulars; of smash and grab border raids by Khmer Rouge revolutionaries and of lines of refugees moving in ghost convoys throughout the night.

Billie gave me an inquisitive look as I took off my earphones post One O’clock News: “You looks like you lost a dollar and found a cent.”

“It’s this place; the war just keeps raging on, no end to it. What the fuck’s it all about?”

"I stopped tryin' to figure that out long ago. Where you guys bin to in this smashed up ol' place anyway?"

"All over: Quang Trì, Huê, Hoị Ẩn, Nha Trang, Quì Nhôn, plus a short spell in Là Drang before moving on to Trệng Nhôy."

"You bin 'round," she said with surprise.

"Command don't like keeping us in one place too long, we might see too much – hell we *have* seen too much. Viet Cong villages bombed out of existence; emaciated children begging for scraps; hordes of bedraggled refugees lining the roadside; Viet Cong rebels beaten and lynched, ceasefire violations on a weekly basis."

"Jeez, you must have a pretty dim view of our GI Joe's out here?"

"Not really, most of the yanks I've met have been fairly decent blokes. Some are a bit naive and I'm not saying there aren't any nasty pieces of work amongst them. But I don't think any of them are really bad. The only bad people are the politicians in Washington, Moscow and Peking who treat this war like an afternoon game of three-card-brag!"

"Amen to that. What do the folks in England think of this little ol' war?"

"They don't mostly, they're too detached particularly people of my generation, to them war's just a collection of moving images on a screen, or an interlude between the tits on page three and the gossip column. You can't blame them for being aloof. Why should they care about a bunch of peasants fighting over their destiny? Truth is the only way anyone's gonna be compelled to think about war is to get a mouthful of it, carry its bitter taste a while."

"Sheeit! you don't sound like any marine I ever met."

"Oh don't get me wrong I love the Marine Corps: the routines, the respect we get, the camaraderie, and the relationships. I don't think I'll ever be closer to anyone as I am to the lads in my Platoon. The only thing I don't like about being a soldier is war. I don't think I'll ever get used to it. So where's that leave me?"

"In a bit of a quandary I'd reckon. Y'all must know you're bein' used just like every other GI Joe out here; 'sides, it sure can't be easy makin' peace—"

"Beggin' your pardon Billie, but as our Lieutenant pointed out a while back we're not here to *make the peace* we're here to *keep the peace*."

"There y'all go then," she returned trying to offer reassurance.

"We don't seem to making a very good job of it."

"Sheeit! yo' gonna have to stop beatin' on yourself. If y'all don't know it the only people that can keep the peace in Charlieville is the Vietnamese. Trouble is too many outsiders bin pokin' their noses in, tryin' to push their ideals and values on 'em."

"Yeah, as if *we* could teach these people anything about values."

"Right-on!"

We could both see Vinegar looking down the ward. The nurses had strict instructions not to fraternise with patients. Billie picked my chart: "You bin takin' plenty of fluids?"

"Drinking like a fish."

"I'll be seein' you," she said, replacing my chart, "I'm off dooty shortly."

I looked at her slender figure as she walked towards the nursing station. I *willed* her to turn round and glance back, but she just kept on walking. Then, just as she reached the office she glanced back and smiled. Just for a moment it made me feel good. In the war in Vietnam, even a moment of feeling good was good enough.

Chauncey started putting up the movie screen at about 15:00. We could see him nervously looking out for Vinegar as he expertly unfolded the sheeting. When he was sure she wasn't around he called out to us with a glint in his eye: "You boys like some Indo-Chinese cuisine?"

"You're joking..." JJ said, "can you really get us some decent grub for once?"

"Sure, the Việt Kiệurie chef owes me…I'll get y'all a special."

"Is there anyone in Rậnlạntoì that doesn't owe you?" Dusty asked.

"Buddy there ain' no one in the 'Nam that don't owe old Chauncey, hot damn!"

"What about Vinegar tits?" I asked.

"She'll be a goin' back to her bat-cave at 17:00," he replied with a chuckle.

Ward staff released us from bed rest at 16:00. We all made a beeline for the ablutions. The bathrooms were as dilapidated as the rest of the building. The sinks were badly chipped, the rose-heads on the shower fittings badly scaled and the ornate tiles that once adorned the ostentatious facility were cracked and faded. Despite this, we all enjoyed our first opportunity to have a decent soak. It was always difficult to bathe on patrol. Most of the time we could only managed to soap our underarms and wedding tackle. Occasionally you could get a river bath, if the threat of ambush was low.

Our prolonged bathing session was followed by the evening meal, Annamese cuisine as promised. Tộnkinese monk fish marinated in ginger and coriander, lightly steamed in a parcel of elaborately entwined kohlrabi and chicory leaves, served on a bed of garlic infused wild mushrooms and chilli fried rice with a lemon grass garnish. Once satiated, we sat round the dining table with a look of total contentment.

"That was magic!" Dinger said.

"Yeah," Dusty concurred, "trouble is it's given me a longing, for a long cool beer, a long soft bed and a long slow screw!"

"Cocksucker-oh-wow!" We roared simultaneously.

"I've told my missus to get ready for me coming back," Tommy said. "I've told her to spend the next few weeks taking a good look at the floor, cos all she's gonna be seein' when I get home is the fuckin' ceilin'!"

"I wonder if we'll get any sick leave after we've been 'ere?" Sugar said. "I'm goin' to *The Pussy Palace* in Big S if we do, book in for a fuckin'!"

The ward was ringing with laughter amid the usual debauchery. Sister Iris [Belinda] came out of the office to see what the hullabaloo was about: "I do declare, all you Limey's do is clown around. We can hear y'all from the office don't-ya-know. I reckons y'all needs another ice bath."

"Fuck that," Sugar said, "I don't want three Adam's apples again!"

Later that evening we spent two hours forty minutes totally absorbed in the classic *Midnight Cowboy*, a touching story about a naive Kansas boy trying to make it as a hustler in New York. It was hard to choose what was best as the closing titles rolled: Voight and Hoffman's portrayals of the hick and the consumptive conman, the haunting flashbacks or Nilsson's wonderful soundtrack. Either way the movie was a real fillip. Some of the lads sat round talking after the film, the usual topics. I decided to retire for the night after adding a small piece to my journal.

I lay in bed replaying Nilsson's *Everybody's Talkin'*. For me the soundtrack would always bring back memories of Rậnlạntoì. I thought of another song before I closed my eyes, Creedence Clearwater Revival's *Fortunate Son*, a number we'd all sung whilst training for the Royal Marine Cadre; boozy nights on joyous weekends. I remember thinking how significant music can be in eliciting recollections. A melody enters your senses, neurones fire, something inside stirs, a warm glow. The feeling doesn't last long and is often replaced by momentary sadness. I wondered how I'd feel later in my life should I occasion those tracks. Would I obtain the same sensation; how would I look back on my time here? A chilling thought brought an end to my self-inquiry – would I have the opportunity?

Sunday 24 June.

I showered on the morning of my twentieth birthday with an almost renewed vigour. I still didn't feel a 100% but at least the all-pervading weakness had subsided. I thought of Lứin Bận Dưìn, it would be her birthday too; I wondered if *she* would be celebrating.

I assumed I wouldn't receive any birthday cards. I felt momentarily sad about the prospect, but considered that reaching twenty in the unforgiving war in Vietnam was enough. I exchanged the customary morning salutations. It was apparent by mid-morning that my muckers had forgotten my birthday.

I thought at least Corporal Farr would remember – his youngest, Rachel, was born on June 24th. I had a right gob on by midday, though I decided in my reserve not to let it get me down.

Most of the lads retired onto the balcony, post lunch; the fact that they never asked if I would like to join them pissed me off even further. 'Fuck 'em!' I thought, as I settled down to read another chapter of a story that brought nothing anew.

"Bazzer!" one of the gang called out from the end of the ward, "…come out 'ere a minute."

'Oh joy!' I thought as I sauntered towards the balcony, '…more bleedin' discussions about the war'—"Yeah," I said, observing the troop lounging round the table each sporting a jocular expression.

"Happy birthday mucker," Tommy said, pulling back a towel to reveal eight cans of Colt .45 on the table.

"You bastards!" I said my voice full of emotion, "I though you'd forgotten."

"Nah, just joshin'," JJ said.

Alcohol was strictly prohibited within US Military Hospitals; being caught in possession was a disciplinary offence. "We'd better be careful boys..." I said, as I sat down unable to hide the delight on my face, "Vinegar's on duty."

"It's cool, JJ and Jumper are gonna keep watch," Dinger advised.

"How did you manage to get hands on some beer?" I enquired, as Tommy carefully poured the amber liquid into eight cups.

"I'll give you one guess," Speedy said.

"Chauncey! pity he can't join us."

We all eagerly awaited our grog. Tommy left half a can extra for me once the cups were full. We were just about to pick up our bounty when JJ alerted us in a semi-hushed voice: "Vinegar!"

Tommy hastily covered the cans and cups as she marched onto the balcony.

"Everythin' alright out-a-here?" she asked in her distinctive Utah accent.

"Yes ma'am, just taking some air," Tommy responded.

Sister Calley perused us, a significant look of suspicion on her face.

"Fuckin' gob on that," Sugar murmured as she departed. "The last time that cunt 'ad her fanny rubbed was when she forgot to pull the breaks on her three-wheeler; ended up arse-over-tit in the fuckin' Christmas tree!"

Vinegar can't have failed to hear the roar of laughter emanating from the balcony. Our chortling was replaced by silence as we each savoured the tepid liquid – beer never tasted so good.

"Fuck-in' Brahma!" Dusty said, as he leaned on the architrave still dutifully on guard.

"Ain't nothin' like a lick of beer," JJ added.

Marine Jeffers' statement was followed by a short period of anticipatory silence, each of us playfully awaiting the inevitable: "Except a lick of pussy!" we collectively hollered.

Howls of laughter followed, Marine Lyle shouting: "Goose, goose, goose!" ('Goose' was Sugar's favourite saying. He'd even shout it whilst firing his weapon – his M16 of course!)

Tommy was suddenly sombre. "Thinking of Rachel?" I asked.

"Yeah, five today…wish I was there to see her face as she opened her presents. I wrapped one of them before we left, big fuck off teddy bear. She'll probably add it to her special collection."

I thought of my own daughter. I had bought her numerous cuddly toys over the years, but only one really mattered to her, a little pink hippo we named Ho'. "It won't be long before we're home."

"Yeah..." Tommy said, offering his cup in a ritual cheers, "all the best mucker."

We sat on the balcony for over an hour talking. The beer didn't last long, but it mattered not. I felt contented as I sat amongst my compadrés.

The social gathering soon broke up each of us going back to our routines. As we adjourned Tommy advised that there was something near my bed I should check out. I hurried to my bed where I could see a small hospital supplies box on the bedside table. I was full of curiosity as I opened the carton. I removed a light layer of tissue paper to reveal a small square Mississippi mud pie containing a single birthday candle. Tucked alongside the delicate patisserie a small note:

Couldn't get another 19 candles on it.
Happy Birthday – Love Billie.

I couldn't contain my happiness as I lifted the miniature cake from the box. But there was more, an oblong object wrapped in paper. I was overcome with emotion as I unwrapped the package, inside, a faded 1950s paperback lovingly thumbed by scholars and part-time readers alike – John Steinbeck's *The Grapes of Wrath.*

I spent the rest of the day writing my journal whilst reflecting on my birthday treats. I wanted to thank Chauncey for his little contribution. Unfortunately he was on 24-hour break. The hospital assigned a relief orderly; a lanky pallid man dressed in dazzling whites. He had tightly curled ginger hair, wild chalky eyes and ashen lips.

"Fuckin' 'ell," Sugar said as the orderly introduced himself, "he looks like a red top milk bottle."

“Dobbs be the name,” the orderly said in a slow deep voice that resembled a tape machine driven by spent batteries. Dobbs [Lon Chaney] was a dour man who would stomp around, as if in slow motion, singing hymns. Sugar asked him if he’d ever been an extra in a Hammer House Horror. Dobbs just gave him a vacant look. “I doe-know what you mean,” he replied in a chilling diction.

Nurse Richardson [Bobbie-Joe] carried out afternoon checks, blood pressure and the like. She added my daily injection to the routine; called it my ‘special birthday gift’. It was only my third jab and my arse already felt like a second hand pincushion. It was another one of those dead afternoons. Rậnlạntoì always seemed quiet.

“There doesn’t seem to be a lot of noise round this place,” I said to her as she discarded the spent syringe, “just empty echoes.”

“Most of the institution’s closed down now. The west wing’s almost completely boarded up; there’s only the psychiatric ward left.”

“Has that got many patients?”

“Its full! …its always full. We used to hear screams comin’ from over there before they bricked up the connecting corridor. The war’s over for most of the guys that come-on through here, at least temporarily. But for those poor suckers it just keeps goin-on.”

I contemplated Bobbie-Joe’s words for sometime. Going off your head was a constant worry. Marine Bomba [Boom-Boom] flipped whilst on border patrol in Northern Ireland. He was taken to hospital under the Mental Health Act – we never saw him again. Some of the more critical members of the section said that Boom-Boom was too sensitive. 'Where did that leave me?' I wondered. Truth is we all have our vulnerability and combat affects those involved in different ways, though we all walked around muttering to ourselves. And I’m sure there were times when I would seem as distant and detached as the rest of my muckers. The fear of being Killed in Action was ever present. Whilst on R&R we’d live life to the full. We’d go out with the intention of drinking every bar dry, frequenting every dope den and screwing ourselves into oblivion in every cat house in Đà Nẵng. It was as if we were trying to live out the rest of our lives in seven days: drink, smoke, fuck, sleep; drink, smoke, fuck, sleep; crazy! We’d board the Chinook back to the bush looking like dead men, a look that had nothing to do with a cosmic-hangover.

Staff Nurse Ebotée came on duty at 22:00, along with Sister David [Collet] and Molly. Vinegar, as always, was loitering around. It was as if she resented handing over the watch. I remember pondering about her life: 'is this ward all she’s got?' I wondered.

Lights out at 23:00, still no chance to talk to Billie. I strolled onto the balcony in my Ran' issue bathrobe as the rest of the lads got their heads down. It was a lovely evening, the kind that made you forget about the armed conflict that ravaged Vietnam. There was a complete stillness in the air, the sort that was forever welcome in war, so quiet that it was almost deafening. The sky was cloudless. The glancing typhoon had likely sucked all of the billowing vapour into its colossal funnel. Lôc Nịnh, like most small towns in Vietnam, had few streetlights; consequently the light pollution familiar to towns and cities was diminished making the stars more observable. I had studied the celestial bodies in the pitch-black skies, particularly whilst on patrol. But this was always against the backdrop of constant ambush. I could never allow myself the luxury of gazing out and truly absorbing the floral display that frequented the everlasting sea of ebony. But on that evening, at last, I had the opportunity and it was well worth the wait. The Universe has always fascinated me. I'd stare out of my bedroom window at the stars and planets wondering what they were made of, how they got there and if I could ever journey to them (as if crossing the Mersey to New Brighton). As a child I imagined the stars in the night sky to be random pinpricks in an enormous black screen their piercing light being radiated from a giant lamp to its rear. I giggled to myself as I remembered an occurrence in '64 when I lay in the snow staring out at the Milky Way. I recall being overcome by a feeling of absolute awareness; one of those rare moments as a child when you obtain 'sentience', the realisation that you are an individual being. I broke off reminiscing. Thinking too much of home was unwise, it evoked too many emotions; emotions that needed to be kept under wraps.

I scanned the empty balcony where I'd earlier enjoyed my birthday drink. A contemporary copy of *Time* magazine lay on the rattan table. Its cover featured a picture of President Nixon with the headline 'What Price Peace?' (Referring to the escalating cost of continuing to support the corrupt South Vietnamese Government.) Someone had penned-in red eyes and the devil's horns and scribed ASSHOLE on Nixon's forehead.

I sensed a presence as I sniggered at the picture; it was Billie slowly walking towards me. She couldn't fail to notice the delight on my face.

"Hello Billie," I said, with a warm smile.

"Howdy birthday boy," she replied in a mild just-passing-the-time voice, "had a pleasant day?"

"It was okay. Nice to have the boys around me, that helped."

"Did y'all enjoy your beer?"

"How did you know we had—?" I stopped observing her knowing gaze.

"I didn't, don't worry, I ain' no squealer."

I looked at her playful expression. She had a pencil-line smile, one that said 'gotcha'! I picked up the much-read copy of *Time*: "It flatters him," I said showing her the defaced picture of their beloved President. “I wonder which member of staff did it.”

“How do you know it was a member of staff?” she returned half surprised.

“We Brits’ spell arse, a-r-s-e, not a-s-s. Don’t worry...” I whispered with a broad smile, “I ain’t no squealer!”

“Sheeit, it don’t make no mind anyhow, he ain’t no asshole. An asshole’s useful. Yo’ Beatles wrote a song that sums him up, *Nowhere Man*.”

We both laughed. She knew I held Nixon in contempt; as far as I was concerned he was a murdering two-faced hypocrite. I asked Billie if it was alright for her to be out on the balcony with me.

“Its okay honey I’m on dooty with Collet tonight, she’s a ‘good egg’ like you Brits’ say.”

“Thanks for the prezzie,” I said, feeling reassured she wouldn’t get into trouble.

“You say what?” Billie replied an inquiring look on her face.

“The mud pie and the book, I’ve started reading it already.”

“It was nothin’. I know you got nothin’ from your folks, least-wise not yet.”

It wasn’t *nothin’* of course. I briefly toyed with the notion of telling her it was something very special but decided otherwise.

“What about your folk and home do you miss them?” she asked.

“I miss my family and I think about home from time to time, but I’m used to being away. It’s my life now, couldn’t really imagine it being any other way. What about you, do you miss good old Alabamie?”

“I miss my kin; I comes from a big family so that makes missin’ them more so. As for Alabamie there’s nothin’ *good* about it, mainly cos it’s stuck in *old* ways. It’s kinda like the rest of the US of A; they don’t want us niggers crampin’ their style. All we be good for is fightin’ their wars!”

It wasn’t hard to discern the understandable contempt in her voice, though as hitherto it wasn’t aimed at me.

“I read an article about your Buffalo Soldiers. It said they’re amongst the bravest troops out here yet the least decorated.”

“Figures, though there’s no difference ’tween black and white once the tracer starts flyin’, they all pray to the same God. That puts me in mind, it say on your medical chart you be a none believer.”

“I don’t believe in God if that’s what you mean.”

Billie gave me an inquisitive look: “Interestin’ you bein’ a Combat Marine an’ all. I heard it say that there aren’t any Atheists in foxholes.”

Billie had hit a raw nerve. I have long despised such suggestions, particularly when made by people who had no concept of what it was like to be under fire.

“There aren’t any cowards either,” I returned, “but I know plenty of card carrying Christians that have got a thick yellow streak running down their backs. Like the eye-for-eye zealots who call for the return of the death penalty, but when it comes to strapping the culprit in the chair and pulling the switch they're the first to run for cover. I don't want to be associated with people like that. Give me an Atheist in a foxhole any day!"

"That's a slur! I'm a Christian and I don't agree with the puttin' people to death—"

"I didn't say all Christians are that way inclined, that would be just as dubious as saying that all Atheists are misguided or bad. It doesn't make you a lesser person just because you refuse to sign up to some spiritual construct."

Billie stared at me for what seemed like an age: "*It matters not whether you believeth in me for I will receive all the children of Israel into my arms... Matthew Eighteen*," she said with total conviction.

"*God is a concept by which we measure our pain... John Lennon*," I returned, likewise.

"Maybe, truth is we all need somethin' or someone to lean on. Ain' none of us an island, no matter how sure we *think* we are about what does or doesn't exist. All's I know is when I pray it makes my sufferin' that bit easier to bear..."

I could have said *touché* but thought better of it.

"...You ever thought about what you'd do or say if you turned up at those pearly gates?" she asked after a brief pause.

"I won't deny I haven't thought of that. If it comes to pass then I've got a whole heap of questions for Saint Peter. Like where was his Lord and Master when the Nazis were dispatching wagonloads of people because of their ethnicity or creed? Or why does he allow innocent children to starve to death on the streets of Sàigòn while their oppressors in the National Assembly grow fat on western aid. And why didn't he knock two phantom jets out of the sky before they had a chance to lay a pattern of napalm on a village in Nha Trang? all before my very eyes. And if Peter should answer with that stock phrase, 'God moves in mysterious ways', then I believe I'd decline an invitation to enter anyway. I'd rather go the other way; at least I'd know where I stood in Hades and who I was standing alongside!"

"So that's it, period. We all just go about our business acceptin' there's no greater power or better place? Sheeit, we all gotta believe in somethin'—"

"I'm not saying we accept anything. On the contrary, I'm saying the exact opposite. And I never said I didn't believe. I believe: in *me*, the love of my family and the boys in my Platoon. Everything else is just paste!"

Billie breathed out whilst slowly shaking her head: "So young...so cynical."

"What do you expect? Who was it that said that this place makes you harsh?"

There was an extended intermission both of us silently staring into the night sky. I suddenly felt rueful; I never meant to be so truculent.

Billie broke the stalemate: "I won't offend you by sayin' I'll pray for you, but when I'm next in chapel you'll be in my thoughts."

"You'll be in mine too."

"Does that mean I ain't paste?"

"You're anything but paste," I said trying, unsuccessfully I feared, not to make my declaration sound too affectionate.

"What are you going to do when this crazy war's over?" I asked trying to introduce another topic.

"Who said it's gonna end?"

"Come on, you know as well as I do, the North Vietnamese Army will overrun this place once the US withdrawal is complete. There's no way the SVA will be able to hold them back. Charlie's day's a comin' and that's a fact."

Billie was taciturn, clearly pondering: "I'll probably stay here. Ain' nothin' for me back home."

"I think it's sad you don't want to go home."

"Who said anything about not wantin' to go home? I just don't want to go back to a place where I'll be spat at and treated like a second-class citizen, no sir! Least I know where I stand out here. Besides, a nation will always need nurses no matter who be rockin' the cradle. It just so comes to be that I like the Vietnamese, no Viet Cong ever called me a nigger!"

"Mohammed Ali said that."

"I knows it," she replied with a smile, "he got it from me."

"Either way, right now there's a lot of angry young men walking the streets of the good old USA."

"Ain't no bad thing. Truth is the folks back home have got a fractured view of this war. They bin watchin' the NBC version. Seem to think Uncle Sam's leavin' with the victory flag a flyin'."

"You say that as if you're glad Uncle Sam's had his arse kicked."

"Uncle Sam ain' had his arse kicked. He be hidin' in the Pentagon, chewin' gum an' sippin' coke. Mullin' over how many more ways he can cheat on his IRS return. It's the conscripts, poor kids, black an' white with not much 'tween their ears but bone that've had their asses kicked, and how. What gets me is there's more good an' genuineness in one of them kids than all those politicians thrown 'gether. I know who I'd turn to if my back was against the wall – no shit!"

I had a sudden feeling of déjà vu. We'd had the conversation before; our views were so alike, a factor that made me desire her more. I was also struck by a realisation that she and her colleagues had likely had traumatic experiences. The content of our conversations were largely about *my* encounters. Billie would often give me a distant look, the kind that indicated that she was detached, briefly interrupted by a passing thought welcome or otherwise.

"I guess you must've seen some things in your time here?"

"Honey, you got no idea. There ain' a month gone by when I haven't seen the real meanin' of war, particularly in the early days. I could paint you one hell of a picture of the boys I saw comin' through this place. Missing limbs, extensive burns, bullet and shrapnel wounds; flesh ripped from the bone like a badly peeled orange. They all got one thing in common; they got fucked-up heads! I've seen some broken bodies in my time, but a broken body ain't nothin' compared to a broken mind."

"Bobbie-Joe said something similar, only she said they were on the psychiatric ward."

"You don't have to be on a psych' ward to have a fucked-up head. The 'Nam's full of boys with their minds' all shot up."

"What about us?" I enquired (not knowing if I really wanted to know the answer).

"You guys are okay though take heed. It's kinda like those bugs that put y'all in here. It'll come when you're least expectin' it; creep up and contaminate your mind."

"I don't know," I said, looking at Billie as if desperate for an answer to a question I hadn't asked. "It's strange out here. Sometimes I feel like it isn't me walking through the bush. I feel like I'm in a dream, like something or someone else is carrying my body. It's as if I'm elsewhere; climbing the hills in the Lakes back home. Is that crazy or what?"

"No, that's just your defence mechanism; we all create them. We need them, particularly in a place like this. The 'Nam's unforgiving, drains you of your reasoning and humanity. We all need to keep a piece of ourselves to one side. Somethin' good we can dip into."

I laughed: "You've got a gift, a way of explaining things, of connecting things up, giving them meaning."

"It ain' a gift," she replied in a way that portrayed total honesty, "it's just somethin' that comes with age. When there's as much of a road behind you as there is still to travel it kinda makes the path less rocky."

"Do you remember your birthdays'?" I asked.

"Honey, you get to not want to remember them once the clock gets past thirty!"

"I remember nearly all mine, 'specially my ninth. Dad bought me a toy commando machine-gun. He didn't like buying me war toys but I'd harangued him into getting me one. It had all the attachments: fold away tripod, grenade launcher, nightsight and a battery driven ammunition belt that made a rat-tat-tat sound. Dad had this second world war Waffen SS German helmet..." I continued to her visible delight. "He used to keep it in a box on top of the wardrobe in his and mum's room. Forbid me to touch it. You'll know the worst thing you can do is tell a child not to touch something. I sneaked it out the house one day along with my newly acquired toy gun. Ended up playing war games in the nearby woods with my mates. There was me, running through the woods with the helmet on. Bloody thing was obviously too big for me. Bounced up and down and twirled like a spinning top on my head. Little John, Simba, Jojo and me were in hot pursuit of some imaginary enemy when I stumbled on a protruding tree root; ended up knocking myself out after nosediving into a tree. I awoke to see my dad stooping over me after Little John had run to get him. He looked like a giant. All I could think of was trying to hide the helmet, but he already had it in his hands. I thought I was in for a shellackin' but dad just gave me a sharp reprimand. Told me in his scary voice 'not to touch it again.' Needless to say I never did. Now, eleven years on, here I am. I've got my own helmet, my own Armalite, only this time it's not make believe, this is for real—"

I could sense Billie at my side. I wanted to look at her but overcame the temptation.

"—As kids me and my mates used to go to the matinées, war films mostly: *The Longest Day*, *The Beaches of Iwo Jima*. John Wayne, Robert Mitchum and the like. Thing is, it doesn't matter how graphic a film is, there are some things that you just can't portray, or that maybe the film makers don't want you to know. Like the sounds of one of your buddies sobbing in the night, burying their head in the pillow to hide their distress. Or the screams from a man who's just had half his face blown away by a mortar shell. You can't depict the real terror of that, no matter how good an actor you are. And the smells of war, you don't get those in the cinema. Burnt or decomposing flesh; the reek of your body odour as you sweat with fear or your vomit after you've just thrown up over your flak jacket. John Wayne never threw up or pissed himself!"

"John Wayne's never dodged white-hot tracer or bayoneted a kid to death. He's like the rest of those American as apple pie actors. All they're good for is talkin' death and glory!"

Billie was right of course, though I already knew this: *The Vietnam War Supporters Club*, my father called them. Rich, privileged and protected. Long distance Generals singing the Stars and Stripes in their Hollywood homes whilst underprivileged conscripts died on the battlefield.

We continued to talk on a raft of subjects. I felt so at ease; as I'm sure did Billie.

“Oh my,” she said, “look at the time. You better get on to bed; you still need to build your strength.”

I felt like a kid at the end of Christmas night as I retired. I could have stood on the balcony until first light. Given different circumstances I would have come-on to her, though I had a sneaking suspicion she was probably glad of the context. As it transpired we simply bid each other goodnight. She must've seen the glint in my eye, I'm sure I saw a twinkle in her's. I lay on my bed gazing into the dark with a broad smile. It had been a good day. I summoned sleep to the inner sounds of a Beatles record—

'He's a real nowhere man
Sitting in his nowhere land
Making all his nowhere plans
For nobody...'

'Yes Billie…' I thought, 'very apt!'

Monday 25 June.

We were moving at a swift pace. I couldn't figure out if we were at the chase or being chased. My heart was pounding, trying to punch its way through my ribcage. I tripped plummeting to the ground. Suddenly I was alone, the Platoon dissipated. Shadows of dragonflies flit weaving elaborate patterns on the hillside, a warning of foreboding. Faceless guerrillas advance, my rifle jams – seemed my rifle always jammed.

“Breech jam!” I cry out, “…dud-round, dud-round!”

I awoke in startled response to see Sugar staring at me. He gave a part smile before turning over to go back to sleep. In war soldiers crying out in the middle of the night was the norm.

Staff Nurse Ebotée quietly walked towards my bed. “You okay?” she asked in a hushed voice.

“Yeah…what time is it?”

“You an' your time, what have I told you, be 'bout 4:30. You bad dreamin' again?”

I thought for a second replaying the closing stages of my night terror. I didn't want to burden her with my torment.

“Shadowdancing,” I replied, though I'm unsure why.

“You say what?”

“Shadows, dancing on the hillside and terraces. Messages, your own choreography though you don't realise at the time. An interpretation of your life past and present, should you care to pursue the performance; continue to follow. But you can't, it's all over too quickly, until the next encounter."

Billie stood at the side of my bed, slowly shaking her head: "Sheeit! where in the hell you get all that from?"

"It's something I saw, a long time ago, or was it?" I whispered still in a semi-slumber.

"I can't figure you…" she said whilst gently pulling over the covers I had discarded, "I can't work out whether you're in constant delirium or just deep."

"It's been a problem of mine ever since I was a kid. My mates used to take the piss cos I used to write all this weird stuff. Do you think maybe you can have someone else's dream?" I asked hoping that Billie would engage my imagination.

"No…" she answered with a chuckle, "dreams be in your own head."

"I know, but when people are really close like me and my mates it's kinda like your dreams are the same. The same context and scenarios, with the same hopes and fears, isn't that like having someone else's dream?"

"That's just like a uniformity I guess though I knows what you mean."

"I wonder what they see in shadows…what do you see?"

"I reckon that depends on the time of the month," she answered, the two us of trying to muffle our giggles.

Billie's presence predictably settled my anxiety: "I like it when you smile," I murmured.

"You polishin' that silver tongue again," she said, pretending to be serious.

"Can't blame a man for trying."

"What I require you to do young man is to try'n get-on to sleep! I'll be here should those *shadows* come to get ya rest assured."

Billie, after bidding goodnight, walked away sporting her everyday grin.

I lay for sometime replaying the previous day's events. The context was different that time. I was weary of restless nights, persistent flashbacks of the shit war throws at you. My twentieth birthday was extra special, more than I could've wished for. 'Yes,' I thought, 'it was good to be twenty; it was good to be alive; it was good to have met Billie Ebotée; it was good to be a part of a unit. It was even good – to be in Vietnam.'

I drifted back to sleep some time before 06:00 shift change. I wanted to catch Billie before she departed for her two days off. I missed the opportunity. I'd like to think she checked on me before leaving. Knowing her, she'd have checked us all.

It would be strange not having Billie around. Who could I speak to now? I thought. Marine Lyle lifted my mood as Lon Chaney came striding onto the ward singing *Rock Of Ages*. "If he dyed 'is 'air black he'd look like a fuckin' dead matchstick," he said.

Tommy tried to engage Dobbs in some banter. He was having none of it. I don't think he could make us out. Apparently, he was on permanent relief; we wondered if this was due to his glum demeanour. Sugar, not wanting to miss an opportunity to rib someone, was on top form. "Hey mate 'ow much do yer charge to haunt a house?" he asked with a serious look.

"I'm an orderly, hauntin' be the Devil's work!"

Sugar was a master impressionist; he could take Dobbs off to a tee. "Fuckin' 'ell..." he said mimicking Dobbs' voice, "who pickled your dick!"

Doctors' rounds took longer than usual. A bunch of Indo-Chinese medical students accompanied the humourless man. An interpreter had been assigned, a young Việt Kiẹư girl who shyly followed the crew. The doctor would launch into a tirade of explanations about our conditions and aetiology. The interpreter struggled to keep up with his tutoring. At one stage the doctor barked at her to, "Keep up!"

"Gí buón xẩu," (*What a fuckwit.*) I whispered to her gesticulating towards the doctor as the grouping walked past. She half-smiled, the doctor glared. 'Fuck him!' I thought; he was nought but an egotistical little prick.

Chauncey came bounding onto the ward at 14:00 turnover: "Yo dudes! y'all missed me?"

"**Chauncey!**" we returned amid a chorus of clapping and whistling.

"Oh boy, are we glad to see you," Marine Jeffers said as Dobbs left without a goodbye. "Lon Chaney's been scarin' the shit out of us."

"Dobbs's all right..." Chauncey told us as conciliatory as ever, "he's spent too much time workin' on the psych' ward 'tis all."

Chauncey asked how my birthday went. I gave him the rundown after thanking him for the grog.

"Ain' no bother, you boys are kinda unique. We ain' had no Limey's up here ago."

Chauncey's attitude summed up the way we'd been treated since arriving at Rậnlạntoì. The care and commitment shown by the staff touched us. Unfortunately, it had also softened us up. We were all aware that returning to full health equalled returning to active duty. After the pampering and soft soap of Ward 6, returning to the front was a prospect that none of us relished.

It was late afternoon. I'd just reached the part in *The Grapes of Wrath* where the family were leaving the dust ravaged farm they'd worked for over a 100 years, each member, save for proud grandma, looking back teary-eyed at the homestead that had seen the birth and passing of generations. I could clearly picture the ramshackle truck loaded with their possessions rolling down the dusty highway, the beginning of a desperate journey for their very survival.

It put me in mind of the refugees we would see on the roadside; from Huê to Sàigòn, dispossessed of everything apart from what they could carry. Each had the same haunted look: resolute yet defeated; indivisible, though each separated within their tormented worlds.

I was so engrossed in my book I failed to hear the dull thud of, not so distant, mortar fire. The whole building seemed to shake as the rounds hit home.

"What the fuck!" Tommy cried out as another report resonated through the building.

Sister Iris rushed out of the office and began shouting to staff, **"Shutters!"** she bellowed whilst clapping her hands.

Chauncey, along with Bobbie-Joe, began hastily closing the large window coverings.

"Are we under attack?" Dinger asked Chauncey as he slammed the last shutter.

"Hell no! it'll be the SVA an' Charlie havin' a fracas. They bin bitchin' over this plot since the ceasefire."

"Sounds pretty close to me," JJ said, a touch of anxiety in his voice.

"Charlie won't lay nothin' on us," Chauncey advised. "He's got a code, he don't attack the sick. He'll frag your ass the minute you mosey on out those gates, but while y'all in here, he'll leave ya be."

We were all visibly relaxed after Chauncey's reassurance. Most of the lads carried on reading or writing letters as the mortar fire and occasional rapid automatic gunfire continued. Sugar could see the pensive look on my face: "What's up?"

"I'm just thinking about the contradictions that keep cropping up in this war."

"Like what?"

"Like the way the yanks have tried to bomb North Vietnam into the Stone Age. Blanket bombing of Vịnh and Hànội, there'll have been hospitals within their targets."

"So," Sugar said, without indifferent intonation.

"So, we westerners keep on spouting about how civilised we are and how backward the Vietnamese are. Yet the Viet Cong won't attack the sick, kinda makes you think don't it!"

The fracas continued for well over an hour. The shutters were not opened until the staff was sure the sortie had abated. Chauncey came strolling down the ward concealing something just as Sister Iris left the office to call for stand down. I'm sure she knew he was up to something; her half-smile gave it away. I can only guess that she wasn't bothered as long as whatever Chauncey had wasn't Class 'A' contraband.

As it transpired the hoard was nought but a selection of girlie magazines and several bars of chocolate. Corporal Farr asked him where he'd got the chocolate (out of concern for Chauncey's job security.) Chauncey said they'd fallen out of a box in the supplies corridor. Judging by the immaculate state of the wrappers they mustn't have fallen far. "Good old Chauncey," we muttered as we wolfed our illicit premium.

Later that afternoon Chauncey delivered a set of – somewhat dated – British newspapers: *The Times*, *Daily Mirror*, *Daily Express & The Guardian*. It had been well over two months since we'd set eyes on newspapers from Blighty, though reading about events from home always brought mixed emotions. Chauncey hinted, before leaving to substitute in the laundry, that there might be some more news "...a-comin' our way later." Chauncey had a penchant for leaving us with little teasers.

Sister Iris brought an end to our speculation at 1950 hours when she stopped mid-ward: "Listen in y'all, Chauncey's organised a liddle ol' surprise at 20:00. Y'all should listen in on Radio Ran'."

We switched on in anticipation. A native hospital worker who spoke in laboriously monotone English was On Air: "Now for a spe-cial favour ask' for by Mister Chaun-cey and his Limey boys on the ward six. I am to tune-in to the B-B-C Worlds Service for the news of the Britain peoples at home and on the world."

We cheered in unison as the recognisable opening tune and pips of the programme filled the air… "This is London 13:00 Grenwich Mean Time—"

We listened to news with the keenness of children learning their A-B-C's.

"—At home, Poulson (a leading architect) has been arrested for alleged conspiracy… Prime Minister Heath, holidaying in the Maldives, refuses to comment on the National Union of Mineworkers' threat of forthcoming industrial action unless fresh negotiations can be opened up on the Government's pay restraint.

Enoch Powell has been admonished by his party for urging the electorate to vote Labour to avoid entry into the EEC. In Ulster the Security Forces have been ordered to clamp down due to a spate of sectarian murders… and Liverpool's John Conteh receives a hero's welcome after securing the World Lightweight Championship.

In Ireland, President Eamon de Valera resigns aged 90; the former President believes that Ireland will be reunited by the year 2000… In Washington, President Nixon refuses, yet again, to hand over the White House tapes to senate investigators. Woodward and Bernstein comment that it is, '...only a matter of time before Nixon would be impeached'. The US Foreign Policy Spokesman has strongly denied CIA involvement in the failed coup against

Chile's President Allendé. Political analysts suggest that support for Allendé within the Chilean Military is waning. In Lebanon, tensions between factions in Christian East and Muslim West Beirût are on the increase. United Nations' forces may be asked to intervene—"

And of particular interest;

"—Government troops in Cambodia have launched an offensive against the Khmer Rouge… and the American withdrawal from Vietnam is all but complete with just a token force remaining." The broadcaster added that the "...ceasefire appeared to be holding on all fronts."

It was with some irony that forty minutes later we would hear another volley of rapid fire. Echoes of continuing gunfire that did not, it would seem, reach the aerials of Broadcasting House in London – or did they?

Corporal Farr and I had a brief post news discussion. We were somehow taken aback by the not unsurprising news of conflict in other regions the world. We suddenly became aware of how insular we'd become, too concerned about what was unfolding in our neck of the woods. There were so many things I could've written in my journal, not necessarily connected to our immediate predicaments. I wanted to avoid that, though the world is inextricably intertwined. I had a habit at end of day of reflecting on events. Re-reading the text I'd often, hastily, scribbled in my journal. Sometimes I'd add to my writings, though more often I would put a line through my ramblings or simply rip out the page. On that evening I reflected at length. So much had happened worldwide in the five days we'd been inpatients, yet within the context of the war, so little. I'd said to Billie that the Viet Cong would win. But winning the battle is one thing and *truly* winning the war another. I had a feeling the Vietnamese would suffer for having the temerity to humiliate the USA. I hypothesised on what would come to pass if, as expected, the Viet Cong secured victory:

'The Americans would put pressure on the countries assembling the South Eastern Triangle to isolate Vietnam; they would punish anybody who traded with them. Vietnam would have their supporters in the Soviet Block, but they hardly had fiscal stability. The Vietnamese economy would nosedive, they'd become more isolationist and unstable. The people would become discontent. The military machine would kick-in and do exactly the same to the populace that the existing oppressive bastards had done. Eventually, in the continuing discord, Vietnam would have to call for help, sign up to the Global Economy. And who's the major player in the world markets? the good old USA!'

I frantically scribbled down my thoughts as the lights went out to signal the end of another day, wondering if my pessimistic predictions would come true; time would tell. Truth is after ten months of living and breathing the war

I was disillusioned with the whole affair. Then, as I lay in the dark, I suddenly felt guilty for being irked. The Vietnamese had been fighting, struggling, for over 9000 days. Nevertheless, when all was said and done I was nought but a small cog in an immense machine. The outcome of the hostility would not be determined or changed by the thoughts of one burnt out Combat Marine. I lay my head down and evoked pleasant thoughts to lullaby sleep. But somewhere in the distance I could hear the sound of crying: a mother who'd lost her son; a family who'd lost their father; a child who burned with hunger; the inhabitants of a village destroyed in a napalm attack. A country in perpetual mourning. I could detect the outpouring of tears; tears that would wet my pillow.

Tuesday 26 June.

It had been sometime since I had written home. I'd been procrastinating since being admitted to the Ran'. Writing home was never easy, I could never decide exactly what to scribe. Do you tell your folks about the war? The hazards that confront you on a weekly basis: claymores that would cut you in two; release–wire satchel-charges tied to trees; fall-pits containing bamboo spikes laced with a thin layer of curare – thin to ensure you died slowly. And high impact pressure–release mines, step on one of those things and there'd be nothing left but the gold in your teeth. Do you disclose the ever-present threat of ambush? Or that you never really knew who your enemy was: a young man with an innocent smile, an old woman with a senile look or a child carrying an innocuous toy that was in fact a grenade? Most of the time I would write somewhere between fantasy and reality, that way, I considered, no one would be hurt or any the wiser. I compelled myself to write with a decision not to disclose that I was in hospital.

My writing was interrupted by the sound of Calley tearing a strip off Bobbie-Joe in the office. Bobbie-Joe looked flustered as she left the room. I felt for her as she walked down the ward intentionally avoiding eye contact. I have always despised bullies, from the schoolyard to adulthood. I've an inclining to give them a message:

'If you've had a lousy childhood, get over it. If your head's messed up, seek therapy. If you have poor self-image, give yourself a personality makeover and if your existence is shit create a life plan that doesn't involve putting the boot in on others!'

I never had the chance to confront Calley; the context never spawned an opportunity. I'd like to think that somebody else gave her a piece of their mind, or that she got her comeuppance. But life isn't like that; the Vietnam War was testament to a plethora of wrongdoing that went unchecked.

The hospital Priest came round at 11:30, looking for lost souls no doubt. There were three other Catholics on Ward 6: Jumper, Speedy and Sugar. The Priest seemed a nice enough guy. He might have been the devoutest of Christians though it mattered not to me, as a confirmed Atheist I took people on different values.

Personally, I'd a bellyful of religion during my time in the Marines, particularly in Northern Ireland. Whilst in Belfast I was seconded to 3: Delta 3 Platoon where I had the misfortune of serving under Colour Sergeant Brady, a Born Again Christian and avid bible reader who seemingly had an attack of dyslexia every time he came across words like love, tolerance, and humility. Brady was a 22-carrot bastard who'd justify his brutish actions by quoting passages from the bible. As a non-believer he had a particular dislike for me, said I wasn't pure – what an arsehole. I thought He and Calley would have made a good match; they say 'misery likes company'.

I was glad that Staff Nurse Ebotée wasn't on duty when the Priest visited. I didn't want to rekindle the semi-heated discussion we had on the balcony, though I was convinced her belief system wasn't far removed from mine. She had only been off for one day somehow it had seemed longer. I spent sometime during private moments wondering about her life. I tried to imagine her as a younger woman or a child. Life can't have been easy in the heat of the racist south. I remember reading about the Civil Rights demonstrations in '61 & '63. Billie briefly mentioned that members of her extended family had to flee Montgomery after persecution from the Ku Klux Klan, how easy my life in comparison. I wondered what else she did besides read during her free time. There were nurses' quarters within the compound; there had likely been some wild nights when the Marine Garrison was in full swing. The firebase was in a perpetual silence by June '73 – other than the squawking of crows and scurry of rats. I knew from our conversations that she'd travelled. I assumed she wasn't married and it was doubtful she was in a relationship. I decided, however, to discard any notions of romance, after all, would she really be interested in a bit-of-a-kid like me?

The afternoon dragged as usual. It seemed worse now that we were feeling better. We spent less time lounging on our beds electing instead to sit in the dayroom or on the balcony talking or reading. My period in hospital had given me time to contemplate a number of issues. Writing my journal sharpened my focus, as did my relationship with Billie. I had spent sometime reflecting on the Platoons' exploits, particularly whilst on R&R. I'd also found myself wishing that the context with Billie was different. I thought of some of the shenanigans we would get up to with the opposite sex. We all considered ourselves lady-killers. Whilst in Đà Nẵng I became acquainted with a young student, Mị Lềa Sận. I had manipulated and lied my way into her bed; promises of a long meaningful relationship and a trip to Blighty. I bragged that I'd 'got her knickers'; what a bastard. How I wished for an opportunity to have time with Billie outside the hospital setting. I would be as 'straight as a die', I convinced myself. I could yearn for all I was worth it would get me nowhere. '*You can wish and dream where's you'd like to go but that don't make it so…*' my grandmother used to say. I'd have to content myself with brief encounters.

Tommy was as engrossed in his book *Bury My Heart at Wounded Knee*, another sorry tail of a people robbed of their land, heritage and freedom, as I joined him in the dayroom.

"You okay mucker?" he asked noticing my thoughtful expression.

"Yeah," I answered, not really wanting to tell him what was on my mind. "Have you ever wished you could turn the clock back, live a day or week again; put right a wrong or stand up to someone who's put you down?"

"No..." Tommy answered with a smile, "*all the time*! What's brought this on?"

"Oh I don't know, this place, the war, where I am in the order of things. I never really thought I'd have time to think things through once in the 'Nam. Didn't think I'd need to. Keep your head down and your mouth shut I told myself. Yet in these past few days my mind's been racing."

"So, think you're the only one? We've all been contemplating: home, family, our duties, the rights and wrongs of this lousy conflict. Some of the boys mightn't be as vocal or seem as passionate as you and me, but that don't mean they're not of that mind. I've a suspicion something else is botherin' you," Tommy said in a way that indicated that it was more than just a suspicion.

I had to think carefully before disclosing my thoughts and feelings: "I'm not sure if I'm cut out for all this and not just peacekeeping, whatever that's supposed to be. I can't look at things and take a neutral stance; it's not in my character. And every time we get close to opening fire all I can think is, 'there must be another way'."

"Sorry buddy I can't help you there; the answer to that's gotta come from within. I thinks maybe a little acquaintance you've made has brought all this to the surface wouldn't you say?"

"I can't deny that Billie's so cosmopolitan, you know. She's got a way of framing things; helping you cut through all the crap, see things for what they are instead of what the politicians and commentators are trying to sell. It's as if I've seen a part of myself that I knew was there but kinda lost or blocked out."

"Oh brother," Tommy said shaking his head, "you've got it bad."

"What?"

"L-o-v-e, my friend that's the only thing that'll make a man start thinking like that. Can't blame you, there's something about Billie. She's got a way, something warm, sparkling and genuine. But if it's advice you want, then get this: you can fraternise and fantasise all you want while we're in here, but soon, maybe very soon, we're gonna be back on the frontline. You're gonna have to ditch all that shit, save it for when we get home. You can't go carryin' round doubts out there, unless you wanna take a bullet and that won't do you or anybody else any good."

"I'll do my duty—!"

"I know!" Tommy replied calming my agitation, "I'm just warning you to get prepared 'tis all. The graveyards full of Combat Marines who had a moment of doubt. Out here we haven't got the luxury of a second shot. Billie Ebotée's still gonna be around when our Tour of Duty's over – just make sure you are!"

Tommy went back to reading his book, leaving me sat in silence. He was right of course. I had to start thinking ahead; doubts were not things that could've been worked through in that arena. As it transpired, I would see further combat in Lebanon, Northern Ireland and the Falkland Islands before I'd acquiesce to the inevitable.

I became drowsy whilst staring at the faded 1950s pictures on the walls. I somehow felt relaxed after our talk. My transitory slumber was interrupted by a commotion on the ward. Tommy also heard the rumpus. We both rushed out of the dayroom to investigate. We arrived to *Fortunate Son* blaring on the Tannoy. Some of the men were up dancing and singing. Sugar and JJ were hitting their pillows imitating drummers. Chauncey also joined the revelry, gyrating as if some dope crazed go-go dancer. Tommy and I enthusiastically joined the communal singing the minute we entered the ward—

"*Some people born*
Spangled banner in their hand
Ooh, they're white and blue.
But when the draft-man
Comes a callin' round
Ooh, they point the cannon at you…"

—we sang at the tops of our voices. Bobbie-Joe came walking down the ward in the middle of our manic soirée. Lance Corporal Bell jumped up and grabbed her swinging her round in some half-baked jive. Bobbie-Joe's face was bright red. She had a beaming smile as she twirled around in the middle of the floor. Vinegar, luckily, was off ward. The crabby bitch would've had a heart attack if she'd set eyes on us. Bobbie-Joe, understandably concerned about the possible return of Calley, said we should cool it. We did of course, out of respect for her, not some over zealous bully.

I spent the early evening dozing whilst listening to Buffalo Springfield on Radio Ran'. The music elicited memories of sun drenched days and steamy nights at the Recreational Facility China Beach: *The Đà Nẵng Fantasy Factory* – everything your heart desires, bar a trip to Blighty.

I awoke to see Corporal Farr sitting with Jumper, Sugar, Dinger and JJ on the bed beside me. Tommy had a ripshit look on his face, a look I had seen many times before.

"What?" I said in anticipation of some revelation.

"I think I've worked it out," he answered with a glint in his eye.

"Worked what out? What the fuck you babbling about?"

"How come *we* got the bug while the rest of the Platoon stayed free…want the low-down?"

"I'm all ears," I said, looking at Tommy and the inquisitive faces of the others.

"We've been within spitting distance of the Cambodian border ever since we started the boundary patrols. Cast your minds back to a week ago. The Detail spent the whole day moving west, we must have covered at least twelve miles. At sundown our sections' established a four-man listening post in the jungle. You, Speedy, Jumper and Sugar were assigned first lookout. Me, Dinger, JJ and Dusty, relieved you at 04:00."

"So, what of it, why's that so significant?"

"Think about it. The Platoon moves *west* all day, that's bound to place us deep inside Cambodia. And our position must have been a good mile beyond the C-P, about a quarter-mile from a network of abandoned paddies. I don't know about you, but I got the hide bitten off me that night."

"But that was three days before we came down with this shit," JJ said.

"Ah, that's were it becomes interesting. I've been reading up on strain, it's not like any other plasmodium. It's got a seventy-two hour incubation period; once in your bloodstream it establishes itself in your liver and spleen. Three days later it multiplies rapidly. That's when you have your first crisis."

"So how come the lads at the C-P didn't get it?" Jumper asked.

"Simple, they were just out of reach. Don't you remember the communiqué: 'M: MTS-7 is only prevalent in the mud-tracts of Eastern Cambodia', and the 'host only has a two mile flight radius'. It all adds up; we were in a high risk area at the wrong time that's the long and short of it."

There was an interlude, broken by Dinger: "What the fuck were we doing in Cambodia? We've got no mandate in Cambodia."

"Politics!" I said with venom, "...fucking politics!" I could see Tommy looking at me with a knowing smile the others a look of confusion. "Wanna know what I mean? Okay, who gives us our intelligence? Who tips us off on border activities?"

"The yanks'," Sugar replied, "they've got the satellites."

"Right, satellites, pretty accurate wouldn't you say? So how come we've been chasing ghosts for the last month? And how come we end up in fuckin' Cambodia? I'll tell you, cos we've been fed a crock-of-shite. Those manipulative pricks have been playing games with us. Feeding us duff grid references so the Khmer Rouge can sneak behind and rendezvous with some CIA Agent to acquire weapons!"

"Come on, you're jokin' me..." Jumper said, "the yanks giving the KR weapons why would they wanna do that?"

"Simple, to further de-stabilise the region. They know they've lost this war, they know Charlie's gonna have his day. What better way to delay the outcome than to stir up trouble between the Marxist Viet Cong and Maoist Khmer Rouge?"

"So what does that make us?" Jumper said, "fuckin' puppets!"

"Pawns! Expendable commodities in the middle of a giant stick of dynamite the fuse burning at both ends, right," Tommy suggested, looking at me for confirmation.

I nodded in silence, scornful of the immoral politicians in high places: "We're nothing to them. We're insignificant, just pegs in an endgame!"

Marine Collins was pensive after our chat. It took a lot to faze him, but on that occasion he looked unusually stressed. "What's up Jumper?" I enquired.

He looked at me: "I don't know. I can't work things out like you and Tommy. I just take what people say on face...you know—"

"Face value."

"Yeah, face value, but I just don't know anymore; I thought we were doing some good out here. I thought we had a purpose. But they've been lyin' to us haven't they? nothin' but fuckin' lies!"

I felt downhearted as I looked at Jumper's youthful face. He still had a kind of innocence, an innate willingness to accept: "We are making a difference. What about the refugees we've helped, like the party of Viet Cong men and women that were being rounded up by the SVA on Route nine. It was obvious what they had in mind. If it wasn't for us those poor bastards would've been decomposing in a monsoon ditch. Sometimes our mere presence is enough."

"Yeah..." Jumper said, without conviction, "I suppose."

I don't know whom I was trying to convince, him or myself. The United Nations had set our mandate; our objectives were, purportedly, clear. But the

Americans' still had a powerful influence in Indo-China; they still pulled the strings. I'd always been suspicious of America's involvement in the war. I had long considered that they were motivated by an arrogant blindness. But that was their lookout. It was obvious, however – if our hypothesis was correct – that they were attempting to covertly drag neutrals into their sordid games.

I momentarily felt contempt for the yanks but then realised, the *politicians* were the pathology, not yanks per se. They, as I've written hitherto, were predominantly good people. The staff on Ward 6: Billie, Phillipa, Molly, Bobbie-Joe, Belinda, Collet, Chauncey; even Sister Calley, she may have been a tyrant but she was still a good clinician. '*Don't judge a nation by its politicians…*' my father once said. I suddenly realised the real significance of those words, as I would on many other occasions as my life unfolded.

Lights-out seemed to come too soon. Maybe it was because I knew I was getting better, hence ready for the frontline. My mind as always was racing as I put my head to pillow. Flashbacks and playbacks of incidents in the 'Nam, thoughts of home; reflections of my young life. 'Should I be so serious?' I thought, 'maybe I should just switch off, let it all hang out.' I couldn't of course – it's not in my nature.

I closed my eyes with an abandoning smile and a wish that I could have just one night of pleasant dreams instead of the constant nightmares of hunting the Khmer Rouge whilst being hunted by Viet Cong.

Wednesday 27 June.

I did have pleasant dreams or at least one, early morning just before waking. I was at home on leave. My mother had just made scones and a fresh pot of tea. The dream was so vivid I could detect the aroma from the freshly baked pastries. We were about to settle to watch *Peyton Place* on afternoon TV. I didn't particularly like daytime television, but I did enjoy time with my mum. I felt sad when I awoke. It was one of those dreams that you didn't want to end; a dream you wanted to pick up again once back asleep but never could. It was with some chagrin that I didn't receive a birthday card from my folks. Inbound mail was always late. The war disrupted everything. Then again what was I complaining about? I had hardly gone out of my way to write home.

After lunch the hospital barber a small Indo-Chinese man with silver-grey hair and black teeth came to the ward to offer us a haircut. He was wearing a standard issue hospital coat that hadn't seen a washtub in years: "You like haircut?" he called out from the middle of the ward, electric clippers in hand.

We all jumped at the chance to have a freebie, queuing in an orderly line

near the ablutions. Marine Lyle was first to sit down.
"You like haircut?" the barber said again.
"Yeah, giz a number two marine crop will yer."
"You like haircut?" the barber repeated with a dumb expression, suggesting it was the only English he could speak.
"Oh fuckin' 'ell. Bazzer, will you tell this fuck-stick I wanna number two marine crop!"
With this the barber suddenly became excited. "Fuck-stick, fuck-stick, jiggy-jiggy…" he cried out whilst jumping up and down, "you like me get you women?"
"Nah, I just want me fuckin' 'air done!"
"Oo-wer…" Jumper said in a camp fashion, "he wants 'is 'air done."
"I'll fuckin' do you when I've got up from 'ere!" Sugar replied amid the howls of laughter.
I instructed him of our requirements.
"Nhần rặ," (*Okay.*) He said, though I had a sneaking suspicion he could speak more English than he was letting on. As it turned out he was an expert barber. He cropped our heads moving the clippers over our scalps without a pause; the eight of us lounged on our beds sporting our new crops.
"Oh jeez!" Bobbie-Joe said as she sauntered down the ward, "…how come you marines always wanna look like you just come out of a stretch in San Quentin?"
I, thankfully, received my last iron injection mid afternoon. Sister David asked us all if we would be willing to give a small amount of blood purely for research purposes?
We all agreed. We were only too willing to contribute towards developing an effective prophylaxis against Strain-7; personally, I wouldn't wish it on my worst enemy.

I kept my eyes open for Billie at the 14:00 shift change. I didn't want to come right out and ask when she was on next. There was no sign of her, indicating that she was likely on the 22:00 turnover. Speedy could see my watchfulness and likely disappointment.
"You lookin' for Billie?" he asked.
"Might be."
"You're sweet on her aren't you?"
"Am not—"
"Come on! the boys all know it. Bit old for you isn't she?"
"I like older women," I replied, deciding that it was pointless trying to hide the obvious. "I've had enough of gymslips. An older woman knows what buttons to press, you dig?"

"Oh yeah! Molly would be my bitch. I know she's a bit big round the hips, but I like that. Fuck those straight up an' down arses. I like a bit flesh, somethin' to get hold of, you dig?"

"It's not just about sex though is it?"

"Isn't it? then again you would say that. We've heard you two talkin' all that intellectual stuff, you like all that shit don't you?"

"Some men like a fag in the afterglow, I like a conversation."

"Bollocks to that! All's I wanna do after I've shot me load is roll over and go to sleep."

"I think you'll find that's a trait in men that women despise."

"Well 'ark at Doctor Ruth!"

Dusty, Jumper and Sugar joined us all wearing thoughtful expressions: "What's up?" Speedy enquired.

"We've just been listening to the news," Sugar explained. "There's been a firefight on the border; NVA by all accounts. The reporter said UN Forces were involved."

"You don't think it was our Platoon do you?" Speedy asked.

"Didn't specify, just said UN Forces."

There was an extended period of silence, each of us probably thinking the same thing. We hadn't really thought of our compadrés since being in hospital. We had each other that was enough. Furthermore, our sojourn was a welcome break from the conflict. Now, we were all reflective, thinking of our buddies; wondering if they'd been involved in the fracas. All of a sudden I missed them.

"Do you think we'll all make it home?" Marine Collins asked, aiming his question at us all.

"Yeah, cruisin'," Dusty answered. "There's only a couple of months left to Blighty."

I remember looking at my buddies wondering if we really would all make it home. We knew from our experiences in Northern Ireland that the first and last weeks of a Tour of Duty were the most perilous. Sometime later I would reflect on our conversation, particularly since it was Jumper who asked the question.

"I just thought," Sugar said, "if any of our lads have been hit they'd be brought here don't you think?"

"Probably," Speedy answered, "though not necessarily this ward."

"We could ask couldn't we?" suggested Jumper.

"Wouldn't be any point," I said, "they wouldn't tell us, not straight away. It'd be a breach of confidentiality."

Speedy stared at me: "Billie would tell if *you* asked, wouldn't she Bazzer?"

"Yeah…Billie would tell me."

Before adjourning I agreed to ask Billie if any of our boys had been brought in though I was unsure, post agreement, if I really wanted to know the answer.

Most of the men participated in a card-school whilst on the ward. No money changed hands. The league table, run by Speedy, was purely sporting. Cribbage was the preferred game, though the absence of a crib-board originally precluded the option.

Dusty Miller was a dab hand at making things. Sugar reckoned he must have spent his entire childhood sat in front of the box watching Blue Peter. Nobody complained when Dusty conjured a crib-board out of flour, water and fat. He'd skilfully moulded the clay-like dough into a block spacing the peg holes in a uniform line. He left his creation on the balcony to bake in the sun.

Corporal Farr and I favoured chess. Unfortunately, the only set in the dayroom was short of 3 white Pawns, a Knight and the white Queen; and a black Bishop, Rook and black King. We attempted a game substituting the missing pieces with salt and pepper cellars but it was hopeless.

Early evening, Jumper, JJ, Sugar and Speedy were engaged in a card game. Dinger was writing yet another letter to his fiancée, whilst Tommy and I read. Marine Miller had disappeared early afternoon – he had a habit of going walkabout. He unexpectedly appeared approaching Tommy and me lounging on our beds: "You two better check something out in the dayroom."

We rushed to the lounge to be greeted by a complete chess set laid out central on the table. "Well feast your eyes on that!" Tommy said.

Dusty had lovingly fashioned the missing pieces out of his flour and water concoction. The white Queen, black Bishop and King were particularly impressive. The black pieces attained their ebony appearance by being soaked in iodine. From a distance you could hardly discern the additions.

We thanked Dusty for his effort and settled after agreeing to play the best of five. We were on the third game, Tommy leading 2 - 1, when he noticed me scrutinising the iodine soaked rook in my hand: "Where you at?"

"Have you read The Colditz Story?" I asked, continuing to examine the crafted piece.

"Yeah, long time ago."

"I read the revised version, five volumes in the Readers Digest. There was a Prisoner of War in Colditz who intricately crafted a whole chess set out of soap. Every piece perfectly honed to scale. He made the board out of matchsticks; used boot polish for the black pieces and black squares on the board. A guard and fellow chess player was so impressed he bought the set off him when the prisoners were liberated. The two of them managed to play a few games before they separated. Struck a friendship; ended up playing chess through the post, over a hundred games. One game lasted nearly eighteen months. They're still playing no doubt. I like stories like that; where good triumphs, uniformity from opposites." Tommy nodded as he went back to studying the game. The interruption was likely a welcome break; I had him on the run. My imagination was in overdrive: "If this place was a Stalag and we were Prisoners of War, Dusty would be the manufacturer. He'd make the tools, fashion the civilian clothes and forge our identities and passports for the escape."

"Yeah," Tommy said, engaging in my fleeting invention, "Speedy would be the banker."

"Sugar would be the conman; that fucker could talk a whole Nunnery out of their knickers."

"Dinger and JJ would be the workhorses for the tunnel," Tommy enthused. "Those two mules could move a mountain between them."

"What about Jumper?" I asked.

"Jumper's a bruiser, he'd be the enforcer. Sort out any guards who reneged on a deal."

"What about us? What would we be?"

"Same as we are in here..." he said with a grin, "a couple of fuckin' smart arses!"

"We ought to take these pieces with us when we leave; souvenirs."

"Nah," Tommy responded, "best leave them for any other Joe's who get the lurgy."

Sister David interrupted our game at 21:00 with our evening refreshments. "There you go," she said gingerly placing our beverages on the table. "You boys enjoying your game?"

"Yeah," Tommy replied after thanking her for the vittles.

"Who's winnin'?"

"Me," Tommy said, raising his hand, "...two–one, though this toe-rag's boxing me in. Reckon I'm for a fall on this'n."

"I've never partaken' in that little ol' game," Collet said, looking at the board. "My daddy taught me checkers when I was a shrimp. Checkers is easy, but all those pieces. Looks too complicated to me."

"You shouldn't put yourself down," Tommy suggested. "We could easily teach you, if we had the time."

With that Collet's facial expression changed, she suddenly became sombre. "I'll leave you fellas be," she said, departing as quickly as she entered.

"How come she went quiet?" I asked.

"Don't know," Tommy replied, re-focusing on the game.

He did know of course – as did I.

By 21:40 we were into our last game. I had indeed secured the penultimate match. The decider was anything but delicately poised; this time I was boxed in. The loss of my Queen exacerbated matters. I wasn't sure if Tommy's bounty was due to a cunning move or a lapse of application on my behalf. Either way it didn't look good, I was swiftly running out of options. My consistent clock-watching didn't help. I assumed Billie would be on duty at 22:00. Tommy noticed my lack of study.

"Concentrate…" he said, "I don't want you blaming your demise on other things."

"I don't know what you mean I'm sure," I replied with a smile.

I tried to focus on the contest. I'd been on the defensive for over 15 minutes. Tommy had astutely affected a pincer movement. My remaining bishops, rook and knight were the only pieces blocking a final move on my King. I attempted a counter attack in a futile endeavour to ward off the inevitable. I needn't have bothered.

"Check," Tommy proclaimed scooping up my knight.

"Fuck-pig! …I didn't see that."

The only alternative was to move my King. I saw the final blow looming. "That's checkmate, mate!" Tommy said, delivering the death-stroke with his pastry knight.

I offered my hand in capitulation: "It had to be that piece didn't it!"

"Never mind mucker," he said, reaching across the table to shake my hand, "…maybe you can get me back tomorrow."

The 22:00 turnover had just been completed as we adjourned. Billie was checking the charts; she smiled as I waved to her. We had to be careful, Vinegar was on duty, she had eyes like a shite-hawk. It was a good twenty minutes before I had a chance to speak to her.

"Did you enjoy your days off?" I enquired.

"It was quiet. Caught up on some sleep; did some readin' an' the like. Truth is it's kinda good to get back on dooty, gets real monotonous in residence."

"Did you hear about the firefight up at Bận Đơn?"

"Sure did, bad skirmish by all accounts."

"We're all wondering if any of our muckers were involved, or to be more precise, if any of our boys were amongst the casualties. Do you know anything?"

"No…" Billie whispered, "though I doubt if any injured were shipped in here. Leastwise I didn't hear any Medevacs above, did you?"

"Didn't think of that. Could they have been brought in any other way?"

"Not in this little ol' neck of the woods, too risky. All casualties come in on birds. Don't you worry your little head, I'll check for ya," she said, checking that Calley wasn't spying.

Billie continued with her duties. It was apparent she'd managed to make a brief phone-call, likely to triage, from the office. She looked at me and deliberately shook her head as she came out of the glass-fronted room. I nodded to indicate I understood. I turned to inform the men that the Platoon had suffered no casualties. The smile on their faces and knowing look in their eyes gave it away, they too had interpreted Billie's message. I wondered if they were as grateful as I of her risky efforts. I concluded of course that they would have been. I knew those boys. I knew what made them tick: their fears and aspirations; their appreciation of good deeds and of how they would withhold their counsel and feelings. They didn't tell me they were grateful because they didn't need to.

Sister Calley disappeared around 23:30. She had an inclination to leave the duty staff nurse late at night. Some of the lads wondered if she had a fancy man tucked away. Sugar reckoned it was Dobbs. "He could bore the fuck out of her, while he was boring the fuck out of her!" he said.

On that occasion I was only too pleased that she'd vacated the ward. I wanted a proper chance to talk to Billie. Most of the men had settled for the night, save for Dinger writing more sonnets to his sweetheart. I felt like a schoolboy bunking off as I made my way through the silent ward searching for her. I eventually found her on the balcony clearing up yet another pile of debris left by our lazy band.

"What you still doin' up?" she asked as I joined her.

"Couldn't sleep, never can in this place. I don't think I've had a decent night's sleep since I've been in the 'Nam. The first thing I'm gonna do when I get home is sleep a sleep of the dead. Put my head on the pillow without worrying about a whole heap of shit coming down on top of me!"

"How long you guys gotta do out here?"

"Just over a month an'-a-half, or six weeks and two days to be precise."

"You lookin' forward to goin' home?"

I paused for a second, I was looking forward to going home or at the least leaving a war zone, how could I not be. I wasn't looking forward to leaving some things behind; Billie was undoubtedly one of them: "Kind of, though there's some things I'll miss."

"Like?" Billie asked with a mystical air.

"The people, the Vietnamese are lovely, when they're not trying to chalk your arse that is. They have an amazing culture, a totally different outlook on life. And I'll sure miss the friends I've made. I've become very close to some, maybe a bit too close. Dad always warned me against that. '*Don't get to close to people; war's got a habit of snatching them away*,' he told me. He was right, except it's not the war that'll snatch some away, it's our duties."

I could see Billie out the corner of my eye. She was staring at me; she knew what I meant, to whom I was referring. I could smell her white rain shampoo; hear her hand gently rustling the keys in her pocket. I could feel her as if she were close to my body. I was sure she felt the same. She spoke just as I turned to look at her.

"You bin readin' *The Grapes of Wrath*?"

"I'm half-way through it, I think I'm beginning to understand its message. How economic chaos impacts most on those least able to influence its outcome. The wickedness of those who exploit people in need and the humanity of those who lend a helping hand. The importance of solidarity in the fight against continuing adversity. And most of all, the *real* meaning of struggle. I've got the message alright. Then again I would have wouldn't I, now that I'm the old bird-dog in the bush—!"

We both laughed.

"—I wish I could discuss it with my dad, right now."

"Write to him; put the words on paper just as you told it then. It'll be somethin' for him to be glad of, that his son has a grasp of somethin' close to his heart."

"You say that as if you know him."

"I've already met half of him," she said warmly, "in you."

Yet another intermission followed. I felt as if in a paradox: comfortable though a little uneasy, composed yet a little impatient. A distant rumble broke the impasse.

"Thunder?" said Billie.

"No, artillery…howitzers, a battery of them by the sounds of it. They're a long way off, maybe even Cambodia."

"Another night of the ceasefire!"

"Huh, another day of lies. The propaganda machine will be in full flow; mendacious robots tapping out the telegraphs. Slaves to the rhythm; peace, victory, peace, victory – we're not really a bunch of double-dealing twats!"

"Hot damn!" Billie chortled.

"This is something else that reminds me of my dad," I said, as the distant barrage was replaced by calm. "He told me of the wonder of serene nights amidst conflict—"

"WW two?"

"Right, couldn't quite work out what he meant as a kid. I got it now though, how nothing surpasses the sound of silence, like silence. Are you the only one in your family who's done military service?"

"I had a brother, Zechariah. Joined the US Marines in 'sixty-six."

"Had, does that mean—?"

"Quang Ngaî 'sixty-nine! Took two bullets; dead before he hit the ground they say. Went home in a crate full of body bags. Came visitin' me down here just before he died. He looked as proud as a peacock in his number one uniform with its gold buttons and marine emblems a glintin'. He'd earned his Green Beret, just like you boys no doubt. I couldn't help but love him, stood there as pretty as a picture even though I was pissed with him for volunteerin'. Truth is Zechariah loved the Marine Corps, that's why your words struck home a whiles back. He told me that for the first time in his life he felt like he belonged!"

I suddenly felt remorseful of my ranting about the war. What is more, I gained some insight into Billie's often distant look, the kind that indicated a fleeting thought, welcome or otherwise, that she would sometimes give whenever I would talk of how I loved the corps.

"How old was he when he got killed?"

"Same age as you, a baby!" she replied without a condescending tone.

"I'm sorry you lost him."

"It's the war, trouble is it ain' *our* war. I reckon you're right what you say about Charlie, though I don't know what drives him."

"Have you read Spartacus?" I asked, still feeling a little uneasy.

"Nope, but I see the film."

"Well I don't know about the film, but in the book Spartacus says, '*Death is the only freedom a slave knows, that's why he's not afraid of it.*' The Viet Cong have got nowhere else to go, nothing else to lose – that's why they'll win. How come you never mentioned your brother before?"

"You didn't ask," she said with a gentle look that re-established my ease.

I thought again of previous conversations. I gave Billie an inquisitive look: "The other day you said you liked the Vietnamese and that you'd consider staying in Charlieville. Aren't you bitter you losing your brother out here?"

"What am I supposed to do hate a whole nation because one or more of their kind killed my kin? I don't hold with an eye for an eye!"

I couldn't help but laugh, acknowledging her belated riposte. I stared into the blackness: "It isn't always easy though is it? Remember I told you about me and my buddies seeing a village being obliterated in Nha Trang? They wanted to seek out the culprits, bend some heads. I repudiated that, said it wasn't the proper response. Fact is I felt the same. It's hard sometimes, standing back, taking stock and thinking things through. Refusing to countenance immediate retribution; rejecting the notion that you should put to death those who've put others to death. And forgiveness, that's something else. I've never had anybody really hurt me or lost a beloved at the hands of another. Truth is, I'm not sure how I'd react, no matter how much of a Humanist I consider myself to be."

"I ask the good Lord…" Billie said with a deliberate smile, "he helps me with the struggle."

I have had altercations with some Christians who, I considered, had used their religion as a smoke screen; a cop out when confronted with sensitive issues or an excuse for their malevolence. I didn't feel that about Billie, I felt sure she was genuine.

"You still writin' that journal?" she asked.

"Yeah, I've written quite a bit since being in here, together with some retrospective stuff."

"What are you going to do with it once it's all done?"

"Nothing probably...most of its pretty private."

"Thought of maybe getting' it published?"

"Nah, no one would be interested."

"Y'all don't know that...some might welcome a different viewpoint. It's good to have different perspectives otherwise history just becomes one book. An' if you write like you talk it'll be different alright."

I felt flattered by her praise and encouragement. Nobody in the Platoon had ever said anything about my journals. Why should they? Most of them were just concerned about surviving day-to-day. Counting the weeks to the flight home, longing to be reunited with loved ones. Billie was the first person I'd ever really confided in, regardless how close I felt to my brothers.

"You're in my journal, you feature quite a bit."

"Sheeit! what do you wanna go an' write about a dumb nigger like me for?"

"You're not that to me," I said my voice full of affection.

Our eyes met in a moment of deep intimacy. I felt as if frozen in time, I wished I could've been.

"Don't look at me like that," Billie said breaking eye contact.

"Why not?" I replied with the awkwardness of a teenager on his first date.

"Cos you shouldn't. It ain't right; ain't the place or time."

"I wasn't aware there was a rule book."

"Some things don't need rule books; some things just can't be written. You'd better get ya self back to bed, Calley could be back at any time."

I didn't see the point in trying to re-establish the intimacy. She'd clearly gone into her professional mode, more out of necessity than choice. I bid her goodnight and turned to make my way back to bed. Billie called out as I walked from the balcony: "I've enjoyed our talks."

"Me too," I replied without looking back.

I wish I had looked back, taken a glance. Then again, I longed for many things as I lay looking at the shadows of the redundant ceiling fans. 'I can't let it go,' I thought, 'I've got to tell her how I feel.' I concluded, as the clock ticked past 01:00, that ruminating would get me nowhere. I closed my eyes with a promise that I would find a way of disclosing my feelings. But as I drifted off to sleep I didn't know that our hours at Rậnlạntoì were numbered; then again, maybe I did.

Thursday 28 June.

I slept longer than normal on that morning. "Good mornin' sleepy head," Bobbie-Joe said, tickling my foot under the sheet. "Where's that smile you normally gimme?"

The lads were already up and about. Most of them had showered and taken breakfast. It took me some time to stir, I felt unusually lethargic. Sugar was babbling away as normal. He tried to engage me in some banter but I had little interest.

I spent much of the morning reviewing my journal. I had written a lot since being on Ward 6. 'Would I really be able to get it published sometime future...' I thought, 'would anyone really be interested?' I doubted it my writings were probably too anti-war. I found myself replaying conversations I'd had with Billie. I must have looked a picture sitting in the dayroom with a permanent pre-glow on my face. There were other things on my mind, I'd still not written home. The half completed letter sat on my bedside table as if awaiting some incantation, a formula to magic its completion.

I was listening to John Lennon & The Plastic Ono Band on the 'Eleven O'clock Album' when Corporal Farr came over: "They're shipping us out."

"What?" I replied, though more through not wanting to accept the statement than failing to hear.

"Fifteen-hundred, it's all arranged. We're linking with the Platoon at Phờn Xuŷen. Doctors' already signed our discharge papers."

"Back to reality aye," Marine Jeffers said as I arrived at my bed.

"Yeah," I replied, trying to hide my despondency.

Our fatigues, neatly wrapped in polythene on our beds, were further confirmation of the end of our stay. The auxiliaries had washed and ironed them with care and precision. Our boots, polished to perfection, lay next to them.

"Have you seen Chauncey?" I asked JJ.

"No, hasn't been around all morning, why?"

"It's nothing," I said, not disclosing that I wanted to ask him what shift Billie was on.

"—Chauncey's covering in the laundry," Bobbie-Joe said overhearing my enquiry.

"Are we gonna be able to say goodbye to him?" Speedy asked.

"He knows y'all shippin' out. He'll get on up here some-hows."

I too wanted to bid Chauncey goodbye, but my mind was on other things.

Lunch went untouched, I was to busy clock-watching willing Billie to be on the afternoon stint.

The rota change bought bitter disappointment. Calley, Staff Nurse Lopez, Molly and Phillipa took the watch. Billie was clearly on another late-shift.

Tommy could see my displeasure as I changed into my fatigues: "I'm organising a collection, wanna get the girls some nutty [chocolates]. Got any cash?"

I only had a few Đồng; we all did the remnants of 8 days previous. I gave what I had and joined the lads collected round the dinning table each putting every last note into the collection. Tommy counted the offering: "Fourteen Đồng, twenty hào – should be enough for a decent box of nutty."

Tommy could see the wanting look on my face. Lance Corporal Bell picked it up too: "What's up with you?" Dinger asked.

I contemplated answering, feeling a little uneasy, unsure of my right to make a personal request. "I'm not sure if I've got the right to ask," I said, the troop looking in my direction, "but I don't suppose you'd let me buy a separate box. Something small?"

"Oh yeah…" Sugar said, "for your fancy piece!"

Sugar was just being his outgoing self. I half expected a rejection at least from some of the boys, but no, just silence.

"Any objections?" Tommy asked.

"Nah..." Jumper said to general nodding from the gang, "it's only a few bob."

"Agreed then, you may as well get them," Tommy said, handing me the pile of crumpled notes.

"Thanks boys, I owe yer."

I was aware that there was a Red Cross shop on the ground floor. Time was moving on, I needed to get our purchase before the Huey arrived.

Staff Nurse Lopez came out of the office at 14:40: "Listen up in here, bird inbound, ETA five minutes, y'all better get ya'selves up top."

Corporal Farr glanced at me: "They're early, you'd better take off; know where the shop is?"

"I'll find it—"

"Bazzer!" Tommy shouted as I hurried down the ward, "…your dog tags, don't forget them."

I picked my tags from the bedrail evoking memories of our first days on the ward. How ill we felt, yet how glad to be in such pleasant company. The cold metal on my skin gave further verification of our return to duty.

The lads were preparing to say their goodbyes as I left the ward. Sugar enquired on the whereabouts of Phillipa. He looked despondent as he was told she'd gone to the med-stores. Clearly, I wasn't the only soldier who was going to miss a particular member of staff.

I searched the labyrinth-like building for the Red Cross shop. The corridors were eerily quiet. Wards, operating theatres, waiting rooms and offices were dark and dusty. The whole thing resembled a scene from *Phantom of the Opera*. I eventually came across a small kiosk. It had a distinctive French design. It was so old that it appeared the hospital had been built around it. A small Vietnamese woman sat on a stool fingering an abacus rack, though it was beyond me how she managed to accumulate any takings in that deserted building. I could hear a faint tune on the radio, a Vietnamese melody: 'Ớ đàu nổi bướn nớ Việt Nâm', a melancholy fable of lost love the squandered object being their very country. She took no notice of me as I scanned the meagre shelves: tobacco, an assortment of confectionery, toiletries, teddy bears (in a military hospital!) and some faded stationery.

"Excuse me," I said, "can you tell me the prices of your chocolates?"

With that the woman jumped up from the stool and placed three boxes on the counter: "Lindts Spec-ial, eleven and fifteen Đồng. Hershey's Select, four Đồng!" she said, banging the boxes down on the faded veneer.

"Haven't you got anything else?"

"What you see you look!" she shouted, though not in an aggressive manner.

I carefully counted the money, though I'm unsure why, I was clearly eighty hào short.

I gave the woman my best lost puppy expression; if Francis Ford Coppela had been around he'd have given me a part in one of his films. "I've only got fourteen Đồng and twenty hào. Can I have your two cheapest boxes for that?"

"Ha! Sold-ier plenty money, you pay good, pay me price!"

I scanned the half empty shelves searching for another option. The absence of any sizeable alternatives left me with the conclusion that I could only purchase one box. I was about to give up when I noticed the stern woman scrutinising the emblems on my combat shirt. "You soldier English," she said, pointing to the Union Flag sewn onto my left upper sleeve.

"Yeah...English."

"Unite' Nation," she deliberately added observing the UN Flag on my right sleeve. "Me Việt Công!" she yelled, pointing to the red ribbon on her arm, "when you go, we win!"

"Yeah," I said with a part-smile, "I do believe you will."

She smiled back; her harsh face suddenly looked kind. "I like Johnny's from England, you take!" she said, pushing two boxes towards me whilst taking the money.

"Cám ơn," (*Thank you.*) I said with a huge grin.

I grabbed my premium and beat a hasty retreat for the ward. The lads had already departed on my return. My footsteps echoed in the huge space as I sauntered towards the office. The ward was barren, except for Staff Nurse Lopez stripping the beds. Molly, stowing blister packs, smiled as I entered the nursing station. Vinegar, who appeared to be completing discharge reports, continued writing.

"Excuse me," I said, feeling awkward. "The lads...well, we've had a bit of a whip-round. Got y'all a box of nutty—I mean, chocolates, as a thank you."

Calley, eventually and somewhat reluctantly, looked up.

"I trust it's not against the rules," I continued, trying to gauge Calley's poker face.

"It's fine," Calley said in an indifferent tone, "just leave them here."

"Thanks babe," Molly said quietly, "real nice of y'all."

"Not at all, you people made us feel welcome. If I had to be sick then I'd wanna be sick in here."

Molly smiled. Calley, on the other hand, continued to stare, her face devoid of expression. I needed to leave the extra box I'd purchased for Billie. Time was running out, the Huey was due at any time. I had a feeling I was in the wrong company to have made a personal request, but I had little choice.

"I don't suppose I could leave a separate box for Billie, just from me?"

I knew I shouldn't have asked the sudden change on Vinegar's face was testament to the fact. "Those chocolates are for the hospital..." she blasted spinning round in her chair, "personal gifts are strictly forbidden!"

"I appreciate that," I said, maintaining my composure, "it's just that there's no other way to leave them for her with the context 'an everything—"

"Is there something wrong with your ears soldier!"

I felt an ascending rage, an almost uncontrollable urge to hit out. I had observed her humiliating her staff: insulting them with her caustic tongue; hiding, like every other tyrant I've had the misfortune to meet, behind her position. I scowled at her desperately trying not to crush the delicate boxes in my hand: "What is your fuckin' problem?"

"Presently you are! I've explained the rules, now I'd be obliged if you'd vacate my ward!"

I was about to respond when I felt Molly gently squeezing the back of my left arm. I wanted for the entire world to give Calley a mouthful. Instead I looked sternly into her glare – which cut into me like a paper knife through frozen butter – determined to maintain eye contact. I couldn't do anything about her bullying the staff; I wasn't going to let her bully me. She turned away and continued to fill in the med sheets.

I continued to stare before dumping the large box of chocolates on the filing cabinet: "Well I suppose I'd better take my swingin' dick out of 'ere!"

"That bitch is in dire need of a good screw," I said to Molly as we left the office.

“She’d get one if she could find a willin’ piece of pussy,” Molly whispered.

“Oh…I see.”

“It was real nice havin’ you boys on here,” Molly said, pecking me on the cheek. “Take care honey.”

“Thanks again girls,” I said as Molly joined Staff Lopez.

I had a mixture of anger and dejection as I made my way towards the exit. Calley’s attitude was untenable. Granted, institutions need rules, but rules are created to act as ‘guidelines’ not ‘tramlines’. I’d an inclination that Vinegar’s renunciation was exacerbated because Billie was the object of my affection. It was obvious Calley didn’t like her. This may have been because of her popularity, or her total dedication to the task. I considered it to be none of these: for I could see it in her eyes, hear it in her voice – it was because Billie Ebotée was black.

Phillipa was coming out of the utility room on the landing as I exited the ward.

“You still here?” she said, surprised to see me.

“We’ve brought you all some chocolates, just dropped them off.”

“Aw, you shouldn’t have, we gals have gotta look after our figures.”

“There’s nothin’ wrong with your figure woman!”

Phillipa spotted the box of Hershey’s Select in my hand: “I got these for Billie. Calley won’t put them to one side for her. Will you take them; give them to her when you next see her?”

Phillipa looked at me; her dismissive expression preceded her verbal response: “I’m sorry Barry; I don’t think I can do that.”

I lowered my gaze, not wanting her to see the sadness on my face. My chagrin was demonstrable. Phillipa clearly knew I felt for Billie. She smiled and slowly shook her head: “It happens all the time soldier, in every hospital in the middle of every war there’s ever been, always has, always will. To us you boys’ just come and go. It’s enough when y’all don’t go out in body bags.”

I looked into her brown eyes, a look that informed her I understood. We both picked up the distant rhythm of the inbound Huey.

“You’d better haul ass,” she said, “you don’t wanna miss that chopper.”

Phillipa put her arms out. We hugged in a momentary silence. I could feel the warmth of her body, her hair pressing on my cheek, her heart beating against my ribs. I wanted to freeze time. Granted, it wasn’t Billie, but it mattered not. Phillipa whispered in my ear: “Y’all keep ya heads down out there. Get ya’selves back-on home to those who loves ya.”

“We will,” I replied, disengaging. “We’ll never forget y’all. You made us feel special.”

“It was nothin’, now go on, get ya’self up top.”

“Phillipa!” I called out as she slowly moved through the double doors onto the ward. “Tell Billie…” I stood in silence unsure of what to say, yet longing to say so much.

“I’ll tell her,” she softly said.

The double doors swung to a close. I stood alone on the landing, fidgeting with the box of Hershey’s Select. 'So what do I do with these?' I thought. The children that frequented the area adjacent the main gate came to mind. I remembered observing them from the balcony, milling around in groups. They’d often be looking through the large, once ostentatious, gates into the compound; scruffy and emaciated, yet always excitable.

I moved swiftly down stairs to the main entrance, the thundering note from the inbound Huey growing ever louder. I dashed across the cracked and weed-strewn courtyard towards the large rusting gates. The western sector of Lôc Nịnh looked even shabbier than the view presented from the balcony. A small pagoda, desperately in need of a fresh coat of paint, dominated the craggy skyline. The children, as always, were gathered round; some playing basket-football, others throwing glass marbles or pitching stones against the pagoda wall. I could see their beautiful eyes shining amid grubby faces that appeared to sport a permanent grin.

“Trê con, chị nhứ kệo,” (*Kids, you like candy*?) I shouted through the gate railings whilst peeling the cellophane from the chocolates. The children assembled with gusto as I poked the open box through the gap; one or two at first then up to a dozen. There were around 20 chocolates in the box enough initially for one each. Word spread quickly; soon the road leading to the gate was teeming with little urchins. None complained when the box was empty. They still smiled, still wanted to know my name and politely asked for souvenirs. I looked at them as they jostled, cackling amongst themselves; their country’s future, the next generation. 'Would they have to fight?' I thought. The downdraft from the helicopter swooping in as if a bird of prey broke my thoughts.

I made a hasty retreat to the entrance, waving the children goodbye. The hall and corridors echoed as my boots thumped on the disinfected floors. I could hear the rotor-thud of the Huey, its damp report reverberating down the stairwell, as I dashed up the staggered steps. I struggled with the access door held fast by the blast from the idling blades, eventually stumbling onto the roof as Corporal Farr guided the last of the troop onto the chopper.

“Thank fuck for that!” Tommy hollered as I ran towards the pulsing Huey. “I was just about to give up on you. Climb aboard.”

I clambered onto the Huey, a Series VI from the 1st United States Air Cavalry. That bird was brand spanking new, spotless and well stowed. Its port and starboard M60 machine-guns lay at a 45° angle, belt-less and sealed, as per the UN ceasefire directive.

“Was Chauncey on the ward when you got back?” Marine Miller asked as I fastened my belt.

“No, why didn’t you see him?”

“Nah, don’t think he could get away from the laundry.”

Tommy climbed in on my left. He gave the pilot a clear thumbs-up after strapping himself in and confirming our fastenings.

The pilot throttled up. The Huey vibrated, shaking violently as its motor ascended to maximum. We were about to lift off when Lance Corporal Bell excitedly pointed towards the port opening screaming at the top of his voice: “It’s Chauncey!”

We all looked, left and right respectively each seeing Chauncey stood at the roof access door his white shirt and trousers blowing in the powerful downdraft.

“**Chauncey!**” we bellowed.

Chauncey stood in the wake of the chopper trying to shout above the reverberating rotor-thud. He cupped his hands round his mouth as the pilot pulled up: “**Goodbye you Limey motherfuckers!**” he roared as the Huey rushed skywards.

We each cheered, our thumbs high and feet rapidly banging on the floor as if excited children watching a pantomime. Corporal Speed tried shouting something back to no avail.

The pilot made a 180° turn. We could see Chauncey standing amid the large red cross stationed on the roof, arms outstretched with a beaming smile. The foliage that wrapped the building fluttered wildly in the rotors gale. It appeared as if a parting wave from a building desperately trying to hold onto life.

I gazed at the ‘H’ block, slowly diminishing as we sped northeastward. I felt a dull ache. “Bye Billie,” I whispered.

Tommy noticed my sombre look. “You okay brother?” he mouthed.

“Yeah,” I said avoiding eye contact.

I thought of Billie as the Huey settled on a regular flight path. How much I admired her; how much I enjoyed our conversations. How much I loved her. At that moment, the realisation that I would never see her again was hard to bear.

I looked at my compadrés sat facing and aside me. Jumper and Sugar were clowning as usual. At that instant, I felt a tad intolerant of their shenanigans, not knowing that in less than seven days they would both be Killed in Action.

Dinger was re-reading his latest creation to his fiancée, whilst Speedy sat with his eyes closed. He may have been praying, though at that moment, it wasn’t obvious. JJ was drumming his knees with his hands whilst mouthing a tune, *Fortunate Son* maybe. Dusty was nervously scanning the plethora of escape drills scattered on signs throughout the cab. Tommy was staring out the port side his thoughts racing as swift as the vista below. I imagined he was thinking of his return to his wife and children, counting the days along with the treetops.

And me: I reflected on the last eight days lamenting the loss of something dear. I reached into my breast pocket for confirmation of our period in hospital. The 1950s paperback, fronted with a single candle taped to its cover by Band Aid, brought the verification required only to satisfy a mind that was trying to prepare for challenges new. The Huey gently swayed, rising ever higher, moving ever closer towards our objective. The hum of its motor brought memories of our nightmare ride, an excursion to hell that turned to a sojourn in paradise. I thought of my birthday and of the dream that followed, the silhouettes of dragonflies skipping on the hillside. I strained, looking over Tommy's large frame, to catch a glimpse of the Huey's shadow. The ground seemed to speed by as quickly as our time in the Ran'. No silhouette transpired; its visit wasn't to be. Then, just as I moved to settle back the Huey banked, the dragonfly appeared. Moving alongside, imitating our every manoeuvre its clandestine messages sealed within its dark frame; bouncing the treetops, skimming the paddies, swinging across the terraces. A dynamic choreography: constant yet ever changing, static yet ever moving. Climbing, descending, pitching, yawing, darting, glancing – shadowdancing.

8: ENCOUNTER WITH THE KHMER ROUGE

In some corner of a foreign field
The gunner sleeps tonight.
What's done is done.
We cannot just write off this final scene…

Roger Walters

09:30: Roughly 2 miles north of Lôn Sín Sịng, Trệng Nhôy, 3 July 1973.

The return to duty for the eight sickly souls of 2: Bravo 6 Platoon was a real culture shock. The steamy and noisy barrack room at Base Camp 9 seemed as if a cattle auction contra to the tranquillity of Rậnlạntoì. Getting back into routine is never easy.

The persistent ribbing about our sojourn from members of the Platoon who'd escaped the dreaded malaria was simple enough to deal with. It was the apparent fractiousness amongst members of the Platoon in general that made reintegrating difficult. Being cantankerous at the tail end a Tour of Duty is, I would suggest, understandable. Whilst in the 'Nam we'd been shot at, spat at, kicked, bitten, put on, rained on, manipulated, lied to and moved from one province to another without explanation. I knew, however, from a tour in Northern Ireland that things would likely get better as our departure neared.

For me, leaving barracks for another reconnaissance was somewhat of a relief. I needed to get my limbs moving and become re-accustomed to outdoors. Spending a night in driving rain was not a relief. The wet monsoon was in full flow. Our new recon' position, the mountains encompassing the western slopes of the central highlands, were renowned for incessant rainfall. We discovered exactly what that meant on the previous night. Yet again, everything was soaking wet. Our elevated position was also cooler than previous locales. The mood of the Detail at the morning briefing was less than congenial. Regardless we had to quickly adapt to our newly designated zone.

The border region, comprising thick forest on the higher slopes giving way to smaller woods and glades, was scattered with small communes and hamlets. The Lôn district, encompassing the villages of Lôn Bịen Tờc, Lôn Bắn Đat, Lôn Sín Sịng and Lôn Thiềt was characteristic of the area. The largely tribal people, the Mới, Rhậde and Sédắng were war weary, cynical and suspicious of anyone who wasn't part of their clandestine collectives. Their hostility was understandable. The strategically important area had been heavily contested throughout the prolonged conflict. The ethnic groups were largely bystanders yet had suffered continual instability and loss. Stray rounds and overshoot from carpet-bombing of the Hồ Chí Minh Trail and concentrated napalm and cluster bombing of peripheral districts had taken their toll. The natives also fell victim to the myriad of antipersonnel mines indiscriminately dropped by American mine laying helicopters. The almost incessant bombing would be accompanied by food drops: sacks of rice, tubs of dried milk, strips of foil wrapped jerky and boxes of water biscuits. The central highlands border policy: bomb 'em and feed 'em, bomb 'em and feed 'em – some policy!

The mountain people differed from their lowland neighbours; they looked more 'Indo' than 'Chinese'. They had a hatred of all splinter groups, with a particular anathema for the Khmer Rouge. The Maoist separatists had long been crossing the border, infiltrating villages in an attempt to recruit new blood. The young and gullible discontented with the continual instability and conflict. Vulnerable people easily open to suggestion. It was somewhat of an irony that Pol Pot hated anyone who was not pure Khmer. This made no difference to the KR recruitment teams spouting Maoist doctrine from their 'little red books'.

Our mission was to patrol the border region between Lôn Sín Sịng and Lôn Bắn Đat. Khmer Rouge guerrillas had apparently been probing areas mid the woods and glades. We had heard it all before. We'd almost stopped asking why we were engaged in monitoring primarily innocuous KR movements. Nonetheless, our chagrin remained. North and South Vietnamese Army Units were breaching the ceasefire on a daily basis. Viet Cong insurgents continued to infiltrate villages in the lowlands and refugees were still being terrorised by all factions. Why were we observing largely non-existent Khmer Rouge movements? Were they really in cahoots with the CIA, if so, why were we monitoring their movements? We decided, privately and amongst ourselves, to stop asking futile questions. What did it matter anyway, the war raged on anyhow.

What we were to do if or when we did encounter Khmer Rouge guerrillas was another area of consternation. We had strict instructions to adopt and maintain a '…non-confrontational stance'. The Platoon could not intervene in disputes unless non-combatants were under threat. If fired upon we were allowed to defend ourselves with a strict policy of '...disengagement once the primary threat had been removed'.

We felt like toothless tigers. Our assignments could have been carried out by a bunch of second ribbon scouts. There were times when the whole affair seemed like an exercise in futility. A seemingly never ending pre-set plot, each day closing the same: blank report sheets, blank rounds and blank faces.

11:45: Approximately 5 miles southwest of Lôn Bắn Đat.

The Detail had been advancing northwestward all morning. The landscape was constituent of a collection of small coppicewoods interrupted by barren grounds. We were subdued in the inevitable monotony that accompanied boundary patrols. Sugar broke the monotony with an occasional joke, though it was Marines Montford and Collins who got the men laughing the loudest.

"Fuckin' boredom's gonna kill me," Mongo said. "Every day the same: up, shave, shit, eat, yomp, eat, sleep – no end to it."

"You missed something out," Jumper added, "pulling your plonker."

"We're not wankers in this Platoon you know," Mongo retoreted.

"Oh right, so I suppose that was a fuckin' jumpin' bean in your sleeping bag last night—"

"Pipe down you lot!" Sergeant Edwards said amidst the laughter whilst half laughing himself.

It was close enough to midday for a break. Buster signalled a halt. Corporal Farr started a brew whilst we opened our bland ration packs.

Lance Corporal Jessop and Marine Miller took the first lookout sitting roughly 15 yards back observing the open ground. Sugar and I were to relieve them 30 minutes later. We chattered amongst ourselves. Our turn to go on watch quickly came, Sugar and me retiring to the lookout post. We sat on the damp ground rifles astride our legs staring at the empty fields. Marine Lyle was deep in thought.

"Penny for them," I said, breaking his daydream.

"Thinkin' of Phillipa, that's one sexy bitch. If I wrote to her, do you think she'd write back?"

"She might do."

"I wouldn't know what to write."

"Tell her you wanna fuck her!"

"I don't think of her like that!" Sugar unexpectedly snapped. "I mean I would, but—"

"Okay, okay! Blimey, I thought I had it bad."

We sat in silence for a short while. I think he felt a little embarrassed disclosing his feelings so openly. "Wait 'til we get home," I suggested. "If she's still on your mind write to her from there."

"Yeah, that's a good idea. It'll be the footie season when we get home," Sugar continued with a grin. "We'll have to get in a few matches."

"Yeah, make a day of it. A drink in the *Blue House*, afternoon at *Goodison Park*, a fuck off Chinky, then a night on the town."

"Oh yeah, sniffin' the fresh pussy down Bold Street, woo'ee! You can stay at ours again if you like, me mam wouldn't mind."

“Yeah...” I said with a smile thinking of possible things to come, “I’d like that.”

Our respite soon finished. The Sergeant assembled the Detachment for a continuation briefing: “We’ll remain on a west by northwest echelon swinging north westerly on the approach to Lôn Bắn Đat. Stay in close formation. We need to take care approaching the woods neighbouring the border. Also, keep your eyes peeled for movement through the glades; we don’t want to get caught napping.”

“Oh yeah,” Sugar muttered, “like this place is crawlin’ with fuckin’ militia. They’re all over the place, like shit in a field—”

“What’s that?” Buster shouted, directly at Marine Lyle.

“Nothing Sarge.”

“Oh good, cos you’re on point!”

The Detail moved out: Sugar on point, Jumper close behind. Jez and Dusty following with the lead General Purpose Machine Gun [GPMG]. Buster, Cowboy, JJ, Mongo, Moose, TC, Vinny and myself in the main group. Tommy and Dinger manned the second GPMG, with Corporals Lane and Speed taking up the rear.

I distinctly remember moving out to our second phase that day. I could see Sugar and Jumper ahead clambering over the rough ground closely followed by Jez and Dusty, a double link bandoleer wrapped around his broad shoulders. I recall smiling to myself. Thoughts of leave in Blighty. We’d earned it, done our bit for world peace. We’d walked 900 miles, at that moment we somehow felt as if we were walking home. How fickle we are; how fragile our existence; how wrong could we be. On that day, we were not walking home – we were walking into tragedy.

14:30: Roughly 2 miles adjacent the Cambodian border.

Soldiers often say that they had a gut feeling before coming under fire, or that everything suddenly went quiet. I had none of these experiences. On the contrary, being confronted with action was the last thing on my mind. I remember thinking that I would have to do something about the irritating sweat-rash on my left groin. 'I’ll have to apply a thick layer of Vaseline,' I thought as we continued to slowly advance towards a large coppicewood fronted by open ground. The sudden clatter of dampened automatic gunfire hit us as if a bolt out-the-blue.

“**Ambush, take cover!**” Buster shouted as the distinctive reports of AK47 assault rifles violated the calm. I needed no encouragement to heed Buster’s command as the gunfire intensified. I dived to the ground lying as close to the thick grass as the strands would allow.

“Sugar’s been hit!” Marine Collins yelled as he leapt from cover towards Sugar’s position.

“Get down you fool!” the Sergeant shouted. It was belated advice; Jumper too had been hit, though I was unsure of the seriousness of either of the strikes.

I lay on my stomach peering through the thick grass and low spreading shrubs trying to assess the situation. I could see pinprick flashes between the trees ahead. Areas of the ground appeared to be crackling before me. Clumps of soil shooting in every conceivable direction; leaves hopping and twirling in the air as if a part of some elaborate dance. The noise was oppressive: echoes of automatic gunfire, the whirr of bullets soaring past or ricocheting on small rocks, the teams screaming target data.

Sergeant Edwards issued orders amid the turmoil: “**Return fire at will, identify clear targets!**”

I was already in the process of preparing to respond; nonetheless, I was briefly startled by the recoil from my M16 as I opened fire. The feeling of cold steel pressing on my right cheek and the rebound of the bolt as it snapped to and fro. I realised that I’d omitted to place my noise-defenders in my ears; the deafening reverberation from rifle discharge temporarily dulled my senses. I grabbed for the earplugs as the rapid gunfire continued. There was a deafening whoosh above our heads, succeeded by an explosion to our rear as I rammed the second plug home.

“**Rockets!**” the Sergeant screamed, “…**RPG, identify location at the next report!**”

“Thirty calibre machine-gun at one-o’clock…” Bronco advised, “RPG to its right!”

The mêlée intensified. Tommy to my left and Jez to my far right were firing the GPMGs with Dinger and Dusty feeding the bandoleers. Some of the lads were becoming overexcited, screaming out to each other in the racket.

“Stop shouting all at once,” Buster yelled. “Give me relevant information only!”

Another whoosh as the RPG discharged. As previous the round landed far behind us. The operator was clearly inexperienced. Jez targeted the discharge position, the GPMG producing a scatter of debris as the rounds hit home.

I steadied myself, aborting discharge until I could identify a clear target. It was difficult in the hail of bullets to get an uninterrupted view of the enemy position. It was essential to identify a positive objective; firing blindly would serve no purpose, save to attain an ambiguous scatter-line. I stretched in my firing position, slowly raising my head above the grass. Our adversaries were dispersed along the treeline with a concentrated group right of my line of sight. 'You’ll do,' I thought amidst my elevated anxiety. I put myself at risk as

I deposited a definitive line on my chosen target. I could see a distinct path of tracer through my sight, the bullets spitting from the barrel. Some of the white-hot rounds ricocheted off the trees or rebounded into the air as if stones skimming on a pond. I experienced a fleeting thrill coupled with a foolish notion of invincibility as the bullets hit home.

Our counter-fire was undoubtedly having an effect. The enemy fire was decreasing, raising our confidence and propensity to take additional risks. Buster hollered above the gunfire: "**Prepare to advance on the position, on my signal!**"

I waited impatiently for the order to advance. The adrenaline rushing through my system had seemingly clouded my judgement. I am gratified I didn't put my fleeting theory of immortality to the test. Leaping from my, albeit limited, concealment in the absence of rapid cover-fire would've been suicidal.

The Sergeant assigned tasks. He would lead a group assault. The GPMG teams would continue to direct cover-fire advancing once the main group reached the edge of the treeline. Mongo would stay put with the Doc' who'd managed to crawl towards Sugar and Jumper to administer medical care.

I leapt from my cover position at the order to attack. We'd been told umpteen times that the repetitive training drilled into us from day one would come to fruition whilst under fire. I quickly discovered this to be the case as the discipline kicked-in: up and advance; move on an irregular course; dive to the ground, roll, right or left; identify target and apply rapid fire. Up and advance ...and so on. I continued running towards the enemy position, screaming like a banshee. I could see lines of tracer flying towards me: 'I won't get hit, I won't get hit!' I convinced myself as I dived to the dirt before discharging a succession of rounds. On one of my runs my rifle bounced off the terrain as I dived for cover, violently recoiling to hit me squarely on the right cheek. Blood oozed from the wound as I cursed whilst continuing to fire. We were within spitting distance of the treeline as the distinctive click on my firing mechanism indicated an empty magazine. I rolled onto my back to change the mag' as a streak of bullets screeched passed missing me by inches.

"**Fuck you!**" I bellowed, as I wrestled with the clip. I rolled back onto my stomach, firing into the undergrowth as if a man possessed, just as the enemy gunfire abated.

"**Ceasefire, ceasefire!**" Buster yelled above our rifle reports.

I lay in the grass adjoining the treeline my elevated breathing the only discernible sound. Blood from the gash on my cheek trickled into my mouth. I gained a strange comfort from its salty taste. I was sticky with sweat. My hands were shaking and the pungent cordite from the abundant gun smoke was invading my nasal passages. The attack team were laying in a row along the treeline. I could just make out the silhouettes of Cowboy and Vinny, left and right. I struggled against the temptation to break cover and scan the setting.

The Sergeant broke the short calm: "You okay boys?"

"Yeah…" we responded jointly.

"Good, now stay on the treeline. No heroics, d'ya hear!"

Our adversaries had apparently retreated from the position. Nonetheless, Sergeant Edwards instructed Bronco and TC to fling a pattern of grenades into the undergrowth. The silence that succeeded the grenade reports and minutia of falling debris confirmed a withdrawal. Buster instructed Bronco, JJ and TC to proceed into the woods to check the ambush position. Dinger and Vinny stayed on the treeline as additional backup, whilst the remainder pulled back to the firefight position.

I couldn't contain my excitement as we moved back. I had forgotten in the furore that Marines Collins and Lyle had been hit. My elation turned to despair as I observed Sugar's prostrate body and face covered with his poncho. Alongside, Medical Attendant Moore was desperately trying to administer aid to Marine Collins. Jumper was coughing, struggling to speak as the Doc' continued to search for a rear exit wound.

Jumper spotted Sergeant Edwards squatting alongside Moose.

"I'm scared Sarge..." Jumper said his voice full of distress, "I'm fuckin' scared!"

"It's okay to be scared, if you're scared that means you can feel, if you can feel that means you're still alive – so hang on in there! Have you called in Medevac?" Buster asked Marine Montford, manning the Radio Transmitter.

"Yeah," Mongo replied trying not to raise his voice, "ETA forty minutes."

"Fuck!" Buster cursed ensuring he turned his face away from Jumper. "He won't last five! Get back on to them, emphasise the priority!"

We squatted around Moose and Jumper's position in a hopeless circle. Jumper's eyes were scanning us. I felt a dull ache, a need to cry out as I observed the pain and anguish on his young face. The Doc' had managed to get a line in and stem the flow of blood oozing from two projectile wounds. But he still couldn't establish the exit portal from a third bullet. Each of us knew what that indicated: that a bullet was lodged in bodily tissue. Some of the men tried offering words of encouragement—

"It's okay mate," Dusty said, "you're gonna be fine, you'll see."

"Birds on the way," Marine Cunliffe advised. "They're wingin' in, d'ya hear me!"

"You're goin back to the Ran'," Corporal Farr enthused. "All those nurses to yourself. Molly, Phillipa and Bobbie-Joe; wall-to-wall TLC!"

Marine Collins continued crying out as Moose pulled his flak jacket and shirt further around his trunk: looking, searching, the expression on his face growing ever pessimistic.

"I'm sorry mate," the Doc' whispered as Jumper groaned and cried out ever louder.

I turned my ashen face away in an attempt to escape the torment only to gaze upon Sugar's lifeless form, the outline of his body clearly visible beneath the cover.

The sound of Jumper weeping interrupted my attempt to escape from the horror.

"Mum!" he cried out whilst grabbing at Moose's flak jacket. "I'm hurt, I'm sorry, I can't get up, my legs—"

His muttering was hindered by a further bout of coughing accompanied by ever increasing wails of pain.

"Its okay son..." Sergeant Edwards said his habitually stern voice full of emotion, "its okay now."

"Medevac's still forty minutes," Marine Montford murmured after closing a transmission.

"Is there anything we can do Sarge?" Lance Corporal Jessop enquired.

"Yeah...pray!"

So, I looked skyward and whispered an appeal: "Okay, if you exist I'll do a deal; let Jumper live and I'll reconsider. I'll do my rosary; go to church. I'll be the best Christian that ever walked the earth just don't take him. He's a good kid; he doesn't deserve to die—"

My request to a non-entity was interrupted by the sound of Jumper crying out. This time his disturbance sounded different. It was incoherent, muddled, as if he was trying to call out whilst gargling. He coughed in an apparent attempt to dislodge something from his throat. As he did a spray of blood spurted from his mouth. He became more and more distressed, grabbing at Moose and Speedy. He wailed, a loud gut-wrenching painful scream, the kind that enters your skull and sits in your psyche hovering as if a foul odour that will not go away. Jumper kicked and struggled grabbing Speedy's flak jacket with so much force he almost ripped it from his shoulders. Then, suddenly, he was motionless. His head and face unmoving save for his eyelids and mouth gradually opening as if in slow motion.

"Fuck it!" Buster cried out.

I looked skyward. "Oh fuckin' great I owe yer one!" I snarled. I noticed Corporal Speed blessing himself. I looked at him my face full of hurt: "Go on, bless yourself again, give another sign of reverence to a fuckwit that either doesn't exist or is just a complete twat—!"

"Knock-it-off!" Tommy said.

We squatted in a circle watching the colour drain from Jumper's face. For some reason we avoided eye contact with each another. I particularly avoided contact with Speedy. I felt regretful for my outburst; I didn't mean to take my anguish out on him.

Our temporary catatonia was broken by the return of Bronco's backup team. They stared at Sugar's covered corpse and Jumper's frozen frame, his widened-eyes gazing at a heaven that should it really exist would've surely accepted him onto its elysian fields. They appeared to be stunned, in spite of the hostile theatre in which we were functioning. Marine Jeffers was notably taken aback. "Jumper...mucker!" he said, as if expecting a response.

Moose knelt beside Marine Collins' body, staring at the blood soaked surgical dressings.

"Where's Sugar's dog tags?" Sergeant Edwards asked looking at the Doc'. Moose took them from his breast pocket, passing them with his bloodstained hands without looking up. "Get Jumper's tags…" he continued coldly, "and re-prioritise Medevac."

Moose pulled Jumper's dog tags from around his neck as Corporal Speed nervously unfurled two body bags.

"Have you got a report for me?" Buster asked Corporal Lane.

"Sarge," Bronco replied, getting back to business. "No further activity at the ambush position. Support crew continuing to covertly monitor the locale from the treeline. We found two dead bodies and an abandoned seven, point, six-two Czechoslovakian machine-gun. No unexploded rounds, booby traps or tripwires – position secure."

We stared as Speedy and Moose silently lifted Jumper's body onto the open bag.

"What's our next move Sarge?" Bronco enquired.

The Sergeant looked at us, then at the bodies of our fallen comrades: "Call in the support crew, and get me the Ordinance Survey Map and a compass."

Bronco handed him the OSM, Tommy a compass. Both squatted each side of him as he checked our position. "That coppicewood is four miles north to south and less than a mile and a half in width. There's a rivulet, a tributary of the Sông Bậ River that cuts the treeline and Cambodian border. Which way would you go if you were pulling back?" Buster asked, directing his question at Corporals Lane and Farr.

"I'd probably head in a direct line for the border," Bronco answered, Tommy agreeing.

"West, me too. Okay you lot muscle-up your gear."

"Are we going after them?" Marine Jeffers enquired.

"Too fuckin' right we are—!"

"**Yes!**" we called out simultaneously.

"Alright calm down and listen carefully. We're gonna attempt to outrun them in a flanking movement. You can bet they've high-tailed it back towards the border. Those pricks know we're UN troops, they think we won't retaliate, well, they're in for a surprise! They probably think they're already home and dry so we've got the advantage."

Tommy gave Buster a look of concern: "What about the directive Sarge?"

"Fuck the directive! They wasted Jumper and Sugar, we're not gonna let them walk from this one. Now listen carefully," Buster said as the support crew re-joined the main group, "...Bronco, you've got Vinny, Dinger, TC and Dusty. Speedy, Bazzer, Cowboy, JJ you're with me. Tommy, you stay here with Jez, Mongo and Moose – stand guard on the position."

The lads detailed to remain at the firefight position had a look of disappointment, though Tommy also looked half relieved. Buster instructed Mongo to contact the nearest SVA Unit with a request for assistance from their Military Police before calling the teams together for a briefing. We eagerly huddled round him as he highlighted our objectives.

"Bronco..." Buster said whilst pointing to sectors on the OSM, "take your team west by southwest arcing right. We'll move west by northwest arcing left. Move at an extended pace. Stay alert and at close quarters. Remember our stealth, hand signals only, got it?"

"Got it Sarge!"

"We'll dispatch our foe on contact, preferably from a dense cover position. Remember to guard against crossfire. Be aware of each teams' position – we don't wanna be shooting the fuck out of each other! Weapons check, y'all got enough ammo?"

We hastily checked our rifles and webbing belts giving verification on completion.

"I've only got one half-clip left," I said.

"Here, take this you trigger-happy bastard," Tommy said, handing me a full metal jacket.

"Okay boys..." Sergeant Edwards said, a stern look on his face, "let's do it!"

We took off on our respective courses. My heart was pounding part with excitement, part anxiety. The guerrillas had at least a half-mile start on us. It mattered not – we were fit and determined, we'd catch them.

We moved at an extended pace over the uneven ground. We needed to adopt a semi-stoop to safeguard against being spotted. The pose put pressure on our hamstrings, which ached as we pushed forward. We progressed through the wood employing all our senses. The insurgents may have used a different route. We needed to be vigilant, ready to take on the faction.

The spacing and density of the wood began to change along with the surface, relatively level ground to a gradual gradient. The undergrowth was becoming more prominent, all indicators that we were nearing the stream. The Sergeant called a halt. We squatted listening for environmental cues. I could hear the sound of the rivulet, fast running resultant of days of heavy rain.

"Y'all hear that?" Buster whispered. We nodded, in expectation of further action. "Okay, crawl towards the bank. Stay in cover; prepare to form an adjacent line. Cowboy, take the far right. Bazzer, JJ, take the middle. Speedy, cover the left side with me. Slowly towards the bank now boys."

We crawled through the profuse undergrowth towards the treeline neighbouring the bank, quickly settling on the rough damp ground. Cowboy suddenly recoiled back whilst frantically brushing at his fatigues. "Fuckin' scorpions!" he said, straining to keep his voice down. "They're all over place."

"They're drawn towards the moisture from the brook," I said.

"I know, I know—!"

"Shit-in-it you two!" Sergeant Edwards growled.

We waited in a stilled hush. The rivulet sounded like a major tributary in the eerie silence. The calmness was interrupted by the sound of muffled voices to our rear. The chatter was accompanied by the scrunching of leaves and twigs. They were close, left of our arrangement.

Corporal Speed strained in his position in an attempt to attain a definite sighting; their voices grew louder. I could hear the sound of my heart beating ever faster as we waited for data.

"Contact!" Speedy said, catching sight of the splinter group.

"Guerrillas?" Buster murmured.

"Yeah, Khmer Rouge!"

"Status?"

"Twenty, twenty-five yards maximum. Single column…four, five, six in number," Speedy whispered observing the growing number of insurgents appearing between the trees. "They appear to be arguing amongst themselves. Eight, nine...that's it I think, nine max' moving towards the stream."

We could hear the insurgents approaching from behind. Sergeant Edwards looked towards me. "Can you get any of that?" he asked as the voices became more audible.

"No, they're speaking Khmer. I only know a handful of words."

"No matter, we're not here to have a fuckin' conversation!"

We lay in anticipation facing the waterway. The situation had reached a critical point. Our actions would be determined on which course the faction took once out of cover. If they elected to turn right we would have a clear line of fire. If they crossed the stream we'd have to creep up and take them from behind. If they turned left we would have to carefully monitor their progress, leaving the task of dispatching them to Bronco's team on our southern flank. Both teams had to be mindful of being caught in crossfire. Buster issued a final briefing. "Remember the drill: identify targets, wait for my order and don't go crazy – three rounds on each target's enough, got it?"

"Sarge," we murmured.

I reduced my outline as far as I could, forcing my body into the damp soil. There was an almost perfect gap in the undergrowth allowing me an uninterrupted view of the stream below whilst giving maximum cover. Cowboy was immediately to my right. I was pleased to be alongside him. He was a crack marksman – fast as well as accurate. He could dispatch a group of close-order guerrillas single-handedly.

The separatist rebels left the cover of the coppicewood slowly turning right in a line reciprocal to the waterway. I held my breath with the realisation of what we were about to do. The militiamen varied in ages; all were adorned in Khmer blood bands and armed with AK47s. One insurgent was carrying an additional RPG launcher with rounds. The troop walked nonchalantly along the bank clearly unaware of our presence; they were indeed in dispute. I surmised that the quarrel revolved around the group retreating without the bodies of their dead colleagues and the .30 calibre machine-gun.

I identified my first target as they walked by; a small man, third from the left in the line. He stopped to light a cigarette; I could clearly see the Zippo lighter in his hand. I released the safety on my M16, pulling the cold metal closer to my gashed cheek. I followed the rebel's slow walking form through my rifle sight. I was surprised at how calm and focused I was. My initial nervousness had subsided. It was as if I didn't see a human soul walking across my field of vision, just an objective. I would go for the kill – no half measures. Once downed I'd dispatch any remaining foe each side, if still standing. I took a deep breath and steadied myself, waiting for the Sergeant's signal. The stream ran, ants and scorpions scurried, my heart beat, as did my adversary's—

"**Engage!**" Buster said.

I opened fire, assuredly squeezing the trigger. The M16 recoiled as I witnessed the man's body convulse in a momentary spasm before dropping limp to the ground. The tributary was dotted with columns of water darting skyward as I shifted left applying a hail of bullets into a man whose body was already convulsing as a salvo of rounds smashed home. His tormented dance concluded with his bullet-ridden form falling into the seemingly boiling rivulet.

"**Ceasefire, safeties on!**"

Echoes of our rifle reports faded restoring the calm. It was over, as quickly as it had begun. I looked below to see a line of prostrate bodies, some face down, some supine; all twisted and motionless beside the fast running stream. The barrel of my Armalite was smoking, adding to the transient pall of curling blue-grey vapours. Shafts of sunlight disclosed their conspicuous presence as they pierced the fast dispersing smog. Our deed was done. It was swift, cold, clinical, final. Murderous? Who could say? Who would say? There was nobody else there, only us, silent, thoughtful, alive.

"Listen up," Buster called, "move towards the stream, proceed with caution. Speedy, signal objective accomplished. Watch out for Bronco's team y'all; they'll be coming in left. And stay alert, we're far from home and dry."

I picked myself up forcing my way through the undergrowth on the shallow gradient. I gingerly placed my thumb on the safety catch of my M16 as I proceeded towards our quarry. We had to take care; we couldn't ease off until we were sure that all our targets had been negated. The Cambodian border was a stones throw from our position. Ambuscade would've been simple within the thick elevated shrubbery on the opposite side of the stream. Two episodes of multiple gunfire in less than 20 minutes made us more than a tad conspicuous. The teams were split and low on ammunition; the last thing we needed was another sortie.

We moved slowly towards the line of corpses. Two of the bodies were part in the stream; one face down, the other on its side one arm slowly moving to and fro in the current as if waving a final farewell to loved ones across the border. The rivulet was stained with a thin line of blood diluting in the cool mountain waters.

I crept towards my kill. The corpse was almost in the foetal position, the AK47 firmly cradled in arms and hands that had lost their mastery. The cigarette I had seen the young man light was still smouldering between his fingers; soon, that too would be extinguished. I stared at the remains unable to remove my gaze. 'Had I really done this?' I asked myself. 'What now, sorrow? No, sorrow was for my muckers. Discredit maybe, why? this was war, hence expected.'

The sound of Marine Cunliffe calling out interrupted my cogitation: "Oh fuck! one of them's still alive!"

We all looked at Cowboy. He was standing astride the young man. The injured revolutionary was lying on his back half looking up. Blood was pouring from a wound in his neck and left leg. He slowly scanned our faces. It was difficult to discern whether the look on his face was of defiance, terror or just a numbed response to our counter attack.

Buster stared at the fallen guerrilla, then at Cowboy: "Do him!"

I felt pitiful as I looked at our fallen victim, Cowboy's tall frame towering aloft. A sudden and unexpected feeling of empathy perhaps, or a realisation that a cold-blooded killing was about to be performed. I expected Cowboy to point the muzzle of his M16 at the rebel's head before squarely discharging one round. He had other ideas. He directed the butt of his rifle downward immediately above the injured man's face. Cowboy wailed a scream of the damned as he brought the metal-lined edge of the butt down on his victim's head. There was a sickening thud as the hardened steel slammed into the man's face. His jaw snapped and teeth shattered as the blow was succeeded by a second and third strike. The man's leg twitched as the butt was brought down with exceedingly brute force in a final blow.

"Fuckin' twat!" Cowboy yelled as he kicked the limp corpse.

A ghostly hush followed. I distinctly remember the sound of the stream as it sped past. We stood staring at Cowboy's handiwork, temporarily forgetting our own kills. I couldn't take my eyes off the corpse. Virtually all of the head had been crushed inward. The left eye had been pulverised, mixed with shattered bone from the eye socket. Blood, snot and saliva dribbled, adjoining a pool augmenting under the matted hair and blood saturated headband. Part of the scalp had been peeled back exposing the cranium beneath; the man was dead, as were the other eight.

I felt like a spectator analysing the scene. I was overcome with a feeling of revulsion underpinned by a strange sexual thrill, a perverse afterglow. Something primal that resides within. A reaction that modern society eschews, masked within the boundaries of our inner worlds. Manifested in private or the confines of the darkened cinema as we watch a gruesome execution, trying not to smile.

"So, what next?" Cowboy asked, as if he'd just finished sipping tea.

"Police-up their arms," Buster said, looking at the bludgeoned body at Cowboy's feet. "Put them in the polythene bags stowed in your webbing. Pick up the AKs by the barrels. Anyone got any disposable gloves?" he enquired to our puzzlement.

"Yeah," JJ said, pulling the thin clear gloves from his pocket.

We stood watching the Sergeant as he donned the gloves before firing a brief salvo of rounds into our ambush position with one of the Kalashnikovs: "Just preparing our story boys!"

We proceeded to collect the weapons. I had difficulty pulling the AK47 away from the arms of my quarry, as if he didn't want to succumb to a final submission.

Speedy collected the RPG launcher. "Fuck me!" he whispered, putting the palm of his hand on the tube, "...the pipe's still warm."

We tied detailed tags onto the ankles of the corpses once the weapons had been bagged. United Nations standard practice: date, time and location of deaths. Methods employed; if the deaths were instantaneous and most bizarre of all 'perpetrators'. I didn't consider myself a *perpetrator*, though I did have first doubts about whether our actions were justified.

Buster pulled me to one side noticing the blood trickling from the cut on my face: "Get the medic to look at that when we get back."

"It's just a scratch Sarge—"

"Scratch or no! get it seen to. You don't want infection getting in there."

Corporal Lane's team linked-up with us as we prepared to leave. "You got them then," he said as the others gazed at the corpses.

"Yeah..." Buster replied, though somewhat sombre, "we got them."

We moved out as a tight pack leaving the remnants of once sentient beings, kissing the soil, staring skywards or at the rampant mottled fungus abreast the bank.

We made our way back to the initial firefight position. All were silent; was our reticence to do with stealth or quiet contemplation? It was likely a combination of the two; though I remember feeling uncomfortable, unable to eliminate a nagging doubt.

Any doubt about the demise of our muckers was soon put to rest as we rejoined the fallback crew sat in the vicinity of the two body bags.

Cowboy launched into a tirade on how we'd "...wasted the little twats."

Tommy had been quite since our return. He could see that I too was introspective. "You okay buddy?" he asked, as I added my spoil-of-war to the growing pile of Kalashnikovs.

I gave an unconvincing nod and shrug of my shoulders before seeking out the Doc'.

Medical Attendant Moore stretched the gash on my cheekbone as he applied a damp swab. The sharp spirit cut into the wound making me wince. 'What have I got to complain about?' I thought, I was still alive. He sprayed a layer of plastic-skin on the area. I felt the skin on my face contract as the film coagulated: "That gash has dissected into scar tissue..." Moose said, "I might have to suture it later."

I remember feeling unconcerned. The abrading of an old scar was trivial given the misfortune that had beleaguered us on that day.

Mongo informed Buster that the arrival of an advanced party of Military Police was imminent, and that a Medical Corps helicopter was inbound to collect Jumper and Sugar's bodies.

'Medevac to hearse,' I remember thinking, a poignant metamorphosis.

Meanwhile Bronco and Tommy carried out an inventory of enemy hardware, reporting the gross to the Sergeant: "Ten Kalashnikovs with seven full metal jackets and eight spent clips; one Czechoslovakian machine-gun with spent bandoleer; one RPG with four rounds, and eleven corpses."

“Don’t you mean thirteen,” Mongo said.

Buster called up his team pulling us to one side. He had a serious look on his face: “Listen up...I guess you don’t need reminding that we crossed the line today; broke the rules. I know it sucks, seems unjust, but the truth is we could be arrested by the South Vietnamese Military Police on a charge of culpable manslaughter. We could even end up being brought before the International War Crimes Tribunal, so we’ve gotta make sure they don’t get a sniff of what happened; that means we’ve gotta be inventive with our reports. And we’ve gotta stick to our stories, no matter what. The basics? simple; Bazzer, you called our identification and directed them to drop their weapons. They ignored our forewarning and moved to open fire. One of them got some rounds off, yeah—!”

We smiled understanding and acknowledging Buster’s little exercise at the stream.

“—We responded with automatic fire, simple as that. Write out your summaries on scrap paper and go through them with me before consigning them to script. Remember, you can’t change an account on a report sheet once composed, no mistakes. Finally, if you’ve got any doubts what we did today then let me remind you, our conduct is determined by a collection of principles and values, the Khmer Rouge’s isn’t! They laid down the gauntlet, took first blood. If you need a reminder of what that means then take another look at the body bags behind us!”

“What about Cowboy’s handiwork; how are we going to explain away that?” I asked.

“Leave that to me,” he answered as Cowboy glared at me. “Cowboy, we’ll sit down, contrive something between ourselves.”

Mongo interrupted proceedings: “Bell-25 [Sioux helicopter] ...inbound, northwest.”

“MPs!” Buster said, “…leave the talking to me.”

The glass-domed helicopter carried four MPs: a Captain, who piloted the aircraft, a Sergeant and two Corporals. We were all taken aback by their appearance. Their fatigues were immaculate; they looked as if they’d just stepped from a fitting room. The Captain’s apparel was particularly impressive. He sported a saffron cravat tucked into his impeccably starched shirt. Sharp creases ran the length of his spotless trousers. His chrome 9mm automatic was buff polished and the metal-wear on his flawless waist and shoulder straps gleamed in the hazy sunshine. He presented as if a model from a catalogue of Jane’s Military Wear.

Meanwhile there we were, in damp, threadbare, mud-ridden fatigues. Tommy gazed at me shaking his head. I knew he was thinking the same as me: 'How come we’re up to our eyeballs in wall-to-wall shit while these fuckwit's lounge in their air conditioned barracks polishing their boots and buckles in-between playing Mahjong?'

Buster told me to stay alongside him as the Vietnamese officer approached. He could likely speak English. Nevertheless, it was customary for translators to be nearby to aid fluent communication.

The Captain was a perceivably odious man. He wore a permanent false smile and was sycophantic in the extreme. He constantly interrupted the Sergeant, patting him on the shoulder saying, "...everything okay. You no be worry, everything fine." Buster concluded his briefing with the offer of an escort through to the second firefight position.

The Captain talked briefly to his men, I covertly listened-in as requested. Sergeant Edwards pulled me to one side as Speedy and JJ guided the MPs to the second scene: "What were those fuck-sticks babbling about?"

"Not a lot, something about the insurgents coming from a paramilitary cell just across the border. They didn't seem surprised."

"Yeah, jumped-up little pricks; they know who they are all right!"

We sat in silence on the damp ground: waiting for the Huey; waiting for Speedy and JJ's return; waiting for the MPs to get out of our faces. We could see a thick pall of cloud developing in the east moving ever closer, its dark cloak shrouding the already gloomy scene. Forks of lightning struck the ground flooding the dismal landscape. It presented as if a camera capturing the closing stages of a tragic drama, its flashlight arresting the last vestiges of two stolen lives.

"Huey inbound east by northeast," Mongo hollered above the claps of thunder.

The speeding bird was on us in no time. The noise from its reverberating blades amalgamated with the intensifying booms of thunder, a rain-dance for the dead. The downdraft scattered everything – save our heartache – as the skids touched down. Moose and Jez loaded the bodies of our dead compadrés onto the Huey. For some bizarre reason I wanted their bodies to remain; as if holding onto them would still make us complete. My transient notion was shattered as the helicopter thundered eastward. The cord had already been cut, our disconnection finalised when their hearts stopped beating. It was a cold and bitter reality: Jumper and Sugar were no more, snuffed out, wasted, hacked down, deceased!

We stared at the Huey gliding beneath the dark clouds, its silhouette diminishing in size. The heavens opened up the clouds finally succumbing to their colossal mass. The rain hammered onto the uneven ground prompting the Detail to gather their ponchos.

I, on the other hand, continued looking east, as if mesmerised in the pouring rain. The Bell Huey disappeared in the deluge. The rainwater bounced on my scalp. I could feel the cool drops: trickling down my forehead, dribbling off eyebrows, splashing on my cheeks, running down my sorrowful face. Billie Ebotée held, '*...if you're gonna cry in the 'Nam best do your crying in the rain*' – so that's exactly what I did.

11:00: Northwestern outskirts of Lôn Sín Sịng, Wednesday 4 July.

Control instructed the Detail to swing southeastward once our duties at the firefight position were complete. The spontaneous directive reminded us of the incident at Tchựin Loy. It had long become apparent that Command dealt with controversial situations by immediately withdrawing as many of the proponents as they could from an area contention. Some of the boys were annoyed that *we* should be considered the antagonists. We were simply carrying out our obligations. Furthermore, why redirect us 180° over ground we'd already patrolled?

I decided to opt out of the mutterings. I was weary of cyclical questions that had no perceivably rational answers. My weariness was exacerbated by my inability to sleep the night before. We'd been up until the early hours writing our reports, the Sergeant patiently trawling through our summaries. Checking and re-checking our accounts. Asking questions and testing our responses. It had been a long day of the soul.

The squads walked past a gathering of South Vietnamese soldiers loafing by the roadside. They were fraternising with a set of, what appeared to be, local hookers. They began clapping as we walked past. Some tried shouting words of congratulation with a clear sarcastic tone.

"Ignore them," Buster said.

Cowboy, as petulant as ever, couldn't contain himself: "Oh yeah, velly good. Chicken flied lice. You fuckwit yeller belly, me number-one sucker; do your job—!"

"Knock-it-off!" Buster roared, glancing back.

"Dinks..." Cowboy muttered, "who the fuck do they think we're fightin' for—?"

Sergeant Edwards turned round and bent a fierce look: "Marine Cunliffe you will shut your fuckin' mouth or I'll put my boot in it!"

I was glad Buster admonished Cowboy; he'd been getting on everybody's nerves since the sortie. He didn't seem to be bothered about the loss of our compadrés or the assassination of our adversaries; for some reason that troubled me. I wasn't aware at the time that people react to trauma in different ways. I'd have been more tolerant should I have known.

We continued on an aimless objective moving beside Lôn Sín Sịng. Buster brought an end to the monotony after he'd received a radio transmission: "Pay attention here, the Lieutenant's calling us back to Phờn Xưýen. Chinook inbound...ETA fifteen minutes."

Our delight at being recalled was tinged with an underlying anxiety. We were likely being called in for debrief – our stories would soon be put to the test.

Sergeant Edwards stopped the traffic, for what it was worth, on the metal road as the Royal Canadian Air Force Chinook prepared to land. People in Vietnam were used to troops holding up traffic to accommodate helicopters. I felt like a VIP at my first experience, but the fascination soon waned.

Buster counselled us as the chopper winged its way to base: "Stay cool now boys they've got nothing on us. Bottom line? We had to defend ourselves. Either way let me do most of the talking."

"Yeah," Cowboy muttered, "fuck 'em—!"

"That includes you Marine Cunliffe!"

15:00: UN Base Camp 9, Phờn Xưýen.

The Chinook took less than 15 minutes to reach headquarters. We returned unused ammunition to the armoury before making our way to Lieutenant Derrick's office. Buster spent a good 15 minutes with the Lieutenant whilst we sat outside in silence. I went through a whole gamut of emotions as we waited to be called in: notions of being arrested by the South Vietnamese police on a charge of murder or of being stripped of our status before the International War Crimes Tribunal. It seemed so unjust; thousands of people had been slaughtered in South Vietnam in the 28 years of conflict. Innocent men, women and children put to death because of their ethnicity, political beliefs or simply because they were different.

Lieutenant Derrick finally summoned One and Two Squads. He sat reading our statements, Sergeant Edwards looking on. He then asked for a verbal chronology of events. Buster opened by explaining our circumstances leading to the first exchanges. Jez and Dusty went on to inform him that Marine Lyle took a direct hit. They told of how Marine Collins rushed towards Sugar's position after seeing that he wasn't moving and under threat from further harm. They notified him that Jumper threw himself across Sugar's body in a desperate attempt to protect him. And of how his firing position left him highly exposed. Lance Corporal Jessop, his voice quivering, went on to explain how Jumper cried out as the bullets smashed home. And of how he continued to discharge his weapon refusing to roll off Sugar's body to attain greater cover.

"Bloody fool!" the Lieutenant said, an expression of sorrow on his face.

The mood was sombre as we continued with our accounts, leading to the teams' effecting a chase.

The Lieutenant dismissed Bronco's team along with Jez, Mongo, Moose and Tommy, leaving Buster's team to continue with the briefing. He sat slowly scanning our reports: "Sergeant Edwards, you state that you went in pursuit of the guerrillas after the firefight to '...keep track of them whilst you waited for the Military Police'. So why pull them up?"

"They were heading for the border Sir; if they'd have crossed we'd have lost the opportunity to accost them—"

"It's the job of Security Forces to accost them. We can only approach and arrest individuals or groups if they've been involved in the mistreatment of non-combatants, you know that."

"I used the discretion authorized in section five of the directive Sir. We had to be expedient, I was unsure of their status. We had to monitor their movements to further protect ourselves. We'd already lost Marines Collins and Lyle—"

"I don't need a reminder we've lost two of our Marines Sergeant – I've got to write to their mothers!"

An uneasy silence followed. Lieutenant Derrick was simply doing his job. He was ultimately accountable; he needed to get things straight.

"Corporal Speed..." he continued, "you say you spotted the guerrillas coming through a cutting and relayed the information to Sergeant Edwards and the rest of the team."

"Yes Sir, we had to wait for them to walk into the clear before confronting them."

The Lieutenant stared at Speedy, a pensive look on his face, before slowly shifting his gaze towards me. He aimed a question in-between scanning my report: "Lance Corporal Morris, you say you identified yourselves and gave the rebels a clear directive to '...stand still and drop their weapons'."

"Yes Sir, in Khmer, I know enough words to be able to—"

"I'm well aware of your language skills young man! How quickly did they open fire once you'd issued the warning?"

"Almost immediately Sir, I didn't get a chance to issue a second warning. It had to be done—"

"What had to be done?"

I froze for a moment regretful that I'd almost let it slip. I had to think quickly.

"—We had to defend ourselves...Sir."

"Marine Cunliffe," the Lieutenant carried through, "in your report you say you were '...forced to defend yourself against an individual attack'. Your *defence* concluded with you virtually pulverising the culprit's skull!"

“He jumped me from behind Sir,” Cowboy responded, “I tried fighting him off but he just went berserk. He was like a man possessed.”
“A man possessed…yes Marine Cunliffe, very apt!”
Lieutenant Derrick scanned the team for what felt like an eternity, occasionally shifting his gaze to flip through our reports. My adrenal glands were working overtime. I became aware that I was twiddling with an elastic band between my fingers. I gripped the rubber strip in an attempt to lessen my non-verbal cues.
“This whole thing smells like Grimsby quayside on the morning of a good catch!” the Lieutenant said, looking at Sergeant Edwards; Buster sat stoically staring back.
Lieutenant Derrick began signing our reports: “We’ve already lost Marines Lyle and Collins, I don’t want to lose anyone else, through ambush, taking off after insurgents or being dragged in by the Military Police! You can all take that worried look off your faces. The MPs have gathered up the bodies and disposed of them, there’ll be no forensic follow-up.”
The Lieutenant took the carbon copies of the signed reports. He gazed at Cowboy, JJ, Speedy and me: “Is this your first kill?”
“Yes Sir,” we replied.
“Are you all okay?”
We each nodded.
“Good,” he said, handing the reports back to Sergeant Edwards. “Okay you lot, go and get cleaned up. Try’n chill tonight, next briefing’s at 0700 hours tomorrow.”
Corporal Farr was waiting outside as we left the room. “Okay boys?” he whispered.
“Yeah,” Marine Jeffers returned.
“He knows doesn’t he?” Cowboy said to me.
“Yeah, he knows alright. Let’s just hope that’s an end to it.”
“I wouldn’t fret…” Tommy said, “a million-and-a-half people have been wiped out in this conflict since ’forty-eight. Nobody’s gonna get wound up about the demise of a bunch of unwelcome militia armed to the teeth.”
We silently made our way to the mess. The stark, but dry, dormitory was welcoming after 4 days and nights in the pouring rain. Our joy was short lived as we noticed Jumper and Sugar’s bed stations; their beds had been stripped and their lockers emptied.
“Fuck me,” JJ said, “they didn’t waste any time did they!”
Dusty stared at conspicuous void: “Jeez, they’re really dead aren’t they. Our muckers...they’ve really gone.”
Nobody answered; instead we went about our business. Unloading our damp soiled clothing ready for the tub; stripping our rifles in preparation to clean

and oil all moving parts; separating our unused ration packs, what to keep, what to bin. We busied ourselves trying not to look at the empty spaces. I tried but it was useless, I could see their faces whether I looked or not. Finding a tin of polish I'd borrowed from Jumper didn't help. He'd scribed a distinctive 'J' onto the lid with his commando dagger. Seeing images of their faces and hearing a ghostly echo of their voices was bad enough, but nothing in comparison to the intrusive flashbacks. They'd started the night before, a series of scenes: Sugar walking on point, Jumper crying out that he'd been hit. Then the pain and anguish; his eyes scanning us, his normally hardened voice crying out. Those final moments of suffering. He wanted his mum. He wanted to say he was sorry. It was as if a film I couldn't stop, the spool constantly playing and rewinding the same scene – over and over again.

I felt angry at Sugar; if he'd have kept his mouth shut he might not have been designated point. My temporary anger was assuaged by a realisation: if he hadn't been on point somebody else would've; maybe even me. Anger, relief, regret, sorrow, bouncing round in my head and stomach – inescapable torment.

Marine Jeffers had turned on his small transistor radio. The music calmed my disquiet. We sat listening to Mott The Hoople singing *All The Young Dudes*. A report on the Five O'clock News, Radio Sàigòn, rekindled my frustration:

"...Yesterday, United Nations' peacekeeping troops killed over thirty Khmer Rouge guerrillas in a border skirmish south of Lôn Bắn Đat," the broadcaster said. "...Regional Administrator, Vịhn Qừi Hựe, commented that this should act as a reminder to all invaders that their presence would not be tolerated. Action would be swift."

"Thirty!" Marine Cunliffe yelled, "...where the fuck did they get that heap of shit from?"

"I couldn't give a fuck how many they said we killed," I scornfully added. "It's intimating that we're their fuckin' cohorts that I don't like!"

An additional Mail Call was arranged post-evening meal. I received a letter from home along with a belated birthday card and an Everton fixture list, Season 1973/74. I scrutinised the list paying particular attention to the opening game – Aston Villa at home. I looked up, scanning the room for Marine Lyle. Realisation cuts the deepest when the barriers of denial finally fall. An absolute reality hit me, concrete in the manifestation of absence; our muckers *really* were dead. I would never again stand beside Sugar cheering our beloved Everton. Jumper would no longer shyly ask me to peruse the drafts of his letters home.

I was overcome by a need to cry. My hands started shaking, I felt myself welling-up. I needed to escape. I rushed outside feeling a need to conceal my disturbance. Dinger said something to me as I left; I pretended not to hear him. I walked in the cool early evening air looking for sanctuary. I observed a perfect retreat, the large water tower at the base.

The tower was of typical United States mid-west design: large saucer-like cylinder perched above thick crisscrossing struts. There was a badly corroded warning sign bolted beside the pin-ladder leading to a narrow unguarded walk way some 120 feet above: **DANGER: UNAUTHORISED ASCENT STRICTLY FORBIDDEN!** We were in Vietnam, the sign wasn't written in Vietnamese so I disregarded it. The view from the top of the tower was breathtaking, the expanse of the Cordillera Mountain Range dissected by the tail of the An Lâo Valley. I felt totally alone as I sat on the weathered boards usually reserved for blue-tailed doves. I strained to gaze at the galvanised tank to my rear. It was apparent that I wasn't the only serviceman who'd disregarded the directive. Former GIs based at the erstwhile US Rangers' Garrison had a habit of leaving their marks in various places, including the forbidden tower. There was an assortment of graffiti, some scrawls scraped in with bayonets, others simply written with marker pen—

MY TIME'S GONE, MY TOUR'S DONE, I'M DONE GONE: MITCH '68
DENZAL'S OFF THE PLATE, GOODBYE TO HATE - HOME RUN '69
THE 'NAM'S A RACKET A FULL METAL JACKET, I DONE HACK IT:
DAY TRIPPER, '70

—I smiled to myself trying to picture the artists. They likely made it home, two of ours wouldn't. The sun hugged the horizon, a beautiful twilight mid my bothersome mind. My cyclical thoughts continued. Being alone wasn't as fruitful as I'd considered. It reminded me of a line from Byron: '*It is in solitude that we are least alone.*' This indeed appeared to be the case as things became even more jumbled. Images of Jumper's distressing death succeeded by the figure of my quarry: the glow from his last cigarette; his body convulsing as my rifle rounds hit home. One was my friend, the other a purported terrorist. But was he? Would I have acted any different if my country had been dragged into military conflict; used as a sparring ground by superpowers? What would I do if my family had been torn apart, my security threatened by continuous instability? How would I respond if my land was plagued by injustice? Would I simply yield to the fist of oppression or would I fight? American B52 Bombers may have been wiped out my quarry's family – revolutionaries rarely emerge from social, political vacuums. I was overcome by a feeling of guilt as I struggled with the continuing conundrums. Jumper and Sugar cared nothing about the aetiology surrounding the region's political turmoil; all they cared about was doing their duty.

My cogitation was interrupted by a loud cry from below: "Don't do it!"
I looked down to see Corporal Farr staring up at me: "Mind if I join you?"
I giggled as he gingerly made his way up the rusting pin-bars.
"What are you laughing at?"
"I was just about to say it's a free country."
"Oh wow!" Tommy said, as he carefully negotiated the walk board to settle alongside me, "…that's some view."
Tommy sat in silence slowly taking in the awesome panorama: "So what are you doin' up here all on your lonesome?"
"You know me and my thoughts. I thought viewing things from up here might clear the fog."
"And?"
"What's there to clear, Jumper and Sugar are dead. I saw one of them die, heard him cry out. So, then what? I went on to kill a man, maybe even more than one. Degsy asked us if we were okay, I said I was, but I'm not. I'm all mixed up: empty yet full of remorse, satisfied yet unfulfilled. Thoughts and feelings bouncing round in my head, turning in my stomach. I feel like we got a result yet nobody's won. How did you feel after your first kill?"
"Same as you; you either want to do it again or you go on questioning. And in the middle of it all you go on doing your duty. You needn't feel guilty about what y'all did yesterday you know."
"I don't know it smacks of revenge. Some sordid reprisal for the loss of our buddies; they're concepts I always eschew. So where do I stand now?"
"It wasn't revenge," Tommy replied with a resolute tone. "Revenge is where you take a guilty party and lock them up for months. Then, on a pre-set date and time you strap them to an instrument and kill them in cold blood. That's what you're against. Happen I'd agree with you. What you boys did wasn't a reprisal it was a necessity. We couldn't just let them take off. That would've given them carte blanche to attack any other UN Detachment they came across. And then what? They'd take out some other poor saps. Maybe even more of our boys, maybe even you. Where would that leave you? Certainly not sat up here admiring the Cordillera Mountains. No my friend those fuckers needed to be taken out. They knew what they were doing; they know we're no threat to them. We're not involved in their pathological doctrine. They could've stayed in cover and watched us walk by, but no, they decided to open fire, cut us down. You can't set up an ambush in this arena and not expect a response. It's a simple matter of 'behaviour consequence', you choose the behaviour, you choose the consequence, end of story!"
I sat contemplating his words. Buster had said something similar. I knew they were right, though the dull ache remained.
"Yeah, I suppose," I said. "It's just that at this moment I feel a long way

from home and a long way from the person I thought I was. Cowboy finished one of them off with the butt of his rifle; it wasn't pretty I can tell you."

"There's nothing pretty about war, y'all know that. The only pretty wars are the ones on the silver screen. There's another way of looking at it. Remember that talk we had in the Ran', about not always having the time to think things through? Well, you didn't need it. You took off after those fuckers without a moment's hesitation. Jumper and Sugar would've been proud of you. You know they'd have gone after them for you don't you. Doesn't make it any more right or wrong, just so happens to be a matter of fact."

"Yeah...they'd have gone after them. I miss them already."

"It'll get easier," Tommy said in a reassuring tone.

"Oh don't tell me…" I said, weary of the persistent clichés, "time's a great healer—"

"No my friend, time heals nothing; it's what you do with it that gets you through. We can start by joining the boys; they'll be wondering where we are. Let's go an' get a beer, aye."

Tommy, as always, helped me to at least partially clear the fog. I cautiously manoeuvred my legs over the walk way feeling for the pin-ladder with my dangling feet. Tommy closely followed as I carefully descended.

"It would be a hoot if we both nosedived off here right now," he said. "Imagine the telegrams home, 'Killed on active service – fucking around'!"

Tommy and I arrived in the NAAFI just as Three and Four Squads returned to base. They had been on general duties in the town, mainly supporting Red Cross teams handing out food parcels and medical supplies. Most of the men from Three and Four made a beeline for the bar. They'd heard about the loss of our compadrés. Macker and Ricky came over to Bronco, Dinger, JJ, Tommy and me. We shook hands, hugged and talked. It was good that the Platoon was together again, we felt so much stronger as a complete unit. The beer flowed, probably too much considering we were unsure of our new objectives. But at that moment we cared not. We needed to chill, to confirm our fellowship; most of all, we needed to talk about Jumper and Sugar. So that's what we did – we talked about our muckers. We talked as if they were still with us, in a strange sort of way they still were.

06:30: UN Base Camp 9, Thursday 5 July.

I'd been awake since before 04:30. I couldn't get back to sleep. I never could sleep in the 'Nam or rather a decent night's sleep would elude me for nights on end. Periods of interrupted slumber followed by one night where I'd sleep a sleep of the dead. I'd wake up on the following morning feeling even more fatigued than after a night of insomnia; I clearly wasn't the only one.

Marine Miller approached my bed sporting a UCLA running top and shorts: "Some of the boys are goin for a run, wanna join us?"

I jumped at the chance as did half-a-dozen others. What started out as Dusty, Ricky and Vinny soon turned into 19 of us.

We left the base in an orderly line. Being Royal Marines I guess we couldn't help falling into rows of three and dressing each other left and right. It was a beautiful morning. Blankets of mist lay like sheaths across the deserted back road. The mist occasionally cleared revealing the splendour of the woods and glades that flanked the road. We ran nearby a pair of wild pot-bellied pigs eating figs that had fallen on the roadside; they carried on munching in dogged determination as we scurried past. An elderly man passed us on a scooter-cart. Two small children were sat at the back, staring at us as the cart overtook the crew.

"Chào người Anh," (*Hello English*!) one of the little girls shouted, the other waving.

"Chào trê cons," (*Hello kids*!) We jointly responded, waving to the tiny waifs.

"Chào người Anh," (*Goodbye English*!) The other girl hollered as the cart disappeared in another sheath of mist.

The playful laughter from the lads said it all. We all loved children, especially Vietnamese kids – they always seemed pleased to see us.

The pace was slow at first. We opened up the warmer we became. Corporal Lane was dissatisfied with the canter. He broke off moving to our left in preparation to whip us into an extended rhythm: "Come-on you fuckin' girl's blouses, lets get into a decent stride!" Bronco opened up with a familiar chant, which we followed with vigour—

"***Sergeant dragged me from my bed***
M16 pointin' at my head
Said Sergeant don't you murder me
Swear I'll tear up my D by P..."

The banter and laughter was discernible. We would have woken the whole neighbourhood, should they've not already been awake. It felt good as we continued along the empty back road. The sound of our boots thumping on the tarmac; the joshing of my compadrés either side of me; the moist air moving over my speeding body; my heart rapidly beating as we extended the pace; the gentle breeze cooling the sweat on my face. As we about-turned to make our way back to barracks I was reminded yet again just how good it was to be alive.

*

The 07:00 briefing was a non-event. Two Squad was assigned base duty whilst One Squad joined up with Three and Four. We would join them on the following day. Being in limbo was the last thing we needed; time on our hands equalled time to mull over events. Nevertheless, those left behind soldiered through: checking light weapons, counting ammunition, cleaning binoculars and removing spent data from the plastic-coated ordinance maps. We'd completed most of the designated tasks by lunch, hence, we were told to stand down for the rest of the day. I decided to take the opportunity to write a detailed letter home. I needed to write, to connect. I had always struggled with missives to loved ones. I was again struck by a feeling of guilt; Marines Collins and Lyle wrote home regularly. Time to make amends.

I wrote with fervour. I didn't write about the incident, that would've been gratuitous and served no purpose save to raise the anxiety of my family. But I did write about my buddies, especially Jumper and Sugar. I wrote as if they were still in our presence. I'm not sure why, maybe it was my way of conveying how much affection I had for them. How important they were to me. How much they'd enriched my life. How sad to write of things that I didn't say to them when they were alive.

Corporal Speed on the other hand was still alive. He was sat on his bed cleaning his rifle for what must have been the umpteenth time. The firefight had spooked us. I guess he just wanted to be sure his weapon was top of the range. I still felt guilty about my outburst after Jumper's death. I'd not had a chance to speak to him since the incident. I moved towards him wondering how I was going to apologise. I stood by his bed as he continued oiling his rifle. He knew I was there but refused to acknowledge my presence.

"Speedy," I said nervously, "listen mate I'm sorry about the other day, I had no right to—"

"Forget it!" he responded without giving eye contact.

I stood there watching him reassemble his M16, continuing to ignore me. I couldn't blame him, I'd added to the hurt he was already feeling, that we were all feeling.

Speedy dropped the spring from his firing mechanism. It slowly rolled across the floor coming to a halt under Jumper's empty bed. We both stared at the 6-inch long object visible through the springs of the bare metal frame. If I was a fatalist or was superstitious I'd have seen it as a sign. Being none of those I simply walked over and picked up the heavily oiled object. He slowly looked up as I handed him the spring: "I really am sorry…I didn't mean to ridicule you. I was angry, hurt. Even so, I had no right to take it out on you. I apologise."

Speedy half-smiled as he gently took the spring from me: "We've all got different ways of dealin' with the shit that life throws at us."

"Somebody else said that to me not so long ago."

"Billie?"

"Yeah...she'd have given me one of her frowns if she'd have heard what I shouted."

"I half expected one of those bolts of lightning to strike you down," he said, "that'll have made you think twice, aye."

Speedy and I talked for over an hour. We talked about our families, our fears and of what we going to do once our tour was over. I had never *really* talked to him before that day. I'm glad I did. We couldn't support Jumper and Sugar anymore, but we could still support each other.

The Platoon was back together again by 1800 hours. Talk inevitably revolved around Marines Collins and Lyle. Would there be a vigil before their bodies were flown home? Where would it be held and could we all attend? The possibility that their bodies had already been flown home also crossed our minds. Corporal Farr put our minds at rest. Apparently nothing could be done until the post-mortems. We wondered when the results would be available. Medical Attendant Moore brought an end to the speculation as he came into the mess, a disconsolate look on his face. Tommy asked what was up. I wished he wouldn't have as Moose gave a summary of Jumper and Sugar's post-mortems.

Marine Lyle suffered one fatal wound; a single bullet penetrated his left cheekbone ripping through bone and brain tissue on its inexorable journey through his skull. The shot was more a lucky strike than a sniper's chosen target, though this mattered not as Sugar's blood and cerebral fluid oozed onto the damp bracken.

Marine Collins took three hits. The first bullet ripped through his left arm; the second below his right collar bone, exiting his right shoulder blade and the third through his left upper shoulder concluding in liver tissue. The last projectile was undoubtedly the killer. The bullet glanced his aorta before ripping through his left lung bursting through his chest cavity and smashing into his liver. Moose could do nothing to stem the surge of blood gushing from massive internal wounds.

If the loss of our muckers was hard to take, the circumstances surrounding their demise was even worse. We were to discover that Jumper's brave attempt to protect Sugar was in vain. Marine Lyle's injuries were so severe he was likely dead before he hit the ground. The high velocity projectile cut through his skull as if it was made of papier-mâché. It was a brutal truth: if Jumper had remained in cover he conceivably wouldn't have been hit.

Biffo briefed the Platoon on the ceremonial arrangements at 20:00. He informed us that their bodies would be flown home on Saturday July 7th after a liturgy at a Catholic church adjacent to the former United States Military Air Strip at Ton Sịa Quran. He went on to tell us that details on the vigil would be posted on the noticeboard. The Platoon was pleased to hear that the service wouldn't be held in a military based church. It somehow seemed more fitting to have the observance in a church outside the clinical environment familiar to barrack-stanchion.

Sergeant Edwards posted the details at 2100 hours. The bulletin included a request for pallbearers. I put my name down along with 21 others – Jumper and Sugar were clearly popular. I was miffed when my name failed to come out the hat, particularly since the majority of the crew were from Three and Four Squads. My annoyance was quickly replaced by self-admonishment. The liturgy wasn't about me; it was about Marines Collins and Lyle, their rites-of-passage. I comforted myself in the knowledge that Lance Corporal Bell along with Marines Clarke, Fox, Jeffers, Montford and Vincent were amongst the grouping. Jumper and Sugar would have been pleased about that.

06:30: UN Base Camp 9, Friday 6 July.

Two Squad linked with Three and Four. We spent the day on the mundane: road blocks outside the base; escorting Red Cross workers from the refugee camp on the outskirts of town and checking movements of individuals purporting to have refugee status. I can remember looking at non-service personnel in a different way, particularly young men. Prior to the firefight we'd considered the Khmer Rouge to be relatively innocuous. The sortie had fundamentally changed our attitudes – the Khmer Rouge was anything but innocuous; they were unequivocally pernicious. All of Two Squad was suffering startled reaction and occasional unexpected attacks of acute anxiety. Nonetheless, it could've been worse; we could've been out in the bush.

The evening dragged, our thoughts were on other things. We spent most of our time polishing our boots and ironing our uniforms. We were determined to give our fallen comrades a fitting send off; it was the least we could do.

I once read that the bereaved rarely dream of a lost significant other until sometime after their deaths, often weeks. I've not found this to be the case. It certainly wasn't the case early evening of the 6th. I was lying on my bed listening to the sound of the rain as it pelted on roof. An oscillating fan clicked as it moved through its perpetual cycle. There were only a handful of us left in the dormitory. Most of the men had gone to the NAAFI or were out doing other things. Dinger was recording a message to his fiancée, his voice more sombre than usual. JJ was lying on the next bed writing a letter home, his radio playing dulcet tunes on his bedside table.

I didn't want to fall to sleep; getting to sleep at lights-out was bad enough. I wanted to save any possibility of uninterrupted shut-eye until then. My body was strong but my soul weak. My eyelids drifted, I fell into a momentary slumber and experienced one of the most vivid dreams I've ever had.

—We were in *The Pussy Palace*, Sàigòn. Beams of psychedelic light darted across the walls in the otherwise darkened, smoke-filled room. The bar was lined with United States Marines spending their last Đồng before the flight home from Tân Sờn Nhứt. I was standing with the lads in a small corner we'd nicknamed the 'sump'. Speedy and Dinger were huddled round a fruit machine. Bronco, Dusty, JJ and Macker were standing beside me laughing and joking. The club was as lively as ever. Drunken sailors brawled whilst the jukebox played Don McLean's *American Pie*. I looked towards a booth to see Jumper and Sugar sitting face to face indulged in their usual tête-à-tête. Two tall glasses of San Miguel and a large burnished ashtray lay central the table. Somehow the scene wasn't right. Sugar was wearing a gaudy Hawaiian shirt. He hated such ostentatious garments. And both were smoking, not just joints, king size filter tips. Very few men in the Platoon smoked – smoking compromised fitness. The Royal Marines demanded high levels of physical fitness 24/7. I stared at them wondering why they were there. 'You're both dead...' I said to myself, 'you shouldn't be sat there.' I was glad they were with us, but confused by their presence. I suddenly became aware of a large wound on Jumper's upper arm. It was raw and weeping profusely. I wondered why it wasn't causing him pain – then again how could it, he was dead.

A youthful bargirl diverted my attention deliberately pushing her body against my side. I could feel her breasts separated by my upper arm, her leg rubbing against my chinos the static from her nylon stocking sparking along with my hormones. Her flawless skin, long black hair and jasmine fragrances were inviting.

"You want me Johnny?" she said, lavishly licking her lips, "...fucky-fucky, sucky-sucky. I good for you, make you cum plenty time."

I wanted to tell her to go away. I wanted to steal time with my fallen compadrés: testosterone raced, my pupils dilated, my skin prickled and boxer shorts tightened.

"Later," I whispered with an enthusiastic air.

I re-focused on the booth as the slender woman walked away, her hand smoothly slipping from my back pocket. The booth was empty, Jumper and Sugar had gone. A cigarette smouldered amid a pool of blood on the table. I scanned the room frantically searching for them. I rushed headlong through the crowd pushing people out of the way, unconcerned about my behaviour.

A Khmer Rouge revolutionary attempted to block my passageway, smirking

'neath his headband.
"Tắm sâqứị," (*Fuck you!*) I barked as I threw him across the room.
Billie and Phillipa were stood near the door, the starched white of their nurses' uniforms distinct. I called out to them: "Have you seen Jumper and Sugar?"
Billie smiled and pointed towards the door; they were about to leave.
"Jumper, Sugar," I called as my legs grew heavy. I could hear *American Pie* on the jukebox the decibels' increasing as the fractured scene slowly fades: "Jumper...**Sugar**—!"
I awoke to see Marine Jeffers sitting on his bed beside me, *American Pie* playing on his radio. The song had filtered into my dream. I was unsure whether the track was the stimulus or a supplement. It mattered not as I lay listening to the last section:

'I met a girl who sang the blues and I asked her for some happy news
but she just smiled and turned away,
I went down to the sacred store where I'd heard the music years before
but the man there said the music wouldn't play,
And in the streets the children screamed,
The lovers cried and the poets dreamed,
And not a word was spoken, the church bells all were broken,
And the three men I admired the most, the Father, Son and the Holy Ghost,
They caught the last train for the coast, the day, the music, died...'

Once again I found myself fighting back the tears. Seemed, that was all I'd done since the loss of our muckers. 'Am I the only person in this fuckin' Platoon that weeps?' I thought as I lay on the duvet. I wasn't of course; others in the Platoon cried, like most men, in private.
JJ looked at me: "Dreamin' about the boys?"
"Yeah, how do you know?"
"You called out their names...was it a good'un?"
"Hard to say, I saw them, but I don't think they saw me."
JJ said nothing in return he just nodded. I think he understood. People grieve in different ways, and dreams are often hard to fathom, particularly when they are about departed loved ones.

11:00: UN Base Camp 9, Saturday 7 July.

We changed into our uniforms early morning, probably too early. The advanced party, Lieutenant Derrick, Sergeant Edwards and the 12 pallbearers had already departed for the chapel of rest. The remainder of the Platoon lounged around killing time. Some of the men played cards; others read or dozed in easy chairs. Corporal Farr and I attempted a few games of chess but we couldn't concentrate.

The lads collected in their common groups. We were all introspective; final goodbyes are never easy. I remember scanning the room that day, looking at the faces of my comrades. I've read myriad books rambling on about the bond that develops between men in combat. There is a bond, how could there not be: there are times when you have to put your life in another man's hands, have him put his life in yours. However, there is I would suggest, a difference between a bond created as a result of common aims and shared experiences, and a connection between individuals resultant of shared values, beliefs or interests. I have been drawn to people through any number of mediums not just fighting alongside them. As for the men of my Platoon, I'd share a foxhole with any one of them, but would only want to share a holiday villa with a handful. We each had our favourites. Bronco, Dinger, Dusty, JJ, Macker, Tommy and of course Jumper and Sugar were mine. I didn't particularly get on with Nasher, Buck or Ronnie, and there was something about Cowboy that spooked me. It wasn't just his perceivably psychopathic tendencies, it was something more, something underlying I couldn't quite establish. We hardly ever talked – come to think of it we hardly passed the time of day. Hence, I was surprised when he came over to me as we waited for the airlift. He sat down beside me breaking a daydream.

"Are you okay?" he asked, with an empathetic expression that took me by surprise.

"Yeah, life goes on."

"Still, it's a sad day."

We sat staring into space, listening for the report of the rotors. Cowboy broke the impasse: "Would you do the same for me?"

"What do what?"

"Cover me if I was down, like Jumper covered Sugar."

"Of course I would, goes without saying."

"Me too," Cowboy said, with a wink. "I'd cover you; lay my life down for you I would."

We stared at each other both wearing nervous smiles. The chopping-beat of the incoming Chinook interrupted our unexpected association.

"Our taxi's 'ere boys," Biffo said, as the roof shook in the 'copters wake.

"See you later mate," Cowboy said, squeezing my arm as we both prepared to leave.

I'd learn a number of things on that day, not least that there are some factors within relationships that can't be defined. As it transpired I would never again see Marine Cunliffe in the same light.

The Chinook banked over the sprawling shantytowns that ringed the outskirts of Sàigòn before landing at Tơn Sịa Quran. The former US Base neighboured the Xuran Noừc district of the capital. Xuran Noừc was a former haunt of the first colonial French. The locality had long lost its opulent appearance; the once palatial buildings were ramshackle. Lines of washing hung from balcony struts that once retained exuberant hanging baskets overflowing with imported flora. The roads were strewn with potholes and the once regularly maintained sidewalks were cracked and hazardous. We made our way to the church in an orderly line. The people milling in the relatively bare streets seemed disinterested by our presence. Doubtless they'd seen servicemen from the locale sauntering to Sunday worship on numerous occasions.

The church was in keeping with its surroundings. The 18th Century house of worship stood in grounds that were once eminent. Bindweed and thistle had long since driven the orchids to inescapable surrender. A tinny bell pealed in the cracked and crooked tower, occasionally drowning the blare of scooters as they scurried through the dusty avenues.

The Platoon mustered each side of the path leading to the gaping baroque doors waiting in silence. The vigil cortège pulled up on a cobbled driveway that looked as if laid by a gang of blind one-armed navvies. The pallbearers walked slowly between the squads. Each coffin was draped with the Union Flag cut, mid-section, by the folded flag of the United Nations. We followed in a silent line shuffling amid the slender nave. The interior was cool yet inviting. I felt light-headed in the overbearing smell of candle-wax, tainted rosewater and incense. The church appeared to be in an inexorable decline. The oak beams were bent and scattered with flight holes. Pinpricks of quartz sparkled in the eroded stone floors. Faded and curled patches of lead dotted the underside of the decaying roof.

A small Eurasian Priest led the pallbearers as a thin grey-haired woman played *Amazing Grace* on a chipped-veneer Hammond organ. There was an impressive semi-circle of stepped candles flickering round the plinth in front of the altar arranged to accommodate the two coffins in an exact fit. The aesthetically perfect pictures of Jesus and Mary dominated the walls each side of a large crucifix. I've often wondered why I've never seen an ugly representation of the purported Son of a questionable God. The church was adorned with stained glass, the colourful illustrations looked incongruous amid the stone washed walls and drab teak pews. The representations were of dramas involving the French. The first Catholic Missionaries; the plague of 1799; the establishment of the first South East Asian Cathedral, Sàigòn 1865 and the visit of Pope John XXIII, 1959. No Indo-Chinese faces featured in the scenes. This was of no surprise: it was to the shame of the Catholic Church that it had done nothing to condemn the injustice and oppression that was a permanent feature within that tormented land. Nonetheless, the context dictated that I needed to put my contempt for the establishment to one side.

The pallbearers tenderly placed the two coffins before the altar. I remember wondering which one was which, though I'm unsure why. The Priest kicked off with the standard sacrament: prayers for the living, prayers for the dead, the Father, Son and the Holy Spirit. He introduced the first hymn *Make Me A Channel Of Your Peace*. I sat in silence as the majority of the Platoon sang. I half expected their collective voices' to sound as if a room full of randy tomcats with chronic cystitis. What a surprise to hear a melodic chorus, even harmonising. Jumper would've laughed, he eschewed sentiment. He always come across as a hard-knock – nobody fucked with Jumper! It was all front: Jumper was one of the most sensitive men I've ever had the privilege of knowing. He loved life, worshipped his mother and father and would have given his heart and soul to have held a child of his own in his muscular arms. Jumper was generous to a fault. He was an honourable man who despised cheats, cowards and bullies. He was a simple man who lived a simple life.

A further selection of prayers was succeeded by the lesson. Lance Corporal Barilla read passages from *Revelations*. Ricky spoke with passion about the river of life: precious, ever changing, flowing with happiness and despair.

Marine Lyle had a zest for life; he always lived it to the full. He didn't dwell on the past and cared nothing about the future – he only lived for the day. He was a natural comedian who made light of almost everything. He seemed to be totally at ease with life and himself. Yet under his façade he was still a boy; insecure, vulnerable and longing to be loved. Truth is, Sugar was loved. Love isn't a word that men like to use when referring to one another. Even so, I can't think of any member of 2: Bravo 6 Platoon that was held in such high regard. Jumper loved him; Bronco, Dinger, Dusty, JJ and Tommy loved him. And I loved him; Marine Robert Lyle was more than just my mate.

The lesson was followed by a second hymn *Oh Lord Our God* (*How Great Thou Art*) my father's favourite. I closed my eyes as the opening verses reverberated through the hazy air; thoughts of home my father singing whilst kneading bread. But home seemed so distant, as if part of a far off universe. It would be a place that Jumper and Sugar would never see again. My emotions suddenly overflowed manifested in tears trickling down my face. As I sat listening to the dulcet tones of my compadrés a strange transformation took place. I was overcome by a desire to sing. I fumbled for the hymnbook resting in the pew leaf. My hands were shaking as I thumbed the pages. Speedy, sitting to my right, intervened instantaneously finding the relevant sheet. Bronco gently placed his hand on the back of my head ruffling my spiky hair as I joined the chorus. I didn't sing with fervour, I hardly added to the decibels glancing the damp walls. Nevertheless, I sang, 'praises to God'.

It wasn't some blinding revelation, some sudden seeing the light. I didn't suddenly feel a need to form an attachment with a spiritual construct so long eschewed. My willingness to participate was driven by respect: a need to honour my fallen comrades and the brothers that surrounded me; to consolidate, confirm that I was still a part of something – even something lost. And a realisation that denial is short-term and reality forever enduring.

Lieutenant Derrick slowly bowed in front of the coffins before presenting the eulogy. There was no talk of faultless individuals; no disingenuous declarations or hackneyed clichés. Just an honest portrait of two Royal Marines who had died carrying out their duties; succinct and to the point. His closing statement was particularly poignant—

"Jumper was the bravest of marines and Sugar, he could make you laugh in the worst of situations. Both these qualities are of equal value, for as well as fighting against the oppression and evil that contaminates this land we must also learn to laugh in the face of those monsters. Jumper and Sugar must now make the trip home. Shortly, we will follow. Until that time we must say our goodbyes and carry through our duties. It's what's expected of us, no less would've been expected of them. As we continue the tasks we will not walk two-down. Marines Gerald Collins and Robert Lyle will still be on point. They will still protect our rear; they will continue to walk alongside us, as we will walk beside them. The spirits of our brave compadrés will be with us now and forever, for *...at the going down of the sun, and in the morning, we will remember them.*"

"We will remember them," the Platoon followed in gentle harmony.

The serenity that succeeded the Lieutenant's address was broken by the sound of a single bugler: Marine Taylor playing *The Last Post.* We knew that Buck could play the bugle, but not with such proficiency. The sharp notes echoing each side of the immense space sent a shiver down my spine. A further hush succeeded the dying notes, interrupted by Colour Sergeant Biffly: "Platoon...fall in outside."

The organist played *Abide With Me* as we departed. I stood behind Corporal Speed amid the pews waiting for the backlog to clear. He curtseyed and blessed himself before the altar; there was no ridicule from me that time. I was about to walk towards the exit when I turned to look at the coffins. I'm unsure why, a final confirmation that my muckers really had gone maybe. I stared at the flags and the two United Nations medals placed on top. I slowly approached the flag draped shapes and placed a hand on each. "I'll never forget you," I whispered.

Tommy smiled as I rejoined the Platoon – there wasn't a dry eye amongst them. Men do cry; in private, in the presence of those who love them enough not to ridicule them and most of all – in the company of their brothers.

The Platoon made its way to a former French 19th Century Meeting House for the vigil feast. The once ostentatious building, the domain of the erstwhile social élite, adjoined the church grounds. The IPSF had organised a room for the lamentations. We were generally critical of the top brass. Sugar used to say that they couldn't organise a hard-on in a Sàigòn massage parlour. What they lacked in logistical expertise they made up for in their ability to organise soirées. The spread in the central room was fit for a state occasion: rows of cooked meats and fish along with an impressive array of salads, breads and patisseries. Lines of bottled beer filled a chilling tray. Two large pictures of Marines Collins and Lyle surrounded by a floral display lay central to the table. They had even organised a compilation tape of their favourite music: Deep Purple, Jimi Hendrix, Led Zeppelin, The Moody Blues, T Rex. The music seemed incongruous in a room formerly used for ensembles and Cajun dances.

JJ had managed to get the PA system working. He stood on the stage mimicking Sugar's voice, telling jokes, taking the piss – it was a hoot!

The lads mingled amongst themselves. Stories of our exploits abounded. My attention began to drift as the beer flowed. I thought of the conversations I used to have with them. Jumper once said: "I wish I could learn things like you and tell stories like you do."

I remember giving him an embarrassed smile, thinking, 'I wish I had your courage.' I lamented that I'd not told him that at the time. Jumper's courage was demonstrable. I thought of a fight he'd once won in an inter-services competition. We'd been chosen along with 5 others to represent the Platoon. Jumper was a 'boxer'; I was a 'fighter'. My strategy comprised of wading in with my fists. Most of the time it worked, that was until the Combined Forces Championships in Hong Kong. I had battled my way through the competition but received a boxing lesson from my opponent in the Middleweight Final. I remember collapsing onto my corner stool at the closing bell, Tony Oxley (the Coach) wiping my battered and bloodied face with a wet sponge. "That was sheer guts!" he said. "He had you beaten in the second round, but you still come out fighting in the third...well done."

Marine Collins was fighting on the same Bill (Light heavyweight). He too struggled in his bout. He'd been knocked down twice in the second round, but came out with a dogged determination in the third. It was then that I witnessed *real* courage. Jumper willingly left himself exposed, enticing his opponent to hit him whilst looking for a defensive lapse. He found one, dumping his opponent firmly on the canvas for a knockout.

My resolve partly originated from a desire not to let the Platoon down, his was from sheer courage. Gallantry isn't something that you can purchase and you can't be coached into being brave – courage is either there or it isn't.

My contemplation was broken by the sound of a large plane taking off from Tơn Sịa Qưan.

Jez gazed at JJ and me: "I wonder if that's Jumper and Sugar's bird?"

"Nah..." Corporal Farr cut in, "they'll be on a winged-chariot to Valhalla!"

The soirée continued, the stream of beer seemingly never ending. I spent much of the time with Bronco, Dinger, Dusty, JJ and Tommy. I talked to Tommy about the last conversation I'd had with Sugar. I asked him if he thought it would be a good idea for me to write to Phillipa to let her know how he felt about her. Tommy put me straight: "Why would you want to do that, for him or for yourself?"

He was right. What would be the point; why add to the pile of those already grieving.

Biffo brought an end to the social at 2100 hours. "Shindig's over boys," he said over the PA, "...time to board big-bird back to base."

We sat in the orange netting-seats of the Chinook; stuffed, well oiled and weary. Most of the lads dozed off through the double rotor-thud. I slumbered in the faint red light glow of the tube-like cabin replaying my last moments with Sugar. I thought of our plan to go to *Goodison Park* to cheer on the Blues. I would have to make the appointment without him. It was then that I made a pledge. I would go to *Goodison Park* as if he were beside me. I would cheer for our beloved Everton. I'd yell for both of us. I would shout so loud that should there be a heaven above, Royal Marine Robert Lyle could not fail to hear me!

14:00: UN Base Camp 9, Tuesday 10 July.

Every soldier counts down. They countdown the months left to passing out at Boot Camp; the weeks to their next period of home leave; the days to the beginning of Rest and Recuperation and the minutes to stand down on the frontline. Counting down is a skill that you acquire throughout your time in the forces. You pick up the fundamentals at an early stage. You learn not to start counting the weeks or days too early, to do so would only lower your morale and make the time ahead seem endless; the psychology of the time continuum.

By our 336th day we were well into RDP (Run Down Period) particularly after being informed that our time in Trệng Nhôy was to end on the 12th of July. Our final police action was to be in the relatively safe streets and peripheral districts of Đà Nẵng; the region had long been under the control of the Sàigòn Government. The territory was still hazardous, but compared to our excursions in Quang Trì, Nha Trang, Quì Nhôn and Trệng Nhôy, we considered any risks to be largely insignificant. We'd also been informed that the Rest and Recuperation Facility at China Beach was still active. We were all looking forward to lively nights and lazy weekends.

The Platoon had linked-up for our last two days in Trệng Nhôy. We had returned to base to pack our equipment ready for the long drive to Đà Nẳng. Morale was high. The lads were in fine form; joshing, singing and taking the piss out of each other's foibles. We felt as if the tribulations of the past eleven months were behind us.

Regardless, I wanted to carry out a little exercise of my own before leaving Trệng Nhôy. I had decided to add to the collection of graffiti on the forbidden tower. I originally considered adding my own name but decided against the act of vanity. Instead, I would leave the names of our muckers so cruelly cut down.

The grounds around the rusting hulk were all but deserted as I ascended the ladder. I knew exactly what I wanted to write as I cautiously crawled along the narrow walk board. I had to take care; the walkway had been designed to accommodate inspection engineers, not maintenance. Workers would be harnessed to safety lines – I had no such luxury.

I carefully squatted writing my chosen testimony with the fluorescent marker pen I'd acquired from stores. The pungent bright orange liquid dried quickly in the arid air. I'd all but finished when I heard the bark of a loud voice below: “Lance Corporal Morris! What the flyin' fuck do you think you're doing?”

'Oh fuck!' I thought as I glanced down to see Colour Sergeant Biffly looking up at me: “Err, nothin' Colour Sergeant.”

“Well you better get your arse down here before I put you on a nothin' report!”

I carefully descended not looking forward to the inevitable roasting I was about to receive.

“Just what the fuck do you think you're playing at?” Biffo said. “Have you got a death wish or something? Do you want to go home in a body bag?”

“No Colour Sergeant—”

“Well you're goin the best way about it, that tower's condemned; apart from that you've just made yourself a target for every fuckin' sniper in the bush! What were you doin' up there anyway?”

I stood looking at the Colour Sergeant, unsure of what to say, desperately trying to remove the hangdog expression from my face. He glanced down and noticed the marker pen in my hand.

“I hope it was worth it,” he said, plucking the marker from my hand.

“It was worth it.”

Colour Sergeant Biffly slowly shook his head. “Get to the armoury...” he said after what seemed like an age, “help Bronco with the weapons check.”

I turned to leave grateful that the affair was likely going no further.

"Lance Corporal Morris!" he bellowed as I turned. "Put this back where you found it!"

I took the marker pen from his hand and scurried towards the stores.

I felt good as left the scene – I had done the deed. The structure may have been condemned. By end of year it may not have been standing; demolished, melted down for razor blades. But dissolving the graffiti of past combatants would not take away the fact that they'd been in the 'Nam, as had Marines Collins and Lyle, and part of them would always remain. I looked up at the tower to see if I could spot any of my 8-inch high letters. I couldn't of course, though it mattered not, I knew what I'd written:

JUMPER & SUGAR
JULY '73
FOREVER YOUNG

'Yes,' I thought as I made my way to the armoury, 'they'd have liked that.'

21:00: UN Base Camp 9.

We were well into a night of boozing. We were yet another marine down. Corporal Farr had been granted special leave after learning that his daughter Rachel was suffering from meningitis. His wife, Jackie had made an emergency radiophone call from Royal Marines Stonehouse Barracks, Plymouth. Tommy hastily packed before boarding a chartered Huey to Tân Sờn Nhứt. I joined some of the lads to bid him farewell.

"No offence mucker," Tommy said as we shook hands and hugged, "but I hope I don't see you 'til Blighty."

"None taken."

It was hard to see another one of our muckers leave. The consolation that time was that we'd soon be following. We already felt as if we were home and dry. Music blared from the jukebox as we continued our penultimate celebrations, thoughts of forthcoming days and nights in Đà Nẳng.

"Oh wow..." Macker said, "RDP in Đà Nẳng, late night strolls down Đoc Mý Street."

"Lounging on China Beach," I added.

"Yeah," Jez enthused, "Tiger beer afternoons and San Miguel evenings—"

"Too right…" TC cut in, "followed by a night of lickin' pussy at Suzy Lò's. My tongue's gonna be workin' overtime, cocksucker-oh-wow!"

"Goose, goose, goose!" JJ added mimicking our late mucker.

The laughter was infectious. I recall having a sudden onset of guilt as I chortled: '…why am I enjoying myself?' I thought, 'I should still be feeling sorrowful, our buddies aren't even in their graves yet.'

Bronco noticed my remorseful expression: "You've got nothing to feel guilty about; they'd want you to go on living, just like you'd have wanted them too."

I wondered how he knew that I was feeling guilty about merrymaking in the absence of our late buddies. It was quite simple of course – he was feeling the same way.

The night rolled on, the jukebox played, the men sung – as did I. One song stopped me in my tracks, *American Pie.* The lads sang with gusto. I sat and listened, memories of my dream, thoughts of my comrades. I enthusiastically joined in as the final chorus struck up—

"*...And they were singin', bye, bye Miss American Pie,*
Drove my Chevy to the levy but the levy was dry,
An' them good ol' boys were drinkin' whiskey and rye
Singin' this will be the day that I die!"

11:00: UN Base Camp 9, Wednesday 11 July.

We were clearing up the last remnants of spent materials when we heard a commotion.

"What's with the hullabaloo?" Lance Corporal Jessop enquired.

We were soon to find out as Colour Sergeant Biffly came into the supply room: "Okay you lot get yourselves over to the Drill Hall, on the double!"

"What the fuck's goin' down?" Marine Jeffers asked as we crossed the vehicle compound.

The dimly lit Drill Hall was filling fast as we arrived. A 10-foot map of South Vietnam dominated centre stage. We each had a sinking feeling as we took our seats.

Lieutenant Derrick mounted the stage a sombre look on his face. "Okay boys, I'll cut to the chase. You may've heard a rumour about trouble around the DM, Zee; well, here are the facts. At least three North Vietnamese companies have streamed across the Laotian border between Đọng Hấ and Khề Sahn. Intelligence suggests they've linked-up with long established Viet Cong Cadres...the Â Shàu Brigade. The SVA and local Montagnards have moved to confront them head-on. All hell's broke loose and there's scores of refugees caught in the middle. Route nine's strewn with them, from Cắm Lô to Thựà Thiện. The poor bastards are being slaughtered. Bottom line, somebody's going to have to police-up the refugees and provide escort to a safe haven. The facilities at Huê and Phư Lắc are on standby to receive additional refugees. There are other units in the area, including a division of

Indonesian Regulars, but we've been handed the poison chalice. I'm sorry boys, there's to be no easy run-down in Đà Nẵng, it's Quang Trì or bust! We're to parachute in early morning twelfth of July. Go back and re-pack your gear, essentials only; you'll have to leave your teddy bears behind—"

The Platoon laughed temporarily arresting our increasing anxiety.

"—The remainder of our equipment will follow in a successive drop, though I'm unsure when. We board the C130 at 0200 hours, Tấlận Chựí Airstrip. Deploy from 4000 feet at around 03:00, Drop Zone north of Khề Sahn; further details to follow at individual briefings."

The Lieutenant was pensive. "I don't need to remind you boys; Quang Trì's a murder hole. I'm not sure what's going to be waiting for us once we get down so we need to be alert. Get a couple of hours shut-eye after the briefing; it'll likely be the last sleep we'll get for at least 48 hours. Chinook to Tấlận Chựí at 22:00; any questions?"

Marine Gypsy broke the silence: "Are we still going to be relieved on August ninth?"

"I can't guarantee that, goddammit I can't guarantee anything at the moment. We'll just have to wait and see."

Yozzer put his hand up: "Have we got time to write a last letter home?"

His question was open to invariable interpretation; an eerie silence followed.

"I don't know about you…but I've got every intention of writing a letter home and no intention of making it my last! nor should you. Given the circumstances I'll sign a chit for a freebie, extra mail collection at 14:00."

No further questions followed, just silence. The Lieutenant summed up: "We've been given the task because we can do the task. We're professionals. More than that, we're superior; coalesced, indivisible and the only thing standing between hundreds of refugees and the almighty. Those poor bastards need to be protected and **we** are going to protect them – yes!"

"**Yes Sir!**" the Platoon roared.

Lieutenant Derrick left as quickly as he'd entered. We sat motionless, muttering amongst ourselves, trying to assimilate a cruel reality. There was to be no lounging on China Beach; no Tiger beer afternoons and San Miguel evenings down Đoc Mý Street; no sensuous nights at Suzy Lò's; no RDP in Đà Nẵng. We were going back, to Quang Trì!

SLAUGHTERED YOUTH

Fresh faced, wide eyed, naive in the extreme
Fervent for the fight to validate their manhood.
Battle cries resonate, young men yell
Thoughts of their sweethearts whom they beguiled
Lost amid the heat of combat.

Swords & lances brandish, as many times erstwhile
Flesh, teeth and testicles soar
Decapitated, shattered to ribbons
Descending the putrescent cavities of inhumanity
Contrived by those bereft of consciousness
Save for malevolence.

Prematurely hacked these rosebuds bursting to open
Their heads cut off as they restrain to unfold
Broken stems emitting the sap of youth
Contaminated amidst the black bile of hatred
Drizzling shadow-like aloft this abomination.

Bullets & grenades rip, young men stumble
Mother! one cries out – mum!
His childhood flashes before him
Final senses fade; the flesh transmutes
Silent screams only the tormented can apprehend
Teardrops dilute amid the flow of blood
Raining, pouring, dripping in the mud.

Colours of conquest, roars of victory
Cheers in the Senate, dispatch papers wave
Media spreads the word: lies will be heard
Dare not tell the truth
'Bout slaughtered youth.

Lance Corporal Barry Morris
Trệng Nhôy, July 1973.

9: RETURN TO QUANG TRÌ

Distrust yourself & sleep
before you fight,
'Tis not too late tomorrow
to be brave.
J Armstrong

02:35: C130, 4000 feet above Khề Sahn, 12 July 1973.

The C130 gently rocked as it winged its way towards our destination. We sat on the canvas bucket seats facing each other in silent consternation. Marine Fox was coming out of a deep sleep – he could sleep on a clothesline. I checked the straps and buckles on my main and reserve 'chutes for the umpteenth time. My mouth was dry and my stomach churning. I kept on rubbing my sweaty palms on my trouser legs. I had an overwhelming desire to swallow; for some inexplicable reason I couldn't. My head was cabbaged with the persistent buzz and whine from the four jet-propellers. Marine Vincent, sitting immediately across from me, was muttering under his breath. He appeared to be nervously going through jump drill over and over again.

Corporal Lane was sitting on my right: "Twenty-nine days to the wake-up and we're still up to our eyeballs in this shit!" he muttered as he too checked his fastenings.

A member of the aircrew signalled that the Drop Zone was imminent. Biffo began walking the central passageway as the aircrew moved aft to make final preparations for our exit. "Hustle up and check your gear. Remember the drill; we establish silent contact once down. Make your weapons at the ready. Do *not* prime unless you encounter resistance. If we get involved in action remember UN protocol – we do no more than defend ourselves and each other. Keep those actions clear! Reserve as much ammo as is practical. If you get separated don't call out. Discipline! Self and collective control, that's what it's about—!"

"Drop Zone three minutes!" a member of the aircrew hollered, "...good luck lads."

"Okay boys, this is it..." Lieutenant Derrick yelled as we all struggled up, "I'll see y'all downstairs!"

The two crewmen designated feed-out duty stood at the two disembarkation points. They began issuing instructions as we re-checked our gear: "Port and starboard, make certain your static-lines, hook up at will!"

I nervously slammed my line-hook on the running release-wire above before turning to face aft. The C130 banked to starboard prompting me grab at the fuselage guide rail as the automatic port and starboard rear doors slowly slid open. The buffeting air stream was deafening. I could just make out the figures of the feed-out crew in the faint red light glow, their safety lines flapping in the vortex.

The whirr from the engines changed, an indication that they were being cut back in preparation for our deployment, only to speed up again. "What the fucks goin' on?" somebody said.

'Maybe the whole thing's been aborted,' I thought. 'Maybe we're going home after all.'

No such good fortune; the crewmen began shouting close up drill: "Port and starboard, carry out final safeguards, check your partners' static-line!"

I checked Bronco's line from behind as the C130 banked again. Lance Corporal Jessop tapped my shoulder after checking mine. I removed my earplugs as we bunched up gazing, as if mesmerised, at the control panel, waiting for the red standby light. The light seemed to take an age; it finally lit, appearing as if a bright red beacon in an already crimson world.

"**Standby!**" the crewmen yelled.

I gripped my static-line, white knuckled. My container slung front and below my reserve chute suddenly seemed to weigh a ton. The drone from the engines slowly changed.

"They're throttling back," Jez said.

I stared at the red light illuminating the back of the control panel. The pitch from the engines continued to drop as my heart raced: 'Change! for fuck's sake turn green!'

My wish was granted: "**Action stations! Go! go! go!**" the feed-out crew screamed as they guided the leading group through the open doors.

The shuffling line moved at a rapid pace, the men offering encouragement to each another. I could see the release-wire above bouncing as we advanced towards the door. The aircrew did not stand on ceremony, the minute I approached the jump-step I was directed out of the rectangular opening. I soared feet-first, plummeting towards the earth at a frightening rate. The blast from the propjets buffeted my body, throwing me at a 45° angle as I screamed out the drill—

"**Thousand one! thousand two! thousand three – check canopy!**"

I looked skyward as the deploying parachute snapped and whacked in the rushing air. I could see the canopy fully deployed.

"**Yes!**" I cried out, catching my breath whilst grabbing the control-lines. "You're open, you big beautiful sheet – you're open!"

I could hear the C130 throttling up as I continued my routine: '…release the container; test your guide lines; carry out a 360-check; beware of collisions!'

My container, attached to a line on my waist-harness, bounced and swung below me as I pulled the release–pin. My senses were racing as I drifted downwards. I caught the silhouette of a descending parachute as I carried out a 360° observation. The canopy was momentarily lit in the moonlight. I could clearly see the ribs and seams as the ballooning sheet passed through the bright beam.

I snapped out of my brief trance. This was no ordinary night jump; the fact that I was gently drifting to terra firma did not negate the actuality that we were dropping into a hot zone. Additionally, I still had to negotiate a blind landing.

I pulled on my control lines to confirm steerage: 'Feet and knees together, legs bent, chin tucked in, elbows forward – concentrate!'

I looked below to see if I could observe any shapes, anything that would indicate I was nearing the ground. I had a forlorn hope that the moonlight would illuminate the landing zone; no such luck. I would have to rely on the sound of my container hitting the ground.

I listened carefully looking into the pitch black. I thought I saw a shadow, a tree maybe. 'I must be near by now,' I thought. Just as did I heard the unmistakable thump of my container hitting the ground. I braced myself ready to roll. The ground thumped against my feet sending a shockwave through my spine—

"Son of a bitch!" I cried out as I tumbled into a heap.

The gently falling canopy shrouded me as I struggled to gain some composure. I temporarily became entangled in the parachute lines. I found myself wrestling in the disarray. 'Calm down!' I told myself as I reached for my hook-knife. I didn't need it; I punched my way through the tangle crawling from beneath the cover.

I released and gathered my 'chute before grasping for my container. I was suddenly aware that I'd misplaced my M16. I began frantically searching for it. I found it under the canopy holding onto it like a child that had just recovered his favourite teddy. I sat in the darkness checking my gear, listening and looking for movement. There was a tomblike silence, apart from the beat of a distant drum thumping out a consistent rhythm. I concluded, through my transitory confusion, that it was the Â Shàu Brigade mimicking Cheyenne and Sioux warriors preparing for battle. *A Memorandum of War*, beating the drum whilst sharpening their tomahawks and chanting their mantra: we the chosen few; we coalesced band of braves; we who stand alone, together. I smiled at the realisation that the thumping was my heart pounding against my ribcage.

A thin layer of cloud had blocked the moonlight. It stirred revealing the silhouette of somebody drawing near. "P'sst!" the individual exclaimed.

“Who is it?” I whispered, holding my M16 tight.
“Cowboy; is that you Bazzer?”
“Yeah, am I glad to see you!”
“Likewise…you seen anybody else—?”
“P’sst!” we both heard just as I was about to answer, “…it’s Bronco and Jez.”
Within a few minutes we’d drawn together a motley crew. The more that congregated, the better we could defend ourselves, hence, the better we felt.
Our team moved north by northwest, as ordered. Sergeant Edwards and seven others approached: “What’s this, a fuckin’ whores’ convention?” Buster whispered. We silently chuckled as one or two others joined us. We were in the process of a roll call when we heard the distant boom of artillery.
“One-o-fives…” Biffo suggested as we scanned the obscurity, “they’re a long way off.”
By 03:50 the whole Platoon had linked for muster. We’d all landed safely. There were no serious injuries and no loss of equipment. After hastily burying our parachutes we made for cover and settled for the night. We squatted on the ground in silence, waiting for the predicted fighting and the expected hordes of refugees; waiting for the sun to rise. I looked at my wristwatch for the umpteenth time. Seconds seemed to turn to minutes, minutes to hours. I thought of our night in the NAAFI some 30 hours previous. Home seemed only a few steps away. As I sat waiting for the sunrise it seemed like a million miles.

20:00: Outskirts of Cắm Lô, Route 9, Thursday 26 July.

Day fifteen of our return to the murder hole, I sat on the damp ground updating my journal. The evening light was fading fast. I scribbled for all I was worth—
‘…Another unproductive day in Quang Trì, our frustration grows. No invading armies, no ferocious battles, no lines of refugees – zilch! There has been fighting. The night skies would occasionally light up, the exhibitions accompanied by distant gunfire. The sorties have undoubtedly involved North Vietnamese Forces, evident by the distinctive hollow reports of AK47 assault rifles and .30 calibre Czechoslovakian machine-guns. At times the forays appeared to be almost on top of us, but most nights have been quiet. Route 9 has become a ghost highway, apart from the occasional truck taking livestock to market. We’re all past asking what the hell we’re doing here…’
I broke off as yet another flurry of distant gunfire filled the air – nobody flinched.
I was forced to stop writing. We’d reached the end of nautical daylight.

Command directed the Platoon to double the watch each night. I did my stint, looking into the fast fading light. As many times hitherto I would have to memorise events and record when able.

It was by far the worst patrol I'd ever undertaken. I felt dreadful; I'd never been so dejected. Water and food had been rationed due to being unable to receive regular supplies. I had two days growth, greasy hair and consistently parched mouth. I had bad guts, blisters on my feet and sweat rashes in the worst of places. My back passage was red raw from days of diarrhoea succeeded by chronic constipation. Defecating was a nightmare, like trying to pass solid stools laced with broken glass. The whole Platoon was thoroughly pissed off – morale had never been so low.

Our soiled and musty gear added to the misery. A C123 dropped our equipment on the 14th; unfortunately the Canucks completely mis-timed the drop. Our packs drifted into a nearby swamp. Everything was soaking wet. We tried to dry out some of our clothes but it was useless.

On the 19th we came across the deserted Khê Sahn Firebase. It was spooky; the former station had been completely flattened. There was no evidence that it had ever existed. Even the concrete foundations to the dormitories, sengers and outbuildings had been pummelled. It appeared that the administration was doing their utmost to eradicate any remnant of the protracted conflict. It was a pity that they didn't do something about the fighting and continued abuse of civilians. We didn't come across any sorties; we did come across the vestiges of battle. We could see the hamlets lining Route 9 smouldering as we sauntered past. People from the villages largely rejected our help; they were clearly afraid of reprisals.

On the 22nd we were reminded that death was a part of everyday living amongst the indigent of that impoverished land. We were moving towards Chừ Mý Shụi when we noticed an ox cart carrying three adults stop on the side of the road ahead. We were on our guard as a young man and woman approached. Our safeguard dropped as we noticed the woman weeping. She was carrying a baby boy in her arms. The child was pallid and limp, its head swinging to and fro as if a rag doll. The 18-month-old boy was clearly dead: "Xin ưt vài trai con. Xin con đau," (*Please help my boy; please help him.*) She said whilst sobbing.

Lieutenant Derrick called the Doc' forward, Lance Corporal Barilla acting as interpreter. "Tell her we'll look at her baby," he said to Ricky.

"What's the point Sir?" Colour Sergeant Biffly cut in ensuring he was facing away from the parents, "…anyone can see the child's dead—"

"I know! but I think we should go through the motions anyway. It could be something they need; confirmation, yeah."

Biffo half-smiled whilst gently nodding.

"Doc'," the Lieutenant whispered as Ricky translated our intentions, "check the little mite over."

Moose took the corpse from the mother. He placed its small body on a groundsheet before placing a stethoscope on its chest. Some of us looked on; others turned away. The child's father stood impassive whilst the mother fell to her knees slowly rocking. She was singing a lullaby. It reminded me of the dreadful occurrences at Tchựin Loy. "Fall to sleep my precious one. Your forefathers' hands to cradle you; joy in everlasting peace…" she murmured.

I looked at Bronco; he too could interpret the song. For the umpteenth time I wished I didn't have a grasp of the language.

Moose pulled the dead child's top down and looked up at Ricky: "Tell them he's dead."

"Chơng tội nổi bựòn, ông áy's chết," (*He's dead – we're so sorry.*)

They already knew of course.

The child's parents took the tiny corpse. We watched as they cradled the tiny body, both openly weeping. The Lieutenant asked Moose if he could determine the cause of death; was it suspicious. It wasn't the right time, but he had to ask.

Moose slowly shook his head: "There's no marks Sir. I don't think it's been associated with violence, probably some childhood disease. There's some evidence of a rash, it's faded now but it's been there, recently. May I scrub now Sir?"

Lieutenant Derrick nodded before directing Ricky to ask the distraught parents if there was anything we could do. They shook their heads.

We prepared to move out as an older woman slowly walked from the cart to join the couple. We silently withdrew, acknowledging that they needed to be left to grieve.

Bronco stared at me as we continued down the highway: "I've had enough of this place Bazzer, I swear, I've had enough! I just wanna go home."

Another outbreak of distant rifle reports broke my thoughts. It was just as well. Thinking of the pain displayed by three more individuals in that futile conflict only added to my misery. The child may've died in spite of the war. But that was little consolation as the reports died down. Bronco had said it all. The clock ticked, our stint continued, the success of the murder hole as unfailing as ever.

19:00: Approximately 8 miles west of Cộ Rơc Ridge, Wednesday 8 August.

Our third day back on the road after a 48-hour break at Biên Dưc. Base Camp 7 looked even more rundown than during our previous visit, but that mattered not as we savoured every minute from our respite. I spent most of my time trying to catch up on sleep after triple washing my clothes and enjoying an extra long soak in a piping hot tub. Unfortunately, the SVA had chosen our first day and evening to pound purported NVA positions northwest of Quang Trì Town. The fact that I was exhausted made no difference. I'd have got more shuteye on patrol.

Things seemed to have calmed in the region. Reports on Radio Sàigòn of daily battles along the Laotian border had changed to sporadic broadcasts about the South Vietnamese Army flushing out the enemy on the reaches and floor of the Â Shàu Valley – they were winning of course. We dug in on our first night back, lulled into a false sense of security. I thought again of my maxim: '*Nothing has happened, ergo, nothing will happen.*'

Reality hit us on the following morning. We discovered the naked corpses of a man, two young boys and a teenage girl lying on the roadside. All had been bludgeoned to death. The culprits had cut off the testicles of the three males. We looked on in horror as we realised that the hacked genitalia had been stuffed into the mouth of the girl. A sharpened bamboo cane had been rammed into the underside of her chin in order to pin her bulging mouth closed. The grotesque assortment resembled the discarded remnants from an obsolete freak show, '...men cruelly robbed of their manhood by a crazed nymphomaniac, doomed by her insatiable appetite. Come take a look at the puffed-cheeks captured in the throws of rigor mortis.'

I thought of our first finds in the murder hole; August '72 seemed a lifetime away. I realised as we waited for the Military Police that my tolerance towards death had become strangely pathological. I looked at the naked and twisted bodies and felt nothing. I saluted the region with a contemptuous smirk – Quang Trì had done its job.

10:00: Outskirts of Tầm Bợi, Â Shàu, Friday 10 August.

We'd been moving west on Route 9 since 07:00. We'd not had a good night's sleep. There had been frenetic activity throughout the hours of darkness. Spotter planes circled the locale dropping illumination rounds. We could hear the distant rumble of trucks moving along Route 9. Extended rifle and mortar reports sporadically broke the semi-hush; so much for a reduction in the fighting. It hadn't escaped our attention that we'd have been flying home if it were not for the hordes of NVA crossing the border. During our tour we'd largely escaped being caught in the middle of intensive fighting. Nobody dared mention that the last thing we needed was to become embroiled in a mêlée between North and South Vietnamese Forces. Our UN status would offer us no favour – both sides would consider us a threat. I tried to put the prospect out of my mind as we progressed down the empty highway.

12:15: Route 9.

My stomach was grumbling it was close to lunch though I still wasn't looking forward to eating. After 12 months we were all sick of the sight, the smell and the taste of C-Rations. I tried to add some flavour to the bland food by adding herbs and mixed spices – all it did was give me chronic flatulence. I thought of Sugar, he would go through the same ritual every time he opened his pack. "Corr, C-Rations, the donkey's knob!" he'd sarcastically say. I smiled wishing he was with us.

We were passing a broad swathe of trees to our left when we picked up an all too familiar whiff: body odour, urine, excrement and vomit – refugees! We cleared the trees just in time to spot the tail end of a large gathering of people to our left fleeing from the edge of the main road into the scrub. Many were crying; all appeared to be in a state of panic.

"Translators up front – standard drill!" the Lieutenant called out.

I joined my fellow translators taking off after the individuals: "Nghe. Khắp thế giời chiến sĩ. Đứng lo an toàn cà bày giơ. Người Anh chiến sĩ. Chơ phếp thưc hiên vàị châ," (*Attention, United Nations soldiers. Don't worry, all safe now. British soldiers – allow us to help you here*!) We called out.

Some of the others followed: "We're UN soldiers, we won't harm you!" they hollered.

There were between 35 and 40 men, women and children; the collection was clearly exhausted. We shepherded them in a flanking movement. Individuals within the group huddled together to offer each other comfort or protection. It was pitiful; the look of terror on their faces was palpable. Many were crawling, still trying to hide in the vegetation. The ragtag compilation had likely come together under the assumption of safety in numbers. As is often the case they'd found ways of supporting each other – homogenising from common aims and objectives.

"Listen up…" Lieutenant Derrick called, "assume a none aggressive stance. Back sling your rifles. Use non-verbal cues. Smile and offer greetings; we've got to get these people calmed!"

We began closing up in a corralling movement. The Lieutenant instructed Lance Corporal McFall to identify a leader whilst instructing Bronco, Ricky and me to await further orders.

Macker identified a recognised principal, a man in his late forties. "Gị tái sảơ. Cơn người," (*What you want with me and these people*?) The man nervously asked after a brief preamble.

Macker reinforced that we were neutral soldiers and that we only wanted to offer assistance. The Lieutenant who began dictating questions joined him. He asked which direction his party had come in from. The principal still appeared reluctant to answer.

"Chûng tôi chuyển đi bặn đêm Chiên sî. Đi bợ bàn chận. Chûng dến vựng Sông Cuầ Việt," (*We move at night to avoid soldiers, travel on foot. We come in from the Cuầ Việt River.*) He said, his eyes scanning those around him. "Chiến Việt Công cư không đồ xế," (*Viet Cong insurgents they chase us persistently.*)

Biffo instructed Ricky and me to accompany Medical Attendants Hughes and Moore, whilst Bronco linked-up with Buster. They both began trawling through the group directing the men to offer non-obtrusive assistance.

The two medics had their work cut out; most of the gathering was sick. The adults looked pale and emaciated and the children were limp; all were caked in vomit and diarrhoea. During a crisis it's incredible how quickly you can become accustomed to things that would ordinarily turn your stomach. The people needed help, and fast. The medics carried out an impromptu triage. Some people appeared to be suffering from food poisoning, whilst one or two presented with overt symptoms of malaria. One woman was shivering and bathed in sweat. "Ask her if she has a sore throat and aching limbs," Moose said.

"Viêm hờng ret?" I enquired. She slowly shook her head.

"I think its malaria," Moose said. "Likely at an advanced stage—"

"Is it strain-seven Doc'?" Marine Jeffers asked.

"Nah…if it was 'seven she'd be brown bread by now. Tell her I'll have to put a line in."

I informed the woman, understanding only too well how she was feeling. She forced a smile as Moose searched for a vein. Meanwhile, Yozzer began attending to a woman with a sprained ankle and a young boy whose feet were badly blistered.

Sergeant Edwards posted two lookouts, Lance Corporal Bear and Marine Bernard, approximately 500 yards on the east and west approaches of Route 9, before creating a citadel. It appeared that the party was becoming more positive about our intentions. The majority were calm as the lads started offering assistance. The people's possessions were scattered over the ground. The scene resembled something out of a disaster movie.

The Lieutenant ordered the Radio Operator, Marine Fox, to contact the Quang Trì Hele'base to arrange an evacuation to an enclave. Wolfie informed him some 5 minutes later that a Chinook was being dispatched; ETA 40 minutes.

Lieutenant Derrick directed Macker to inform the leader of our intentions.

"Xếp an toàn día điểm. Chûng tộị bát dầu liên hợừn chựyển cạ bày giơ, an toàn vựng," (*We've arranged a safe place. We'll soon move you to a sanctuary.*) He told him.

The elder looked at the Lieutenant and Macker: "Đao phât đối vơị, càm cấ," (*May Buddha sanctify you.*)

The medics continued offering aid. Our confidence was growing, especially since hearing that a Chinook was inbound; our trek through Quang Trì had suddenly become worthwhile.

By my 367th day in Vietnam I should have realised that nothing was that easy. My translation skills were about to be sorely tested as Marine Gypsy approached with a distraught woman carrying her drooping six-year-old daughter.

"Doc', Bazzer! this little'n needs help," Tinker called out as he coaxed the woman forward.

I asked if she knew what the problem was as Tinker and Moose looked on: "Bệnh đáị đường, bệnh đáị đương!" she said, holding her child tight.

I started frantically flicking through the translation manual. I knew that *đường* had something to do with sugar. I trawled the pages of the medical section; the information was meagre.

"Bệnh đáị đương, bệnh đáị đương!" she repeated becoming more distressed.

"Come on Bazzer!" the Doc' whispered, "...that kiddie looks at death's door."

My hands were shaking as I scanned the pages. I was just about to beckon Lance Corporal McFall when I struck lucky: "Bệnh đáị đương! Diabetes, its diabetes mellitus!"

"Are you sure?"

"Yeah, can't be anything else!"

Medical Attendant Moore looked at the floppy girl: "It measures up...she could be hypo'." He rolled up the girl's sleeves finding what he was looking for. "Ask her how insulin dependent her daughter is. How many injections per day? And ask her if she's got any other medical conditions."

I started asking questions, the woman gave me a blank stare. It took a good 5 minutes to acquire a coherent thread. Moose was looking at me eager for information.

"She doesn't know," I said.

"What, how come—?"

"Her husband used to administer care. He's gone; dead."

The Doc' looked at the girl and her mother, then at me: "Tell her I'll need to carry out some tests, and that I might need to get a line in."

"Thuc hiên cần hiêt đô côp. Vầ chuyển bệnh vịên," I advised trying to reassure her with a gentle smile.

"Vâng, vâng không vấn đề. Xin không trê con là chết," (*Yes, yes, not a problem. Please, I don't want her to die*!) She cried.

Moose carried out a pinprick test on the tiny girl; she hardly flinched. "Her bloods are rock bottom, she's hypo'. Dextrosol! [Glucose tablets] I need Dextrosol!" Moose yelled.

We called out asking if anybody had any tablets.

"We're out, been out for days," Tinker followed.

"Fuck it!" Moose screamed, "…I need glucose, we've gotta get some sugar into her! Anybody got any chocolate, sweets, anything containing simple sugars?"

We started frantically searching through our packs. It was unbelievable – we appeared to be completely out of the substance.

To our joy, Marine Rippley excitedly approached us: "Spangles! I've got some Spangles!"

Moose unwrapped one of the sweets. He tried to put it in the girl's mouth; she turned her head away. He tried rubbing the sweet on her tongue but she kept on spitting it out.

"It's useless…" he said discarding the sweet, "boil some water, we'll melt some of the sweets, give her a drink."

Blue, hurriedly pumped up his stove whilst JJ unwrapped the sweets.

"Not too many!" Moose advised, "we don't want to send her bloods the other way."

Lieutenant Derrick and Buster joined us as the billycan simmered.

"We could ask the Chinook to divert to a med' station to pick up some insulin," Buster suggested.

"No…" the Lieutenant responded, "we haven't got the time."

"But Sir the little girl—"

"It's about the needs of the many Sergeant, you know that as well as I do! The area's crawling with troops – it could go critical at any time." He was clearly trying to justify his actions. He didn't need to; everybody understood, glad they were not the ones with the responsibility. "Is she going to be alright?" he quietly asked Moose.

"She needs insulin Sir…without it her organs will start shutting down."

Lieutenant Derrick looked at his pocket watch; it had been 30 minutes since we'd contacted the hele'base: "Goddamn it, where's that Chinook? Sergeant, get on the RT, give them an update and tell them to open the throttle!"

The young mother continued cradling her daughter as Moose searched for a vein, eventually forcing the cannula into a blood vessel in her tiny foot. The flaccid little girl cried as he penetrated the vein. "Sorry little one," he whispered.

The Spangles had finally dissolved. Moose cooled the contents before offering a cup to the girl's lips. She slowly sipped the warm liquid.

"Chũng tới bệnh sốt rét," (*We'll soon have her in a hospital.*) I said to her mother.

I scanned the scene. Most of the group were squatting in the scattered vegetation. The Platoon continued offering support; sips of water, help in sorting and gathering items. We were all listening for the report of the rotors. I thought I heard a distant hum, I couldn't be certain – I just thought I did.

I heard the reverberation again; it seemed to be emanating from our right. Marine Miller and one or two others heard it too. Dusty looked at me wearing the same inquisitive expression. The noise was more a rumble than a hum. I gave him a nervous half-smile, returning my gaze to the distraught mother. My concentration was broken by the sight of Marine Bernard sprinting through the grass towards us, a look of alarm on his face: **"There's a column of tanks comin' down the fuckin' road!"**

"What!" Lieutenant Derrick returned, "who?"

"Don't know..." Bruiser said, trying to catch his breath, "NVA I think, I didn't 'ang 'round to find out!"

"How many?" Colour Sergeant Biffly enquired.

"Too many! A company maybe, supported by ground troops, 'undreds of the bastards—!"

"Did they spot you?"

"No way, the minute I pinged them I made like Jessie Owens!"

"Judas Priest!" the Lieutenant said, "...nearly a month of nothing and we bump into a heap of shit with this lot!"

The news spread like wildfire, the men anxiously muttering to one another.

"Calm down..." Biffo said trying to keep his voice low, "you're gonna spook this lot!"

I stood upright looking at Biffo, waiting for advice: "There's a wood a half mile back," Biffo said to the Lieutenant. "We could try'n make a dash for cover—"

"We haven't got time, besides we'd struggle with this lot. We'll have to make the best of the cover we've got. Get everyone back another two hundred yards, no more. Marine Bernard, get off after Lance Corporal Bear, and stay low!"

Bruiser took off as we began directing the group to move back. The principal wanted to know what was wrong. Macker, told him not to worry. He needn't have bothered; the party couldn't fail to hear the approaching convoy. The rumble was getting louder: tank tracks have a distinctive squeaking–rattle. The grinding screeches of the metal merges with the drone of the engine, as if a symphony contrived by an ensemble of manic percussionists. The sometimes high-pitch whine sounded like a pod of singing whales.

We struggled back as the noise intensified. The trees that blocked our view of the refugees on our way in offered cover as we moved back. Moose strained to carry his equipment along with the little girl, her mother tagging behind. He'd crafted a makeshift 'T' frame to accommodate the saline drip. JJ ran alongside him ensuring he held the bag aloft.

We dumped ourselves back on the ground. We instinctively started smearing camouflage cosmetic on our faces. Some of the children started crying, there was no way round it; we would have to provide cover for everybody. Lance Corporal Jessop and Marine Miller playfully smeared some cosmetic on two of the children, but it did little to calm them. The poor mites were terrified – they weren't the only ones.

We noticed that some of the refugees' belongings were brightly coloured. Some of the teams began covering them with army-issue fatigues and hastily cut grass and scrub. We created a 2-line semi-circle, the refugees behind us. I was in the support line. Speedy, Cowboy, Dusty and TC were to my left. Dinger, Jez and Vinny on my right with Moose behind with the sick. We were all focussed on the trees to our right. The road dipped to our left; there was little cover apart from occasional long grass and scattered shrubs.

Bruiser and Huggy approached in a squatting position from the left; they made it just in time. Biffo turned to us as the increasing thunder from the procession indicated they were almost past the trees: "Keep calm now. Remember UN protocol – stay down and button it!"

I cocked my M16 and concealed myself in the grass, lying as close and tight as possible whilst peeking through and above the strands. The lumbering vehicles created a subtle vibration – it cancelled out the feeling of my heart pounding. The first vehicle in the convoy appeared from behind the trees. It was a half-track travelling at no more than 5 MPH. We could clearly see the North Vietnamese Flag waving in the gentle breeze. Our worst fears had been realised. The SVA had scant regard for UN Forces – the NVA had none! A soldier was perched on top of the cab with a tripod mounted .30 calibre machine-gun. 'He's got to see us…' I thought, 'he can't miss us from that vantage point.' Fortunately, he continued looking forward.

The pack was likely on a search-and-destroy mission. They were travelling west, back towards the Laotian border. The half-track was followed by 3 Russian T-65 Tanks, succeeded by a line of APCs and Lorries. Many of the open topped vehicles contained an array of weapons: 40mm Grenade Launchers, 56mm Mortars and Russian Katyusha Rockets. The array looked more than just sinister.

I slowly turned to look at the refugees, wondering if they'd remain motionless. I needn't have been troubled – they were obviously seasoned; they needed no guidance from us.

The line progressed, the replicate pod singing louder than ever, signalling their intent in melodious rhythms. Soldiers and Viet Cong militia hitched a ride on the sides of the tanks. Some of the vehicles contained flash scars; they'd clearly been involved in combat.

I was beginning to think we'd avoid detection when a soldier jumped from a lorry almost directly in front of us. He walked towards our position stopping to take a leak. We all held our breaths: 'Just one,' I thought, 'that's all it would take, just one to spot us!'

The soldier was urinating profusely.

"That fuck-stick must've drunk arf a dozen party sixes," Vinny whispered.

Under normal circumstances I'd have chuckled. Somehow my vocal chords had frozen.

After what seemed like an age the piss happy soldier tucked away his tackle and turned towards the vehicles. A baby started to cry just as he moved away. Its mother did her utmost to muffle its wailing to no avail. The noise from the lumbering vehicles turned to our advantage. He jumped onto a slow moving tank to sighs of relief.

We were all breathing again. I had forgotten in the heat of the situation about the inbound Chinook. Wolfie frantically signalled that he'd received a communication: "Sir, Chinook inbound, ETA five minutes."

"Fuck! talk about timing. Get on the horn, tell them to double-back and take up a delay pattern. And adjust the vector – south by southwest to immediate southeast!"

I wondered how close the chopper was; had anyone from the convoy spotted it? Continuing anxiety and uncertainty. Our disquiet was exacerbated as we spotted a division of heavily armed Viet Cong insurgents flanking the column. They were walking on the verge, talking amongst themselves. Four or five others joined them as they maintained the course. One of them broke off and began walking in our direction. My heart missed a beat; it was as if he was looking straight at me. My head was spinning…thoughts of the ultimate: 'So this is it! This is what all the training's been about – to battle against the odds, face the unassailable. Well, if I've gotta fight, I'll fight! I've got 36 rounds and I'm gonna use every fuckin' one of them! When they're spent I'll use my bayonet, the butt of my rifle, my fists…you're not taking me alive; you're not cutting my balls off—!'

The militiaman stopped and bent down. He must have been less that a 200 yards from our front row. He picked something up, a garment, likely left by one of the grouping.

I wasn't the only one hyping myself up. Cowboy was muttering: "Come on cunt-weasel, go for it! If they open up I'm gonna waste every livin' thing that ain't gotta fuckin' tail. I'm not gettin' my arse fragged—"

"Shit-in-it you…" the Colour Sergeant growled, "save it for the NAAFI!"

The insurgent stared in our direction. Little did he know he had at least a dozen M16s targeted on his frame. If he started he sure wouldn't finish. One of his comrades called to him. He turned, dropped the garment and rejoined the band.

I closed my eyes and took another deep breath as a further line of closely grouped lorries and APCs tagged behind a flash scarred T-65. 'How much longer can we evade detection?' I thought. 'Our luck has got to run out!'

I considered moments in my young life when I had lost in the closing stages. A sucker punch in the dying seconds of a hard fought bout; a star-crossed strike in a fencing final and a last minute drop goal in a wildcard match we had sewn up. They were nothing in comparison. I looked at the slow moving line waiting for the inexorable that last greasy rung – so near yet so far.

Another battle-scarred T-65 closely followed a loaded troop carrier. Its turret was facing aft, an indicator that it was the tail-ender. An assortment of combatants sauntered behind the apparent rearguard; then, nothing – a clear road.

"Oh wow! I think that's it," Biffo whispered.

The noise diminished as the rearguard moved out of sight. The tracks on the tail-ender let loose a screeching pitch, a final salute from a lone tenor.

We lay in the grass awaiting orders, our ears ringing. Lieutenant Derrick stirred: "Well gentlemen, that appears to be that. The murder hole shall not have us; not now, not ever! Colour Sergeant, send out two men to check the highway. Marine Fox, contact the Chinook, call standby. Keep it down now boys, we're not in the clear yet."

Bruiser and Huggy took off as we checked the refugees, staying low and quiet. Moose and JJ had dutifully stayed with the diabetic and her mother. The children were holding onto caregivers, some had fallen to sleep. Some of the refugees focussed on us. I tried to raise a smile but it was difficult. It was our narrowest escape since Tchụrin Loy. I daren't let my guard down, not until I was sure.

Bruiser and Huggy were back in no time: "Road and immediate locale clear, all points."

"Right..." the Lieutenant said, "Marine Fox, call in the Chinook, original grid. Tell them the area's still hot. We'll have to guide them in without smoke."

Lieutenant Derrick pulled us in for a briefing. We eagerly surrounded him and Colour Sergeant Biffly: "Listen up, we're gonna have to get these fuckers onboard that Chinook in record time. We proceed the minute the ramp's down. Then, we hightail it out of here, get as far as we can from the jaws of that armoured column, got it!"

"Yes Sir!" we responded.

We hastily guided the refugees towards the landing zone, a patch of ground to our rear. We could hear the clearly identifiable double rotor-thud of the approaching Chinook. The refugees were silent – they looked understandably stressed. For many the nightmare was continuing, they'd likely never experienced air travel. We helped them carry their belongings. Some of the Platoon carried the sick; others acted as a rearguard pulling back whilst scanning the landscape. The chopper appeared skipping the treetops of the nearby wood. The pilot banked hard; he turned the 'copter a 180° dropping the rear hydraulic door as he dumped the wheels on the ground. The downdraft blasted us; some of the people became distressed as we abruptly ushered them onboard.

A Canadian Aircrew Paramedic came running down the ramp as we marshalled the refugees through the giant gale sucking portal: "Where's the medic, the one treating the diabetic?"

Biffo pointed towards Moose. The ACP rushed towards him: "You've got a diabetic, yeah!"

"Yeah…" Moose replied still supporting the girl, "this is she, why—?"

"Insulin!" the Canuck said holding up a plastic pack.

"What, oh you beauty!" The delight on the Doc's face was manifest. He handed the sick girl to the ACP, tenderly squeezing her mother's hand as he ushered her onboard.

The last of the refugees reluctantly embarked. The pilot lifted the ramp as we pulled back; we'd loaded the group in record time. We watched the Chinook as it thundered skyward winging its way towards Phư Lắc.

Lieutenant Derrick called as we were in the throws of group-congratulation: "Hustle up your gear, objective southeastwardly – let's get the fuck out of here!"

We took off, our bergens bouncing on our backs. Some of the lads were muttering under their breaths, they felt as if we were running away. Who could blame us? It would have been suicidal for 29 of us to take on an Armoured Company inclusive of ground troops. Nonetheless, in many ways we were running away, though at that moment I didn't care!

12:30: Eastern reaches of Cô Rớc Ridge, Â Shàư, Tuesday 14 August.

Our death-defying act of mercy was succeeded by a return to the mundane, though a novice onlooker would've been at a loss. For some unknown reason local radio stations began presenting daily reports of intensive fighting: '…a rerun of Tết'. It was all hogwash. North Vietnamese Forces had crossed the border but not in the mass originally reported. The incursion likely involved less than a handful of regiments. The exercise was nought but an incursion to test out South Vietnamese defences.

We'd stopped for lunch. Breaks had become the only part of the day we looked forward to, despite the unpalatable food. Our inactivity had given us time to reflect; the episode on Route 9 was a reminder of our vulnerability. I took every opportunity to update my journal. I wondered if it would be discovered alongside my corpse post battle – the daily ramblings of a peacekeeper. I scanned the Platoon as they passed the time. Many were writing letters home. They may've already told the story; my writings nought than old news. I checked my own hastily half-written letter home. I'd never written that 'last letter'. Some of the men compiled a final correspondence to their loved ones to be sent only in the event of their demise: unspoken words, apologies or messages to their children. Some considered it fateful, others too spooky to contemplate – a memorandum from the grave. "Some things are best left unsaid," one of the lads told me. I convinced myself that my failure to write had more to do with laziness; truth is it was more to do with my inability to disclose my feelings. I'd never actually told my mum and dad I loved them. Kids brought up on the streets of Liverpool were not in the habit of being demonstrative. I had to confront the fact that I went through a raft of regrets as I looked at the armoured convoy through my rifle sight. After some consideration I tucked my unfinished missive away. 'I'll finish it,' I convinced myself, 'sometime later.'

I perused my journal as the watch changed. I'd written in detail about the rescue of the refugees. I wondered just how much of a safe haven the refugee camp would be, memories of Camp India – the squalor and the injustice. Then again, surely anything was better than being exposed to the defencelessness of the open highway. As hitherto, I couldn't get the images of the distressed people out of my mind. During my tour I had to constantly admonish myself for becoming too involved. At times I felt as if my anger would boil over. How I hated power-crazed bullies. How I wished I could come forth with a panacea to deal with the injustices and how I sometimes detested being human. I had been on the frontline for too long, either that or I was too sensitive.

I had also written about my compadrés. I felt even closer to them than previously. We'd shared so much. I wondered how my life might change once we got home; if we got home.

My cogitation was broken by Colour Sergeant Biffly calling muster – back on the road. Route 9 looked even more deserted. I deliberated over my letter as we formed yet another seemingly pointless echelon. 'I won't finish it,' I decided in a weak capitulation. 'I'll save what I need to say until I get home: if I get home.'

*

14:30: Approximately 9 miles west of Mệ Tẩy.

Command issued orders for the Platoon to maintain a westward echelon. North Vietnamese Army Regulars had apparently been accosting refugees attempting to cross the Laotian border. What we were supposed to do if we spotted troops abusing refugees in a purportedly neutral country was beyond us. Furthermore, we were aware that the SVA were also accosting refugees attempting to move in the opposite direction. All in all, we were long past caring.

The weather had changed. We'd thankfully enjoyed dry periods since our return. The skies had unexpectedly become overcast, squally showers that drenched our already dampened spirits. Wolfie had been busily receiving radio broadcasts all day. He called out to Lieutenant Derrick: "Sir, it's Command…for your ears only."

"Hold up!" Biffo called out as the Lieutenant held the handset whilst taking notes.

We squatted on the wayside, 'Oh fuck, what now…' I thought as we stared at the Lieutenant. He passed the handset to Wolfie, a serious look on his face. You could hear a pin drop as he prepared to brief us: "Gentlemen, we have fresh orders with immediate effect. A brigade of Indonesian Regulars has just assumed responsibility for the northern sector. We're to board a Chinook at Mệ Tẩy for a flight to Huê-Phu Baì, rendezvous 1700 hours. We board a C130 post debrief for a direct flight to Tấlận Chựí, Sàigòn; then sometime tomorrow…"

We stared at him as he broke off. He seemed to take an age.

"…we board a VC10 for Blighty – it's all over boys, we're out of here!"

"**Yes!**" We cheered.

"Okay that's enough!" Biffo yelled after a few seconds, an ever-growing smile on his face. "Listen up now."

Lieutenant Derrick scanned us: "We'll set off for Mệ Tẩy in five. We've got just over two hours to walk nine miles, I'm sure we're up to it. Let me remind you, we're not clear yet. We could still bump into something. Don't let this go to your heads. Stay on your guard."

Colour Sergeant Biffly dismissed us. We couldn't contain ourselves.

"We're goin' home Bazzer," Bronco said throwing his arms around me. "I'm gonna see my missus and my little girl!"

I could feel his body against mine as I soaked up the atmosphere. I wanted to let go, to cry out in celebration, but I felt somehow inhibited.

The lads were in their element – nervously laughing, looking skyward in hushed prayer or sitting in quiet contemplation. I moved away from the hullabaloo electing to sit in momentary isolation. A feeling of foreboding suddenly overtook me: 'Maybe it's a ruse, a cruel joke, that fateful trip with the finish line in sight.' But no, there was no trickery, this was for real, we were going home.

What transpired next was a scriptwriter's chance and cynic's amusement. The overcast sky suddenly cleared, the sun floodlighting the gorge. If I'd been a believer in the afterlife I would have supposed that Marines Collins and Lyle arranged the lightshow. Though eschewing such possibilities I still smiled, the experience was one to savour. I sat on the ground listening to the continuing celebrations. I scanned all that was around me in a minute of private wonder. I looked at the landscape, illuminated by a new dawn: to the west I could see the massif assembling the Laotian border; to the north the plains staggering the De-Militarised Zone; to the east the gentle hills ascending the coast and to the south the rolling peninsula of South Vietnam. At that moment, the Â Shàu Valley never looked so beautiful.

SONGS FROM THE 'NAM

Final Echoes

JOAN BAEZ *The Ballard Of Sacco & Vaanzetta; I Shall Be Released*

THE BEATLES *Hey Jude; Fool On The Hill; Nowhere Man*

BUFFALO SPRINGFIELD *For What It's Worth*

CREEDENCE CLEARWATER REVIVAL *Fortunate Son*

DEEP PURPLE *Child In Time*

ARETHA FRANKLIN *Respect*

JIMI HENDRIX *Hear My Train A Comin'; Stone Free*

LED ZEPPELIN *Black Dog; Stairway To Heaven*

JOHN LENNON & THE PLASTIC ONO BAND *Give Peace A Chance; Working Class Hero*

DON MCLEAN *American Pie*

THE MAMAS & THE PAPAS *California Dreamin'; It's Getting Better*

MOTT THE HOOPLE *All The Young Dudes*

HARRY NILSSON *Everybody's Talkin'*

SIMON & GARFUNKEL *Bridge Over Troubled Water; The Boxer*

JAMES TAYLOR *Fire & Rain; You Need A Friend*

T REX *Children Of The Revolution; Hot Love*

NEIL YOUNG *Alabama; Harvest; Heart Of Gold*

10: GOODNIGHT VIETNAM

1 *Did the people of Vietnam use lanterns of stone?*
2 *Did they use bone & ivory, jade & silver for ornament?*
3 *Were they inclined to quiet laughter?*
4 *Did they distinguish between speech & singing?*

1 *Sir, their light hearts turned to stone. It is not remembered whether in gardens stone lanterns illuminated pleasant ways.*
2 *A dream ago, perhaps. Ornament is for joy.*
3 *Sir, laughter is bitter to the burned mouth.*
4 *There is an echo yet of their speech which was like a song. It was reported their singing resembled the flight of moths in moonlight. Who can say? It is silent now.*

D Levertol

05:30: UN Base Camp 1, Bìen Hoâ, Sàigòn, 16 August 1973.

I lay in bed listening to the sounds of aircraft taking off and landing from Tấlận Chựí. The almost total withdrawal of US troops had done nothing to lessen the commotion. A flurry of machine-gun fire filled the air at a lull in the air traffic – déjà vu. Charlieville had dealt us one last twist. Our VC10 developed an electrical fault forcing a 24-hour delay. Under normal circumstances I'd have taken pleasure in the possibility of further testing out the delights of a city, but nothing during our Tour of Duty had been normal.

We'd all hit the town on the previous evening, save for Yozzer. Some of the lads nicknamed him the Olympic Torch cos he never went out. My final jaunty through Big S had been memorable to say the least. It started off okay: a boat trip on the Sàigòn River followed by a meal in the Đon Bế Market. Bronco, Dusty, Dinger, JJ and I then decided to test out the Thừín Tưa district. We bumped into Cowboy and Jez who were on the lookout for arm candy. Unfortunately, Viet Cong revolutionaries began mortaring the area from the outskirts of Chơnlôn. We were perilously close to the reports. A cluster of rounds landed near the bar we were sitting in. The blast shook the foundations sending accumulated dust from the 1950s light fittings. We beat a hasty retreat electing to try out the *Hựng Doấ & Rex Hotels*. The hotels were the journalists' havens. We, conversely, were unwelcome. The porter at the *Hựng Doấ* told us it was nothing personal, they just didn't want obvious targets drinking in their presumably peaceful hostelry. I considered it was more to do with snobbery.

We met up with more of the Platoon down Tư Đô Street. The boulevard hadn't changed, though some of the déclassé had to look for other establishments in an attempt to regain their status. We sat in the early evening air observing the street opera that was Sàigòn. Street traders moved down the thoroughfare: shoeshine boys, barbers and a man purporting to be a mobile tattooist. We examined his box of tools with fascination. He had a pact with some of the bar owners who'd allow him to plug in his electric pens for a slice of the take. The pen tips were as grubby as his fingernails. We all declined the offer of a special deal.

We met up with the remainder of the Platoon in *The Pussy Palace*. It was there I foolishly accepted the offer of some yellows from Corporal Alan. He and Corporal Biggs had purchased the pills from a former US Ranger who looked like something from the psychedelic '60s. I was stupid beyond belief to trust the two of them. Nasher was a churlish man who rubbed up just about everybody in the Platoon, and Ronnie, with his android-like persona, was always on the make. If there were two marines I wouldn't want covering my back it would've been those two. The yellows had likely been manufactured in a back street chemist.

I sat listening to Buck singing *Little Old Wine Drinker Me*. He had a deep croaky voice, as if he'd spent his life gargling with white-hot gravel, yet when he sang his voice sounded like velvet. The yellows started to kick in; cloud nine and climbing. I went through an extended period of giggling followed by inconsequential babble. Bronco and Macker could see what was happening. They ushered me through the door as two MPs patrolled the bar. I broke free from them running down Lế Chừí Street. I felt like a sprinter in an Olympic Final, my senses in overdrive. I recall people staring at me as I whooped for joy, Bronco and Macker in pursuit. They caught up with me, frogmarching me to a nearby café to force piping hot coffee down my gullet. The upper didn't last long and was succeeded by the inevitable downer. I found myself hallucinating in the middle of the crowded café: fireballs rolling over fields strewn with corpses; mummified figures reaching out to me; the sounds of children crying amid rapid gunfire. My muckers dragged me into the alleyway. I sat on the ground desperately trying to sort out my spinning head. I reattached to reality some 15 minutes later. The lads supported my weak frame back to *The Pussy Palace*. I spent the rest of the evening talking to Huey on the big white telephone. It was a bitter lesson – the upper was ecstatic, the downer demonic, it would be my first and last.

The Platoon started to stir. We still didn't know what time we'd be boarding our flight home. Bronco asked me if I was alright. I nodded after apologising. I spotted Nasher some 5 minutes later. He skulked past my bed on the way to the bathroom. I noticed he had acquired a large bruise on his cheekbone and a split lip sometime later. Apparently Marine Cunliffe had laid into him. The lads had to pull Cowboy off to stop him pouring the remainder of the yellows down Nasher's throat. Six other members of the Platoon ended up on a high. The biggest low, however, belonged to Corporal Alan.

10:00: Tấlận Chựí Military Air Strip.

We finally mustered for our flight home. The other Platoons had just left; they too had a delayed departure. Fighting on the outskirts of Sàigòn continued. We tuned in to Radio Sàigòn for a final news report. During the night Viet Cong insurgents had overrun two SVA positions north of the Sàigòn River. Morale in the SVA had declined since the departure of their Yankee cohorts. It appeared they simply didn't have the stomach to continue the fight. Their illustrious leaders issued a warning that deserters would be sentenced to death without appeal. It did nothing to cauterise the flow.

We boarded a clapped out charabanc for our transfer to the RAF VC10. We sat in the rust trap for over 45 minutes. We could see the VC10 in the distance. It was frustrating not knowing what was going on. We eventually learned that the delay was due to reports of Viet Cong guerrillas setting up Sam-6 Heatseeking Missiles on the periphery of the airbase.

"Oh that's just fuckin' great!" Dusty muttered, "…blown out the heavens on our way home."

I gazed at the airbase fence and perimeter road out of the steamy windows. There was a collection of large billboards lining the road. As usual the signs were extolling the efficiency of the government and, predictably, somebody had covered the propaganda pieces with lampooning graffiti and cartoons. One sign had an enormous map of South Vietnam with the caption—

SOUTH VIÊT NAM - NO SURRENDER TO THE NORTH!

The map was inset with a representation of the happy South Vietnamese populace encircling an icon-like picture of President Thiều, the South Vietnamese, French and American flags flying like a semi-halo around his glowing head. Someone had overlaid a less than flattering caricature of the beleaguered President and daubed—

AU REVOIR À MÉNAGE À TROIS. NÂM VIỆT NAM TOUT FINIS!

(*Goodbye to the three associations. South Vietnam all finished*!)

—across the bottom. I smiled at the cheek of the artists.

We finally took off for our bird. We scurried onboard and quickly settled.

The whine of the engines sent some of the lads into a frenzy; they started banging the seats whilst singing *The Wizard Of Oz*. We taxied to the far end of the runway and, yet again, waited.

I stared out of the small window at the flashing runway lights. I'd placed the final book of my journal on my lap; there was less than a page left. 'What now,' I thought, 'how do I finish?' I considered concluding with a collection of clichés. I didn't see why not, the text was full of them. I thought of how I had landed in that tormented nation as a boy, and how I was leaving a man. Without further ado I wrote—

'...We are leaving Vietnam behind; soon it will just be a distant memory alive only in the pages of this book and the celluloid of my mind. I've learned many things in my time in this place; of the inhumanity and compassion of mankind. Most of all, I've learned about myself. In war a boy can do one hell of a lot of growing up, and a man one hell of a lot of breaking down. I think I've probably done both.'

That was that, I closed the book as the VC10 sped down the runway. We were homeward bound, flying over the craggy rooftops of Sàigòn. As the VC10 climbed I whispered a silent farewell: "Goodnight Vietnam – I'll never forget you."

The metropolis of Sàigòn disappeared in a swathe of cloud. I closed my eyes unknowing just how prophetic those words would be.

15:50: Lime Street Station Liverpool, Friday 17 August.

The 13:15 London Euston – Liverpool Lime Street pulled in on time. I eagerly made my way down the platform, the smell of diesel fumes and triple echo from the PA system entering my senses. There was only a small queue at the taxi rank. I stood behind a middle-aged man who looked as if he'd spent the entire afternoon on the sauce. He looked at my uniform: "Just back from Northern Ireland son?"

"Something like that."

He climbed into a hackney cab: "Be safe now."

I nodded as his cab pulled away. I felt safe. I was safe, almost home.

I thought of Marine Lyle as I threw my kitbag into the next taxi. If he'd made it home we would have shared the train journey and had a few pints before separating.

"Where to mate?" the taxi driver asked.

"Southdene, Kirkby please. Go via *Goodison Park* will you."

"It's your fare lad."

I gazed out the taxicab; life in Liverpool had continued during our 373 days. We passed *Goodison Park*. "I'll keep our appointment Sugar," I mumbled. I spotted the driver looking at me in the rear-view mirror. He may've thought he had a nutter in his cab though I cared not. The cab sped along the A580, memories of Vietnam sealed within my head and my journal.

If I could bottle experiences then homecomings would be near the top of the list. Those first few moments are extra special. My parents' house always looked bigger. I would spend the first minutes soaking up the atmosphere; the sounds, smells and textures. Within a very short time it would seem as if I'd never been away.

Royal Marines HQ had sent my family a telegraph on the 9th explaining that we'd been delayed. Mum and dad were planning a welcome home party. I'm glad it didn't materialise. I was happy to be home but I felt ambivalent. Mum was naturally excited to see me: "Why didn't you tell us you were coming? I'd have made some scones and a chocolate cake."

I smiled at her. Throughout my time in the 'Nam I'd thought of many things connected with home. Mum's baking was amongst them, but it faded into insignificance compared to just being in the house that had offered me so much love and protection as a child.

I sat talking to my mum, or rather she talked to me – so much to catch up on. My sister was away on holiday with her boyfriend. Nothing much had happened in the neighbourhood, other than Bob from across the road being involved in a serious car accident: "…it was touch and go at one stage," mum said, "he hasn't been the same since."

I sat back as she went through a raft of gossip. It all seemed so insignificant contra to the enormity of the war. I had to remind myself as I fought to keep my eyes open that life goes on, at a different pace and in many different ways. Bob's family would have found the experience of almost losing him in a car accident just as traumatic as the incident at Tchựin Loy – maybe even more so.

I checked out my bedroom; it didn't look any different from the day I left. The Star Trek wallpaper and Airfix models reminded me just how child-like a part of my bedroom still was. Mum and dad didn't want to redecorate. Maybe they wanted to hold on to those last memories of a mischievous little boy who'd do his utmost to do the unusual. I scanned the room: on one side my old toy box containing battered Dinkies, a train set that had long been derailed and a Dan Dare Radio Set, its worn valves possessing memories of inter-galactic conversations across the landing. On the other, symbols of adulthood: records and tapes, bottles of aftershave, my boxing trophies and a collection of classic literature. I had never really noticed it before, a time-line around my bedroom. I sat on my bed and looking at the 3-by-2 *Sky at Night* chart I'd pinned to my ceiling as a teenager. I scanned the Celestial Ocean thinking of that night on the balcony in Rậnlạntoì. 'Was that really 8 weeks ago?' I thought – it seemed so much longer.

I'd decided to leave my unpacking until later; dad was due home from work. The sound of the backdoor latch signalled my father's return. Mum was in the kitchen as I rushed downstairs: "There's a surprise in the living room," she said.

"Ah, you're home, you made it out of there!" Dad said rushing towards me.

"Yeah…I made it."

We held each other in a lasting embrace. I thought I saw a tear in his eye; maybe it was in mine. Dad and I decided to go the *Globe* for a pint. We sauntered along in the warm early evening air. I absorbed all that was around me. We passed my primary school and the fields I used to play football on as a youngster. Dad did most of the talking. I wanted to tell him about my journal, but thought I'd leave it until later. I thought again about the things I was going to say to him and mum – I would leave those until later also.

A car backfired as we neared the pub. I jumped; dad didn't flinch. He smiled at me, a smile that said he understood. As a war veteran he already knew something I was yet to learn. War comes at you full in your face, peace comes more slowly.

POST SCRIPTS

POST SCRIPT:
THE JOURNAL

One who never turned his back but marched breast forward,
Never doubted clouds would break,
Never dreamed though right were worsened,
wrong would triumph,
Held we fall to rise, are baffled to fight better,
Sleep to wake.

R Browning

08:30: My parents' house, April 1974.

I towelled myself down in the steamy bathroom. I was looking forward to breakfast. I'd completed my early morning run – 8 miles, I was pretty pleased with myself. I was determined to enjoy my last weekend leave before redeployment. The Platoon was due to start a United Nations Peacekeeping Tour of Lebanon at the end of the month – from Sàigòn to Beirût. I always enjoyed Saturdays during the footie season. Dad and I were both looking forward to going to the match. We'd go through the same routine: a couple of pints in the *Blue House*, followed by a scouse pie, an Eccles cake and a large beaker of tea once in the ground.

The remnants of an early morning dream popped into my head as I dressed; something about Vietnam. Mum shouting that my breakfast was nearly ready broke my train of thought.

Dad was already sitting at the table reading his *Daily Mirror*. Mum had a smile on her face, the kind that says 'go on, ask.'

"What?" I said as I poured milk on my Frosties.

"I had a funny dream last night," she said. "We were in this bookshop, you, me and your dad. You were sat signing copies of a book. I was all dressed up. I had this big hat on; I must've looked like the Queen Mother—"

"God forbid!" Dad cut in.

"—Funny thing is your Uncle Kevin was there, (Kevin was Killed in Action during the Korean War.) He left for Korea long before you were born; he asked me what you were doing. 'He's signing his book,' I said. 'He's written a book about his time in Vietnam.' There was this big queue, people we knew and strangers. You weren't in uniform, you had a suit on – it was really vivid."

My mum was still smiling as she finished cooking the sausage, bacon and eggs. 'Mum and her dreams,' I thought. I was about to tell her not to get her hopes up when I remembered my own early morning dream. "That's funny," I said staring into space, "I had a dream about Mợi Phần Bý, only we weren't in the *California Bar*, we were in the *Blue House*. Billie was there too…yeah, she was sat in the lounge."

"Who are they?" Mum enquired.

"Oh, they're just some people I knew. Funny thing is they both asked me if I'd ever consider turning my journal into a book."

"You never know," Dad said lowering his paper.

"Nah, they're just dreams."

"Dreams are as much about possibilities and probabilities as they are about the weird and the wonderful."

"I'm no writer—"

"Oh, so what do you call that lot stacked in a box in your room?"

"That's just scribble."

"George Orwell started with scribble," Dad said returning to the sports page.

I sat in silence, part replaying my dream, part thinking of dad's words. It was typical of him. He was the eternal optimist: no mountain's too big, no crossing's too wide – all you need is the will.

"Don't you think there's something in that?" Mum asked, breaking me out of my trance.

"What?"

"Both of us having a dream about the same thing at the same time."

"Yeah Mum I do…it's called coincidence."

'Mum and her dreams,' I thought again. But as I tucked into my fry up I couldn't help wondering if I really would write a book one day.

POST SCRIPT: *SHADOWDANCING*

What is the worst of woes that wait on age?
What stamps the wrinkle deeper on the brow?
To view each loved one blotted from this page,
And be alone on earth, as I am now.

G Byron

Matthew Street, Liverpool, Friday 22 January 1993.

The cold easterly wind blew down the narrow street scattering the day's debris. The locale was full of the usual tourists congregating for photographs in front of the Cavern Club. *The Coffee Machine*, a popular local café was crowded as usual. The warm air infused with the aroma of ground coffee beans was inviting as the swinging door closed behind me. I had just completed a jaunty around the shops. I was cold, tired and ready for some refreshment. The young café assistant smiled as I approached the counter: "Double bacon and tomato on toasted rye, jumbo chocolate muffin and a large cafetière of Colombian deep roast, right?" she said.

"Am I that predicable?" I answered returning the smile.

"Sit yerself down, I'll bring it over."

Fridays were always special, more so since I'd been attending College to complete a specialist social work course. Fridays equalled 'study afternoon', a strange title for something that very few students practised.

I settled in my familiar seat. The café contained the customary mix of people. Japanese and Korean Beatles fans chatting amongst themselves; an elderly couple taking afternoon tea with jumbo homemade scones. A bored and apparently mute middle-aged couple, the table between them an additional barrier in their seemingly moribund relationship, and a collection of young girls bunking off school. The girls had taken off their school ties in an attempt to look less conspicuous. One blew smoke out of her mouth in a deliberate manner. I smiled recalling my own adolescence.

There was something familiar about a stocky black gentleman sitting at the third table to my left. He was sitting next to a younger man, likely his son, who reminded me even more of a past acquaintance. The man broke off interactions with a small woman facing him. He gazed over with a half-smile before continuing the conversation. Something within me stirred, as he looked my way; a strange feeling of déjà vu. Something from my past, sounds and feelings, an experience to which I couldn't quite reconnect. I put the conundrum to one side electing instead to scrutinise my newly acquired CDs.

I saw somebody approach out the corner of my eye as I tucked into my double bacon and tomato sandwich. It was the black gentleman towering over my table.

"Excuse me Sir..." he said in a deep southern United States accent, "I hope you don't think me to be rude but I've a feelin' we've met sometime a whiles back."

"It's alright," I replied, "I've the same feeling."

"Did you by any chance spend anytime in Vietnam?"

"Yeah, 'seventy-two to 'seventy-three."

"Did ya spend anytime in hospital whiles you there?"

"Yeah, the United States Marines Hospital, Rậnlạntoì—" It was then that it struck me, the face, the accent, the smile. "Chauncey? Chauncey Leigh...is that you?"

"As I stand here a-breathin'. Hot damn, you be one of them Limey boys we had on the ward six in 'seventy-three!"

I leapt from my seat to shake his hand. We couldn't contain ourselves as we stood hugging and backslapping each other in the middle of the café. For a moment we were oblivious to others, including Chauncey's family sat looking at us in disbelief.

"Come on over and meet my kin," Chauncey said his face glowing.

I made my way over to his table. Chauncey introduced me to his wife Verity and his son Nathan. Nathan was beginning his second term of a student exchange, Louisiana State University and Liverpool University. Chauncey and Verity had flown over to spend a week in Great Britain with him. I still couldn't believe I had bumped into them. I wouldn't have if, as originally planned, they had taken another voyage on the Mersey Ferry. For Chauncey and me their change of plan was fortuitous. The two of us sat facing each other trying our utmost to stop giggling.

"Oh jeez, did we have us some time when you boys were on the ward," Chauncey said to the visible delight of his wife and son. "All we did was laugh the whole time."

"Do you live in this little ol' town?" his wife asked.

"What soccer team do you support?" Nathan added. I couldn't get a word in edgeways, though my silence was partly due to the continuing surprise.

"I live outside Ormskirk just up the line. I support Everton and yeah, we sure did have us a laugh on ward six."

We ordered a large pot of coffee and a plate of Maryland cookies. We sat talking about any manner of things. Nathan was keen to know why I'd been in the 'Nam. Chauncey said that he should '...leave questions of that kind,' though I told him I wouldn't have minded answering. Verity could see that Chauncey and I were engrossed in conversation.

"Honey..." she said sensitively, "why don't you an' your ol' buddy go get yo'selves a beer. You ain' talked to a vet' for a whiles now it'll be kinda nice for ya both. Me an' Nat' can go on back to the hotel and catch ya's later."

Chauncey and I agreed. I partly felt as if interrupting a family get-together as Chauncey and I sauntered off to the nearest pub. I asked Nathan if he would like to join us once he'd escorted his mother back to the hotel, but he declined. I think he too could see the delight on our faces. He didn't want to impose.

Chauncey asked me about my life as we sat drinking in *The Bee Hive*. I gave him a potted history before asking him likewise. Chauncey told me that he had left Vietnam in October 1973 and that Rậnlạntoì had finally closed in December the same year. He went on to work in a number of US Military hospitals throughout the 'States before training to be a Youth and Community Worker in New Orleans. He had four children, two girls and two boys, Nat' being the youngest. He was content with life but missed his old friends. I asked him about staff from Ward 6, did he know where they were? Had he kept in touch with any of them?

Chauncey smiled before giving me the rundown. "Now there's a story. Molly, she married a marine from up Idaho way. Bobbie-Joe, she went on home to Pennsylvania. Sister Calley got herself a posting up in Utah while Belinda worked a Veterans' Hospital in Washington DC. I met up with them all briefly in 'eighty-nine but I ain't seen them since. Phillipa, you remember Phillipa don't you?"

"Who could forget her," I replied with a lustful intonation and expression.

"Right-on! Well, she stayed in Charlieville, signed off the Corps – signed up for the Red Cross. She stayed on through the Communist take-over, the recession that followed and the war with Kampuchea. Last I heard she was workin' in Hànội."

"You're jokin' me! Phillipa stayed on...well I'll be. She wouldn't have looked out of place on a catwalk."

"Don't life throw up surprises; truth is she loved the Vietnamese as much as she loved nursin'."

Chauncey went quiet for a second. I wondered why he hadn't mentioned Billie: "You've forgotten somebody, Billie Ebotée, what happened to her; where's she at?"

Chauncey put down his glass and looked ahead: "I worked with Billie for nearly six years after we all got home. She became a Sister, ended up in charge of a ward at the United States Navy Hospital, San Diego. She was a pleasure to work for that's a fact. She must've been one of the only Sisters I knew that never had a bad word against her name."

"Yeah..." I said with a smile, "that sounds like Billie. Where is she now?"

Chauncey looked at me, I knew from his sorrowful expression that he was going to deliver bad news: "Billie got the cancer, New Year's 'eighty-nine. She put up one hell of a fight but it wasn't to be. She was dead by the fall."

I was hit by a dull ache, yet another untimely demise of a past acquaintance.

"That's real sad," I said staring into my pint glass.

"She was buried in a little ol' churchyard in Alabama. We all gave her a real good send-off. Quite a few of the old guard came – Molly, Bobbie-Joe, Belinda, Yvonne—"

"Yvonne?" I asked, unsure to whom he was referring.

"Calley, Yvonne Calley."

"Calley! She went to Billie's funeral."

"Sure, flew down from the Air Force Base she was workin'. She was real nice too, said some real nice things about Billie. I guess in war you gets close to people whether you likes it or not."

Chauncey continued talking for a while though I found it difficult to concentrate. It had been almost twenty years since I'd seen Billie, though at that moment, it seemed as if only twenty months.

I suddenly became aware that Chauncey was staring at me with a huge grin: "You were real sweet on Billie, wasn't ya."

"Yeah," I replied deciding it was pointless trying to hide my hurt, "she had a way about her; a charisma like I've never seen. Funny, I don't think I've come across any one quite like her since."

"Yeah," Chauncey said chuckling, "Billie had a way alright, just about as human as a human can be if you get my drift—"

"Oh I get your drift, even the coldest of people could've warmed to Billie."

I thought of our discussions on the balcony: the sound of her anodyne voice; the smell of her cologne carried by the moist monsoon air brushing across our faces. And her smile, a smile that filled me with warmth and wanting. "After we'd gone, did she ever..." I stopped mid-sentence unsure of whether I wanted to finish the question.

"Talk about you?" Chauncey said with a knowing expression, "...sure, with just about the same look you both used to crack when ya'll would talk on the ward. What in the hell did you used to talk over anyhow?"

"All sorts, the war, politics, literature, family; life in general I guess. It's funny, I dream about now and then, only in my dreams I've caught up with her—"

I spotted Chauncey out the corner of my eye staring with an inquisitive expression.

"—age wise I mean. She was older than me, quite a bit older. But in my dreams I'm the age I am now, whereas Billie, she's still in her thirties. And we're in England – Plymouth, walking hand-in-hand along the front in the warm summer air. It's timeless, comfortable. There's no sickness, no war, no rules; nothing to come between us. It's like one of those candy floss dreams you have as a child, fulfilled, untroubled. Like a summer vacation you never want to end."

"Jeez..." Chauncey said shaking his head, "you really did like her."

"More than that," I said comfortable that Chauncey would understand.

We sat in silence for a moment. Chauncey broke the quiet: "Say, what did you do with all that stuff you used to write?"

"My journal, oh, it's tucked away in a box somewhere."

"Sheeit…I remember you sittin' on the balcony on your lonesome writin' all that shit. You never did tell what y'all put."

"I told Billie."

"Hot damn!"

"Uh huh, I wrote about her; wrote about you too."

"No shit! It must be real neat to be able to flick through those pages an' look back. I occasion to think about my time in Charlieville. Sometimes it seems like another lifetime, others, like it was just yesterday."

I nodded, understanding exactly what he meant.

"So…" Chauncey went on, "tell me about the boys from the ward six. How in the hell are they all doin'?"

Up to the news about Billie the conversation had been jovial. I was reluctant to add to the change of mood, but genuine questions require genuine answers. I thought carefully before responding.

"Well, you remember Corporal Farr, Tommy; he was the big guy in the bed on my left – the Platoon spokesman."

"Think so," Chauncey replied with a look that belied the fact.

"He's a lecturer now, Brunel University, 'Post Modern Philosophy and Twentieth Century Politics'. He's a granddaddy five times over and still as in love with his wife as on their first date in High School. Marine Jeffers, JJ, he's still in the Marines, Colour Sergeant. They'll have to throw him out kicking and screaming. He loves the life, kinda worries me, it's as if it's all he knows. Marine Miller, Dusty, he owns a couple of garages across Doncaster way. He makes a living but I'm not sure if it's what he really wants. Reckon he misses being a Bootneck—"

I stopped for a second: "Do you remember Sugar, Marine Lyle, brunette hair and a permanent cheeky grin; and Jumper, Marine Collins, blond hair, muscular frame, more scars on his face than Al Capone?"

"Yeah, they come to mind. Yo' guy Sugar was a real comedian."

"Right, they didn't make it out the 'Nam, got killed in an ambush less than a week after we'd left Rậnlạntoì."

"Sheeit! God-damn, that's a real shame."

"It was a real blow to us all, but a bit more so for me and the guys who shared time at the Ran'. I was one of last to talk to Sugar. He asked me if I thought he should write to Phillipa. I said that maybe he should wait 'til we got home; he never made it."

"What about the others?" Chauncey asked after a moment of reflection. He'd obviously remembered there were eight of us on the ward.

"Lance Corporal Bell, Dinger, and Corporal Speed, Speedy – they were both Killed in Action during the Falklands War."

"Aw jeez, it gets worse," Chauncey said shaking his head, "I remember that little ol' war. Were you guys involved in that too?"

"Yeah, the whole fuckin' thing was a mess, nothing like the media reported. We lost a lot from 2: Bravo 6. As for those two boys, I don't know which one of the losses was the worse. Dinger bought it on one of the first exchanges. I didn't know 'til the following day. And Speedy, he was killed two hours before the Argentinean surrender. Took a direct hit from a hundred-and-five millimetre shell; blown all over the fuckin' place. I helped collect his belongings, what was left of them scattered 'round the crater. A busted wristwatch, his wedding a ring, and his dog tags with a crucifix attached; the same crucifix I saw him holding onto in the Huey to Rậnlạntoì. He kept his faith to the end for all the good it did him. Kinda makes you think doesn't it; there's Billie and Speedy devout Christians taken before their time, and me, a born again Atheist still kicking."

"Maybe you still got a purpose."

"How do you mean?"

"Well, I reckons we're all put on this earth for a reason and taken the same. Ain't your time; you still got things to do, for yo'self or maybe others. As for Billie an' yo' buddies, well, I reckons they're lookin' down on us right now, smilin' at us sat here reminiscin'."

"I'm sorry Chauncey I don't believe that, though I respect your right to."

We sat in silence for a short period gazing at the clientele partaking of their Friday night rituals. I think we both wanted to rekindle the conversation, though with a less sombre topic. I can't recall who kicked things off again. As it transpired we sat for over an hour talking about any manner of things. The clock soon ticked round to 20:30. Our glasses were empty and it was my round.

"Same again?" I asked scooping up the glasses.

Chauncey gave me a thoughtful look: "I'm gonna have to take a rain-check on that if you don't mind. We be flyin' back the-morrow and I wanna spend some last time with my boy."

"Of course not..." I replied, feeling a tad guilty, "I'll walk you back to your hotel."

We strolled down Water Street towards the *Atlantic Tower Hotel* the stiff breeze from the Mersey cutting through our conversation. We touched on Vietnam yet again. I guess we couldn't help it being veterans of that distant conflict. Chauncey asked me how we all got on post homecoming. I informed him that for us it was simply a relief. Nobody, save our families, were any the wiser. I added that on returning from the Falklands we were treated like heroes, and in many ways that was worse.

Chauncey had a different experience. Like numerous Vietnam Veterans he had to keep his mouth shut. Being a vet' may've been hip in the '90s, but it could get you a kicking in the '70s, particularly if you were black.

Chauncey was pensive. "The Veterans' Association's got one hell of a job. There's a lot of angry men with too many questions and not enough answers, '*...to the US of A the 'Nam's a gapin' wound that ain' ever gonna heal.*' Billie Ebotée said that."

"Figures!"

I could have informed Chauncey that I had some difficulty adjusting post Falklands but thought better of it. I may've had some problems, but at least I wasn't spat at!

We were at the hotel entrance in no time. Chauncey invited me in to say my goodbyes to Verity and Nathan.

"Would you like stay for a bourbon or a coffee maybe?" Verity asked me.

"Thank you kindly, but no, I've imposed enough, I should leave you all now."

Chauncey gave me a melancholy look as we walked to the door, his eyes almost glazing over: "Isn't time cruel...don't it always go so quick."

"Yeah, but at least we had some. If you'd have all got on that ferry we'd likely never have met again."

"Be sure to look us up if you ever get on out to Louisiana…" Chauncey said as we exchanged addresses, "you'll be welcome in my house anytime."

"Likewise," I replied with a smile.

"Goodbye my old friend," Chauncey said offering his hand.

We hugged in a lasting embrace. As we disengaged I whispered into Chauncey's ear: "Goodbye you Yankee motherfucker."

"Hot damn!" he cried out, remembering that day on the hospital roof.

I stood in the lift looking at Chauncey's face down the corridor. The doors slowly closed. As they did he cupped his hands to his mouth: "Keep ya head down out there!"

The doors met as I waved with a smile the elevator descending. I stood alone with my thoughts, the hum of the lift-gear my only companion. In the background, I swear I could hear the rotor-thud of a phantom Huey winging its way to the ghostly corridors of Rậnlạntoì.

The half-empty train sped down the tracks. I sat looking at its moonlit shadow on the darkened fields. It was nice meeting Chauncey, I had hardly thought of my time at the Ran' prior to our rendezvous. It was good to talk over old times. Billie and four of my muckers whom I'd shared those days with were dead, but somehow that didn't numb my exultation. They would have wanted us all to go on living.

As the train progressed memories came flooding back. The roars of laughter and Radio Ran'; *Midnight Cowboy, The Grapes of Wrath & Fortunate Son.* Still days and typhoon nights; my birthday drink; chess games with pastry pieces. Distant thunder, distant artillery and a not so distant love that could never be. The rocking motion of the train lullabied me into temporary slumber. The sound of the wheels clattering on the track seemed to beat out a rhythm: Vietnam, Vietnam, Vietnam – yes I was there.

POST SCRIPT:
BAD DAY AT TCHỰIN LOY

Yes, my guard stood hard when abstract threats
Too noble to neglect
Deceived me into thinking
I had something to protect
Good & bad I define these terms
Quite clear, no doubt, somehow,
Ah but I was so much older then,
I'm younger than that now…
Bob Dylan

Town Green, Aughton, Sunday November 26 2000.

In June 1972 some ten weeks before the first of a succession of ceasefires in the Vietnam War a young Vietnamese girl Kim Phuc, caught the imagination of the world through the lens of a Photojournalist. Kim was photographed running naked, screaming and horribly burned from the village of Trằng Bậng after becoming victim to a napalm attack. Many people believed that the images of Kim, transmitted in news reports worldwide, hastened the end of the war.

Almost seven months after the outrage that followed the violation of Kim Phuc the village of Tchựin Loy would also be engulfed in a napalm attack. But on this occasion the telegraphs of the world would not buzz. Reuters would not issue a priority news item; the cry '…hold the front page,' would not be heard in the pressrooms. There were no journalists or film crews in the Tchựin fields on the morning of 15th December 1972; consequently, the act of mass murder perpetrated upon the people of Tchựin Loy would gain no prominence. Tommy's assertion, it appeared, was indeed prophetic. The peasants of Tchựin Loy remained largely forgotten. Just another set of names in that abstract chronicle: Casualties of War.

Nonetheless, those souls from the commune who, subject to working the paddies, survived the attack and the 16 men of One and Two Squads 2: Bravo 6 Platoon, would not easily forget that act of State Terrorism and its aftermath.

Still, time as they say is a great healer. As you get older memories fade like a picture exposed to too much sunlight. But some memories remain as sharp as the day they were etched upon the psyche. The incident at Tchựin Loy will continue to be with me for the rest of my days, though it features less as the years mount. As I've continued my journey through life I haven't had any particular reason to think of that tragic day. I touched upon it briefly, along with other memories, after my chance meeting with Chauncey in '93. I confess to having the occasional nightmare featuring Vietnam and other conflicts. And I have occasioned to talk to people about some of my experiences. Notwithstanding, nothing had prompted me into revisiting my journals. That was until November 2000, when Stephen (Bronco) Lane's daughter Julia invited me to her Graduation Ceremony at Birmingham University. Regrettably, her father could not accompany her on that day. He was Killed in Action during the Falklands War, another loss of life in another avoidable conflict.

It wasn't a particularly good period for Julia in spite of her success in gaining a Degree. She had recently separated from her husband after their increasingly stormy marriage had finally turned into a hurricane. Regardless, she didn't want anything to spoil her special day.

Julia and I assisted by numerous bottles of wine, spent graduation eve discussing a plethora of topics. Invariably a conversation ensued about the time I'd spent with her father. Julia was delighting in the many yarns I had about our exploits.

I can't exactly recall when the talking became more serious. When it did one request stopped me in my tracks. "Tell me about Vietnam," Julia said, "I need to know what happened there—"

I remember staring at Julia, unsure and a little uneasy.

"—I know about Northern Ireland and I think I know what happened in the Falklands, but Vietnam is a mystery to me. When dad came home in 'seventy-three he was distant and moody. Sometimes I'd hear him screaming out in the middle of the night. Whenever I asked mum what was wrong she'd just say that he 'wasn't himself,' or that sometimes he'd get 'very bad headaches.' What really hurt was that I thought it was something that I'd done. It wasn't until about six months later that he started doing things with me again. I remember it distinctly. He took me to *Saint Andrews* to watch the football. Tell me about Vietnam…please."

Her appeal was irresistible. I considered she had the right to know; hence, I took her through the journal of antipathy firmly lodged in my mind:

I enlightened her on how emaciated children would approach us begging for scraps whilst the SVA sold rations at inflated prices on the black market. And of how we'd walk through Viet Cong villages that had been persistently razed to the ground, trying to avoid eye contact with people who had an immovable look of savageness cut into their faces. I explained how Command would move us from province to province constantly testing our resolve. And of how we'd drive past hordes of refugees lining the roadside;

dispossessed, stripped of everything, save their dignity. I told her about the bloated bodies floating downriver; the disappeared covertly disposed of in the thick of the jungle. I informed her of the incident in Quì Nhôn when we discovered the two Viet Cong women hanging from a tree. Of how we had to stand idly by whilst the South Vietnamese Military Police cut the women's bodies down whilst joking about their plight. And of how we had to struggle to keep the revulsion that we felt for those nauseating creeps, delighting in the torture and execution of fellow human beings, to ourselves. I enlightened her on how we had to battle to keep the poison of hatred at bay and maintain a grasp on our humanity.

I became aware that Julia was gaping at me with a look of horror. I suddenly felt uncomfortable, regretful that I had disclosed so much: "I'm sorry, I didn't realise. It just came out—"

"Don't stop…" she said in a determined voice a stern look on her face, "I want to hear it – I want to hear it all!"

So, after a moment of contemplation I told her. I informed her about that fateful day in Nha Trang Province. I took her through the incident at Tchụrin Loy; from the first reports of gunfire to the enduring cries of distress as we exited the obliterated site. I talked about how the incident impacted upon our lives; of how I saw her father fighting back the tears as he gazed at a crayon drawing she'd sent him. And I informed her of how on the following day, we had to pick up our rifles lock and load and just carry on.

Once I'd finished we hugged each other in floods of tears.

"He never told me..." Julia cried, "why didn't he tell me? Why did he keep it all in?"

"He couldn't tell you – you were seven years old! He wouldn't have told you if you were twenty-seven. We had strict instructions not to disclose anything about the 'Nam outside the Platoon. To have done so would have resulted in a court martial and certain dishonourable discharge."

We sat in silence for what seemed like an eternity. Julia eventually broke the reticence: "It still hurts doesn't it?"

"War never stops hurting. It kicks you in the guts, takes all the wind out of you. You never really fully recapture your breath, there's always a part missing. Maybe I'll get that last bit back on my deathbed. Maybe that ultimate gasp will fill my soul, a final atonement for all the shit I've been involved in—"

I noticed Julia giving me a sad empathetic look.

"—Don't look at me like that guilt's no bad thing. Nothing reminds you that you're still alive more than guilt and as you can see, I'm still standing!"

We finished the evening on a lighter note and her graduation day, I'm delighted to say, lived up to its expectations. Bronco, I thought privately, would have been proud of the strong assertive woman standing before me, his *little girl*.

Before I made ready for home Julia, after thanking me for attending the ceremony, broached the subject of Vietnam. She stopped me as I tried to apologise: "There's no need. I asked you, you told me, end of story...or is it?"

"How do you mean?"

"Dad used to talk about you. He said you were forever reading and always writing; so write about it. Write about Tchựin Loy, for you and for dad—"

I stood for a moment thinking, unsure of what to say.

"—Do you know what else he said to me?" she continued with a smile, "…he told me that a good friend once said: '*A candle's not a candle 'til it's lit, a path is not a path 'til it's walked, a story is not a story until it's told.*' You know who told him that, don't you?"

"I'd like to think I know *him* better than anyone else, although sometimes, I wonder. Did he really tell you that?"

"He told me lots of things especially about his pals; you, JJ, Jumper, Sugar, Tommy, Dinger, Dusty. What an ornery bunch of motherfuckers you lot must have been!"

We both roared with laughter relieved that the theme had been lightened.

We said our goodbyes. Julia placed a manila envelope in my hand just as I was departing. "Don't open that until you get to Liverpool," she said.

After agreeing to her request, I set off for home.

The drive up the M6 Motorway was surreal. I found myself reflecting on the night before. I was astounded by how much had come out about our time in Vietnam particularly that day in Nha Trang Province. I realised that my disclosure was the first time that I had talked about the incident outside the Platoon for over 27 years. Moreover, there was so much more I could have told her – not all bad. I could have told Julia how students in Đà Nẵng and Quì Nhôn would delight in our presence: "We like you Britain people, number-one friends. Not kill like Yankee. Beatle music very best: Penny Lane, Yellow Sum-barine, Mr Pepper, very best sounds." Or of how people in the outlying provinces would ask for their photographs to be taken alongside us: "You take home English, show people Vietnamese can smile. Much joy on our faces when ÂK not in hand."

I also could have told her of the sad day in Trệng Nhôy when we lost Marines Collins and Lyle.

Regardless, nothing characterised the repugnance of war more than that day at Tchựin Loy. But would I have the notion to put pen to paper? I thought once again of the running journals I'd kept throughout each conflict in which I had been involved. They were stacked in a box at my parent's house. Threadbare notebooks containing daily recordings, anecdotes and my first attempts at war poems. Grubby pages stained with gun-grease, dirt and tears. Northern Ireland, Vietnam and the Falklands, each page a portrayal of all things common to armed confrontation. Despicable acts, commendable acts, indifferent acts; the malevolent, the benevolent and the 'I just don't give a goddamn'. Could I, should I peruse my journal? Would I be awakening old ghosts or simply putting long, assumed, forgotten demons to rest?

On arriving home I concluded that I'd need to give the proposal further consideration. Then before I retired for the night, I remembered the envelope Julia had pressed into my hand. As it transpired its content would be the key that would unlock the chest; the final piece of an abstract conundrum less than five hours old.

I was full of curiosity as I opened the envelope. The faded pink piece of paper inside had been doubled over so many times it was held together by Sellotape. As I unfolded the paper the sketch became instantly recognisable: a house with a smoking chimney next to a tree. Alongside, a mum, a dad, a *little girl* and a dog. A crayon drawing, by Julia Lane, aged seven.

***

Saturday 12 August 2001.

In January 2001 I wrote to Claude Van Danbrok of the International War Crimes Tribunal, The Hague, requesting a transcript of the enquiry into the bombing of Tchựin Loy, 15th December 1972. Mr Van Danbrok replied in April 2001 stating that the enquiry had been held under the auspices of the IPSF on the 12th & 13th March 1973, and that the findings were: '...subjected to the 50 year ruling'. Mr Van Danbrok closed by inviting me to resubmit a request for the transcript prior to February 2023.

In my frustration I wrote a letter in the Vietnamese text to Bảnh Thận Lhờn, President of the Social Democratic Republic of Vietnam. I explained my circumstances in December 1972 and my reasons for wanting details on the enquiry's findings, plus information on how the survivors of Tchựin Loy coped after that disgraceful act of mass murder.

I felt somewhat uncomfortable once I had posted the letter. During my time in Vietnam I always felt as if an intruder. An unwilling intermediary in an ever-unfolding drama: the Montigues and Capalets of Indo-China. Was the outcome of the enquiry really any of my business? Why did I need to know about the survivors? Was it a genuine desire to ascertain what had happened to the distressed individuals who endured the wake of that cowardly act or was I simply trying to assuage my own guilt?

Regardless, in July 2001 I received a reply to my correspondence, on behalf of President Lhờn, from Commissar [Chủ tích] Lâm Chì Phơm, Chief

Administrator of Nha Trang Province. Chû tích Phơm thanked me for my missive and for the interest I'd shown in his people. He explained that the presiding administration did not have details on the outcome of the enquiry into the incident at Tchựin Loy. He advised that I should be assured that the former corrupt leaders of South Vietnam had received a comprehensive programme of re-education. And that their instruction was inclusive of gaining an understanding on the ways of the Viet Cong.

Chû tích Phơm went on to write a précis of the events following the bombing of Tchựin Loy. He stated that their comrades in the villages of Tchựin Điêt and Tchựin Khômn gave the survivors from the commune shelter and protection. The people from the Tchựin collectives went on to form an active coalition to clear the bombed site and rebuild the settlement. Tchựin Loy was re-established in the dry season of 1973 and continues to thrive to this day.

Lâm Chì Phơm concluded by inviting me to visit his country. He wrote that should I take up his invitation then I would be welcome to contact him at his office where he would be only too pleased to arrange a visit to the Tchựin fields. He assured me that the people of Tchựin Loy would embrace my presence. And that some of the older members of the commune would not have forgotten 2: Bravo 6 Platoon and the help and generosity we offered them on that fateful day in 1972.

I read and re-read the letter. I checked and re-checked every sentence. I wanted to be sure the words were real. That those traumatised, bewildered and bedraggled people really did lift themselves above the spectre of evil; that the village of Tchựin Loy was alive. Actuality hit home, when it did I felt as if a weight had been lifted from my shoulders. More than this, I felt exalted; as if our presence on that sorrowful day had in some way served a purpose. I no longer felt like an unwilling witness to a hundred executions, more a witness to the character of resolute people who, in the face of persistent adversity, refused to acquiesce. I felt like a courier conscripted to issue a memorandum to those tyrants who endeavour to repress their fellow man and woman: '*You can napalm the body, but you cannot napalm the spirit*!'

Awakened, I revisited the aftermath of that momentous occasion. So much was said in the days that followed that monstrous act, yet so little. Of particular note was the assertion by Lieutenant Derrick: "Sometimes the only way to deal with the unacceptable is to accept it..." He was right – sometimes you do have to accept the unacceptable, but that doesn't mean you have to like it!

Moreover, those who, by choice or misfortune, become embroiled in monstrous acts have I believe a responsibility to convey what they've seen to others. If systems cannot or will not deal with those despots who seek to restrain the self-determination of people and their communities then opportunities should be sought to inform as many people as possible of the *real* evil that lurks within this fragile world.

Be that as it may, when all is finally laid down the incident at Tchựin Loy is history. Memories will live on and will be passed on. Still, Vietnam is at peace and although we should not forget the past neither should we let it nullify our future.

As for me, Lâm Chì Phơm had the goodwill to invite me to his country. No doubt, maybe sometime soon, I will take up his offer. Until that time I have contrived my own way of moving on, of bringing some closure to that grievous event. I have accomplished this by creating 'my perfect day', a collection of moments in time when all is right. A final journey constructed to release me from the after-effects of an *assumed* forgotten event that has left a scar that only those who have ventured close to me will recognise. And now Dear Reader, as I bring this section to a close I invite you to share my dream:

'...It is a warm and pleasant morning in the Tchựin fields. I walk alone now, but unafraid, for I carry the memory of my brave compadrés. I stroll a familiar trail excavated by the boots of invading armies and hopeful peacekeepers; the sandals of fatigued workers and the gentle feet of playful children. To my right the Sôn Kơi Woods, which are quiet now, save for the sweet sound of bird song.

To the west I stare at the peaceful mountains reflected in the rice pools and observe the silhouettes of people working the fields. No longer their ears vibrate to the echoes of gunfire those sounds are removed now.

A young Vietnamese couple pass me in playful pursuit of Annamese golden hornets, hopeful for a sign that their love for each other will last forever. Miniature rattan reeds lightly sway in my wake. I swear I can hear a welcoming note as their delicate fingers rustle.

I am aware of the presence of long lost brothers. Ahead I see Marine Collins forever prepared to go on point, always 'rifle at the ready'. He gives the semaphore for, 'all ahead clear, no present danger'. I stop him mid-signal: "It's okay Jumper, I know."

Behind me I hear Sugar, laughing as always: "You got your head off Jupiter yet?"

"Not quite…but I'm working on it."

I become conscious that somebody is walking alongside me. I turn to see that it's Bronco: "Hello my old friend."

"Wot-ya Bazzer!"

"Come to walk into the village with me?"

"No, not today, this is your road. You go on ahead…take it on home for both of us."

I turn to tell him about Julia but see that he has gone – though he's still with me.

I progress the Sôn Kơi treeline. The faint shade lifts as I draw near the outskirts of the village. Tchựin Loy appears rousing recollections that once enlightened and numbed my senses. I saunter to the burial ground to pay my respects. Ten thousand days of ultraviolet light have faded the charring on the headstones, just as our memories have faded in the cycle of time. Yet the cracks, as the underlying sadness, remain. I stop at the village boundary. The commune as always is a bustle of activity, each individual working to a common objective – their continuing survival. Behind me the workers are slowly returning from the paddies. There is no urgency on this day, no cries of distress, only mutual jesting and familiar chatter.

The village elder greets me as I walk the bamboo bridge across the monsoon ditches. He gives me the Mahayana Buddhist sign for peace and harmony, which I return alongside other salutations. I look at the elder with expectancy and wonderment. There is a brief interlude broken by my expression of sorrow for what happened in '72. I explain that given the opportunity our Detail would have stopped that cowardly attack. And of how we desperately wanted to do more to help his people in the aftermath. In my nervousness I suddenly stop temporarily lost for words. I struggle to re-establish the context. As I prepare to speak the elder brings three closed fingers up to his lips. (The Vietnamese gesticulation for, 'silent now, all is well'.) I realise this wise and good-natured man needs no explanation from those whom he knows to be genuine.

I am reminded of a Viet Cong precept: '*In Vietnam there are more eyes and ears than heads and hearts, so first we look and listen, only then do we think and feel.*'

The honcho sensitively takes my arm and invites me into his commune. I look at the peoples' faces with interest, as they do mine. Children come running with excitement. Who is this newcomer who can speak their language? What does he want on this day? Why does he delight so at our presence? Tender questions that deserve only one answer, an answer that only the genuine warmth of a human smile can portray.

I walk amongst the populace. Some hold out their hands in a greeting. As I touch them I feel a connection. I casually scan the settlement, which is smaller now. I look towards the livestock enclosure; there, I see a young Vietnamese girl tending a water buffalo. She smiles and gives a gentle wave reminding me that when all is said and done – life goes on. I observe a gathering of people near the community centre preparing the midday chow.

The elder invites me to join them in the communal meal, an offer that I gratefully accept. The Viet Cong, it appears, are back to their hospitable ways.

On arriving in Vietnam an American counsel gave 2: Bravo 6 Platoon an unsolicited lecture on '...the ways of the Viet Cong': "Don't ever show Victor Charlie the back of your head," he said.

I always considered this advice to be somewhat misguided. I've been in plenty of bars and walked numerous half lit streets in this world where I would not turn my back on strangers. Personally, I've always found the Viet Cong to be honourable people who would look you in the eye if they had a grievance. Their principles are firmly grounded in existence (their lives are dependent upon congruity with all living things each with its value within a system that is undiminished).

The Viet Cong collectively cherish their children and revere their elders. Their regard for each other is the foundation that binds their community, all else is just paste easily washed away in the rain of despair. But despair has not broken these people, it served only to bond them further. Their mosaic, once shattered, is rebuilt.

I once read: '*The beauty of simplicity is in its complexity.*' My experience has given birth to a different view, for no people I have ever met are more *complex* than the Viet Cong, though none lead more *simple* lives. They are truly unpretentious people who strive only to collectively better themselves.

I join the commune for the midday meal. As I sit amongst my fellow humankind I gain a feeling of total acceptance, for on this day I visit not as a soldier of the United Nations, but as a citizen of the world; not as a peacekeeper, but as a man of peace. The honcho smiles at my amazement and reverence. He moves close to me and declares: "You are at one within the 'Cong commune. You join us as an equal; you do not move down, sideways or up, only *in*."

And so, I move in: ever nearer to them, ever deeper into myself, in so doing I finally find the peace that has eluded me.

I elevate my senses in an attempt to absorb every nuance on this significant day. I look skywards and see only peaceful cumulus, their amorphous forms as if memories of dreams dreamt or wishes yet to be fulfilled. I gaze at the children; their sloe-eyes no longer reddened, only filled with curiosity for this stranger in a not so strange land. I listen to all that surrounds me: no more the sounds of people crying with anguish, only the sounds of children's babble and the laughter of inhabitants that have returned to peaceful ways.

I probe the encompassing fragrances. Gone are the odours of burnt napalm and the reek of scorched flesh, on this day, only the sweet essence of warm rice and coriander permeate the air. I release my inner self: no more a feeling of fear, only calm, no longer a feeling of remorse, only acceptance for what we did amidst that carnage. No more a feeling of sorrow, only joy.

It is a wondrous day. On this occasion nothing will shatter the serenity. And so, I close my eyes and drift ever deeper into reconciliation with myself, into contentment with my being, and I relax in the sure and certain knowledge that this time my visit will not turn out to be a Bad Day at Tchųrin Loy.'

POST SCRIPT:
ENCOUNTER WITH THE KHMER ROUGE

I have grown past hate & bitterness,
I see the world as one,
Yet though I can no longer hate,
My son is still my son.
All men at God's round table sit,
And all men must be fed,
But this loaf in my hand,
This is my son's bread.

M Gilmore

Wavertree, Liverpool, Saturday 22 September 2001.

I pulled up outside the small terraced house full of trepidation. It didn't look any different from my last visit some 29 years earlier. I thought of my phone conversation on the previous Thursday, the voice of Mrs Edith Graham answering the phone…

"I'm sorry to bother you..." I said after the faint voice answered, "I'm trying to get in touch with Mrs Lyle."

"This is Mrs Graham," the woman said after a moments hesitation.

"I'm sorry; it's an old number I've got. You don't happen to know a Mrs Lyle? She used to live at that address—"

"Lyle's my widowed name. Who am I speaking to?"

"Oh, it's an old friend of Sugar's, I mean Robert—"

"Robert? Robert's dead, been dead near on thirty years."

"I know I was with him when he got killed." My belated disclosure was followed by an eerie silence. I could hear my heart beating amid the back echo from the handset. I sat waiting for Sugar's mother to say something.

"Robert was in Vietnam..." Edith said a clear note of surprise and confusion in her voice, "who did you say you were again?"

"I'm sorry I didn't. Barry, my name's Barry. I was in the same Platoon as Sugar, I mean Robert. I was on tour with him in Vietnam."

"Oh, I see. What do you want?"

It was a fair question, what did I want? I thought I knew, but at that instant I was suddenly unsure. What on earth was I doing phoning Sugar's mother 28 years after his death? I was overcome by a feeling of regret. '*Best let sleeping dogs lie,*' bounced into my head; too late now, the beast was awake.

"I'm sorry, I just wanted to talk. I know it's been a long time but...well, I need to clear things up—" I was digging myself further and further into a hole. The silence on the other end of the phone didn't help. "I apologise...you must think me crazy," I said with a nervous laugh.

"No, just a bit surprised – I thought I was past being knocked off my feet!"

The tone of her voice settled my nerves: "I know, I guess I'd feel the same. Listen, it doesn't matter if you don't—"

"Oh no you don't young man! You've fired up my curiosity. If you want to talk about Robert then that's fine and dandy with me."

I thanked her for understanding. We would meet – 14:00 Saturday.

...So, there I was, stood on the doorstep. I stared at the doorknocker as if willing it to rap without my assistance. The door opened just as I was reaching for the tarnished knob: "Mrs Graham?"

"Edith please, come in."

I gave her the bunch of flowers I had purchased as we silently entered the front room.

"I don't suppose you recognise me?" I said trying to initiate conversation.

"Should I?"

"No, not really, it's just that I stayed here one night in 'seventy-two. Me and Sugar, I mean, Robert—"

"It's alright; I'm aware that was his nickname."

"—Thanks. We went out on the town; I crashed here. You made us one of your famous Saturday morning fry ups; he called it 'the works'."

"He was always bringing round waifs and strays," she said with a chuckle.

Edith went off to make a pot of tea after we'd spent a few minutes breaking the ice. I sat scanning the room to the sound of a grandmother clock slowly ticking. Family pictures adorned the walls: photographs of his sisters' weddings, pictures of children, presumably grandchildren, and a photograph of Edith and her second husband. A crucifix lay central one wall beside a large 1970s picture of Royal Marine Robert Lyle in his number one uniform. '*They shall not grow old as we who shall grow old...*' I thought as I looked at the fresh-faced youngster: his cropped brunette hair, blue eyes and perpetual cheeky grin. A glass case was screwed to the wall below the photograph. The small cabinet contained the Northern Ireland medal along with the United Nations medal I'd last seen resting on his coffin 28 years previously.

Edith poured the tea and invited me to tuck in to some of her homemade fruit cake: "Don't be bashful now take as many slices as you want, I like to see a man eat."

"Bashful," I chortled, "it's a good job my mates aren't here, they'd be doubled over! Don't you worry none, I won't be bashful."

Edith laughed with me. We were both at ease it seemed.

"So..." Edith said, "what's your story?"

“There’s a question,” I said with a sigh. “I’m not even sure where it begins. When I perused my journals for the first time in over twenty-five years; when I bumped into an old acquaintance from ’Nam a few years back, or when I attended a recent graduation. Truth is, it probably starts in ’seventy-two. Maybe even before that…”

I became aware that I was playing with words; stalling. I needed to cut to the chase.

“…Thing is, I came here to talk about Sugar. I guess I should really start with an apology for being twenty-seven years late.”

Edith smiled: “It’s never too late; you’re here now.”

“Thanks for that, but I needed to apologise if only to assuage my own guilt. Our Commanding Officer asked me if I’d be willing to call round whilst on leave. I said I would, but I kept putting it off. I was a lot younger then; words don’t come easy when you’re a bit of a kid. I’d have probably started blubberin’ if I’d have come round. So…how much do you know, or want to know, about his death I mean?”

Edith was silent for a short time. “It was such a long time ago, though I remember the day I was told the news. I was coming back from the shops when I noticed this limousine parked across the road, Mercedes I think. There weren’t as many cars on the roads as nowadays so it stuck out like a sore thumb. I remember looking at it as I opened the front door. Two Royal Marines got out, a Captain and a Sergeant. They walked towards the house. 'They haven’t come to see me have they?' I thought. I’d convinced myself they’d either come to see somebody else or to tell me how Robert was doing. It didn’t hit home until they were right on top of me. The Sergeant looked at me; a long sorrowful look. I knew then...I knew. ‘It’s Robert isn’t it?’ I said. ‘Is he dead?’...‘*I’m so sorry*,’ the Sergeant said. I opened the door to let them in. Then, I froze; stood in the hallway unable to move. Next thing I remember was the Sergeant putting a hot cup of tea up to my lips. I was slumped on the settee in the living room. He was an older man. The Captain was a bit of a kid, not much older than you and Robert likely. Sam [Sugar’s father] came in from his shift at Ford’s just as I was coming around. That’s when the wailing started. The rest, as they say, is history.”

“Did they give you any details about the incident?”

“Oh the usual stuff. They said his Platoon was involved in an ambush; that he fought bravely and that he was killed instantly; said he didn’t suffer. They would say that wouldn’t they?”

I thought for a second before giving her a resolute look: “I was there when he got hit and I can report that he was dead before he hit the ground – he didn’t suffer.”

She half smiled a smile that said *thank you*, as if a relief 28 years in the making. I considered telling her that we'd got the culprits who cut down her son but decided against it. It wouldn't bring him back. Besides, I'm still not a 100 per cent sure that what we did was justified.

We talked for over an hour, or rather, I talked. I told Edith about my time with Sugar. About days and nights in Northern Ireland and Vietnam; of our support for one another and our shenanigans with the rest of the lads. And of our talks: discussions about our families, our hopes for the future and our beloved Everton.

Edith replenished the teapot before producing a box full of photographs, cards and letters. She handed me some of the faded pictures, their corners curled up. A picture of 2: Bravo 6 Platoon and a print of some of the men from One & Two Squad; Sugar, Jumper, Bronco, Dinger, Dusty, JJ, Speedy, Tommy, Vinny and of course myself.

"That was taken on China Beach…" I said staring at my 19-year-old face, "blimey, where did that kid go?" I suddenly felt regretful. I'd lived on; Sugar had died and there was I reminding his mother. She noticed my woeful expression.

"It's alright..." she said with a gentle smile, "life goes on."

"It's crazy," I said continuing to stare at the photograph, "the war continued all around us, every day, every night; almost constant dread. There were times when I was sick to the stomach. Couldn't eat or sleep. Yet, I can't help but feel wistful looking at this picture. Truth is they were some of the best days of my life."

"You'll probably think the same thing in another twenty years when you look at a photograph taken now," she advised.

I nodded, acknowledging that I understood what she meant. I felt comfortable enough at that stage to disclose my feelings, talk in more depth: "You know I'm old enough to know that you should move forward in your life. Cherish the good times, accept the bad and consign them to the past. But when I look at this picture I can't help wishing I could go back. Just for one day. Not to the war, I'd never want to revisit that. The good times; a day in Đà Nẵng on R and R, or the day we spent on Nha Trang Beach. Even a day at the military hospital we were in. I'd take the opportunity to say unspoken words; particularly to the muckers I'd lost…just one day."

"A day wouldn't be enough, you'd want more, take it from me. And you couldn't just block out the war. It was part of you then it would have to be a part of you if you went back."

Edith was right of course. I smiled: "Your son never told me you were a philosopher!"

"Did I hear you say you were in hospital with him?"

"Rậnlạntoì, yeah, I was there."

Edith rummaged through the box before producing a faded envelope. "This was his last letter," she said a hint of emotion in her voice. "He wrote it from there...yeah, you're Bazzer aren't you," she continued, scanning the pages, "he mentions you and the other boys."

Edith read excerpts from the letter. Sugar wrote that he was fine and that she shouldn't worry. He added that he and the lads were having a scream. And that there was a "...real nice nurse that he was sweet on—"

"Phillipa!" I said with a chuckle.

Edith carried on reading, filtering out the more private segments.

"Thanks for that," I said as she finished. "It brought back memories."

Edith gave a thoughtful expression as if unsure if she should ask a question: "They said another boy got killed in the same action. And that he'd tried to protect Robert. Can you tell me about that?"

"Marine Collins, Jumper...yeah, I can tell you; it would be my pleasure."

I took her through the details. I didn't elaborate on Jumper's painful death, that would've served no purpose. But I did talk of his courage.

"Which one's Jumper?" she asked picking up the photograph.

"There he is..." I said pointing him out, "between me and Sugar."

"What about his family have you visited them?"

"I tried, spent some time in the Northeast a few years back. I searched through the Telephone Directory, there's a lot of Collins in Newcastle I can tell you. I never found his family, though if the truth be told, I didn't really try that hard. I visited his grave though. He's buried in a small church cemetery in Jarrow. The Royal Marines' Chaplaincy got me the plot number. His grave was overgrown, unkempt. Maybe I wouldn't have found his family after all. I returned a couple of weeks later with a bottle of soapy water and a scrubbing brush. Cleaned up the headstone, raked out some weeds, laid some fresh flowers, said a few words. It felt good doing that...just like it feels good coming here."

"Was he decorated for what he did? ...Jumper I mean."

"No, you'd have to exercise some pretty extraordinary gallantry before being decorated in the Royal Marines, believe me. But it's more than that; Jumper couldn't be decorated for his courage because he was involved in an action that we should never have been involved in the first place."

"How do you mean?"

"It's simple, we were never an official part of the 'Supervisory Force or the United Nations. We were a gift from the government of the day; a token to demonstrate our country's commitment towards world peace. There were only a hundred and twenty-eight of us for pity's sake; four Platoons in total. Whilst there we wondered why Command were constantly moving from province to province. It didn't become clear to us until much later. That's only a half of it, wanna know the real irony—?"

Edith nodded in silence.

"—there never was a proper ceasefire. The whole thing was a ruse; a licence to allow the Americans to withdraw with honour. Richard Nixon called it his 'Ace in the pack'. Some political commentators said he obviously didn't look hard enough because it turned out to be a 'Joker'. The joke was on us; the whole thing was a sham. We spent three hundred and fifty days walking through South Vietnam monitoring a ceasefire that didn't exist."

Edith became pensive, clearly engrossed in my disclosure. Yet again I felt regretful, aware of my unfortunate habit of communicating factors that were often best left under wraps. Nevertheless, I believe people have the right to know the details on the loss of a loved one. But how much do you disclose? I decided, as I looked into Edith's thoughtful face that I had said enough, at least about the politics of the conflict.

We talked some more. I told her about my last moments with her son; of how we'd planned to go to *Goodison Park.* And that I'd have likely turned up on her doorstep for a crash, followed by *the works*. I told her about the church service in Sàigòn and the lamentations that followed. Of how the lads talked so fondly about him: his cheeky grin and comical impressions, and his jokes. And I told her about the graffiti on the water tower. Most of all, I told her of a particular episode in 1971:

"We were on the Commando Assault Vessel HMS *Fearless*," I said, Edith nodding, likely remembering her son's draughtings. "We'd been in port for just over a week. I was skint, stuck onboard like most of the lads. I'd just split up with this girl I'd been seeing. Like most men I put on a brave face. Said I wasn't bothered, the usual clichés '...plenty more fish in the sea' and the like, but deep down I was cut up, miserable. Robert could tell. Oh he joked with me, took the mickey. But sometimes you can glean more from the unspoken word. He asked me if I fancied going ashore for a few pints, just him and me. I didn't have any money, neither did he, but somehow we managed to scrape together some pennies. We looked through our lockers, checked our pockets. Sugar called in a few favours. We ended up with just over three-quid, quite a bit for 'seventy-one. So, we went ashore. It was a warm September evening. We sampled the pubs along Portsmouth Hard. Had a few pints, chatted up some fanny, I mean women—!"

Edith laughed calming my embarrassment.

"—Made our way back to ship around ten-thirty. We were both a bit peckish. We counted out the kitty – just on thirty pence. Wasn't enough for a portion of chips each or a Chinky nosh. So, we bought one portion of chips and one sausage. There we were sat on the quayside in Portsmouth Docks an open wrapper of chips and split sausage between us, gazing at the lights from the ships, talking, laughing. I think that was the first time in my life that I understood the true meaning and value of friendship. I liked Sugar...he was my mate."

Edith suddenly started to cry. "I'm sorry," I said, "I didn't mean—"

"It's alright, its just Sam. He'd have loved to hear you say that. Sam loved the girls, but Robert was the apple of his eye. He took his passing away really bad; became depressed. I don't think he ever really got over it."

We both sat in silence alone with our thoughts. The five o'clock chimes interrupted the repose. It didn't seem like three hours. I was aware that Geoff, her second husband, was due back from his allotment. She'd consigned him there for the afternoon so we could talk in peace. Edith looked at me: "Well, it's been interesting. I'm glad you came round. It was nice to hear you talk."

"Thanks for that. You know, as I was sat here talking I couldn't help wondering if I was just doing this for me—"

"Both of us..." Edith interrupted with a smile, "for both of us."

I made ready to leave. I momentarily considered informing Edith that I was in the process of writing a book about my experiences in Vietnam. I thought of asking her if it would be alright to include our meeting. I'm unsure why; I'd hardly asked anybody else. In the midst of my cogitation I suddenly thought of Marine Collins' family. What if the book got published? What if *they* acquired a copy and read of Jumper's distressing death? Too many questions, I would have to think things through.

I bid Edith goodbye. She insisted I take the rest of her homemade fruit cake, which I thankfully accepted. She gave me something else before I departed: the plot number of Sugar's headstone in Toxteth Cemetery. I didn't visit his grave, I probably never will. I have already said my goodbyes: in a small church in South Vietnam, to the dulcet tones of *How Great Thou Art*.

GHOST VOICES

The small child looked at me his eyes full of wonder:
Tell me of your present, future & past.
My present is much the same as yours
What you see, feel & hear.
My future, I cannot tell; nor my past
That resides in voices within my head
And you, little one, must acquire your own.

Vietnamese Fable

Town Green, Aughton, Sunday 15 December 2002.

In September 1998 I watched Steven Spielberg's *Saving Private Ryan* with a fellow war veteran. We discussed the opening scenes over a pint, both agreeing how refreshing it was to see a motion picture that portrayed the true horror of war. *Saving Private Ryan* is one of a collection of films based on World War II. The Vietnam War has also spawned a plethora of movies. Lamentably, most of the representations have been about the ordeals endured by American soldiers. I've often wondered why there has been no authentic reference to the abuse and murder of non-combatants within that struggle. Oliver Stone's *Platoon* came close. Regrettably, the stark depiction of the horrors committed in a Viet Cong village was followed by the affect the incident had on the very perpetrators.

Saving Private Ryan rightly depicted the sacrifice made by brave young men fighting against evil. In my view those of us who enjoy freedom *should* be reminded of the sacrifices made by men and women in the fight for a better world. But any chronicle that leaves out the pain and anguish suffered by innocents is not worth the celluloid upon which it's etched.

Some three years after watching Spielberg's war epic, I stood in my local watching the Six O'clock News, or rather watching the horror on the faces of the patrons as they tried to assimilate the unbelievable spectacle of two planes plunging into the World Trade Centre. For most, the September 11th attack was a traumatic experience; their certainty of a relatively safe world crumbling along with the concrete. For me, it was simply another reminder of mankind's inhumanity. I had already experienced my own 9/11 – Nha Trang Province, December 15th 1972. Now, as we come to the end of another year, I wonder just how much we've learned from the 9/11 attack and the ravages of war in the 20th Century. I sit listening to the news with dismay: George W Bush and his lap dog cronies preparing to attack yet another sovereign state.

To me, it sounds all too familiar. Countries in the so-called *responsible* free world condemning supposedly reckless nations for developing weapons of mass destruction. Politicians reviling a state for the oppression and torture of its citizens whilst sucking up to neighbouring countries with equally inexcusable human rights records. The support of tyrants in ostensibly friendly nations whilst naming and shaming terrorists, many of whom would later be greeted in champagne receptions.

One could suggest that it would be naive for me to expect the fragile world in which we live to be any more at peace than in those heady days when I walked through South East Asia. Though I claim to be no more at liberty than others of my age or peer group, I do foster a belief that I have a right to expect our learned politicians to be more responsible with whom we choose to cosy up to, and hand weapons and technology to!

As for the unified Vietnam. I have taken great interest in that country since boarding the plane home. The whole region continues to struggle. Vietnam has signed up to the global economy and the good old United States of America still hold the keys; so, who really won? Former US Secretary of State, Robert McNamara commented on the Vietnam War on his retirement stating: "*We were not fighting Communism in South East Asia, we were fighting Nationalism.*" In my view he was wrong on both counts. The USA were interfering in the struggle of an indigent people who simply wanted self determination; to live their lives within their chosen belief and value systems and rid their country of decades of tyranny. United States Forces did nought but protract the conflict and add to the tyranny, hence, many of those who took up arms turned to increased levels of cruelty. You can be sure that if you fight tyranny with tyranny then all you'll be left with is tyranny – George W Bush take note.

Notwithstanding, my life has moved on since those days. As I look at the faded and curled pages of my journal I can't help wondering if the whole thing was real. Although most of the above text has come from those pages, some has come from memory. The problem with our memories is that they sometimes play tricks on us. We act as if our recollections are like a tape that can be simply rewound. We reframe experiences, put in additions to events that didn't happen, or see negative experiences in a different way. We need to keep in mind that what is attainable on a magnetic strip is not achievable within the neurons that make up our recognition. Nonetheless, what I've written here is as true a reflection as possible.

Many things have happened since my return – some good, some not so good. I've survived further armed conflicts, travelled extensively and made friends throughout the world. But continuing to exist manufactures other consequences, survivor-guilt being the most prominent. I've tried to put the bad things behind me, ignore the nightmares, the occasional awful reminders and painful anniversaries. The trouble with anniversaries is that they're there whether you remember them or not. It's not without irony that I have chosen to bring an end to this narrative on the 30th anniversary of the bombing of Tchựin Loy. As mentioned hitherto, the images of that burned settlement are as fresh in my mind as the day we walked the Tchựin fields.

Significant milestones are other reminders of those who fell. Jumper was only a few months older than me and Sugar a few months younger. As I move towards my half century I wonder what their lives would've been like. Would Jumper have had the son and daughter he so yearned for, and Sugar have found that special woman he so wanted in his life. They both came across as hard knocks with a streak of the charlatan. How men play games, hide their true feelings. It's been almost 30 years and I still miss them.

As for that cruel conflict, my feelings towards the justification for the war and the injustices that took place on a daily basis have not changed. Though it was easier for me to support the aims of the Viet Cong there were undoubtedly wrongdoings on both sides. As a Humanist I have never – and believe will never – endorse the philosophy of one wrong negating another.

I think of my fellow survivors on a regular basis. I wonder what their thoughts and feelings are towards that far off struggle. I'd like to imagine that most foster the same attitudes and believes as myself, but everybody has differing experiences and perspectives. I'd be surprised if all my comrades would feel the same as me 30 years on. Nevertheless, it doesn't take away the fact that they were there. We all contributed in separate and collective ways.

Some things haven't changed since those halcyon days. I'm still an Atheist; I still despise bullies, bigots and cowards. Age has done nothing to assuage my intolerance of long distance Generals and armchair executioners; people who expect others to kill on their behalf. I continue to believe that the strong have a duty to protect the weak; that all societies have a corporate responsibility for the care and protection of children; that no human has the right to be another's master, and that there is evil in the finest of people and even the slightest soupçon of good in the worst. I have seen mankind at his best and most unpleasant, though not wanting to be conceited I believe I'm more than qualified to make these declarations.

A track on my self-edited completion album breaks my concentration. I sit back and listen to Neil Young's *Heart Of Gold*; the track elicits memories of R&R in Đà Nẵng. Jim Croce's *Time In A Bottle* follows the melodious piece. If I could save time in a bottle would it include some of my time in Vietnam? Probably, though I was much younger then, time seemed endless as if desert sands in a bottomless hourglass. Truth is I would probably include a lot of things – I'd need a pretty big bottle!

Time has taught me many things: that you shouldn't hold back on things that need to be said; that nothing is more precious than real friends and that the trick of life isn't getting what you want, but continuing to want it once it's in your possession. I missed the chance to really talk to my father and there have been times when I've had precious things within my grasp and not realised they were there. Given a second chance I'd likely do many things in a different way, including my actions as soldier. But none of us can exhume the sands of time; they can only be stirred in the abstract of acceptance or regret. As for this chronicle, I must now bring it a close. I feel content with what I've produced; I feel it was necessary. The text is nought but a small part of an augmenting Library. It may end up gathering dust on the shelf of a backstreet bookstore counting its days. Regardless, it will not negate the fact that it has been written.

I may still have nightmares about my time in Vietnam, but I also have dreams not just nocturnal. In my dreams I float on the China Winds over the peaceful mountains of Quang Trì and take pleasant walks through Quì Nhôn. The thunderous rains replenish paddies that are free from oil. There are no tented cities, only peaceful towns and villages where people can walk in safe grounds and children can play. The dark days have gone; the only illuminations dotting the skies are the lantern balloons carrying the wishes of a peaceful people. I have more good mementos and memories of that beautiful land than bad; this book is nought but one part. I have numerous photographs, on print and within the images etched upon my mind. I have discussions with others who survived the war. And I have the voices: the accents of the Vietnamese in the bustling streets; the melodious songs of the workers in the fields; the babble and laughter of children who never failed to offer a smile and the banter of my compadrés; countless words from countless voices – Ghost Voices.

REFERENCES

Armstrong J (1968): in – *Voices: an Anthology of Poetry*, Harmondsworth, Penguin.

Brooke R (1989): in – *The 'Cohen' Book of Quotations*, London, Bloomsbury.

Browning R (1970): in – *The Classics II*, London, Cramer.

Byron G (1971): in – *Poets' Corner*, Liverpool, Riverside Press.

Crosby D (1967): *For What It's Worth*, USA, Columbia Broadcasting System.

Dylan B (1964): *My Back Pages*, USA, Warner Brothers Music.

Levertol G (1975): *Images of Conflict*, USA, Veterans' Associated Press.

Gilmore M (1968): in – *Voices: an Anthology of Poetry*, Harmondsworth, Penguin.

Goresky H (1969): in – *Letters from the 'Nam*, USA, Veterans' Associated Press.

Herr M (1977): *Dispatches*, London, Picador.

Joel B (1980): *Goodnight Saigon*, USA, Columbia Broadcasting System.

Lennon J (1972): *Imagine*, London, Capitol Records, Incorporated.

Owen W (1962): *The Collection of Poems*, London, Chatto & Windus.

Sassoon S (1970): in – *The Golden Treasury*, London, Collins.

Simpson L (1967): in – *Amid The Carnage*, London, Hammersmith Free Press.

Walters R (1979): *The Gunners Dream*, London, Pink Floyd Music.